ONCE A
CROOKED
MAN

ONCE A CROOKED MAN

David McCallum

Minotaur Books

A THOMAS DUNNE BOOK

New York

This is a work of fiction. All of the characters, organizations, and events portrayed in this novel are either products of the author's imagination or are used fictitiously.

A THOMAS DUNNE BOOK FOR MINOTAUR BOOKS.
An imprint of St. Martin's Press.

www.thomasdunnebooks.com
www.minotaurbooks.com

The Library of Congress has cataloged the hardcover edition as follows:

Names: McCallum, David.
Title: Once a crooked man / David McCallum.
Description: First edition. | New York : Minotaur Books, 2016.
Identifiers: LCCN 2015037864| ISBN 9781250080455 (hardcover) | ISBN 9781466892484 (e-book)
Subjects: LCSH: Actors—Fiction. | Organized crime—Fiction. | BISAC: FICTION / Crime. | FICTION / Humorous. | GSAFD: Mystery fiction. | Humorous fiction.
Classification: LCC PR6113.C3586 O53 2016 | DDC 823/.92—dc23
LC record available at http://lccn.loc.gov/2015037864

ISBN 978-1-250-11206-4 (trade paperback)

Our books may be purchased in bulk for promotional, educational, or business use. Please contact your local bookseller or the Macmillan Corporate and Premium Sales Department at 1-800-221-7945, extension 5442, or by e-mail at Macmillan SpecialMarkets@macmillan.com.

First Minotaur Books Paperback Edition: January 2017

10 9 8 7 6 5 4 3 2 1

This book is affectionately dedicated to
Corporal George Whitney Carpenter, USMC.
1946–1967

A man I never met.

There was a crooked man and he walked a crooked mile,
He found a crooked sixpence upon a crooked stile.
He bought a crooked cat, which caught a crooked mouse.
And they all lived together in a little crooked house.

ONCE A
CROOKED
MAN

1

Until he pulled open the door of the Starbucks at 50th and Lexington, Carter Allinson II had only experienced crushes on the fair sex in his early years and minor infatuations in his teens. Some of the latter had led to wild sexual exploits but Carter had never fallen deeply in love.

The line was mercifully short and he soon had his usual fix of a regular coffee with a double shot, along with a slice of lemon cake with white icing. He looked around for somewhere to sit, and that's when the Fates took a hand in his future.

She was seated at a table in the far corner reading a book. In front of her was a small beaded purse and a mug with a Chamomile tea label hanging out. On the far side was an empty chair. The only one in the whole place.

Carter threaded his way through the crowded room.

"May I?" he asked, and pointed at the chair.

"Of course," she replied, and moved her purse.

"Thanks. Busy here this morning."

"Yes," she said.

As he sat down she looked at his face for the first time.

Poets have tried to capture in words that rare and magical moment when eyes meet and lives are permanently changed. Some come close in both prose and verse. It is one of the world's great tragedies that some people never experience it. The animal kingdom knows it well: bald eagles, beavers, wolves, and vultures mate for life, just to name a few.

On the fourteenth of July 1998, Carter extended his hand and said simply, "Carter."

"Fiona," she replied, taking it and marveling at the intensity of his blue eyes.

For half an hour they sat in silence, but before parting company they exchanged the briefest of pleasantries and he invited her to have dinner with him. The whole encounter was so natural to both of them that there was no need for any beating around the bush or subterfuge. He had asked and she had accepted.

Over dinner she discovered that he had recently graduated from Vanderbilt and was now going on interviews. Most of these had been unsuccessful, not only as a result of the current state of the financial world but also because the young man with the deep blue eyes was not particularly well organized and definitely in need of feminine guidance.

Perhaps if she had known just how much guidance that would be she would have nodded politely, got up from the table and walked out of his life. Instead she invited him to meet her father, who just happened to run a Wall Street investment firm.

On the following Friday evening in the paneled library of the family apartment Carter found himself before Charles Maitland Walker, Fiona's father and the founder of the firm of Walker, Martin, Pomeranz and Fisher. In his hand he held the young man's résumé.

"I see you went to Deerfield. Great school. One of my partners went there. But that was back when it was all boys," he said wryly.

"Yes sir, that was before my time." Carter took slow deep breaths.

"And then Vanderbilt, I see." Charles Walker looked up. "Why did you head south?"

"I think it was the weather, sir. I had had enough of snow and cold."

"And I see you did a stint over in the UK."

"Yes sir, in England. Bristol University. I got to play a little rugby."

"That must have been interesting. I saw a great game at Twickenham once. Fascinating. So simple by comparison to what we do here."

Carter crossed fingers on both hands as he watched the pages turn.

"I get the impression from what I read here that you have all the necessary qualifications for this line of work, but lack the motivation. Apart from sports. It makes me wonder whether you are cut out for a career in finance. My daughter thinks otherwise." He sat down on the sofa. "If you were in my shoes, what would you do?"

Carter took a deep breath and forced himself to relax before he answered. "It is true, sir, that my efforts in the past have been less than satisfactory, but I can assure you that need no longer apply if you put your faith in me. I shall work hard to learn the specifics of whatever you choose to give me. I can promise you enthusiasm, loyalty and a strong desire to succeed, both for my own future and more importantly to justify the trust that your daughter appears to have in me."

Fiona and her mother rose up when the two men came out of the study. They spoke in unison: "Well?"

Charles Walker laughed aloud. "He starts tomorrow. In a very minor capacity I might add," and he kissed his daughter on the cheek. "Then, as my mother used to say: 'We shall see what we shall see.'"

Carter put his arm around Fiona. "Thanks," he said. "I'm afraid I'm a little shell-shocked. This is all happening so fast."

"Welcome to the Walker clan," she replied. "Let's have some wine and toast to your success!"

"Our success," said Carter with a broad smile.

The next weeks were extremely hard for him. The pace of his life tripled as he learned the pleasures and pitfalls of investing other people's money. But in six months he had proved his ability. As he was the constant companion to a partner's daughter, he was given his own small office on a lower floor.

The young couple were inseparable and it came as no surprise when they married at the Church of the Heavenly Rest and honeymooned in the Swiss Alps. James was born the following year and Amanda fourteen months later.

No one in the family at any time had the slightest idea that Fiona's new husband had a sizeable skeleton in his cupboard.

2

It was an odd coincidence, but on the fourteenth of July 2015 it all began for Harry Patrick Murphy in Bloomingdale's as he tried to figure out what to send his mother for her sixtieth birthday. He settled for her favorite perfume, a bottle of Chanel No. 5. And in the section marked "Intimates," he worked his way through an endless number of racks that held every size of style, color and material known to man. He chose a black satin robe that was perhaps a little too sexy for someone her age. Not to worry—his dad would get a kick out of it.

He liked to keep in close touch with his parents, but as he had lived in New York and they had retired to Florida, this was more of a sentiment than a reality. As a child he had respected his father's authority and willingly accepted his mother's cooking and constant care. It was only when he was older that he was able to appreciate what a great job they had done. Mike and Bridget Murphy had made him a man of principle with a strong set of values. They had given him the confidence to face the world and handle most situations that might come his way. Or so he believed.

As an actor, he was well established with most of the ad agencies. His voice had the essential ingredients of sounding authoritative and at the same time friendly. He was fortunate to be sent to a considerable number of commercial auditions. Once in a while he was successful and the resulting income combined with the odd movie and television part kept him solvent. When he was really fortunate, he landed a role on Broadway.

Over the past month however, he had gone on several promising auditions and had not been selected once. These rejections were beginning to erode his confidence.

Harry took the elevator down to the gift-wrapping department on the lower level, where he stood in line to pick up a box, two sheets of white tissue paper, a length of ribbon and a big red bow. Five minutes later he ran across the street to Chase Bank.

The balance of his checking account was precariously low, a situation not uncommon with actors in New York, particularly with the quixotic economy and ever-growing demands of daily living. Harry was forced to take out only two-thirds his weekly allowance from an ATM. The notes were folded in his money clip and he headed home.

Most people might find living in a fifth-floor walk-up a nuisance. Harry felt it an excellent way to keep fit and he was able to save on the expense of a gym. The West Side location on 56th Street was prime. It was also relatively peaceful as he was the only tenant on the top floor.

He unlocked the front door, went in and put the Big Brown Bag on the sofa. As he moved into the kitchen his cellphone played the march from *Star Wars*.

"Hi there, sport," said the familiar raspy voice of his agent, Richie. "We're emailing you a new play by an up-and-coming young author. They're doing it at Ninth Stage. Mike Zergenski is producing. He's the one who caused the stir last year with the naked Coriolanus." Richie took a drag on his omnipresent cigarette. "You may be a little old for the part but I think it's worth a try. It's an anti-war, anti-America sort of piece. Scale, of course, but it's only a six-week run and with Zergenski, highly visible and a good career move. The office is emailing you a script. Audition's Monday."

Harry chuckled to himself. It was amazing how people in the

business talk about off and off-off-Broadway. No one had any idea how successful a production would be, but always assumed it would transfer to a large Broadway theater for a long and profitable run.

"How much rehearsal?" he asked.

"Zergenski wants three weeks but there's some discussion about getting it on in two."

"What else has this guy written?"

"No idea. I could ask."

"Have you read it?"

It would snow in Tahiti before Richie read every page of an off-Broadway script. "I plan to get to it this weekend when I have some free time."

"Sounds fascinating," said Harry.

"Look at the part of Tex. He's the one in the box."

"What box?"

"You'll see when you read it. They also emailed you the address. It's somewhere in Queens."

"Sure. No problem. Thanks, Richie."

"You're welcome. Oh, I just had a thought. Are you free right now?"

"Yes. Why?"

"We got a last-minute audition for a voiceover at Roz Lewis. Two national TV spots for Mueller's Mayonnaise. Could you make it over there within the hour?"

"Sure."

"Great. You see Wendy on the sixth floor."

"Great. Thanks, Richie."

Every voiceover audition was a crapshoot. Unless one of his interpretations made half a dozen people sit up and listen he wouldn't get the call back. On a spot like this he would be competing with the best in the business and star names often got the lucrative contracts.

Once in the casting office, he signed his name on the list and picked up the copy. The Mayo creative team had been brief. The text was simple:

Mueller's Mayo! It's in the bag!

Familiar faces came into the room. He nodded hello and shook a few hands before seeking a quiet corner to sit down to wait. Five minutes after his appointed time, Wendy came out, glanced at the sign-in sheet and called his name. He walked into the little studio, placed the copy on the black music stand and put on the headphones.

"Just your name and slate, Harry," she said. "This will be take forty-two."

She pressed buttons and gave him a wave.

"Harry Murphy, forty-two," he said in his friendly voice. After a short pause he read the text intimately, enthusiastically, and as a news announcer.

"Thank you," said Wendy flatly. "That was great."

"You're welcome," he replied.

He replaced the copy where he found it and left the agency feeling not particularly optimistic about his chances.

3

When he was sixteen years old, Carter Allinson regularly traveled down from the family home in Westchester to the Bronx to to buy his supply of weed. Several other boys at Deerfield Academy were users and he had become their provider at the beginning of his second year. This enterprise made him popular and gave him a much needed supply of ready cash. As social mores changed, his supplier was able to sell him whatever was currently in vogue to pop, smoke or snort. When he graduated and moved on to Vanderbilt he established another select group of customers and had the merchandise triple-wrapped in plastic and sent to him in a FedEx box. During the short time he was studying at Bristol in England, a trusted Nashville friend took care of the distribution.

Studying at college allowed Carter little time for casual recreation and he personally stopped smoking. But on his return to the States he continued to supply his close friends as he considered it harmless.

Carter was not the sharpest knife in the drawer and he knew it. To succeed in life and business he needed guile and luck. He soon taught himself the first and never missed an opportunity to take full advantage of the second.

The day the Walkers announced that Carter and their daughter Fiona were to be married, the young man felt it prudent to contact his customers to tell them the store was closed. Everyone understood his position and most wished him well. Then he called his own supplier and gave him the same message. This time the reaction was not so understanding.

"How the fuck am I going to explain the loss of so much fucking business!" came the scream on the other end of the line. "Don't you realize my boss may decide to fucking kill me? Or do me a serious goddam fucking injury?!"

Anxious to avoid involving others, Carter made the egregious mistake of offering to explain the situation to the man's boss personally. An hour later he found himself in the Fiery Dragon, a nondescript Chinese restaurant in Queens, seated across a table from a neatly dressed cigar-smoking Sicilian who told him politely that there was no way he could walk away unscathed.

"You are in too deep, my friend. And if you make a big fuss, you will be driven upstate to a remote forest, cut up into little pieces, fed to a pack of starving Dobermans and crapped out among the pine trees."

Carter sat silently, agonizing over the sudden and terrifying prospect of losing everything he had managed to achieve.

"However," continued the little man, "a deal may be possible. Our organization has never had anyone to officially take care of our business affairs. You are in the perfect position to rectify this omission. If you agree to become our financial advisor and tell us what to do with our money you can carry on with your cozy life with nobody any the wiser. Otherwise, I am sure the press would jump at the chance to publish a juicy *segreto vergognoso* about the drug-addicted tycoon with the beautiful fiancée and who works at a prestigious Wall Street firm. The choice is yours. We will of course come to some financial arrangement mutually agreeable to us both."

Carter weighed his options. Right away the challenge of investing large sums of cash began running through his mind. If he played his cards right he could do what this man was asking and keep his head above water.

The Italian leaned towards him. "Believe me, Mister Carter Allinson, there are many who make a very respectful living off of the weaknesses and needs of others. My brothers and me are not like those you may have seen on the big movie screen."

And then he lowered his voice and spoke the words that would be embedded in Carter's mind until the day he died.

"Most people in this great country have an illusion about the criminal mind that is based on what they watch on their television sets and read in their newspapers and gossipy magazines. But contrary to popular belief, crime pays, and pays well. The trick, my friend, is not to get caught. This is a lot simpler than people think."

The man leaned back and smiled. "The law enforcement agencies of this country are not omnipotent. They only succeed in uncovering a very small percentage of what goes on in the so-called underworld. And they achieve prosecution even less often. Trust me, if you just treat us like any of your other clients, no one will ever be aware of what you're doing. Keep it in that smart brain of yours that the law with all its money and manpower only catches the stupid, the impetuous and the greedy."

The deal was settled with a handshake and Carter left. Two weeks later in his little office he began to receive bundles of bills in small denominations from his newfound clients. To be able to bank the cash he immediately created a bogus company with a chain of nonexistent self-service laundries across the country. At all times he was careful to keep the deposits below federal reporting limits. As the flow increased he simply created additional fictitious cash-heavy companies.

The Sicilian's name turned out to be Salvatore Bruschetti and he had two brothers: Enzo and Max. At a subsequent meeting with all three in the same Chinese restaurant, Carter made arrangements to take over control of the Bruschetti assets, reinvesting most of them in legitimate low-risk companies. He insisted the brothers be named as owners, pointing out to a reluctant Enzo that they would be more anonymous doing this than in the old way of obscuring their identities and going about with pockets full of cash. Over time Carter made them use Social Security numbers, file corporate returns and pay all the required taxes. As the balance sheets were within acceptable limits, there was nothing in them to flag an IRS audit.

The Bruschettis collected street money for the Colombians and held it in stash houses in Manhattan. For this they were paid an agreed amount.

When he was at a reunion with classmates in Bristol, Carter met Julian Evans who had become manager of a bank in the Channel Islands. Carter took the hapless fellow out to dinner and offered him a small percentage of the money that he and his associates wanted to pass through the bank. Julian took two days to make up his mind but eventually agreed, stipulating that on no account was he ever to be told the source of the cash.

This meeting also serendipitously led to a way to get the money from the United States to the Channel Islands. Julian's sister was married to a diplomat who traveled without scrutiny across borders. At first the amounts were kept small, but as the pattern was established the sums grew larger. Once Julian had processed the cash, the funds were transferred electronically through banks in several countries until they found their way to offshore accounts, most of which were on Grand Cayman. All these were under the direct control of Carter Allinson at Walker, Martin, Pomeranz and Fisher.

As the years went by, the brothers themselves became like many of Carter's regular clients. The only difference was the records of these early dealings. Carter kept them tucked away in a private safe to which only he had the combination.

4

Harry took a beer from the icebox, flipped off the cap and made himself comfortable on the sofa with the Zergenski script.

"FAR, FAR AWAY"
BY ALBERT HALLENBECK
A PLAY FOR OUR TIME

Below this were the name and address of the producer and a warning of dire consequences if anyone dared copy a word. Below this was a note from the author:

> *Apart from the imprisoned Texan, all the other twenty-seven parts will be played by two actors and two actresses.*

Harry chuckled. Anything to save a buck.

Act I began with Tex the Prisoner being dragged on to the stage by an Arab guard and stuffed into a small wooden crate. He remains there through much of the play. The crate is slatted so that the audience can see him and hear what he says.

As he sweats in the hot tropical sun Tex remembers his life back home. The crate becomes the kitchen table where his mom

gets him ready for the school bus. Then it's a bench at the ball-
park and his father shows him how to throw a curveball. His
sister sits on it as it becomes her bed and she teases him about
his acne. By the eighth page Harry was getting really bored. But
then at the age of fourteen Tex drops out of school, leaves home
and takes to the road for a series of exciting and well-written
adventures. But then life becomes reality and things get tough. To
ease the pressure he borrows money that he can't possibly repay.
To escape his avaricious creditors he joins the army and ends
up as a grunt in an unspecified country in the Middle East.

Act II and Tex is with his buddies in the desert. Violent,
bloody battles. Great camaraderie and a good time is had by all.
But then his tour is over and Tex is repatriated. Back in the States
he is made to conform to a stultifying suburban existence and
he goes slowly crazy.

In the last moments of the play, Tex screams that he wants
to go back and spend the rest of his life alone in the crate.

As the audition was to be held in Astoria, Harry headed for
the subway at Columbus Circle taking with him a neatly wrapped
package for his mother that he intended to drop off at the post
office on the way. However at 58th Street the light was changing and he made the stupid mistake of running across the
road. At precisely that moment, a cab accelerated away from
the sidewalk to his left.

When he saw it coming, his brain told him there was no way
he could get clear. So to prevent severe damage to his legs, he
leapt upwards. His body was slammed over the hood where his
head hit the windshield and his left hand tangled briefly with
the wiper blade. Immediately the driver banged on the brakes
and that sent him sliding back off the hood and down to the
roadway. There was a momentary pause and then the cab drove
off with a squeal of tire treads.

The whole incident took a matter of seconds. As he staggered
back to his feet, he checked his body for damage and mercifully
felt no broken bones. A gash in his left hand was bleeding badly

and his left shoulder throbbed from the impact. Taking out his handkerchief, he bound the wound. A few passersby paused to look at him but none offered assistance.

At the moment of impact, his mother's package had flown out of his hands in an arc and landed on the sidewalk. The destruction was total. Brown soggy paper held clinking pieces of shattered glass and reeked of Chanel No. 5. Harry looked at his watch. Replacements would have to wait.

It was time to go to Queens.

5

From a double-locked drawer Max Bruschetti extracted three sets of stapled papers, put them in his briefcase and set it down by the front door. He walked across the hall into the bedroom and lay down on the king-size bed. Beside him was a naked young body, her glossy skin lit by the golden morning rays of the sun that shone through the window. The girl was sleek and curvaceous and blessed with a mass of curly dark brown hair. Max stroked the soft fuzz on her brown ass. She didn't react to his touch. This was hardly surprising after their exertions of the night before.

This encounter was somewhat of a milestone. One month earlier Max had collapsed in the shower. Nino, his driver, had found him and dialed 911. In the local Emergency Room the doctor had told him the attack was not life-threatening. However, he should take it easy for a while both physically and, more important, mentally. His attack most likely had been brought on by a high stress level. Max had tried to take the doctor's advice but was totally ill equipped for the passive lifestyle. Within days he became restless and frustrated. As he didn't want to die of boredom, he made up his mind to take a few risks. The girl beside him was the first.

A phone beeped on the bedside table. Reaching over the prostrate girl, he picked it up.

"Yeah?"

A male voice at the other end said, "I'll be there in five."

"Thanks, Nino," said Max, and he replaced the phone, grabbed the girl's shoulder and gave it a shake. "Get up, babe," he said.

The young girl shivered herself awake, knelt up on the crumpled sheets, stretched her arms to the ceiling and thrust her taut body back into the world. Images of the night before flashed through Max's brain. She gave him a knowing smile.

"Not now, babe," he said. "Sorry to say, we got to go."

The long-legged creature slipped off the bed, gathered up her scattered clothes and disappeared into the bathroom.

Max pulled on a pair of khaki pants, a denim shirt and a Windbreaker, walked through into the kitchen and poured himself a cup of black coffee.

Five minutes later, Nino opened the doors of the black sedan parked out front. Max got into the front passenger seat, and as they drove off his anonymous female companion curled up like a kitten in the back.

The trip to the Edgewood Boat Marina took only minutes. The waterfront was silent and deserted. Max climbed out of the car and walked slowly across to the edge of the dock carrying his briefcase. Nino, his driver, switched on the radio. The sounds of "Summer in the City" wafted across the empty parking lot. An odor of fish and engine oil rose from the dense mass of flotsam that had collected against the riverbank.

The girl materialized beside him hugging herself in the morning air. Together they watched as an impressive cruiser appeared throwing up a wide bow wave. The helmsman passed upstream, cut back on the power and steered around in a tight circle. Judging the distance perfectly, he glided along the dock and cleared the concrete supports by less than a foot.

Max stepped on board, lifted the girl up and swung her to

the deck as if she were a doll. Immediately the twin Caterpillar 475 horsepower engines roared to full throttle and the big boat plowed through the calm waters of the Hudson and headed south towards the city.

A deckhand in a dirty Mets cap held open the aft door.

"Thanks, Karl," said Max. Taking the girl by the arm, he propelled her inside, where they squeezed past boxes of supplies, life jackets and other marine paraphernalia.

In the main cabin, his brother Enzo was sitting in one of two swivel armchairs before the wide front cabin window. In contrast to Max, he was dressed in a suit and tie.

Max pointed to a ladder that led to the cabins below. The girl reached down, pulled off her high heels and silently disappeared.

Enzo got up and the two men greeted each other with a back-slapping hug. Enzo held on to his brother's arms. "Who's the chick? Cora's new girl?" he asked.

"Yeah," said Max.

"She pass the test?"

"Cum lauda." Max grinned at his own pun. "Coffee ready?"

"Sure," said Enzo with a nod. He walked to the back of the cabin but turned in the doorway.

"What's up, Max?" he asked. "Why the meeting? Something go wrong with the stuff at Kennedy?"

"No," Max replied evenly. "They used four intermediaries and clean cash."

"What about the Times Square construction project?"

"Siegel got his money. Fletcher got his contract. Client was very pleased."

"Then what the hell is going on?" asked Enzo. "Something's up, right?"

"No more questions," said Max firmly.

"Okay," said Enzo with a shrug. "I'll get the coffee." And he stepped into the rear cabin.

Max stood watching the world go by on either shore and

wondered how Enzo would take the news that they were about to change the way they did business. Although they were a close-knit family, Max had never really got to know his younger brother in any depth. Enzo lived a solitary life and kept very much to himself. There were rumors that he indulged in weird sex but Max dismissed these as malicious gossip.

Three weeks earlier he had met with Sal and briefly outlined his plan. His older brother had given him the go-ahead and told him to get back to him when he was ready to talk details. The meeting today was called for ten thirty. Hopefully Sal would be on time. Of the three brothers, age had changed him the most. Punctuality had been one of the first things to go with Sal.

Max wished that he had someone outside the family whom he could talk to about his deeper reasons for wanting these changes. The decision was not simply for medical reasons. He harbored a nagging feeling that that he was missing out on what life had to offer. He couldn't put his finger on what this was, but he was determined to broaden his lifestyle and give it every opportunity to make itself known.

He was also aware that there were serious risks involved in what he was about to do. The past three weeks had been an exercise in anticipating what these might be and taking all possible measures to avoid them. This included discussing his decision with no one. In spite of a fraternal urge to put Enzo in the picture Max decided to wait until they were all together and in a safe and controlled environment.

Enzo carried in two steaming mugs.

"Something's changed in here," said Max. "What is it?"

"Very good," replied his brother. "It's the chairs. I had them re-covered. And the curtains are new too."

"What was wrong with the old ones?"

"Nothing. I just like to take care of my *Gazelle*. Makes us both happy."

For a while they both stood side by side.

"Gonna rain later," said Enzo.

"Yeah," replied Max.

The *Gazelle* passed beneath the immense span of the George Washington Bridge. Headlights flickered on the road. Max was glad he was down on the water. He liked his bridges like his women, young and pliable. The older structures were to be mistrusted. They'd been around too long and had begun to creak.

The helmsman steered into the Harlem River between the buildings of the Bronx and the island of Manhattan. They glided under the Triboro Bridge and alongside the green fields of Randall's Island. Finally they bobbed alongside the rickety dock of an abandoned factory and the two brothers jumped off. Max led the way around the building and across Vernon Boulevard. A thin man in a brown suit waited at the side of a Town Car.

"Good morning, gentlemen," he said, opening the door.

"Everything in order, Benny?" asked Max.

"All present and correct, my friend" was the answer. Once the brothers were safely inside, Benny slid into the driver's seat and locked the doors. The car sped off down the road in a cloud of summer dust.

6

A paper taped to the door fluttered in the breeze. Harry held it down and read: *Far Far Audition 2nd Floor.* The casting instructions below were to **be on time** and for actors to **read carefully** the monologue that made up the last two pages of Act I. Pushing open the graffiti-covered door, he climbed the narrow stairway to the theater lobby.

On the ride from the city, he had removed the bloody handkerchief and put pressure on his cut finger. Thankfully the damage was minimal; it could easily have been so much worse. Once the bleeding had stopped, he had taken out the script pages and gone over them again. Although he had memorized the lines the night before, he wanted to make sure he had them word for word.

Eight people were standing around the little space. An unsavory odor from a unisex toilet at the far end pervaded the atmosphere. Two actors sat on the floor. A tall actress spoke her lines aloud with her head pressed against the shutter of the refreshment counter.

A blonde came out of the auditorium. "Fucking asshole!" she muttered, and headed down the stairs.

At 10:50 he was the last one called up to audition.

The casting person, as Lenny liked to be called, gave him a warm smile and apologized for keeping him waiting. A young man with a shaved and polished head sat in the second row scribbling notes on a clipboard. Harry climbed up and walked over to center stage. Lenny settled back in the shadows.

After a long pause, bald-head looked up and gave him a cursory glance.

"Don't you have the sides?" he asked testily. His accent was from somewhere in the Midwest.

"Yes," replied Harry. He touched his forehead. "Up here."

"Oh," said the young man. "I like to work with my actors from the script. But never mind, just show me what you can do." He returned his attention to the clipboard.

When he arrived at the theater, Harry had been nervous. Now he was mad. He lay down on the floor, curled into a fetal position and delivered the lines with venom. If there had been an audience present he would have received a standing ovation. For a moment he felt the euphoria that comes to actors when they are performing well on a stage. The young man leaned on the seat in front of him.

"No, Harvey," he said with a theatrical sigh. "Not that way."

"Harry," said Harry.

"Harry," the man said as if it could matter less. "Imagine you are totally bored with life. Take all the energy out of your voice. Give me the feeling you have accepted your fate. Try it again.

And slower." He sat down. "And get up off the floor; we can get to all that crap later."

Harry had come across this type before. A petty dictator who wanted to know up front which actors would conform and submit. A control freak who had no doubt worked at a university or in regional theaters where young inexperienced minds could be impressed by his bullshit.

But Harry needed to get this part. He could put up with being paid less than $400 a week. He could stand being confined for two hours in a crate and overcome his dislike of this tedious, egotistical director. The theater was remote and drab. The stage cramped. But Harry felt an affinity to Tex. With any luck the cast would be supportive. He might even get a favorable review in *The Times*. It could be a wise career move.

He delivered the text just the way the man asked and hurried down the stairs into the real world.

Out on the sidewalk Harry had a sudden urge to take a leak. It was not surprising after two cups of coffee, a bottle of water and the adrenaline pumping through his nervous system from the encounter with the cab. But relief was a few steps away.

Across the road was a convenient Chinese restaurant.

7

Max told Benny to pull the car up opposite the Fiery Dragon and take the usual look around before he and Enzo went inside. A red neon sign flashed: *Good Food! 24 Hours!*

Benny crossed the road and disappeared briefly inside. Both brothers waited until he came back. "Just Sal and the kitchen staff," he reported, opening the door.

Salvatore Bruschetti was in the farthest corner at a table allowing him to keep an eye on the whole room. Red-striped pajamas poked out from beneath a gray sweatshirt and baggy

trousers. A bottle of Cutty Sark stood on the table in front of
him with three empty glasses. An unlit cigar butt dangled from
his lips. Max and Enzo threaded their way through the tables.

"You look like shit, Sal," said Max. "Someone steal your
clubs?"

"The way I been playing lately I should be so lucky," Sal
croaked. Years of cigar smoke had wreaked havoc to his vocal
cords.

Max slid into the booth opposite his older brother. Enzo
pulled a chair up to the end of the table.

The waiter hurried over. "You like to try the special?" he
asked. "We got spicy shrimp on menu today."

"Bring me a cup of black coffee," said Max, "and then disappear. Don't come out until I call you. Savvy?"

The cook called out something in Chinese from the kitchen.
The waiter twitched in understanding and scampered through the
beads. He came back with the coffee, set it down with a trem-
bling hand and looked inquiringly at Enzo who shook his head.
The little man bowed and withdrew. Max poured a stream of
sugar into the mug and gave it a stir.

Sal unscrewed the cap on the whisky and filled the glasses.
He pushed one over to Max. "You want to tell him, or shall I?"

"Why don't you?"

"Max and I have been talking about getting out," said Sal.
"Putting an end to everything illegal. Calling it quits."

"What!" said Enzo.

"Bastard put up a good argument," added Sal. "In the end I
agreed with him. I told him to put some figures on paper. Give
us an idea of what we got."

Max lifted the clipped papers out of his briefcase. He handed
one to each. Sal took out a pair of half-glasses from a pocket and
perched them on the end of his nose.

"Page one," said Max, "is a summary of our current investments. The figures are from the end of March. Pages two and
three show where our income comes from: bonds, real estate,

overseas investments, stocks. Page four is what we're worth. This doesn't include any cash we got stashed away. As you can see, the Bruschettis are in pretty good shape." He took a swallow of coffee. "Page five is why I decided to talk with Sal."

All three turned to the last page. "Seven percent!" said Enzo. "Is that all it is now? I work my ass off for seven percent? I spend my life updating the books, handling the payouts and keeping this organization running for seven percent?"

"Yeah. That's all it is. Take a good look. It's the last time you're gonna see it on a balance sheet."

Enzo was irritated and bewildered. "That smart-ass money-man put you guys up to this?"

Before Max could reply the front door banged open. All three heads turned. A rugged individual stood in the doorway, blinking at the dimness. From the beaded curtain the waiter trotted out carrying a menu.

"We're closed," said Max.

The man declined the offered menu. "No. Sorry. I just need to take a leak."

There was an awkward pause.

"You heard," said Max. "We're closed!"

There was a moment of silent confusion.

"Get the fuck out!" yelled Sal and Max in unison. The waiter and the man in the doorway obeyed fast.

8

Harry had no desire to pee his pants. Out on the sidewalk he frantically looked around for somewhere he could relieve himself without being seen. Mercifully there was an alley on one side of the restaurant. He hurried down it unzipping his fly as he ran.

A heap of black plastic bags of garbage were piled up beside an overflowing Dumpster. Harry squeezed past them, leaned against the wall and soon became oblivious to the world as all the tension and discomfort of the past minutes flowed to the ground.

Through an open window directly above his head he became aware of the voices of the men inside who had just told him to fuck off. At first he thought they were talking about the plot of a new action movie. Then he realized that these guys were the real deal. They were talking cold, hard facts. The prudent thing to do would be to leave. Quickly and quietly. But he didn't.

Curiosity overcame good sense.

Harry Murphy stayed perfectly still and listened to every fascinating word.

9

"That 'smart-ass moneyman,' as you call him," said Max, "doesn't know about any of this."

"Bastard will be pleased," said Enzo. "Carter's wanted out ever since we nailed him."

Max gathered up all the papers. "We got enough ready cash to keep us fat and happy until we're too old to care." He put them back in his briefcase. "Your great-grandkids will be able to buy all the candy bars they can stuff down their throats. Our legit businesses can provide jobs for every cousin and nephew we got." He snapped the case shut.

"More important, we stay clean. There is no record anywhere that links us to illegal activity of any kind. If we get out now and stay legit, we'll never have to worry about asshole cops busting down the front door at five o'clock in the morning."

As if to emphasize his point a police siren wailed past outside.

Enzo frowned. "You know we've never been on that side of the fence," he said. "It's not gonna be that easy."

"Give me a break," said Max. "We got ninety-three percent on that side of the fence. Shut down the cash pickups, the adult merchandise, and we're one hundred percent clear. Everything else is nickel-and-dime operations, favors for old friends that don't mean shit."

"How long ago was it?" asked Enzo suddenly. "How long's Carter been with us?"

"Fourteen . . . no, his little girl's gotta be fourteen . . . what's her name?"

"Amanda."

"Right, so it's sixteen years now."

"And he's done quite a job," added Max. "The Feds begin an investigation tomorrow, by the time they fumble their way through the files, like I say, we'll be drooling in our oatmeal."

"What about your pal Julian in the Channel Islands?" persisted Enzo. "You really think he'll keep his mouth shut?"

"Of course he will. He'll just make a few changes in the bank books. Go on about his other business."

"Basically, we got three things to deal with," said Max. "First is the Colombians. Shouldn't be a problem. We're not the only ones doing business for them in the Northeast, so they'll find a replacement real easy. Then there's the adult merchandise. Not a problem. I know someone who'll take over the whole operation."

"Who?" asked Sal.

"Ramon Rivas," replied Max.

"Rivas?" Sal raised an eyebrow. "That Latino cunt? You sure?"

"He's an ambitious bastard and he already controls a major part of what's sold on the East Coast."

"He'd pay cash?" asked Enzo.

"You have to ask?" said Max, and he sat back down. "That

leaves the guys in London. We have to give Santiago and Colonel Villiers their marching orders. I figure if we give them generous severance pay, they won't give us any trouble."

"We never talked about Cora and the girls," said Sal, pouring himself another shot. "You gonna close Mazaras?"

"What the hell for?" replied Max. "Nobody gets arrested for fucking."

"What are we gonna tell Rodrigo?" said Enzo. "We've been doing business for fourteen years. Those guys don't take kindly to change."

"I'll go down to Bogotá and meet with him," said Max. "Face-to-face."

"When?"

"I haven't figured that out yet."

Enzo hesitated for a moment and then asked, "What about Vic and his computer business?"

"They'll have to pack it up too," replied Max. "He's your son, Sal. You want to tell him or shall I?"

"You." Sal took a drink. "He listens to you."

Enzo asked, "How much are you going to give Villiers and Santiago?"

"The Colonel picked up a shipment in Canada this morning," said Max. "Close to a million and a half. I'll get a message to him not to make the usual delivery. I'll tell him to keep it with him and wait for instructions."

Enzo was unconvinced. "Won't he be curious?"

"About what?"

"Where the money's going."

"Give him a reason. Make one up. You don't have to be specific. Keep it vague. Tell him we have to take care of some strategic planning at the airport; he'll believe that."

"Okay," said Enzo. "But what about all the guys who work for us here in New York? What are you gonna do with them? Give them a fucking reference?"

"They don't work for us, Enzo," replied Sal. "They work for a guy who hires them with a cellphone. No names and no connection to us. Remember, we always picked good people. They won't have trouble finding jobs."

Enzo shook his head. "We made a lot of enemies over the years. You think they forget? Soon as the word gets around we gone soft they'll come running."

"Most of them have quit, are dead or inside," said Sal and he began to laugh.

"What's so funny?" said Max.

"I was just thinking about Papa Aldo," Sal explained. "What he'd say if he was here now."

Max grinned. "Yeah. He wouldn't know what the fuck we were talking about. We'd have to sit him down and give him . . . what was the name of that drink he liked?"

"*Fernet Branca*," replied Enzo. "Battery acid."

Sal gave a throaty grunt. "Yeah, that was it. His *aperitivo!*"

All three men smiled at the memory.

Sal leaned back in the booth. "Hey, Max," he said, "remember when the big boys tried to put Papa out of business? There was no *amici degli amici* for him. He did it alone. Beat the bastards at their own game. It took him years, but he did it. Our name meant quality."

"Quality! Give me a break, Sal," said Enzo. "Our old man established power by terror and intimidation. He wouldn't survive five minutes in today's world."

"So what do you say, little brother? Are you with us?" said Max. "Tell us what you're thinking."

Enzo just gave a shrug.

"It's time we got out," said Sal assertively. "Okay?"

"Okay," said Enzo. "I agree."

Sal delved inside his sweatshirt and pulled out a fresh cigar and cutter. He nipped off the end, carefully lit it until it was glowing red. Then he stood up and walked over to the curtain.

"Hey! You two. Get the fuck outside," he said. "Like now!"

The cook and waiter shuffled out through the front door as Sal came back and stood beside the table.

"When Papa died he put me in charge," he said. "Right?"

"Right," agreed Max and Enzo in unison.

"There is a conception I don't take much interest in the business. Some people even think I'm getting senile. And that's good. Keeps them off my back." He blew a huge cloud of smoke into the air. "We gotta move fast, Max. We ain't gonna get no second chances. We gotta do it right the first time."

He pointed his cigar at Max. "You go to South America right away. Meet with Rodrigo. You can work out what you're gonna tell him on the plane. Send Rocco to London tonight. He should keep in touch same way as usual through that same Internet café in Kensington.

"I'm sorry, Max, but I don't agree with giving Santiago and Villiers severance. They know too much. Tell Rocco to get rid of them both. Permanently."

Max hesitated before asking, "Dead meat? Both of them?"

Enzo shook his head. "Santiago has been our point man in Europe for a very long time. He's proved himself to be extremely useful. When the Colonel's needed help moving the cash, he's been right there. He's never let us down. He's reliable. Aren't we better off with him alive rather than dead?"

"Enzo's right," added Max. "Shouldn't we wait . . ."

"*Madonna!* Are you both deaf? No fucking delay!" said Sal vehemently. "We got no choice if we're going to sleep nights."

He put a hand on Max's shoulder. "Tell Villiers we're sending someone to the Mews to pick up the million and a half. Don't tell him it's Rocco. We don't want him to get suspicious. The fewer people that know Rocco's there, the better. Go ahead with Rivas. Work fast, but get the best price you can. Then you send the girls packing. Shut Mazaras down."

"No need to shut the place down," said Max. "We'll just run it as a restaurant. Family-style."

"Okay, if that's what you want," replied Sal, and he flicked the ash off his cigar. "Enzo. You take care of all the little jobs we got going. Do what you gotta do to get rid of them all. Call me when you're done."

"All of them?" asked Enzo.

Sal nodded and banged his glass down. "Meeting adjourned," he said, and dropped two twenties on the table. "Now let's get out of here. I hate this place. I don't know why the fuck we ever bought it."

10

Amidst the garbage, Harry stared at the little screen on his cellphone. Soon after he had begun listening under the window he had quietly retrieved it from his pocket, turned on the Notepad app and tapped out names and phrases as he had heard them.

A good five minutes passed before he ventured back to the sidewalk. To regain his composure he began to walk. After a few blocks he came across a coffee shop. In a booth by the window he ordered a bagel with a side order of bacon and a cup of coffee. Switching on his cellphone he read through the list.

One thing was clear. Someone in London was about to be terminated, someone with the name Villiers. Presumably by an assassin named Rocky.

The waitress came back with his order. Harry added some cream and sugar to the steaming mug of coffee.

Had he got it all wrong? Could it be a hoax? Or a stupid television game show of some sort? Who were these guys? Who was Villiers? And what had the poor man done to deserve being turned into dead meat? And what the fuck did it have to do with Harry anyway?

He balanced some bacon on the bagel and took a big bite. As he munched away he gazed once more at the list and came to the sad conclusion that there wasn't much an out-of-work actor in New York could do to help a doomed bastard on the far side of the Atlantic.

11

Max settled back into the soft worn leather seat of the Town Car. "Can you believe that Sal!" he said. "The old bastard can't wait to take on the whole fucking world! Still gets a buzz out of killing."

"It's ironic." Enzo shook his head from side to side. "Furella managed to change everyone but her own husband."

Max smiled. "Yeah. I never thought of it like that."

"*Dio ce la mandi buona!*" exclaimed Enzo. "We're quitting!"

Max put an arm around his younger brother's shoulder and pulled him close. "Sorry I kept you in the dark."

"No, you were right," replied Enzo. "*Come sempre.* Keep the surprise. Quick and clean. The fewer who know what we're doing the better." He leaned forward and opened the liquor cabinet. "I had the impression that you were in favor of payoffs." Ice cubes clinked into a crystal tumbler.

"I am," replied Max. "I figured it would be easier to deal with Carter if we didn't have too many bodies lying around."

Bourbon flowed over the ice. "I suppose if we don't take them out we take a big risk."

"Killing isn't risk-free either. But Rocco will take care of it. He's a pro."

As Enzo took a drink, Max asked, "You got a phone with you?"

"Sure."

Enzo reached in his pocket and pulled out a disposable

phone. Max dialed Continental Airlines Reservations, where he was put on hold.

"The new guys gonna use our stash houses?" asked Enzo, taking a big drink. "Cash comes in every day. Piles up pretty damn quick."

"How many apartments we got?" asked Max.

"Four."

"Four? I thought we only had two."

"We just signed leases on two midtown, one east, one west. I was going to get rid of the others at the end of the month."

"Let's decide when I get back," said Max. "By then I'll know who's taking over."

"What do you know! No more hassle with bagmen," Enzo mused. "You know I'm not gonna be able to make the changes overnight."

"How long do you need?" said Max.

"I dunno. A week. Two maybe."

An agent answered and Max checked on available space on flights to Bogotá. Turning off the phone, he handed it back.

"As soon as you get home," he said, "call Rocco and tell him to go to London. Tell him what Sal said."

"Okay." Enzo sipped his drink. "You meeting with Carter in his office?"

"No way. Carnegie Deli."

"How d'you get him to see you there?"

"I told him he had no choice," replied Max with a grin. "I think I scared him."

"You gonna tell him Sal is, shall we say, cleaning house?"

"No fucking way," snorted Max. "I'm only gonna tell him we're making changes."

"He's bound to find out," warned Enzo.

"He'll find out when they're dead. *Tutti morti.* That's when I'll take him into a quiet corner and explain the facts of life."

12

Carter Allinson II was in fine spirits. At the office he had met with a group of investors from Europe and persuaded them to put their financial future in his capable hands. If all went according to plan, this acquisition would substantially increase his personal wealth.

The evening before, his wife announced that the board of the hospital, to which she dedicated most of her time, had asked if they could give a cocktail party in her apartment for their major donors. The news had so thrilled Fiona that she had seduced her husband before breakfast and given him a big bear hug before he left. Carter understood her happiness. Her diligence over the years was not only appreciated but now formally recognized.

The only blot on the day was a call from Max Bruschetti. But even that failed to dampen his mood. Only when he saw Max standing in the doorway of the Carnegie Deli surveying the crowded room did he face reality. He raised his hand, waved and watched as his nemesis threaded his way through the tables. Carter was surprised to see how thin and drawn Max looked.

"I took the liberty of ordering," said Carter affably.

"This won't take long," said Max. "How's Fiona and the kids?"

"She's in fine form, busy fund-raising for her hospital," said Carter, doing his best to hide his discomfort. Even after all their years together he still hated these face-to-face encounters. "The kids are with their grandmother. James is driving everyone mad. Growing up too fast in this crazy world."

"I thought Amanda was in Europe," said Max.

"She goes next week. Tuesday, I think, or maybe it's Thursday." He picked up a menu from the table and held it out.

Max shook his head. "Just coffee."

"You okay?" Carter asked.

"I have a big day ahead of me," answered Max with a sigh. "Got a lot to do. I have to go down to Colombia later."

"There a problem?" Carter sensed the possibility of trouble.

Max lowered his voice. "I'm going down there to tell them they have to find someone new to do their pickups and deliveries. The Bruschetti boys want out."

This was the last thing Carter expected Max to say. But was it necessarily good news? Why the sudden change in their operation?

The waiter set down his corned beef sandwich.

Max asked for coffee and continued quietly, "I had a meeting with Sal and Enzo this morning. We made the decision to go one hundred percent legit."

For a moment Carter was at a loss for words. Then he asked, "Are you saying what I think you're saying?"

Max smiled. "Enzo said you'd be in favor of the change. He feels you would have been a happier man if you had never met us."

"He doesn't still say that does he?"

"He thinks you got a conscience," said Max. "Always have. Always will."

"And that makes me someone who could never fully be trusted. Is that it?"

"It makes you someone who has always wanted out. That carries its own baggage."

The waiter arrived with a mug of coffee for Max and refilled Carter's.

"In my experience," said Carter, "quitting is not that easy. Things can jump up and bite you when you least expect it no matter how prepared you think you are."

"Thanks. I'll keep that in mind," said Max.

Carter took a bite of his sandwich and chewed for a moment. "I take it you'll want me to get in touch with the Channel Islands?"

"There's no need for Julian to know," replied Max. "Not yet."

"What about the others? What about London?"

"Not a problem," answered Max. "We will take care of them. We're still working out the details."

"I've always wanted to ask if you know that Villiers steals from you."

Max smiled. "I wouldn't call it stealing. Skimming perhaps. The amounts are nominal."

"How much do you suppose he's taken over the years?"

"Enzo has a pretty accurate figure and he simply puts it down to the cost of doing business. For that matter, in our line of work everybody has sticky fingers. How do we know your friend Julian doesn't take a little more than we agreed?"

Carter laughed aloud. "Julian has always been a bit weird but he'd never do that."

"You sure?" asked Max.

"Absolutely," said Carter with finality.

Max paused for a moment. "Why have you never brought this up until now? And what do you mean Julian is weird?"

"Flaky," replied Carter. "A little odd."

"Flaky? What the fuck is 'flaky'?"

"Well, last year when I saw him in London, I had the impression that he was more relaxed. Less uptight. He was with another 'guy,' if you know what I mean." Carter emptied his water glass. "I take it you'll be closing down Mazaras."

The waiter materialized to see if they wanted to order anything else. Both shook their heads. Tearing off the check, he tucked it under the ketchup. Max retrieved it. "Why would I close the club?" he asked.

"I just feel that you need to be aware the 'club,' as you call it, is a direct access to your whole organization. If you've made up your mind to close all the loopholes you sure can't leave that one open. We both know what goes on there. People talk. If the city ever decided to run an investigation . . ."

"Thanks for the lecture," said Max, cutting him off. "So what else do you need to know?"

"Nothing," said Carter with a shrug. "I need to know nothing. You and your brothers are comparative strangers to me. All the work I do for you was set up by correspondence a long time ago. I simply follow orders and invest your money. Statements are sent out on a regular basis according to those same written instructions. I keep the books and file the taxes on time. The only difference now will be that the money coming from certain accounts has ceased. I will simply assume they've become inactive. Happens all the time." He leaned across the table. "I don't need to know anything because I don't have to change a goddam thing."

Max got to his feet.

Carter asked, "Why did you decide to do all this now?"

"Lots of reasons."

"Not wasting any time are you?"

"I see this as a surgical operation," replied Max. "I make the incision. Work as fast as possible to minimize the pain. Hopefully there won't be too much bleeding."

Carter watched Max as he stood in line to pay the check, unable to grasp what had just happened or how he felt about it. On the one hand, he was hugely relieved that the Bruschettis were going 100 percent legit, but on the other, he had an irritating feeling that everything could start to unravel. As he had just warned Max, change often produced unanticipated consequences.

13

Out on the sidewalk Max pondered the disturbing fact that Carter Allinson had apparently eliminated every tie to the Bruschetti family. If there ever was an investigation of the Bruschettis and he became involved, the bastard could easily turn state's evidence and cop a plea. Max glanced at his watch. It was only one fifteen.

At the Fiery Dragon Sal had decided it was necessary to kill Santiago and Villiers in London. From what Max had just heard it might be wise to get rid of Carter, his pal Julian and maybe a gay boyfriend. And what about Carter's wife? How much did the lovely Fiona know?

Could be a fucking massacre.

14

In a modest hotel room in West London chosen for its obscurity, Rocco Martinelli finished his daily exercise routine, showered, toweled himself off and dressed casually in dark clothes. With the Do Not Disturb sign on the door, he slipped down the stairs and out onto Westbourne Grove. The evening sky was cloudy, but the breeze was warm. In five minutes he entered Paddington mainline station, pushing his way through the throng of commuters.

Whenever a dead body is found in odd circumstances, the police assume foul play. Rocco thoroughly enjoyed creating evidence that would change that assumption to accidental death or suicide. When the medical examiner pronounced that his victim had died from natural causes Rocco was thrilled. The latest challenge of disposing of Percy Santiago and the Colonel was giving him much pleasure.

Both of his targets knew him well, so the approach would be easy. But what then? How to dispose of the Colonel came to him while he was watching the movie on the flight from New York. Santiago's demise proved to be a tougher proposition. It wasn't until Rocco was making the long walk from the plane to the luggage hall at Heathrow that the means of Santiago's death came to mind. The idea was sparked by a poster on the wall of lurid London nightlife, and a guidebook bought at a newsstand had given Rocco the information he needed.

Now the plan was well developed in his mind.

A Circle Line train took him to St. Pancras where he connected to the Northern Line and the ride out to Belsize Park. As he emerged from the depths he bought a copy of *USA Today*.

A short walk brought him to the southern fringes of Hampstead Heath, where the guidebook suggested he could find receptive male companionship. Rocco selected a park bench at the edge of a small copse, sat down and opened the paper as if to read it.

In the evening light there was little activity. Only when dusk truly fell did the mating begin. Roaming males circled, glanced, paired up. Rocco strolled about and observed the ritual. If the couples headed for the shadows beneath the trees, he went back to his bench. If they left the park, he followed and made a note of exactly where they went.

Eventually he had the addresses of three male prostitutes. One was a young boy with streaky blond tints in his hair who lived in a basement close to the park. He wore shorts and a sports shirt. His clean appearance made him stand out from the others and apparently brought him the most business. As the first light of dawn flecked the sky Rocco took a taxi back to Paddington and enjoyed a deep sleep.

The next night he was gratified to see that his diligence had not been in vain. The young man again walked the paths. Now Rocco timed how long his flat was left empty between tricks and found that it was never less than twelve minutes.

A huge oak tree directly across the road from the boy's dwelling gave Rocco good cover. His quarry arrived with a tall man with a limp a little before midnight. Neither of them spoke a word. The metal gate squeaked open and the two disappeared below street level. The front door opened and closed. In thirteen minutes, the man came up the steps and hurried away as fast as his lame leg would allow.

Ten minutes went by. Rocco began to wonder if he'd left it too late. Perhaps the limp had been the last customer and the boy had packed it in for the night. But the door opened and closed and he reappeared. Freshly combed hair glowed orange under the streetlamp as he left. As soon as he was out of sight, Rocco went across the road and down the steps. Uneven flagstones covered the ground. Three dustbins stood against the wall. The door to the flat was made of wood and had a Yale lock.

To the right of the door was a casement window with a center latch. Rocco took out his pocketknife and eased it in through the gap in the old frame and pushed the hinged metal to one side. The window slid up silently and he was able to climb up over the sill.

A heavy green blanket was tacked to the ceiling in place of curtains. Rocco closed the window and eased the covering aside to give himself some light.

The room was a square box with a bed, a chair and a table. Two doors in the back wall stood open, one to a bathroom and the other to a closet. Makeshift shelves held books and a microwave. The place smelled of damp and sweat.

As his whole plan depended on there being a telephone in the room, Rocco looked around to find one. Mercifully there was a portable on the floor by the bed. Rocco picked it up and dialed the code to retrieve the number. Tearing out a page from one of the paperbacks, he took out a pen, wrote the numbers down and replaced the phone exactly where he had found it.

A quick check of the room assured him it was unchanged. Releasing the blanket, he let himself out, closed the window and slid back the catch before climbing the stairs.

The next day a hardware store provided him with a flashlight, a coil of galvanized wire, a small black tool bag, a pair of cutters, a screwdriver and a lock that was identical to the one in the basement door. In Haberdashery at Marks & Spencer, an assistant helped him to pick out a pair of black socks and leather gloves. In Cosmetics, a vivid red lipstick and a tube of brown mascara were added to the assortment. In Ladies Underwear, a black garter belt, queen-size stockings and a pair of red panties completed his purchases. Rocco paid for everything with cash.

The hotel provided stationery for its guests. Rocco sat at the small desk by the window and took out an envelope and a sheet of notepaper. Folding the blank paper, he slid it into the envelope. On the outside he wrote: *Percy Santiago*. The glue tasted of peppermint as he licked the flap. The next part of his plan called for him to get in touch with Continental Delivery Motor Services.

When the receptionist answered his call he said, "Mister Santiago, please."

There was a click and almost immediately a cheerful voice said, "Percy here. Who's that?"

"It's the messenger boy from the States." Rocco leaned back. "I've some interesting news from the boss in New York. I need to share it with you. I'm staying at a friend's flat here in town and wondered if you could meet me there."

"Nice to hear your voice. When do you want to meet?" Santiago asked.

"Tonight? Say eight thirty?"

"Sure. Where?"

"At the entrance to Belsize Park underground station at eight fifteen. Okay?"

"Sure. No problem is there?"

"No. Just a few changes. I have a list for you," said Rocco, and before he got any more questions he hung up. Right away he telephoned the Dorchester Hotel and asked to be put through to the message desk.

"Hi! My name is Herbie Smith and I will be checking in later. I just wanted to make sure that if anyone calls, you'll take a message for me?"

"What did you say the name was, sir?"

"Smith, Herbert."

"If anyone calls we'll be sure to take a message, Mister Smith."

"Thank you."

Rocco pulled out the torn page from the paperback and dialed the numbers. A young voice answered. "Yes?"

"This is a bit embarrassing," said Rocco quietly. "I need to make sure I'm talking to the right person."

"That's okay. What is this about?" He sounded Cockney, cautious but friendly.

"I'm over here from Chicago and I'm looking for some . . . some . . . well, some companionship this evening. A friend of mine gave me this phone number but didn't give me a name. He said he was very satisfied with the . . . service provided when he was here."

"What did your friend tell you about me?"

"He said you were about five eight, one hundred forty pounds. You have streaky blond hair."

"Anything else?"

"Yeah." Rocco smiled. "You have a great ass."

The boy chuckled. "That's me all right."

"Would you be free this evening?" Rocco closed his eyes and waited.

There was a slight pause. "Yes" came the reply.

Rocco opened them. "How much?" he asked.

"Five hundred quid. Or seven hundred fifty dollars or seven hundred euros. Cash. Any of those is okay with me."

Rocco paused for a moment. "I take it that much is for all night."

"Absolutely. Or until your prick falls off. Whichever comes first." The boy laughed crudely at his own witticism.

"Great," said Rocco. "I look forward to meeting you. My name is Herbie Smith. I'm at the Dorchester. Come around eight and we'll have some dinner."

"The Dorchester?"

"Yeah."

"Cool. I'll be there."

At 6:30 P.M. Rocco was behind the same convenient oak tree across the road from the basement flat. A pair of surgical gloves covered his hands and the leather gloves hid these. Everything else he had bought was in the bag by his side.

The boy appeared at just after seven and headed up the hill in the direction of the station. Wearing a Windbreaker over a white shirt and khaki pants, he whistled as he walked. Rocco remained where he was for five minutes before he crossed the road. Once he was down the steps, the window catch flicked back easily and he climbed in.

He now worked with swift precision. Taking the screwdriver, he removed the lock from the door, loosened the restraining screws and rotated the cylinder until it dropped out. He placed this one into the plastic bag and took out the cylinder from the new lock. Once this was installed, he replaced the whole mechanism on the door. The new key turned smoothly. Pulling it back out, he put this key in the left pocket of his coat. In the right he stuffed one of the stockings.

He straightened the bed, tidied up the books and closed the bathroom and closet doors. Satisfied that the room looked normal, he placed the envelope in the center of the bed with Percy's name uppermost and pushed the bag out of sight under the bed. Letting himself out, he ran up the stairs and over to the subway station.

Santiago was already there waiting. A short man with a thick head of dark hair who always wore flashy suits and sported a flower in his buttonhole. A tie was optional but the gold chains and bracelets were not. Unlike the Bruschettis, he had adopted a highly ostentatious lifestyle. His photograph appeared frequently in the newspapers at horse races or on his yacht or at antique car rallies. His art collection was famous. He gave the overall impression that he was a man who had once been poor but through entrepreneurial skill had managed to become wildly rich and now was determined to enjoy it to the fullest.

Not all his wealth, however, was legally derived. Percy Santiago was a scrupulously careful and successful owner of several car dealerships that collected and delivered new and stolen cars all over the continent of Europe. Colonel Villiers had met him while buying his classic Jaguar. The two had become close friends and it wasn't long before the Colonel was able to make use of Santiago's network to sequester large sums of cash until the propitious moment arose to deliver it to Julian in the Channel Islands.

The moment Santiago saw Rocco he gave him a hug and kissed him on both cheeks.

"The messenger boy from New York! What a pleasant surprise! Good to see you my friend. How long have you been over here? My God! You are looking so very fit. Are you still running all those miles around the streets of New York? Which way do we go? Up or down? Should we take a taxi?"

"Up," said Rocco. "We're just going around the corner. It's not far."

Santiago spoke loudly and gesticulated with his hands. "I want you to know that I appreciate what you do for me," he said with feeling. "You and Max, the Colonel too, and so if there is anything I can do for any of you, be sure to let me know. Anything you want."

"Thanks," said Rocco. "You're not making this easy for me."

"Try me," said Santiago with a smile. "I won't bite."

"Why don't we wait until we're inside the flat?"

"Why? Who's going to hear you besides me?"

Rocco gave a nod and said abruptly, "Max has a health problem."

Santiago stopped in his tracks. "You're not serious. No, I didn't know."

Rocco continued walking. "The brothers got together and decided it was time for a few changes. They felt it was time to take the pressure off."

"And?" Santiago had to run slightly to catch up.

"They're gonna get out of the business."

Santiago went silent. The two men turned onto Pond Street. "Does the Colonel know about all this?"

"I'm meeting with him later," continued Rocco as they neared the basement flat. "But I'd like you to keep this conversation to yourself until he calls you. Max has a plan to offer you guys severance with an additional payment later. He gave me a list to give you of all the changes we're making."

"What kind of health problem?"

"A heart attack in his shower at home. He was lucky, though. Nino was with him when it happened. He got him to the hospital real quick."

"You got to be kidding. Where's this list?"

"In my room." He unlatched the gate. "Just down here."

He led the way down the steps to the boy's basement flat, reached into his left pocket, pulled out the new key and unlocked the door. As he did, his fingers curled around the stocking in his right. Santiago walked past him and into the room. Rocco followed and switched on the light. This illuminated the envelope on the bedcover. Santiago saw his name, assumed it was the list and reached over to get it. As he leaned over, Rocco slammed him down, placed his right knee firmly in the small of his back and slipped the stocking around his neck. With both hands he pulled it just tight enough to cut off the air supply but not enough to cause bruising or internal damage.

Santiago was completely immobilized in the soft bedding so he couldn't struggle. With his windpipe cut off he couldn't cry out. His body became tense, then rigid. For a moment it spasmed. One by one, his muscles jerked and then relaxed. Rocco waited a full three minutes and then slowly eased off the pressure.

All life in Santiago was gone.

Rocco switched off the light, turned on the flashlight and propped it on the floor. He pulled out the bag from under the bed, set it carefully on the coverlet and picked out the screw-driver and old cylinder. In less than two minutes he had the orig-inal lock back in place. With the door closed he turned on the overhead light.

Opening the closet door, he scooped up all the clothes from the floor and threw them against the back wall. He lifted a white metal chair from the bathroom into the closet. With the cutters he fixed loops of wire to each of the front legs and an-other at the top of the backrest.

For the next five minutes he undid all the buttons and zip-pers on Santiago's suit and shirt and eased them off, carefully folding each piece of clothing and laying it neatly at the foot of the bed. Santiago's Jockey shorts were soiled with body fluids. Rocco used them to wipe Santiago as clean as he could and then stuffed them into the bag.

With some difficulty he slid the garter belt under the waist and connected the two hooks and eyes. He then grabbed an ankle and lifted up one of Santiago's legs. Rolling up the other stocking, he attached it to the suspenders. A little pink bow on the panties showed him which way round they went on.

Pulling the body up into a sitting position, he bent down and let the inert mass fall over his shoulder. Using a fireman's lift, he carried Santiago to the closet and set him down on the chair. One of the prepared wire loops went around his neck and the others were soon fastened to his ankles.

Santiago's head lolled back. Rocco fetched the lipstick and mascara from the bed and painted the man's mouth, being care-ful not to touch the drool that trickled down Santiago's chin. He applied mascara to both the upper and lower lashes and pressed a finger and thumb of the dead man's hands onto the tubes of makeup before taking them into the bathroom and plac-ing them by the washbasin.

As Rocco turned to leave he noticed a crumpled and wet Kleenex in the wastebasket. He retrieved it, carried it to the closet and swiped it over the dead man's inner thighs. Then he replaced it where he had found it.

The lock parts, screwdriver, cutters and wire went back into the bag. To make it appear as if there had been strenuous coupling, he crumpled up the bedding.

Taking a satisfied look at the grotesque figure on the metal chair, he shut the closet door.

He was just about to go out the front door when he remembered the envelope. A quick search revealed it lodged under the pillow. Rocco put it in the bag and left the flat.

Running up the steps from the basement two at a time he felt that he had created the perfect setup. He was sorry that he couldn't wait to see the expression on the young man's face when he came back home from his uneventful and no doubt frustrating Dorchester trip and opened the closet door.

It was a pleasant evening and perfect for a walk across town to his Paddington hotel. There was no hurry now. Max was on his way out of the country and Enzo never liked being called unless it was a dire emergency. The call could wait.

As he crossed a small bridge over the Camden canal he leaned over and dropped the screwdriver and cutters into the murky water beneath. These were followed by the lock parts and wire wrapped in Santiago's shorts. Rocco watched as they sank out of sight.

A bum lay sleeping outside Madame Tussauds. Rocco left the leather gloves at the old man's side.

The fresh air made him suddenly feel very hungry. In a pizza café on Edgware Road he chose a slice with sausage and onion. The cooks behind the counter wore plastic gloves and periodically discarded them in a metal bin at the end of the counter. As he waited, Rocco took off his surgical gloves and flipped them among the others.

15

Max drove into the city early the next morning and took a moment to gaze up at the chipped and uneven redbrick facade of Mazaras. The old building had been a part of his life for as long as he could remember. He would be sad if it ever left the family. His father Aldo had bought the original building when Max was ten years old. For a long time it was just a spaghetti joint where friends and occasional enemies met, but after Aldo died, Max had redesigned the dining room and changed the menu to encourage a more affluent crowd.

Later on he turned the two middle floors into a select social club for his close associates. A nice place for them to play a little poker with their friends and relieve any tension with his personally selected girls. The top floor was set aside for him to use as an office and a place to crash whenever he was in town.

At first the patrons of the restaurant and the men visiting the girls had shared the same entrance. Then Max bought the garage complex that backed up against his building and knocked a hole through the second-floor wall. This provided Mazaras with a discreet rear entrance and more than enough parking for the restaurant.

He opened the street door with his key and locked it behind him. The place was silent but for the hum of the iceboxes back in the kitchen. None of the staff had yet arrived but the white cloths on the tables were fresh and neatly laid. No matter how late they closed, Max made it a rule that everything be set up for the following evening.

He went up the stairs. As he reached the top landing he stopped. A strange man and a woman were talking inside his office. He moved noiselessly across the hall and leaned his back against the wall. Then he recognized the voices, relaxed and opened the door.

In the far corner of the room a woman lay full length on the big leather sofa. Her black sleeveless gown had fallen open to reveal long silken legs. Two sling-backs lay on the floor. She was lit by the flickering television screen where the complaining Lucy and her voluble Cuban husband were nose to nose in black and white. Max crossed to the window, drew back the heavy curtains and flooded the room with light.

Max had met the sleeping figure on a working trip to Las Vegas when he had ordered up dinner and a hooker. She had spent the next two days on his arm, the nights in his bed. It was at a time when Max sought someone to look after the girls at Mazaras. He offered her the job on the condition she change her name. He couldn't deal with "Penelope Wainwright." Over the ensuing years Cora Hunt had become his loyal friend and trusted advisor.

"Hey," said Max close to her ear. "Wake up!"

Cora gave a slight start. Her head rose stiffly off the cushion and she brushed back a tangle of dark red hair. The bright daylight made her blink. "Jesus, Max. It's you." Her voice was husky. "You frightened me! What time is it?" She looked around and asked blearily, "What are you doing here early?"

"I was about to ask you the same question."

"I asked first."

"I had a meeting with the boys yesterday at the Dragon and we made some decisions," he answered.

Cora was confused. "What are you talking about?"

Max walked over and turned off the television. "What are you doing here?"

"Darlene wanted to meet this morning and talk before she went to her day job. I thought it best we do it here. I lay down after she left. God! I'm tired." She swung her legs to the floor. "This is cruel and unusual punishment."

"You can catch up with your sleep later. Pack me a bag. Just a shirt and some underwear."

He bent down and flipped over the corner of the rug.

"What did Darlene want?"

He removed a square black metal plate and spun the dials of a small floor safe.

"To get married."

Cora put on her shoes and crossed the room to the bedroom.

"She says she's met the perfect guy. He's taken her three times to the Bronx Zoo. Can you imagine? Seems on the last visit he proposed to her in the monkey house. 'Very romantic,' she says. We talked for hours. I still wasn't able to change her mind. I'm sorry, Max. I know how much you like her."

Cora returned with a carry-on. "How was the other night?" she asked unzipping it on the table.

"The other night?" There was a click. Max opened the round door.

"Carmen. Remember?"

"Who the hell is Carmen?" Reaching in, he pulled out two manila envelopes.

"The girl you took home with you."

"Oh, her. Fine." He crossed to the table and emptied the envelopes out bedside the case. "Her name was Carmen?"

She gave him an exasperated look and headed back into the bedroom muttering, "You men!"

She pulled open the chest of drawers. "Where is it this time? Hot or cold?"

"Colombia," replied Max, sorting through a bunch of passports. "If anyone calls I need you to cover for me." He found the one in the name of Perez and picked up a wad of money.

"Why the deception?"

"Things go better in New York when everyone thinks I'm around." He selected a small packet of papers and envelopes held together with a rubber band.

"What should I tell them?"

"Nothing. You know nothing."

Cora got a brown leather toilet bag from the bathroom and

finished packing. Max picked up the phone and told Nino to take the rest of the day off.

In the bathroom, a brief shower washed his mind and body clean. He was now Fernando Alejandro Perez on his way to South America to see his cousin Raul. Not only did Max speak excellent Spanish but he would also be carrying papers that confirmed his identity. None of the passports the Bruschettis used were fakes. A great deal of cash had passed through a great many hands to procure the genuine articles and more to keep them up to date. Any one of them would take him across borders, without question, anywhere in the world.

Cora stood in the bathroom door and watched Max as he dried himself. "So what about Carmen? You want me to hire her?"

"No. Not right now." He dropped the towel and went past her into the bedroom. "When will you be seeing Darlene?" he asked as he took out a pair of pants and a jacket from the closet.

"Tonight. She'll be here tonight." Cora opened a drawer and selected a pair of socks and briefs and held them out. "Why?"

Max pulled on the underpants and sat on the bed to put on the socks. "You can tell her she can leave. It'll be okay."

"I see," said Cora, nodding her head. "No Carmen and Darlene can go. I don't get it."

"You will." He stood up and put on the shirt and pants.

"Max, what the hell's going on?"

"Later."

Cora took out a belt and laced it through the loops. "I thought we agreed not to keep things secret from each other."

"Secret? This isn't a secret." Max reached for a hairbrush. "I just can't tell you right now."

"You can't tell me? This is Cora, remember?" She pulled the belt tight.

Max sighed. "There's gonna be some changes."

"What sort of changes?" She fetched the jacket and held it out.

"Look," said Max as he put his arms into the sleeves. "A lot depends on what happens in the next couple of days."

She spun him round and held him by the lapels. "When people start talking about changes it usually means for the worse."

"This time it's for the better."

"You're taking that doctor's advice, aren't you? That's why you're doing this, isn't it?"

"Not now, babe," he replied.

"Have you told Sal and Enzo about your little trip to the Emergency Room?"

"Not yet," he replied. "Nino may have told them."

"Don't you think they deserve to know?"

"No. It would show them I was worried." He went towards the other room. "I don't need that right now."

"Rocco knows, doesn't he?"

"Shut the fuck up!" Max growled, and stuffed the wad of cash into his coat pocket. The passport and papers were tucked into the case and it was zipped shut.

"You're right," he said. "My little dance with death is the main reason I'm making these changes. But remember what the man said: I have to reduce the stress in my life. Fat fucking chance!"

At the doorway he turned.

"So I get up this morning. I have everything worked out. No pressure. I've come up with a real neat solution. But then every fucker I meet gives me shit. Little bit here, little bit there. Even Sal. But that's okay. I say to myself I'm a big boy, I can work it out. So enough already. When I get back you'll be the first to know."

He walked back over and kissed her on the forehead. "That is, assuming I make it back."

16

Carter had started the morning in a good mood. Fiona's father had invited him to play a round of golf at his club on the North Shore of Long Island. They had teed off with two friends at noon in bright sunshine and with a cool breeze. The course was in immaculate condition and Carter's swing had been loose and easy for the first nine holes. Then he had begun to think over what Max had told him the day before and specifically about all the things that could go wrong. That opened up a Pandora's Box of possibilities. His body tensed and the ball flew wildly to all the wrong places.

When it was over he didn't stay for the usual farewell drink at the bar but jumped in his car and headed to the city. On the journey back he tried to concentrate on the positive aspects of the proposed changes. As he went up in the elevator his mood had improved.

Soon after Fiona and Carter were married her parents had given them the apartment as a wedding present. Her mother took great pleasure in overseeing the interior design. The result was classic Upper East Side: carpets by Stark, curtains by Belfair, a hidden sound system and a paint job that cost what the average citizen pays for a house.

The living and dining rooms were at the front overlooking Park Avenue. The kitchen, laundry and maid's room were sensibly arranged in the center with the four bedrooms off a rear corridor. The smallest of these was fitted out as a gym.

Since the birth of their second child, Fiona had made it a rule to work out for an hour every evening. All forms of sweeteners were scrupulously avoided and at social occasions she only drank lemon-flavored Perrier. The result was a young body and a sharp mind. Carter headed to where his wife would be pounding away on the cross-trainer in her red leotard and black tights. He stretched up and gave her a kiss on the cheek.

"Hi, sexy. How much longer?" he asked.

She glanced at the clock on the wall. "Couple more minutes. Did you hear about Valerie?"

"No. Who's Valerie?"

"Geoffrey Johnson's wife. You sat next to her at the Special Surgery benefit."

"Oh, her. Thin, blonde and on continuous transmit."

"That's the one."

"What about her?"

"She's been arrested. Isabel told me."

"This sounds fascinating," he said, handing her a towel.

"Well," said Fiona, wiping her face. "It seems that for about a year she has had her own secret little brokerage account that Geoffrey didn't know about. She keeps it on her laptop."

"Nothing wrong with that."

"Yes, but Isabel said that she's been taking notes when Geoffrey is on the phone, or when he's having clients over for dinner. Apparently she went online and used what she had overheard to update her portfolio. About a month ago she made a real big killing and the flags started to fly at the Securities and Exchange Commission. They started to monitor her trades. Wasn't long before they figured she was using inside information. At eleven this morning the Feds came and arrested her."

"You're kidding."

"Isabel said Geoffrey got a call at the office in the middle of a meeting and had to leave to post bail. He's hopping mad. Isabel says even if she gets off it's going to cost them a fortune in legal fees. And there's the publicity. It's going to be all over the papers tomorrow. They might even have to resign from the clubs. I feel so sorry for the kids."

Fiona switched off the machine and headed into her bathroom. She stripped off her clothes, stepped into the shower and closed the curtain.

Minutes later Carter stood in his own shower letting the water cascade down his face. His wife had just put into words everything that he feared. She had just described what would happen to the Allinsons if Max and his brothers fucked up.

Valerie's husband, Geoffrey, was not one to ever give in easily. His aggressive personality would never let him suffer the consequences of his wife's idiotic transgressions. He would engage the best lawyers and put the whole matter to rest swiftly. No one in the Johnson family would be dragged into court and the limelight. No one would do jail time or even submit to one of those stupid ankle bracelets under house arrest. Geoffrey would skillfully handle the press and his marriage would remain intact.

As Carter and Fiona dressed for the evening he learned the details of his daughter's upcoming trip to Europe. Also, James had called to let them know he had done better than expected on his science exam and could he please have money for a new lacrosse stick? For the moment at least, everything at home was normal.

Carter slipped on his jacket as Fiona gave her neck a light spray of Floret.

In the kitchen Mathilda was sitting in front of her little television watching the Catholic Channel.

"We're off, Mattie," said Fiona, checking the contents of her sequined black evening purse. "We should be back by midnight."

"Shall I be leaving a little something for you in case you get hungry?" Mathilda was from Limerick.

"No, there's no need. We're having supper out."

"Right you are. Have a lovely evening now."

A limo was waiting in front of the building to take them the short ride across the park to Lincoln Center. The doorman opened and closed the door and respectfully touched his cap as they drove off.

17

The long flight down to South America had been endless with strong headwinds. On the connecting flight from Bogotá to Medellin, Max Bruschetti had been seated next to a fat woman smelling so strongly of fish and cheap talcum powder that he wanted to puke. As he walked from the plane into the terminal his neck and shoulders were stiff with tension. In the swaying taxi from the airport he had reminded himself that this was his last trip to this godforsaken place. It was too hot, too humid and too dangerous.

Once in his hotel room downtown he threw his case on the bed and went into the bathroom. Switching on the light, he washed his hands and face.

Minutes later in front of the hotel, Max approached two taxi drivers who stood smoking and waiting. He pulled a piece of paper from his top pocket and said in Spanish, "I want to go to the Finca de los Caballos Blancos on the main road into Llano Grande. It's close to the Hipico Club."

Max noticed the younger driver give a flick of recognition at the name of the house. He asked him, *"La conoce?"*

The young man shrugged. *"Sí, la conozco."*

Max nodded towards the two vehicles. *"Que taxi?"*

Both of them pointed at the first. Max opened the rear door and climbed in.

The young man flopped in behind the wheel. Using his horn to clear the roads ahead, he raced at breakneck speed through the streets as if challenging his passenger to ask him to slow down. Max ignored him and sat back in his seat. The road rose up through the valley and corrugated iron gave way to red brick and space began to appear between the buildings. Minutes later they crested the ridge and sped down towards Llano Grande. Max's driver grunted and pointed to the right.

The Finca de los Caballos Blancos lay on a gently sloping hillside and at the end of a long sweeping driveway. Flanked by tall trees and fields of verdant grass, the walls were white, the doors and windows painted deep green. Around the main building stood stables, barns and a large circular exercise arena with a high pointed roof of Roman tile. The walls of the Finca were taking on a dusky orange hue as the sun lingered on the brow of the far hillside.

Some of the staff wore khaki pants and white open-necked shirts with brown leather cases for Ray-Ban sunglasses on every belt, the flaps trimmed off for easy access. A few wore ties and sports jackets. The menial tasks were being done by workers dressed in blue overalls and straw hats, some tending the gardens, others grooming or exercising the horses. One washed a white Jeep Cherokee parked in front of the main house.

To the casual observer this appeared to be a well-run horse farm. To Max it was an armed camp with no shortage of firepower. The Finca was said to possess a state-of-the-art torture chamber, but no one had ever come forth to confirm or deny the rumor. Several people had allegedly disappeared without a trace on the orders of the man he was about to meet. But all this was hearsay. The Hernandez family kept a low profile and avoided the flashy and fatal lifestyles of certain other families in Colombia.

The pastoral scene before him was a far cry from his last visit to the country. In the early days of their association, the Bruschettis only did small jobs for them along with a few black-bag operations. Nevertheless, Rodrigo Hernandez wanted Max to be aware of all aspects of the drug operation. It was at a time when the DEA was stepping up the pressure in the Miami sector. Max had been flown down to attend a meeting on the need for alternative routes.

The barred gateway swung open and they were waved through by a short man in a green jacket who spoke into a two-way radio. Max watched as the automatic gate swung behind them and sealed out the rest of the world. The taxi pulled up beside the Cherokee and Max leaned forward and paid his driver. As Max climbed out, the local insect population gave him an obstreperous welcome.

A green jacket stepped forward and signaled to the driver to leave. A second took Max's bag and with a nod indicated that he should precede him up the front steps.

The high-ceilinged room into which Max was ushered was filled with magnificent upholstered furniture. Arrangements of flowers were everywhere. Wide-open arches ran the full length, giving a view of the garden. Two attractive women in their mid-thirties stood talking animatedly in Spanish. On the floor, four small children played with a toy garage, driving little cars noisily up and down the ramps, the eldest imperiously telling the others what to do.

On a terrace outside the last of the arches, a chef in a white hat was cooking at a built-in brick barbecue, sending clouds of white smoke into the surrounding ornamental bushes.

Although no one in the room was smoking, a suggestion of marijuana mingled with the rich odor of the roasting meat. A Persian cat licked itself high up on a sunny window ledge and two Saluki dogs lay draped on the rug in front of the vast fireplace.

A short man in casual white clothes sat at a table in the far corner with his concentration firmly fixed on what was passing from his plate to his stomach. Next to a plate of *crepas* was a long dish filled with a mixture of chopped meat, tomatoes and peppers. On a wide wooden board were piled freshly barbe-cued chorizo sausages, colorful salads and a variety of hot and cold vegetables. As this was not the man he had expected to meet, Max took a quick look around to see if he could spot anyone else, either in the room or out on the terrace. The man looked up, wiped his mouth with a huge white napkin and gave Max a wave.

"Señor Bruschetti! It is good to see you." His voice was reedy and nasal. "Please take a seat. You must be hungry after your long flight. Please, come join me in a little sustenance." He waved again, this time to a chair across the table.

"Thank you," said Max, sitting down. Immediately a waiter in a white coat placed a rush mat in front of him. On it were neatly arranged cutlery, a napkin and two long-stemmed glasses. As one waiter left, another arrived with a tray on which were a small glass of *aquardiente,* a glass of water and a small plate of coconut. Max drank down the strong liquor in one gulp, ignored the water, but slipped a piece of the white nut into his mouth to reduce the heat.

His host smiled. The gold fillings in his front teeth glinted as he spoke.

"No doubt you are surprised to see me. I am sure you were expecting Rodrigo. Regrettably, since the extradition and incarceration of certain prominent members of our little fraternity and the demise of several others, it has been necessary to change the way we operate. But I hasten to assure you we are in business as usual; it is only some of our methods that have changed. Did you know we are now in the gold business? Yes, of course you did. A commodity that is proving surprisingly easy to control. I never thought that one day I would be concerned with the safety of miners!"

He laughed a little too loudly.

Max speared a couple of sausages, helped himself to some fresh sliced pimientos and took a bite. The flavor of the meat was delicious. Chorizos in Spanish Harlem never tasted like these.

"Good, eh?" his host asked proudly.

"Excellent," answered Max, mopping the fat that trickled down his chin.

An arm waved towards the terrace. "Roberto is an artist at the grill. He's from Venezuela. They make the world's finest butchers and cooks." Giving a chuckle, he whispered, "I had to strangle his last employer to get him!"

Max smiled. After exchanging a few pleasantries about the weather in New York the little man quickly came to the point.

"Your message spoke of changes. As you are no doubt aware we do not take kindly to change. It leads to trouble and we prefer to avoid trouble whenever possible."

"I've come to talk about ending our relationship," said Max laying down his knife and fork. "I'm also aware that we're only a part of your East Coast operation. You have many others who can take over. The time has come for the Bruschettis to hand over to someone else. I'm here to work out the best way to do it."

His host raised his eyebrows and then after a moment asked, "And what made you come to this decision?"

"We are concerned about our moneyman," said Max.

"Señor Carter Allinson?"

"Yes. I have a feeling he's planning to quit. To retire. I think he's had enough."

The little man gave Max an amused smile. "As I remember, Señor Allinson was never too happy about the manner of his recruitment."

"You know about that?"

"I try to know as much as I can about everything, Señor Bruschetti," he answered. "Are you telling me he's now a danger?"

Max continued. "No. Not at all. I don't think so. It's only that the time has come when we might have to replace him. That would mean setting up a whole new financial arrangement. I'm not absolutely sure we could do that securely."

"I see."

"The whole problem, and what it would take to solve it, makes us nervous. If you agree to what we are asking, I can guarantee a smooth changeover. Your security will not be breached at any level."

A maid in a pale blue uniform appeared and shepherded the children off to bed. High-pitched protestations echoed along the corridor. A door was closed and order was restored.

His host folded his napkin and put it on the table. "What about the people that work for you? Can you trust them?"

"Anyone who works for us knows his job and only his job. They have no idea what anyone else does either above or below them," replied Max. "There are one or two exceptions, and we're making arrangements to terminate all of those."

"Excellent," said the little man, and he rose from the table.

"I appreciate your taking the time to make this trip, Señor Bruschetti. It is a long way to come for such a brief meeting. But better this way than all those 'bits and bytes' out there for all the world to download and analyze. So, my friend, Señor Rodrigo will be in touch one way or another. Do I make myself clear?"

"Completely," replied Max,

A proprietary arm was draped over Max's shoulder as they strolled across the room. "Now is there anything else we can do for you while you're here? Any indulgence you might care to amuse yourself with before you leave? You have only to ask."

Torture was not the only myth attached to the Finca. Sex was another. It was whispered that the big white house had seen some imaginative orgies. Max would have gladly indulged his fancy with either of the two women by the fireplace. Or both. But the reality of the offer would more likely be a whore in a seedy room back in town.

"You are very generous, señor," he replied. "But I'm afraid I have to get back."

"As you wish," said his host with an understanding shrug.

They walked down the front steps to where a driver waited in the Cherokee. The two men shook hands and his host perfunctorily wished him a pleasant journey.

The center of the town was thick with traffic and they crawled along to the hotel. Until it was time to leave for the airport, Max lay on the bed fully clothed. Only on the plane back to New York did he finally catch up with his sleep.

At Newark Airport Enzo stood by the barrier outside the

customs area. Benny was waiting for them in the parking lot. Both men climbed in.

"What did he say?" asked Enzo.

"Who?" said Max.

"Rodrigo," said Enzo.

"I didn't meet with Rodrigo," Max answered. "It was another guy. Looked a bit like him. Probably a cousin. Tight little bastard. Never even told his name. I'll tell you what happened, but first, you tell me about Rocco."

"Good news," said Enzo. "Santiago will be found in a male prostitute's room. Sure to be a verdict of accidental death. Weird sex game gone wrong. "

"Jesus! He's a clever bastard," said Max, shaking his head. "What about Villiers?"

"For our friend the Colonel, Rocco is gonna make his death look like a political hit. He got a hold of a man called Eddie Ryan to carry it out."

"A political hit? What the fuck is that all about?" asked Max.

Benny paid the parking and swung the big car out into traffic.

"Before he got married," continued Enzo, "Colonel Villiers did active duty in Northern Ireland and apparently made himself pretty unpopular. It's a good cover. Rocco asked me to ask if you thought he should wait a couple of days. He's worried about the two killings so close together."

"I don't pay him to worry! Jesus! Why can't anyone do what I ask?! When does Villiers get back?"

"I think he's due back Thursday morning. First thing."

"Then he gets whacked Thursday morning! First fucking thing!" said Max angrily.

"Max! We should . . ."

"For once will you just shut up and give me a goddam fucking phone!"

18

The *Star Wars* march rang out in the living room. Harry walked over and picked up his cellphone. Call-waiting showed him it was his agent, who came straight to the point.

"Sorry there, sport, but Lenny the casting person called to say that you didn't get the part of Tex. Zergensky loved your interpretation and is looking forward to working with you on another project in the near future."

Harry thanked Richie, hung up and sat motionless for almost a minute absorbing the rejection and accompanying bullshit.

Then he gave a deep sigh of frustration.

Did he really want to spend the rest of his life putting himself on the line at auditions only to be summarily rejected? Was that to be his future?

Not for the first time he wondered if it was time to quit. Move out of New York. Go somewhere a little more cost friendly. Possibly change his life completely. There must be something else besides acting that he could do in this world. But what?

To relieve a growing physical tension he went for a jog in Central Park. As he ran, he tried to concentrate on reasons to continue his career as an actor. Then he noticed his hand had begun to bleed. This reminded him of the jarring impact of the taxicab and the possibility that if he hadn't had the presence of mind to leap upwards he could have been killed. This made him think that perhaps he had been too hasty in his decision to do nothing to prevent this Villiers being killed. But what could he do?

Taking the escalator down into the Whole Foods market on Columbus Circle, he chose a packet of large Band-Aids and covered up the open wound. He then took the opportunity to pick up a six-pack of Stella Artois and a few groceries.

Once back at his building, he extracted a wad of letters and magazines from his mailbox and climbed up. Dumping them onto the living room table, he went into the kitchen and put away the groceries and beer. His freezer compartment was almost full, so it was necessary to chip away some of the excess ice before he could squeeze in three packets of frozen macaroni.

Retrieving his cellphone, he located the list of things he had overheard and sent it to the printer on his desk. Picking up the single sheet, he flopped down on the sofa:

Carter
Julian
Amanda
Papa Aldo
Rivas
Rodrigo
Colombians
A colonel
A million and a half (dollars?)
Santiago
Bogotá
Max
Mews
Europe
Villiers
Dead meat
Rocky
No delay
Channel Islands
Internet
Kensington

As he stared at the words it suddenly occurred to him that he could put in a call to Villiers. How stupid! Why hadn't he thought of that before? Glancing at his watch, he made a quick calculation. It would be late afternoon in London.

Harry had worked on location in the UK many times and

knew that Kensington was in West London. As he didn't have international calls activated on his cellphone, he walked back into the bedroom, sat down, picked up the landline and dialed 411. It took only a few seconds to be connected to overseas directory assistance.

"What number do you require?"

"Villiers," said Harry. "In Kensington, London."

"One moment please." A pause. "There is more than one Villiers listed, sir. Do you have any other information?"

Harry thought fast. "Yes, I do. It's in a Mews."

"Thank you, sir. We show one in Kensington Mews."

As Harry wrote down the number and address the operator asked, "Can I assist you with another number, sir?"

"No thank you," said Harry. He pressed down the cradle, released it and without hesitating dialed the fifteen numbers. A phone on the other end began to ring. Harry was wondering what to say when a female said, "Villiers residence. May I help you?"

She sounded very proper. Very upper-crust.

Harry took a deep breath. "Yes. I'm calling from New York. For Mr. Villiers."

"*Colonel* Villiers," she corrected with emphasis. "I'm afraid he's out of the country. Won't be back until Thursday morning at eight thirty. Would you care to leave a message?"

"No. Thank you. No, I don't think so. It can wait," said Harry and he quickly replaced the receiver.

19

Detective Sergeant Ivan Sapinsky was pouring himself an espresso from his old and well-used thermos. In his haste to press the record button when the overseas call came through to number 4 Kensington Mews, he almost knocked over the little metal cup.

The police officer was surrounded by a highly sophisticated level of electronic eavesdropping devices. If the cup had gone over, it would have been an extremely expensive accident. However, Ivan managed to catch it in mid-tip. Only a few drops of the dark liquid spilled on his overalls. To make absolutely certain that nothing had been damaged, he played over the conversation he had just recorded and then pressed more buttons.

Three swallows later a telephone number appeared on one of the screens in front of him. Next to it was a name: "Murphy, H. P.," and a New York phone number.

20

The beer in Harry's hand grew warm as the implications of what he was doing percolated down through his head. This wasn't a script for a movie. It was fact, not fiction. An actual Colonel Villiers lived in London. Someone was going to try to knock him off. Once he was a corpse on the ground no one would come along and help him up. He'd be dead meat. And so would Harry if he stuck his nose in. Real murderers don't leave clues. The person who killed them both would never be caught. Harry would suffer an anonymous death in a foreign country. Only a fool would get himself involved.

Then his cellphone rang in the living room. Once again it was Richie.

"Hello there, sport," he said cheerily. "Sorry about the play, but we just got some good news. You have a booking at Nutmeg at nine A.M. tomorrow for Mueller's Mayonnaise."

"Wow! That's great!" exclaimed Harry.

"They loved your reading. When you get there, ask for BJ." And he hung up. Richie was a man of few words.

It was a sign! The recording fee would cover the flight and hotel and the residual payments would cover any additional expenses. He would drop by the Mews and knock on the door. If trouble arose he could always improvise. Harry had played dozens of shady characters and with so much firsthand experience he would know exactly what to say and do. Once he had done his duty he would relax for a while. Go sightseeing. Visit a few of his favorite restaurants. Take in a couple of shows.

Maybe he would pop over to Paris for a naughty weekend. Or Copenhagen. Copenhagen was naughtier. And if the whole thing turned out to be a hoax, he would simply have enjoyed a memorable vacation and would be able to come home with a whole new perspective on life.

Aware that time was of the essence, he went online and found several last-minute low-fare options to Heathrow. He chose a flight out of Kennedy on American Airlines.

The next morning the commercial turned out to be an animated cartoon. Harry's enthusiastic reading of "Mueller's Mayo. It's in the bag!" had thrilled the client as it was perfect for the talking sandwich that leapt in and out of a kid's lunchbox. Soon after noon everyone had convinced themselves they had the definitive reading of the cute little voice.

Harry left extra time for the taxi ride to Kennedy Airport in an effort to avoid the rush-hour exodus from the city. As always, the Van Wyck was a parking lot. But check-in and security went relatively smoothly and he was able to get himself a bite to eat before it was time to board. At the gate he was delighted to find that due to overbooking he had been upgraded. This was clearly a sign that he had made the right decision to go and warn Colonel Villiers.

The seat in Business Class had a series of levers that would angle the head, body and feet to any desired position. A touch-screen television and Bose headphones were provided for the inflight entertainment. As Harry sipped from the little plastic glass of champagne, he amused himself by reading the safety pamphlet telling what he should do if this massive plane came down unexpectedly in the Atlantic.

"Good evening," said a voice, soft and low.

Harry looked up.

Settling into the seat next to him was a woman with deep violet eyes. Elizabeth Taylor eyes. She wore a smart suit and a Hermès scarf. The current issue of *Vanity Fair* poked out from her carry-on.

"Good evening," he said, marveling at his good fortune.

Harry took a moment to check out the other passengers in the cabin. Could one of them be on his way to eliminate the Colonel? And need a hired killer necessarily be a male? There had been several movies in the last few years with diabolical women assassins. Would she, or he, be traveling in Business? The more successful could certainly afford the comforts of First, but Economy would be the most anonymous. Then Harry reminded himself that what he was doing was not fiction but reality. He should stick to facts.

Before takeoff, seat belts were fastened, the empty glasses were collected and everyone was made aware of the necessary safety instructions. The cabin gave a slight shudder, and right on schedule the big jet was pushed back from the gate and slowly trundled over the bumpy concrete like an elephant. But as the wheels left the runway the great jet flew into the air like an eagle.

About twenty minutes later the Captain's voice over the intercom announced they had reached their cruising altitude. Harry's companion pushed the scarf from her head and said, "Excuse me."

"Of course," he replied.

"Do you know what time we land at Heathrow?" She had an odd accent that Harry couldn't place.

"About nine thirty," he answered.

She smiled her thanks revealing teeth that were toothpaste commercial material. She stretched out her hand. "Marisa Vargas." Her hand was strong and cool.

"Harry Murphy."

The flight attendant appeared with tablecloths and they both pulled out their trays.

"Are you traveling on business?" Marisa asked, dropping the magazine at her feet.

Harry took an instant to ponder the question. The last thing he wanted to talk about was show business. He was sipping champagne next to a drop-dead gorgeous woman en route to Europe. It was unlikely they would ever meet again. Here was an opportunity for a little fabrication. What could he be? Then he remembered, like the Blues Brothers, he was on a "mission from God."

"I'm in law enforcement," he said confidentially.

"Really?" The dusky way she replied gave him goose bumps. "INTERPOL?"

"Well, not exactly," he said, and added, "I'm with an agency that deals with a select number of cases that are out of the normal areas of police investigative work."

"Really?" She was impressed. "Drugs?"

"Computer crime mostly."

Harry was on a roll.

"The criminal mind has become smart and sophisticated. It's tough to catch them these days."

"Is what you do dangerous?" she asked.

He gave a slight shrug and smoothed out his tablecloth. "It's a living."

As he had waited to board the flight Harry had passed the time reading an article in *The Week* describing the deplorable foreign-policy decisions of the current administration. All through dinner he talked fluidly about his work as an undercover operative, using plots and dialogue from scripts he'd done in the past. Two more glasses of champagne and two of Sangiovese oiled his willing tongue. Marisa was a good listener. The creative fiction only ended when the overhead lights were darkened. The efforts of the last two days and the flickering images on the screen in front of him combined to lull Harry into a deep sleep.

"Mister Murphy."

He opened his eyes to see a tray with a glass of orange juice. A polyester blanket had been draped over him in the night and he felt hot and clammy. First light streamed in through the uncovered windows. The seat across from him was empty. "You were dead to the world," the flight attendant said smiling. "We'll be serving our continental breakfast in just a moment."

Harry drained the glass in one gulp. His companion reappeared carrying a small leather case. Her hair was held back with a gold clip. Harry grabbed the complimentary kit from the seat pocket and lurched to the toilet. Inside, he slid the bolt to Occupied and the lights blinked on. Unzipping his fly, he relieved the considerable pressure on his bladder and pushed the little lever. A swirl of blue water flushed the toilet with a loud thud. When he returned to his seat Marisa was now wearing the Bose noise-canceling headphones and reading *Vanity Fair*.

The captain throttled back as he began the descent into Heathrow. The landing was smooth and they soon pulled up at the ramp.

Once off the big jet Harry walked as fast as he could through the tunnels in the terminal as he knew from past experience that seconds could make a difference in the time he would have to wait in the immigration hall. Unfortunately, a Dreamliner had disgorged hordes of passengers who not only didn't speak English, but also carried sheaves of papers that needed careful checking and loud stamping. Harry shuffled along in the line.

It took him another ten minutes to find his suitcases at Carousel 4 in the baggage claim. For some unexplained reason they had been taken off the conveyor belt and placed on the floor with luggage from a flight from Miami. The smaller of his two bags had sprung open to reveal his freshly laundered shirts and underwear. He shoved everything back in, closed it up and wheeled his trolley under the octagonal green sign marked: Nothing to Declare.

A customs official motioned him to stop and indicated he should place his bags on the counter.

"Had an accident, have you?" he said and pointed at the broken zip.

Harry shook his head. "The catch is broken."

"Open it."

Harry unzipped the lid and lifted it back.

"On business are you, sir?"

All his life, Harry's parents had lectured him on the need for conformity. In matters of paying taxes, obeying the law and passing through Customs, he was taught to respect authority. Antisocial behavior was the swift route to eternal damnation. The cells of Harry's brain were filled with residual religious guilt. Fear of consequences kept his feet firmly on the straight and narrow.

Nevertheless he thought it prudent to avoid the real reason for his trip. "On vacation," he answered casually.

The man gave the case a perfunctory search and then nodded that he was free to go and turned back to his colleagues. Once again Harry stuffed everything back in and trundled his way around the corner of the wall that separated the customs area from the free world. Harry headed for Cook's and changed two hundred dollars into sterling.

The Heathrow subway station was at the end of an exceedingly long passageway. At the ticket booth, Harry bought a runaround ticket. Once inside the compact carriage he felt as if he were traveling in a toy train. Outside the window, the narrow streets, the shops, the little houses, the back gardens and parks of suburbia all flashed by, bringing back a kaleidoscope of memories from earlier visits.

On those trips, Harry had stayed at a small hotel not far from the Portobello Market that was popular with actors, writers and musicians. It was stylish and expensive, but the company always paid the bill. But a reservation had to be made well in advance. This time, with such short notice, a room wasn't available, so it had been necessary to look elsewhere. Larry Parker, his accountant, could always be relied on to come up with a bargain. He had made a suggestion. Harry had called and booked a single.

The walk from the subway station to the hotel took him less than ten minutes. Once checked in, he took a cramped little elevator to his floor.

The layout of the diminutive space under the eaves was most ingenious. On the right-hand wall was a wooden bunk. Built into it were two drawers for storage. Beyond the bed were a narrow closet, a folding canvas chair and a table with kettle, plate, cup and saucer. The tiny minibar was attached to the wall at eye level. The TV was on a bracket perched high above the end of the bed. The control lay on the little pillow.

The left wall housed the bathroom unit that was entered through a sliding door. The basin folded up to reveal the toilet. To take a shower, it was necessary to sit on the toilet and hold the little plastic spray. This was also used to fill the basin for washing and shaving. Folding this back up sent the dirty water down into the toilet.

Daylight came into this snugly decorated cell from a window high up in the end wall. Harry comforted himself with the fact that it wasn't barred.

Like many men, Harry liked to spread out in a state of orderly untidiness. Some of his clothes went into the drawers beneath the bed. The rest he piled where he could. Once undressed, he edged his way into the little bathroom and sat down on the toilet. With shower in hand he turned on the water. The light spray sprinkled over his hair. As it ran down over his face he closed his eyes and tried to recall the voice of the woman who had answered the phone. Who could she be? Mrs. Villiers? Or perhaps a maid? Someone who worked for the Colonel? A relative?

Although the pressure was pathetic, a great deal of water leaked out of the unit. Harry dried himself off and mopped up the floor as best he could.

Once dressed, he retrieved the S—Z telephone directory from under a pile of shirts on the window ledge and ran his finger down the columns until he found: *Villiers CJ 4 Kensington Mews.*

On his way past the front desk, he did his best to explain to the smiling gentleman from Pakistan why he needed new towels. In spite of all the friendly nodding, Harry had no idea whether the man had actually understood what he was saying. Leaving the hotel, he walked to the end of the street and flagged down a passing cab. When they arrived at Kensington Mews, Harry paid the fare and stood for a while on the pavement to get his bearings.

Opposite was an ornate and somewhat worn Victorian archway that framed the entrance to a narrow cobbled street. Carriage houses lined both sides. Most of these had been converted into upscale dwellings. A few were used as garages. Lush green ivy grew everywhere. On many of the windowsills were boxes of geraniums. Harry had grown geraniums on his sill in New York but they were deformed dwarfs by comparison to these strong and healthy creatures.

As Harry passed under the archway a FedEx van swung past him into the Mews and drew up at the second doorway on his left. Someone somewhere was practicing a Bach fugue on a piano. In a second-floor window two Siamese cats watched a flock of pigeons as they squabbled over a scrap of bread in the gutter. Midway down the block an elderly gentlemen in tweed trousers, a loose sweater and Wellington boots was washing a blue Bentley with a garden hose.

As Harry walked by, the man looked up from his chores. "Lovely morning!"

Harry smiled in reply.

Two steps later he saw a polished brass plate that read Colonel C. J. Villiers. As he stared at it, a distant church bell struck the hour.

He moved closer to the windows. The interior was obscured by net curtains. Not wishing to draw attention to himself he sauntered past.

At the end of the Mews, a yellow British Telecom panel truck was parked close to the wall. A ladder led from the truck to a roof. At the top of it, a worker in overalls was tinkering with a TV aerial. Inside the cab, a girl with closely cropped black hair sat reading a newspaper. Cigarette smoke drifted from the window. Both glanced at Harry as he passed.

The Mews turned out to be a dead end, so Harry turned back. But for the truck, the street was now empty. The car washer had turned off the faucet and gone indoors and the FedEx van had driven away.

Harry hurried over to the window and peered through the gap at the edge of the curtain but all he could see was the top of a piano covered in photographs in silver frames. As he held up his hand to shield the light, the same upper-crust voice from the phone conversation surprised him with "May I help you?"

Harry looked around but couldn't see anyone. Then a short woman with spectacles and clutching a rolled newspaper straightened up right beside him. "You are?" she inquired with raised eyebrows.

Harry didn't know what to say. Parental indoctrination took over. "Harry Murphy," he said politely.

"Ah yes," she said. "And you have come to—?"

"From New York," he said quickly, deflecting the question.

"Ah yes," she said with a knowing nod. "We've been expecting you."

Harry was totally lost.

"Enzo called Charles. Said we should be getting a visitor from New York. Come in and have a cup of tea." She gave him a smile. "Or no doubt you would prefer coffee?"

"No, tea would be fine," he said with a silly laugh. "Thank you."

She handed him the paper, reached into the depths of her purse, took out a key and opened the front door. A silk scarf tied under her chin covered most of her head. Here and there, wisps of gray hair stuck out. She wore a light green Mackintosh and sensible brown walking shoes.

Harry wanted to ask questions but being totally ignorant of who he was meant to be and what he was supposed to be doing, he didn't dare risk saying the wrong thing.

Carefully wiping his shoes on the doormat, he followed her inside. The entrance hall was tiny. A narrow carpeted stairway led to the upper floors. Holding out a hand for the paper she waved him towards a doorway to his left.

"Go into the drawing-room and make yourself at home," she said. "I'll be with you in a jiffy. You can put your coat anywhere. We're really quite informal here."

The bright and cheerful room ran the full depth of the building. A marble mantel dominated the far wall with wicker baskets on either side, one for logs, another smaller one for kindling. A chintz sofa faced the fireplace, flanked by two matching armchairs. French doors led out to a lawn that was surrounded by well-tended flower beds.

Harry took off his coat and laid it on a chair by the piano. Maybe he could get a clue from the photographs. He bent over to get a better look.

His hostess called out from the kitchen. "Have you had lunch, Mr. Murphy? Can I fix you a plate?"

"I haven't really settled down from the journey yet," he replied. "A cup of tea would be fine."

There were two principal themes on the piano: the army and equestrian sports. A photo of the Prince of Wales amidst a smiling group of riders in polo gear. A faded photograph of a bridal couple on church steps, the groom in dress uniform and the bride in a white lacy gown. A group of men in battledress linked arm in arm with a tall, handsome man in the middle. No doubt the Colonel. Across the bottom of the frame was engraved *Falkland Islands 1986*. There were no pictures of kids.

The kettle in the kitchen whistled and was turned off. The water was poured into the teapot and the top replaced with a clink.

Harry picked up the bridal couple to take a closer look. When he heard footsteps crossing the hall he put it down.

The little woman sailed into the room like the *QE2* entering harbor. She carried an enormous oaken tray laden with Spode Butterfly Garden china, linen napkins, a plate of cookies, a sponge cake, a milk jug, a sugar bowl with tongs, a tea strainer and a floral cozy covering the teapot.

She nodded her head for him to move the magazines off the sofa table. He gathered them up, put them on the piano and took another quick look at the wedding picture. Her height gave her away. *QE2* and bride were one and the same.

Mrs. Villiers perched herself in the center of the sofa. "It's Charles's own mixture. Typhoo and Earl Grey," she said with pride.

Harry said, "Fantastic!" and sank into one of the deep armchairs.

"From when his dear father was stationed in India. So long ago now." She sighed and poured a little milk into the cups, followed by the dark brown tea through the strainer. "Charles told me he was expecting you on Thursday."

Harry thought this an appropriate cue for him to explain his reasons for coming to London. "No doubt you're wondering why I'm here," he said, and leaned forward.

"Oh no. Enzo explained it all," she replied pleasantly.

Harry paused. Enzo? Who did she think he was? Could it be a mistake to tell her his true identity? Why he was there? Perhaps a more cautious approach was called for. He settled back in the cushions and asked nonchalantly, "How is Charles?"

"Doing wonderfully well, thank you," she replied. "How many sugars?"

"Three please."

"A sweet tooth! Then you simply must try one of these. Our neighbor Mrs. Perkins makes them. She's Irish too." She handed him his tea and held out the cookies. "Take two. They're really only a mouthful."

They looked very much more than a mouthful to Harry. "Do I sound so Irish to you?" he asked.

"No, of course you don't," she replied. "But no one from America ever sounds the way they should, do they? Incidentally, why did you come here today and not tomorrow?"

"I was checking where you lived," he lied. "This is my first time here. I wanted to be sure I knew where to come. I make it a habit to be prepared."

"When is your birthday?" she inquired.

"September 20," he answered.

"Ah, you see!" she said. "You're a Virgo. I thought as much. Always so careful and organized with everything in its place."

Harry sipped his tea and ate his cookies. The curtain was up and the show was going great. As the conversation proceeded it became clear that the engaging Mrs. Villiers was not a main character, only a supporting player. Clearly he would accomplish nothing by revealing his mission to her.

For another half hour he stayed and chatted about the deplorable parenting skills of the royal family, the vicissitudes of the British weather and the finer points of astrology.

He followed the cookies with two slices of sponge cake.

21

Back at the hotel, a large pile of towels had been placed on Harry's bed with a note: *Hope these are what you wanting.* He moved them into a corner, lay down and switched on the television. The BBC was showing a replay of a cricket match. Five minutes of Middlesex versus Glamorgan and Harry was dead to the world.

Raucous laughter awakened him. Above him, a fat comedian dressed as an aging nun leered at him from the screen. Harry didn't find this style of British humor at all amusing. As if to prove him wrong, the studio audience screamed with merriment. He pressed the mute button. The ensuing silence was total.

Lying there, he wondered whether he should just pick up the phone, call Mrs. Villiers, tell the nice lady all he knew and take the first plane to Copenhagen. But if something really bad happened to the Colonel, the call could be traced back to Harry's hotel. Possibly to this room. Fear of consequence called for a little patience. And a degree of caution. He would go back to the Mews as planned in the morning and find a spot where he could watch without being seen. As soon as he saw the Colonel coming back he would intercept him and tell him what he had heard. Then he would beat a hasty retreat.

Water was running somewhere in the depths of the building. Far up in the sky, a jet made the approach to Heathrow. Harry stared at the odd patterns on the wallpaper, his conscious mind slowly drifting into the unconscious. When he awoke with a violent start he had no idea where he was.

The tiny room was lit by flickering blue light from the television. Then everything came back in a flash. He glanced at his watch. Time for dinner.

A stroll along Oxford Street took him to Regent Street, where he spent a leisurely time looking in the windows, marveling at the prices. In the alleys of Soho he was sad to find that the lively old red-light district was now somber and dark.

A little Italian bistro seemed adequate, so he went in and ordered a bottle of red wine and a Milanese with a side order of spaghetti. After some inedible spumoni he drank an espresso. At the tables around him, several couples happily shared their evening, making him feel conspicuous in his solitude. It would be wonderful, he thought, to have someone with him.

The nearest Harry had come to tying the proverbial knot was with Colleen O'Herlihy. Colleen and Harry had grown up together in adjoining houses in South Brooklyn after their grandfathers had traveled over from Ireland on the same boat. The O'Herlihys sprang from Cork. The Murphy family tree had its roots in the town of Blackwater in the County of Wexford.

The Murphy transplant to America had nothing to do with potatoes or poverty, or even political unrest. For many years, the eldest Murphy, one Sean Patrick, had insisted that his wife make his tea using Holy Water from the natural spring at the entrance to the church. Not only did it make an excellent brew, but, as the old man pointed out to everyone who shared his pot, God exulted in making such a practical contribution to human comfort. God also decided one rainy night to cause the church horse to stumble and fall on top of the unfortunate elderly parish priest and squeeze the breath out of him. His pale replacement was a zealous youth, fresh from the seminary.

Invited to tea, the young man almost asphyxiated when he was told the source of the water in the pot. A passionate discussion followed in the confines of the Murphy parlor with both men quoting liberally from the scriptures to support their arguments about the use of Holy Water. Three days later the irate priest took the dispute public and denounced the terrible desecration from the pulpit. It was, he thundered, an unforgivable heresy. The eighty-four-year-old Murphy rose from his pew and led his considerable family down the central aisle. Five days later he took them aboard a boat to Boston. From there they traveled by coach to the city of New York where the male offspring joined the police force. The eldest was killed during Prohibition and another died of a mysterious illness on a trip to California. Harry's grandfather managed to survive both violence and disease.

Harry remembered vividly the day Colleen was born. For a fifth birthday treat he'd been promised a trip to see the precinct house where his father worked. The outing was called off at the last minute when Colleen came into the world a month early. From that day on, Harry harbored a deep-rooted resentment towards the little brat next door and over the years they were never really friends, only neighbors separated by a garden fence.

That all changed when Harry came back from college at the end of his junior year. The premature little O'Herlihy girl had blossomed into a stunning beauty. That same night, he invited her to go with him to the movies.

What Harry didn't know was that Colleen had set her sights on him the first day she had gazed up into his big brown eyes from the safety of her baby carriage. Now she was a ripe and dedicated virgin who was genetically skilled in the art of enticement. Each time they went out on a date she drew him closer and closer. With a knowing smile she would allow him tantalizing glimpses of her pretty white lacy panties. At the same time she made it abundantly clear that the only way he could enjoy what lay beyond was with a proposal of marriage. In no time at all she had him climbing the walls. The poor lad's sexual strings were stretched far beyond the limits of safety. All four parents prayed regularly to God and asked Him to encourage the union. It came as no surprise when Harry posed the question, a date was set for the wedding and the banns were posted. Harry returned to college a happy man.

Throughout his senior year at Albany State he tried to study for a degree in business, but it became increasingly clear to him that the world of finance had no appeal. At graduation, Harry told his father he wanted to look around before settling on a career. Both parents told him he was making a big mistake. Harry was adamant. He wanted to see the world.

The world turned out to be a fifth-floor walkup in Greenwich Village that he shared with two friends from college seeking work as actors. One month later, Harry announced to his family that he too was going to try the theater. Colleen's father heard the news and withdrew his consent to their marriage. Somewhat to Harry's surprise, the love of his life sided with her father and handed him back the engagement ring. When pressed for a reason, she took refuge in the excuse that she was not the kind of girl to defy her father. Harry understood. He too was the offspring of an Irish immigrant.

With his good looks, a strong voice and a natural sense of the dramatic, Harry soon worked regularly on and off Broadway. He acquired an agent and made the move into television and film. While he was acting in a regional production of *Amadeus* the O'Herlihy family moved out and contact with Colleen was lost forever. Two years later Harry's father retired from the police force. Mike and Bridget Murphy relocated to the sunshine of South Florida. Brooklyn was home to Harry no more. But he never forgot the image of those lacy white panties.

Sipping a Sambuca, he imagined how he and Colleen would have shared the evening. To get himself another glass of the sweet liquor he moved over to the bar where he spent a considerable time talking with a vivacious young girl from Birmingham. He flirted with the idea of inviting her to his hotel but she gave him the distinct impression she wasn't the type. More relevant was the fact that he had a life-saving job to do the next day.

Leaving the bar, he went over to Covent Garden, picked up the papers from an all-night newsstand and then walked briskly back through the deserted streets to his hotel.

22

Carter Allinson experienced a vivid dream that made him sit up in a sweat. The images were fleeting but powerful. His body was being carried along naked in the swirling water of a tsunami and he struggled to get to the surface for a breath. In the milliseconds before he consciously awoke, the water swiftly receded and he found himself lying spread-eagled on the wet sand.

He sighed audibly. His subconscious mind apparently knew more about what was happening than he did. Perhaps it was trying to warn him. Like animals that run or fly away when an earthquake or other natural disaster is close, a sixth sense of impending doom. But he shrugged off these thoughts as crazy and told himself to stop being paranoid.

Nevertheless, after a quick breakfast of coffee and toast he went to work and spent the entire day cloistered in his office making absolutely sure that the early Bruschetti records and accounts were sufficiently abstract and complex. When he was satisfied, he packed everything back into boxes and locked them away. He disliked keeping such damning evidence around but there was no other choice. The Feds would have a hard time following the trail, but if they succeeded Carter had to know exactly what to say if he was ever called to testify.

After being cooped up all day he needed some fresh air so he walked home. In his absence, the apartment had been transformed for the hospital benefit.

A maid was laying out plates of food on the dining room table and a tall man was setting up the usual bar in the far corner of the living room.

"Good evening, Mr. Allinson," he said.

"Good evening, Peter," replied Carter. "Everything okay?"

"I think we have everything under control. Can I get you something?"

"Yes, please. A scotch. Just a little ice."

In the corridor to the bedrooms Carter was assailed by Amanda.

"We need to talk," his daughter said imperiously, sounding exactly like her mother. Carter often couldn't tell their voices apart.

"You do surprise me," he said.

"I need to get away tonight by eight."

"What for?"

"Marcie's got tickets for the new group playing at the Bowery Ballroom. I said I'd go with her. A bunch of us made plans to meet at her place."

"What time does it start?"

"Nine."

"Nothing ever starts on time at those places. The party will be over by nine. You can leave then."

As Amanda dashed out of the room he called after her. "And not a minute sooner, you hear?"

"Be sure to tell Mom?" she shouted back. Her bedroom door slammed.

Carter smiled. Their daughter had a new boyfriend. Unknown to Amanda, her mother had already checked out the young man and reported that he came from a very acceptable family.

He was picking a tie from the rack when Fiona came flying in.

"There you are!" she exclaimed. "Thank goodness! I'm going to need a few more minutes. Dear Mitsuko took forever to dry my hair. And then it was impossible to find a free cab. I finally took one of those extortionate limo people. Be a pet and welcome everyone for me."

"Take your time, darling," he replied. "Leave it to me."

A quick check in each of the rooms assured him that all was as it should be. Using a mini iPad in the living room he programmed

Sonos for light classical music. Haydn's Symphony no. 94 began to play softly from invisible speakers. Carter enjoyed being the host on these occasions. It made him feel accepted and part of the New York social scene. Among the guests would be several faces and names whom most people only read about in the newspapers and magazines.

The first guests arrived a few minutes after seven fifteen. By eight o'clock the apartment was full. The hors d'oeuvres were passed and as the alcohol flowed the decibel level rose.

At the epicenter of this gathering was Charles Walker. Fiona had deliberately weighted the guest list with his cronies and business friends and every one of them made it a point to go up and reminisce with him.

At a quarter past eight, his wife made her way to the fireplace. Carter tapped on a glass to get everyone to stop talking.

"It gives me very great pleasure to welcome you here this evening," Fiona said, speaking clearly so that everyone heard every word, "and to be able to tell you that as a result of all your generous efforts, the wonderful new wing of our hospital will be completed as planned and, what is truly amazing, on time!"

There was a smattering of applause, but Fiona raised a hand and continued. "I have asked Doctor Richards to give you an idea of what this will mean for our little patients."

Doctor Richards stepped forward. Young, handsome, immaculately dressed and with a Marine Corps pin in the lapel of his jacket.

"Well," he began, "I wish to thank the Walkers for their generous hospitality this evening. My particular thanks go to Mrs. Allinson for her extraordinary tenacity and charm, which has culminated in our celebration tonight. The other day I witnessed one of our staff perform delicate MIS surgery on a baby boy's heart. I am happy to tell you the repair was successful. That operation is truly miraculous. And what you have done here is also a miracle. On behalf of the hospital staff, my sincerest thanks to you all."

The room broke into loud applause. A tall woman in sensible shoes, gray suit and pearl choker stepped forward.

"I have one small but happy announcement to make," she said. "In recognition of the many years the Walker family has dedicated to our hospital, the new facility will be formally recognized as the Walker Pediatric Suite."

At the other end of the room, Carter felt proud of his beautiful and talented wife as she gave her father and mother warm hugs. The three then stood together as the guests thronged around to congratulate them. At the same time a little voice inside Carter reminded him that pride goes before a fall and the next few days and weeks could prove critical.

If he wanted to avoid disaster, it was vital he keep a close watch on the Bruschettis.

23

A little after dawn the next morning Harry was back at the entrance to Kensington Mews where he waited on the steps of a block of flats on the far side of the road. An awning over his head sheltered him from the rain and made him less conspicuous. The Mews was empty apart from the Telecom truck that was still parked at the far end.

At 8:25, a dark green Jaguar approached from the left. Harry only had a brief glimpse of the driver, but from his appearance there was little doubt that it was Colonel Villiers. Harry ran across the street to number 4, leaned down and rapped hard on the passenger side window. The glass slid down.

The photographs on the piano didn't do the Colonel justice. The man was dashing as well as handsome and his military bearing was clearly evident. He wore a smart double-breasted sports jacket, regimental tie, cloth cap and neatly pressed gabardine trousers.

"Colonel Villiers," Harry said, panting. "I have something to tell you."

"Oh, do you now?" came the barked reply. "And who the hell are you?"

"Murphy. Harry Murphy from New York."

Villiers's whole demeanor changed. "Ah yes, Murphy, from New York. Rhonda told me you were here. Where the hell is Rocco? Gone AWOL has he?"

Harry shook his head. "Never mind that. There's something you should know."

"And what pray is that?"

Before he could answer Harry noticed a black motorcycle turn under the archway into the Mews, the helmeted rider cruising slowly towards them.

"Get on with it man," said the Colonel.

"It's a long story but I have reason to believe there's going to be an attempt on your life."

"Oh? Do you now?" He laughed. "And when might that be?"

The man on the bike stopped, reached into his bag and pulled out something metallic and black.

Harry screamed, "Oh shit! Oh shit! I think it's now!"

Villiers looked in his rearview mirror and saw the rider aiming his weapon.

"Get in!" he shouted.

Harry wrenched the passenger door open and dove onto the seat. The powerful engine was still running. Villiers floored the gas pedal. Harry and the man on the motorbike were both taken by surprise. The Colonel had put the Jaguar in reverse. The heavy car hurtled backwards.

"Head down!" commanded the Colonel.

Bullets tore into the metal and shattered the back window. Glass pellets showered down on both of them. Fear crawled through Harry's whole body. The adrenaline in his system soared.

Harry had done a lot of scenes with guns but these bullets

produced a totally different sound from blanks. Less of a bang and more of a crack.

Villiers yanked the steering wheel hard to the right. The Jaguar smashed into the would-be assassin and pinned him and his bike against the wall. Harry crashed against the dashboard as the attacker let out an agonized scream. The black helmet was jerked off revealing a young man with red hair. His weapon flew in a high arc before hitting the ground. The impact set it off. Bullets shattered the pot of geraniums on the nearby window ledge and they clattered down on the roof of the car.

Villiers was amazing. Now that he had dealt with the immediate threat, he slammed in the gears and drove the Jaguar down to the end of the Mews, sliding past the Telecom truck. With a twist of the wheel and a light touch to the brakes, he spun the car around until it faced the opposite direction and then accelerated smoothly.

As they flashed past him, the would-be assassin was trying to lift himself up on one elbow. A pool of blood had already formed on the wet cobblestones beneath his legs.

Moments later the Colonel drove the Jaguar up the ramp to the Motorway and adjusted the rearview mirror.

"I'd do up your seat belt if I were you, old boy," he said calmly. "I'm afraid we've got company. We appear to have upset British Telecom."

24

Confident that he had arranged everything to perfection, Rocco sat in his rented car at the end of Kensington Mews and watched his plan as it was carried out. Villiers drove up close to eight thirty. One minute later Eddie followed him into the Mews on his big BMW motorcycle. What Rocco didn't expect was the man in a flapping raincoat who ran across the street to warn the Colonel. Seconds later, Eddie was pinned against the wall as the Jaguar roared past him followed by a big yellow truck.

Starting his engine, Rocco drove around until he spotted a phone booth. Inside, he entered the prearranged number and code. When he heard the beep on the other end he punched in the number in front of him. He stood with the receiver held to his ear and the cradle held down with one finger. When the phone rang he let it go.

Max listened to him as he briefly reported what had happened.

"Have you any idea who the man was who warned Villiers?"

"No," replied Rocco. "Never seen him before."

"The guy you used. How bad is he?"

"Eddie? I don't know. An ambulance just went to pick him up. He was lying on the ground when I left."

"Then he's still alive?"

"Yes. His legs were smashed pretty badly. He could die from loss of blood."

"Find out where they take him and call me back."

Max gave him a new number to call and hung up.

25

Villiers was barking orders again: "Knock out all those damn bits of glass will you? We don't want to draw attention to ourselves, now do we?"

Harry climbed over into the backseat and pushed out the rest of the shattered rear window. Rain dripped in through the gaping hole. About two hundred yards behind them, the big truck was weaving from lane to lane and slowly gaining on them.

Villiers muttered, "I wonder who those buggers really are. Got any ideas?"

"No. Who do you guess?" asked Harry.

"No idea. But whoever is driving is definitely not an employee of the telephone company."

He double-declutched into second gear and gunned the car forward. Harry pitched backwards and sideways as Villiers drove off the Motorway and down to the Marylebone Road. Making two quick lefts and a right he plunged down a ramp into a garage of a large block of flats. The alleys of parked cars pulsed past on either side.

Behind them, the truck was forced to stop at the top of the ramp. It was too high for the garage entrance. Framed in a rectangle of bright daylight, the driver and his passenger climbed out and ran down after them.

The Colonel was not one to be caught with his back to the wall. The garage had ways in and out at either end and he bounced up a second ramp. As soon as they emerged into the light he turned hard right and was zigzagging through traffic half a mile away before his pursuers could determine which way he and Harry had gone.

"Thanks for the warning," the Colonel said. "You cut it a bit close though, don't you think?"

Harry's brain was working frantically with zero results. "It all happened so fast," he said lamely.

"Usually does, old boy."

A big grin spread across Villiers's face. He put a finger through a bullet hole in the doorframe. "Bastard came pretty close. That's the damn trouble with MAC-10s; they're apt to be a bit wild. Fortunate for us though. Look, I usually don't ask questions. Always seems to me that in our business, the less you know, the longer you live. But I am very curious to know how you became privy to the fact that I was about to be eliminated?"

A disquieting thought struck Harry. Villiers could be one of the bad guys. When he found out that Harry wasn't who he thought he was, he could take it unfavorably. For the moment it might be wiser to continue avoiding the truth.

"Well, it was like this," Harry said. "I overheard a conversation. Put two and two together. Can't say more than that, I'm afraid, without getting myself in too deep."

"I don't suppose you'd care to give me a hint."

"If I could, I would. But I can't."

"You're not one of Rocco's regulars, are you?"

Rocco? Where had he heard that before? Of course! He had written the word "Rocky" on his cellphone app. Apparently, Rocco had billing above the title. Villiers was waiting for an answer.

"Sorry, Colonel, that's classified," he bluffed, as if he were under orders not to talk. The ruse worked.

"Understood," said the Colonel. "So. What's the next step?"

Harry's mouth dried up in just the same way it did on those rare occasions when he forgot his lines on stage. He had received his cue. It was his turn to speak and his brain had no idea what was next. Milliseconds felt like minutes. Panic flowed through his veins and beads of sweat ran down his spine. As he did on stage, he improvised.

"I suggest . . . well . . . it would be best . . . if just we proceed as arranged."

"Fine," Villiers said brusquely. "I'll give Max a call. Let him know we've made the transfer."

The last thing Harry wanted was for Villiers to call New York to tell them all about the nice man who'd just saved his life. "No!" he replied a little too loudly. "You don't have to do that; I'll take care of it. Rocco will be expecting me to . . . eh . . . report . . . in."

Villiers accepted this without further comment and turned off the highway and up another incline leading to yet another garage. By now the rain had stopped. Leaning out of his window, he pulled a ticket from the machine and the orange barrier rose up and let them through. They wound their way up the scarred concrete spiral and stopped in the far corner of the fourth level beside a battered old gray Ford Escort. The number plates were very dirty and the radio aerial a twisted wire coat hanger.

"This is where we change vehicles, old boy," said Villiers as he switched off the ignition. "Excuse me." Stretching across, he flicked a catch on the dashboard and a panel flipped down revealing a Browning 9mm complete with silencer and two spare clips. When he pressed a second catch the whole apparatus dropped into his hands. Cradling the mechanism under his arm he climbed out and walked over to the Escort.

Harry joined him as he opened up the trunk. Inside were the spare tire, a tool kit, a brown leather suitcase and a battered cardboard box. Villiers handed Harry the keys and told him to unlock the doors. Once they were open the Colonel handed him the suitcase.

"Here you are," he said. "Put it on the backseat for now."

The case was heavy. Harry opened the rear door and heaved it in. Villiers rummaged about in the cardboard box and pulled out a black broad-brimmed hat and a furry object.

"Put those on!" he barked, throwing them over.

Harry pulled on the hat as far as he could but it was a tight fit. The fur was a fox stole with a little shiny snout and a pair of beady eyes. Everything reeked of mothballs. Villiers donned a workingman's cloth cap and a dirty old coat. He took out a bushy mustache, peeled off the backing and stuck it on.

With a large rag he gave the Jaguar a thorough wipe, both inside and out. "Just a precaution," he observed. "You never can tell." He threw the cloth back into the trunk of the Escort and banged it shut.

A billowing cloud of blue smoke followed them down to the exit booth. Villiers produced a second ticket from his pocket and paid the required fee. The attendant would remember little of the elderly suburban couple who motored sedately away.

In the distance the metallic ringing of police cars and ambulance sirens crisscrossed. After about two miles, Villiers drew into a deserted side street, stopped the car and pulled on the handbrake. From his belt, he pulled out the Browning, pushed off the safety catch and cocked it with a snap. In the confines of the car it was a very loud noise. It made Harry jump, fart and shit his underpants ever so slightly.

Like the trained soldier he was, the Colonel was simply making sure the mechanism was in working order. The gun disappeared into the depths of his clothing.

Harry hoped he didn't smell too bad. It would take a lot of explaining.

Mercifully, Villiers got out and slammed the door. Hanging from the rearview mirror, a pair of fuzzy dice and a Saint Christopher medallion swayed together in protest.

The Colonel bent down and spoke to him through the open window.

"I'll leave you here. I'm going to disappear for a while. Make myself less of a target. I'll be in touch later. Leave the car in Myrtle Road. It's close to Hounslow East tube station and from there it's only a short ride to the airport. Throw away the keys. I have others if I need them."

He reached in and shook hands.

"It's all yours now, Murphy," he announced. "The best of British luck to you! And thanks again. I owe you one. Be sure to give my best to Max."

Rising to his full height, the Colonel strode off down the street humming his regimental march.

Harry got into the driver's seat. The glass eyes of the stole stared accusingly from his lap. He snatched it off and flung it into the backseat, the enormity of his predicament throbbing in his head. What the hell had he got himself into? In less than an hour he'd been an accessory to two attempted murders, two witnesses knew his name and four people had seen his face. Two of those had even given chase. So much for avoiding trouble.

Although the damage in his pants was minimal, the inside of the car was beginning to smell like a blocked drain. The hotel would be the safest place to change. Harry glanced at his watch. It was only ten minutes to nine. Checkout was at noon. Nobody knew where he was staying except Larry Parker, and he certainly wouldn't give out information to anyone. Larry would never do anything that could be bad for business.

Harry moved to the driver's seat, checked out the controls, started up the engine and headed west. Miraculously, he found a free space two blocks from the hotel. From the parking meter he purchased a ticket for two hours and left it on the dash. Grabbing the case, he shuffled along with his legs slightly apart trying to ignore a growing itch. He collected his key from the deserted lobby and climbed up the narrow stairs to his room, where he dropped the case on the bed and stripped off all his clothes. Wrapping his dirty pants in the sports page of *The Telegraph,* he dumped them into the wastebasket.

The shower felt great after his exertions and he lingered under the hot water, careful to direct the flow towards the inner wall to avoid another flood. Common sense finally urged him to get moving.

He was about to pull on some socks when he remembered the suitcase. He tried the catches and they sprang open with a snap.

The sound that came from Harry's lips when he lifted back the lid, suggested to an elderly gentleman three rooms away that a guest of the hotel was in the throes of passion. When the cry died away Harry lifted out bundle after bundle of hundred-dollar bills. Turning the case over, he dumped them out on the bed and let the case fall to the floor. He figured each packet was about ten thousand dollars.

There had been three rows of five with ten in each pile. The case contained about a million and a half dollars in US currency.

There was a knock on the door. A key was thrust into the lock and turned.

Harry pulled the towel from around his waist, threw it over the money and grabbed his hairbrush. The door was opened by a young freckled-faced maid in a white apron.

Harry turned full frontal and casually brushed his hair.
"Come to do the room, have you?" he asked.

The elderly gentleman three rooms away heard another strangled cry which confirmed his earlier suspicion. This time the
pitch was female and decidedly orgasmic.

26

Rocco was angry. He was not used to failure. Santiago's killing
had gone so smoothly, and now this fucking Villiers fiasco.

The important thing was to keep himself focused and avoid
any more mistakes. When the ambulance left the Mews, it had
come right past where he was parked, sweeping by him with
bells clanging and lights flashing. Rocco had waited only seconds before following. When it had finally pulled into St. Mary's,
Rocco had driven past the entrance and pulled to a stop where
a mother balanced her baby on her hip as she fumbled with the
keys to an old Volvo wagon. The moment she had driven off he
had reversed into the spot and paid for three hours of parking.

Once inside the hospital he had watched as the motorcyclist,
plus his police escort, was wheeled out of the main corridor.
Presumably on their way to an examination room.

Now as he waited, Rocco checked his watch. Before they
operated, the medical staff would stem the bleeding, begin a
transfusion and give the patient a thorough check before they
dealt with the broken bones. In the States they would certainly
take the time to MRI the patient. But not here. You never knew
with the British health system. He definitely had time to report
to Max. In a dilapidated telephone cubicle he dialed the code
and number.

"Well?" said Max.

Rocco described exactly what he had seen and heard.

Max swore loudly. "You think you could deal with him?"

"Yes," Rocco said. "But are you sure?"

"You bet I am," said Max. "But no loose ends this time! *Capish? Don't leave a fucking calling card.*"

"Ti penso io," said Rocco confidently. *"Lascialo a me."*

In the hospital cafeteria he bought a ham sandwich and a carton of milk and sat at a corner table to think and plan. Around him were several staff. As luck would have it, the security badges clipped to their white coats were not unlike the New York State driver's license.

He looked at his watch. There would be another delay between the time the police figured Eddie was important and the time reinforcements arrived. Until then, there would only be one cop keeping an eye on him and he would not be alert. With both legs crushed, the semi-conscious perp wasn't going to run away.

Rocco went back out to the street, walked to Edgware Road and located a hardware store. Three paces inside the door was a padlocked cabinet of Messermeister professional cook's knives. Rocco asked the helpful assistant for a six-inch flexible boning knife. When it was brought out he was careful not to touch any part of it with his bare hands.

A medical supply store supplied a box of powderless surgical gloves. As he paid, a rack of white canes by the register caught his attention. One that telescoped was added to his purchases.

At Ryman's he got himself a nameplate holder almost identical to the ones he'd observed at the hospital. From a street cart he bought a pair of cheap round dark sunglasses. As he walked back to the hospital, he slid his driver's license into the holder and distributed the rest of the stuff among his pockets. The knife still with its protective sheath went point down into his left inside jacket pocket.

Eddie was nowhere to be seen. To find out where he had gone Rocco would need to go into the Emergency Room. For this he needed a disguise, so in the gift shop he bought a bunch of flowers and went up the central stairway. Anyone who passed

him would simply take him for a visitor. At all times he was careful to keep his face averted from the security cameras.

On a hook in the corner of a pediatric ward he found a white
lab coat. Discarding the flowers, he slipped on the coat, pinned
the holder to the lapel and pulled on a pair of the rubber gloves.
From a nearby bedside table he picked up a small towel and
tucked it into his left coat pocket. In the right he put the knife
with the blade pointing down. In another ward he lifted a clipboard off the end of a sleeping patient's bed and retraced his
steps to the Emergency Room. Confidently he pushed through
the swing doors.

A well-upholstered black nurse passed by and Rocco stopped
her. "Where'd the shooter go?" he asked.

She frowned. "What d'you say?"

He explained. "The guy with the fractured legs."

"Oh, him." The nurse shrugged and she nodded towards the
far end of the room and a green curtain. "He's next. Soon as
they call for him."

Rocco returned his attention to the clipboard and glanced
around. No one was watching as he sauntered towards his
target. Fifteen feet away he put the clipboard under his arm
and reached into his coat pocket. His fingers clasped the handle of the knife.

The doors at the end of the room wheezed open. An operating room orderly came in accompanied by a young policeman
in a helmet and short-sleeved shirt. Together they drew back the
curtain. Eddie was wheeled out of the room. Rocco let go of
the knife and followed the gurney, keeping his head bowed as
he flipped through the papers on the clipboard.

The little group trundled along a short corridor and stood
waiting by the elevators. None arrived.

The orderly repeatedly pushed the button. "Bloody hell! They
say they're going to fix the bloody things but they take their
bleedin' time about it. Come on, I know another way."

Eddie was wheeled along a slightly longer corridor to a second bank of elevators. Rocco followed a few paces behind. These doors opened immediately and they all trooped aboard. Rocco stood at the back. The orderly selected a floor and turned inquiringly to face him.

"Same," he answered.

Up they went to the operating room floor. The gurney was pushed out and over against the wall.

"Wait here," said the orderly to the policeman, and he disappeared through a pair of double doors with frosted windows.

Rocco walked away and turned right. The first door on his left was a storage closet piled with supplies. Quickly tearing open a box of gauze pads, he used his lighter to set them on fire, made a small pile of paper towels next to the door and placed the now blazing box on top.

With the door slightly ajar he ambled back. The cop was still waiting beside the prostrate Eddie. Rocco pushed the down button for a fast getaway. Once more his fingers clasped the knife.

The orderly came back through the doors.

"Why don't you go wait in the Doctors' Annex?" he suggested to the policeman, and pointed down the corridor. "Last door on the left. I'll give you a call when they're done with him."

"Thanks, mate. Don't mind if I do."

The policeman walked away. The orderly took hold of the gurney and turned it to face the operating room. Wisps of smoke came drifting through the air.

"Blimey! What we got 'ere?" he said to Rocco, and hurried around the corner to investigate.

Rocco pulled out the knife and drew it from its sheath. With a sharp descending blow he pushed it through the sheet and into Eddie's abdomen. In one swift downward move, followed by a thrust upwards behind the heart and a circular twist of the blade, Eddie's aorta was sliced into pieces. Blood pulsed out, flooding his abdominal cavity. Numbed by trauma and medication, the body on the gurney didn't even flinch. Rocco took the towel from his pocket, wrapped it around the knife, pulled it out and tucked it back in his pocket. It would be several minutes before anyone would notice anything amiss. Not until much later would they discover what had been done. Rocco chuckled at the thought of the subsequent autopsy and the puzzled look on the pathologist's face.

The elevator opened behind Rocco and he backed in. The third-floor corridor took him to the emergency stairs. As he ran down them two by two, he removed the ID holder and retrieved his driver's license. Slipping off the coat, he rolled it and the knife into a bundle under his arm, tossed the clipboard into a corner, donned the dark glasses and extended the white cane. Out on the second floor he slowly tapped his way along towards the first bank of elevators. A kindly nurse pushed the ground-floor button for him and guided him out. She then insisted she hold his arm until he was safely out into the street.

As he stood at the pedestrian crossing, another Good Samaritan, an elderly lady with white hair, stepped forward and escorted him across. Three blocks from the hospital and before he returned to his car, Rocco slid the coat and knife into the bottom of a convenient Dumpster. The glasses and folding cane followed. The rubber gloves, which now contained his sweat and DNA, were the last to be stripped off and stuffed into his hip pocket. These had to be carefully disposed of far away from the scene of the crime.

27

It is so easy to carry two suitcases and so awkward to carry three. Harry stood on the sidewalk in front of the hotel trying to solve this problem. No matter what combination he tried, the cases were either too heavy or too big. A throat cleared itself behind him and Harry turned. The Pakistani was standing there with an even larger smile.

"Are you in need of assisting, sir?" he asked.

"No!" Harry gripped the case of cash firmly. "I can manage, thank you."

The man was politely insistent. "I would be happy to accompany you to your transportation, sir. I am not busy at this time of the day and you appear to be having more suitcases than you are having arms."

The logic was irrefutable so Harry relented. "Okay. You're right. Thank you."

The two men made their way in silence to the Escort. Harry opened up the car. The Pakistani packed the cases in the trunk. Harry propped Villiers's case in the front passenger seat and secured it tightly with the seat belt. He handed over five pounds and the man bowed slightly and left.

Harry got in behind the wheel and put the key in the ignition. Then he remembered his A to Z London Guide was in one of the bags in the trunk. Climbing out, he retrieved the little book and then had to repack. This was more exercise than he'd endured in a long time.

No matter how many times he drove on the left he found the mental adjustment unnerving. The guide showed that the journey to Myrtle Avenue necessitated navigation across a spiderweb of streets. None of them was straight. As he pulled away from the curb he muttered a brief prayer to the dangling Saint Christopher medallion and did his best to concentrate on the road in front of him.

As he drove along, however, the images and sounds of the last few hours ran through his head, particularly the conversations with Villiers. Especially intriguing was when the Colonel had said, "It's all yours now."

He had three options. He could go to the police and tell them everything. He could return to number 4 and give the cash to Mrs. Villiers. Or he could take a little time to think.

Harry knew the consequences of involving the police. The paperwork alone would take days and the investigation would drag on endlessly and he'd probably have to stick around until they told him he could leave. His violent encounter with the Colonel would likely end up in the press and that would be an end to his anonymity. If he wanted to live, it might be in his best interests to return the money before they came looking for him. Not to mention the Colonel who had a howitzer tucked into his belt and seemed to relish the prospect of using it.

On the other hand, Harry had accomplished his mission and saved a man's life. Next to him on the passenger seat was well over a million dollars in cash. Should he keep it as payment for services rendered? Possibly. On the negative side of that equation, suitcases of cash usually meant drugs. Drugs involved money laundering. That meant the big time. That meant big trouble.

Clearly, if he made the wrong decision he would kick himself for the rest of his life. A little thought was called for, and preferably in a calm, safe, remote spot.

After all, a million dollars could buy a great deal of pleasure. He could get himself an RV and travel the country, an Airstream pulled by a Ford 150. Or a boat big enough to cruise the Caribbean. He could put a down payment on a Jimmy Buffet–style beach house in the Florida Keys. Perhaps he could . . .

Harry made a turn to the right and found himself facing four lanes of oncoming traffic. He stopped, made a two-point turn and sped across to where he should have been in the first place. With all thoughts of the money out of his head, he gripped the wheel firmly and managed to arrive at his destination in one piece.

Myrtle Avenue was a quiet suburban street lined with parked cars and garbage cans. At one end was a space beneath a tree and he pulled in. With the towel he wiped the steering wheel, got out and did the same to the paintwork and door handles. With the cases on the pavement, he carefully locked the little car and put the keys in his coat pocket, determining to throw them away in a more discreet spot. Fashioning his belt into a sling to carry one of his cases, he slowly made his way to the subway station. To keep his pants from falling down he had to stick out his stomach.

The illuminated sign on the platform indicated that the train on his left went to Heathrow Airport and the one on his right to central London. Which one should he take? He paused. Somewhere out there was a secluded English country town where he could hole up and give himself time to think. The subway map on the wall showed him that he was not far from the Main Line station that served the West Country. Down there were lots of little villages that would be surrounded by fields full of sheep and cows.

Ten minutes later in the huge vaulted terminus of Paddington Station he stared up at the departure board. The Exeter Line looked rural and remote. He procured a trolley and wheeled the suitcases over to the ticket window. With a First Class ticket to a town called Taunton safely tucked in his pocket, he made his way to the platform. In the carriage he chose a seat facing front. The case of cash and his raincoat went on the overhead shelf. The others on the luggage rack just outside the automatic door.

A father and mother and their two children took over the table across the aisle. From their conversation Harry gleaned they were on their way to visit Grandpops in Falmouth.

The guard came past the window checking his traditional timepiece. Once he had taken a final glance at both ends of the huge train, he waved a hand and let out three sharp blasts on his whistle. At the same time there was a minor commotion at the entrance to the platform. A gentleman in a blue suit and bowler hat ran round the barrier and managed to scramble aboard Harry's carriage.

Relief showed on the man's ruddy face as he dropped into the seat across from Harry.

"Just made it!" he said, and without further comment extracted a copy of *The Times* from a worn briefcase. Throughout the journey, he silently filled in the crossword puzzle.

Harry watched as the city gave way to the suburbs and then to the verdant English countryside. They passed through a vast field of tall waving grass as a flock of geese flew overhead in perfect formation. Bright rays of sunshine pierced the clouds. The aromatic smell of fried pork sausages filled the carriage. The father and son returned from the buffet car laden with food and drink.

"Now who ordered what, darling?" the mother asked as the little cardboard boxes were laid on the table.

"Yours is the bacon roll, darling. The bun is Lucy's," the father replied. "Did you want tea or coffee? John couldn't remember."

"Tea please, darling. But only if you have a spare one."

"Well, actually, darling, we brought a spare one just in case."

Harry watched as brother John took a big bite from the roll with the sausage and began to munch.

Harry loved British bangers. Two of them at that moment, preferably in a crusty white roll and accompanied by a can of Guinness, would hold him over nicely until dinner. But he didn't dare leave the leather case. Taking it would draw unwanted attention. By the time the guard walked through the carriage and announced they were about to arrive at Taunton Station, Harry had made up his mind to find the best accommodation the town could offer and treat himself to an Epicurean Feast.

The gentleman opposite stood up and put on his bowler hat. "Need help with your luggage?" he asked politely.

"No. I can handle it, thank you," said Harry. "But I could do with the name of a good hotel. Can you recommend one?"

"You'll like the Waterside," the man replied without hesitation. "It's down by the river on Wicket Green. Best food for miles around. Excellent cellar too." In true British style, he touched the brim of his bowler as they parted company.

The Waterside stood in extensive gardens with decorative battlements running along the top of the main building giving it the appearance of a fortress. There was even a turret at one end. The walls were covered with ivy. The white of the window frames peeked through the dark green foliage. Harry mentally thanked the man in the bowler hat for the perfect hideaway. He paid his taxi driver and went in through the portico.

The interior was a blend of the old and the modern. Without destroying the atmosphere of Victorian England, every amenity and comfort had been skillfully installed within the original Gothic architecture. Magnificent arrangements of roses sprang from every surface. Three venerable clocks ticked away in the hallway. A demure lady in a white blouse and black neck ribbon welcomed him from behind the polished oak counter.

"And how long will you be with us, sir?"

"I'm not sure," he murmured as he filled out the registration card. "Can I let you know later? Or would that be a problem?"

"Not at all, sir. Not at all." She handed over a large key on a brass ring. "Number fourteen. It's on the top floor overlooking the river." She lowered her voice. "One more thing, sir, how will you be settling your account?"

Harry hesitated. Should he use a credit card? That would mean a physical record. Perhaps it would be better to pay in cash. But if she required a deposit, that would mean opening the suitcase. This called for a compromise. The lady took an imprint of his American Express card but assured him it would be no problem if he wanted to pay by cash later.

"One more thing, sir," said the lady. "What paper would you like with your morning tea and what time would you like to be knocked up?"

Harry smiled. "*The Daily Telegraph* and eight o'clock please."

A tap of the bell on the counter summoned a scrubbed young porter in a green baize apron who took the key and expertly picked up the three cases. Harry followed him to the elevator and they rose steadily upwards to the penultimate floor. A short flight of stairs took them to a narrow hallway. At the far end the porter opened the door to number 14 and stood politely to one side. Harry walked into the little room beneath the eaves.

Apart from the bed, the furniture was small in scale. There was a padded armchair, a circular table with two chairs and a cabinet. On top of this were a television set and a bowl of brightly colored flowers. A card was propped against the bowl indicating that a Well-Appointed Gymnasium was available on the third floor.

The closet was well stocked with wooden hangers. A paneled door led through to a white and chrome bathroom. Two thick white bathrobes hung on the back of the door.

The young man put one of the cases on the stand and the others on the floor by the bed. Harry gave him a five-pound note, closed the door after he left and turned the key in the lock.

As he suspected, the cabinet was a cleverly disguised mini-bar. Harry seized the half bottle of Moët champagne and eased off the cork.

Once he had poured it into the glass, he opened the case from Villiers, set it on the floor in front of the armchair and sat down. Gazing at the bundles of money, he savored the cool champagne and the limitless possibilities that could now present themselves to him.

28

Life was suddenly very complicated. Max leaned heavily against the wall by the phone taking deep breaths. Goddam it! His whole plan had been compromised. And by a total fucking stranger. Some shithead not only knew his plan but also had managed to warn the Colonel. But how? Beside himself, only four people knew the plan: Rocco and Eddie, Sal and Enzo. And Enzo hadn't been told anything until the very last minute.

The decision to tell Rocco to get rid of Eddie Ryan could have been a mistake. Ryan could have been the one who had talked. Max had never met the man. Nor would he. Not until judgment day when he'd be arraigned with all the others who had been killed. That would be some crazy lineup.

Nino was waiting in the car.

Max waved at him. "Follow me," he said. His voice was hoarse. "I need to walk."

"The hell you do," his driver said getting out and opening the rear door. "You look like a ghost. I'm taking you home. After you have some coffee and something to eat you can walk your ass off."

"Not home, Nino," said Max. "Take me to the club."

"Now you're talking."

They drove up into the garage behind Mazaras just after six. Max was hitting the buttons on the back-door keypad when his phone bleeped. He read the screen and muttered, "Shit!"

He ran up the stairs to his office. Taking a phone from the drawer, he dialed a series of numbers and held it to his ear.

"I am sure you have heard the latest by now," said Rhonda Villiers, clearly suppressing her anger. "One attempt has been made on my husband's life and I see no reason to believe that there will not be another. As soon as you know anything about this attack I would appreciate a call."

"Don't worry. I'll get back to you. Soon as I can," said Max.

As he ended the connection his own phone bleeped again and so he repeated the procedure. This time it was Villiers himself.

"Is this a secure line?" he asked brusquely. "Or should I call back? Use a different phone?"

"It's okay," replied Max evenly. "I just spoke with your wife. She told me you have a problem."

"What the blazes is going on, Max? I picked up at the drop-off as usual, then I got the message from Rocco, but it did not contain instructions to expect enemy gunfire." He chuckled. "I must admit it was rather exciting in a way. Great to hear the snap, crackle and pop of the MAC-10."

"Who do you suppose was behind it?" asked Max.

"Ah. Glad you ask. Well, I've tweaked a few noses in the past. Particularly in Ireland. Lots of possibilities there. And elsewhere of course. Thank God for your man Murphy. He warned me just in the nick of time. How long has he been working for you? He's a good chap. Thinks on his feet. Rhonda found him a delight."

So the stranger had a name. Murphy.

"Call me back tomorrow," snapped Max.

The Colonel paused and then asked, "Do I sense you are as much in the dark as I am?"

"Let's just say there are a few unexpected complications," replied Max. "How did you leave it with him?"

"Murphy?"

"Yes."

"He headed for Heathrow with the cash. I told him where to park the car. I'll pick it up later. Have you heard from him?"

"Not yet," said Max, trying to control his confusion. "You say you gave him the cash?"

"As per the instructions. Any problem with that?"

"No," said Max.

"How was Rhonda?"

"Worried. I told her you'd be fine. Why didn't you call her yourself?"

"A truck in the Mews. I'm sure your fellow told you about it. Telecom be damned. Surveillance if you ask me. Phone taps. Didn't want to take the chance."

Max hung up and sat down on the sofa.

Who the fuck was Murphy? The shit-faced asshole had put the charm on the usually astute Mrs. Villiers and fucked off with one and a half million dollars.

Nino appeared in the door with a plate of scrambled eggs and some heavily buttered toast.

"Here," he said, and set it down on the table. "Get this into you."

"What the hell are you doing?" said Max. "You know what the doctor says about . . ."

"Forget the doctor," said Nino, handing him a fork and napkin. "You need protein. You need—"

"Okay, okay! Enough with the lecture," said Max. "Go get Enzo and bring him here."

Nino nodded and left. Max ate slowly and then wiped the plate clean with the last bit of toast. By the time he heard his brother coming up the stairs he had made a pot of coffee and was getting out the mugs.

"In the kitchen," he called out.

Enzo came straight to the point. "Now what the hell is going on?"

Max poured out the coffee and added cream and sugar for his brother. Moving into the main room, they sat down at the table.

"As you told me in the car, Rocco intended to make the hit on the Colonel look like it was politically motivated. For that reason he set it up with a man on a motorcycle, similar to attacks in Northern Ireland. Great plan until someone turned up to warn Villiers at the last minute. To make matters worse, the hit man, one Eddie Ryan, was pretty seriously hurt by Villiers backing up his car."

"Where is he now?"

"Ryan?"

Enzo nodded.

"He's in a hospital. Don't worry. Rocco's taking care of him."

"Who was it who warned the Colonel?" asked Enzo.

"Someone by the name of Murphy. Mean anything to you?"

"No."

"Villiers called. Told me he gave Murphy the money."

"What!"

"The Colonel obviously assumed Murphy was sent by us to pick it up."

Enzo remained silent as Max continued. "Then I had a call from a Rhonda Villiers, who is clearly concerned for her husband's safety. Odd thing is, this Murphy seems to have hit it off with both of them."

There was a long, significant pause.

"Good coffee," said Enzo finally.

"Thanks," said Max.

"That's a lot of shit hitting a big fucking fan," said Enzo.

Max put his cup down. "Maybe not," he replied. "Think about it. What's the worst that can happen?"

"Well," said Enzo, "Villiers is not gonna incriminate himself. He'll keep his mouth shut."

"You're right there," said Max. "If he opens it he'll be breaking rocks until he's old and gray."

"And nothing has happened over there to change things here."

"Not that I know of."

Enzo shrugged. "Well then, with Ryan out of the way we have containment."

Max leaned back in his chair. "Up to a point, yes. We still have to deal with Villiers when he surfaces. Right now I see no reason to change anything here. I'm meeting with Ramon Rivas tomorrow as planned."

"Sal know about all this?"

"No. But he soon will. I'm curious to see what he'll say we should do."

"About Murphy?"

Max said bitterly, "Murphy, whoever the fuck he is, has enough of our cash to keep him happy for a very long time. The bastard also knows the money belongs to people who do not have his interests at heart. Unless he's a complete idiot, Mr. Murphy is long gone."

"Wait a minute!" said Enzo loudly. "You're gonna let him keep it? Shouldn't we . . . ?"

"What do you suggest I do? Send in the Marines? Don't get

me wrong, little brother; if I could, I would. And anyway, he's three thousand miles away."

Enzo raised his hands in the air. "So what do you want from me?"

"I want you to have everything ready so we can make the transition when we hear from Rodrigo. We need to show the Colombians we are efficient and reliable."

"You got it," said Enzo. "Anything else?"

"No," replied Max.

Enzo gave another resigned shrug and went out the way he came in. Max went into the bedroom, kicked off his shoes and lay down. Talking to Enzo had made him feel better. Now it was time to back off and consciously relax. Follow the doctor's orders.

29

Harry's martini was cool and dry and he ordered a feast that began with local brook trout served on a bed of watercress. This was followed by a rack of lamb, normally prepared for two, cooked rare and accompanied with a selection of homegrown vegetables and an expensive bottle of Château Margaux. For dessert he threw all caution to the wind, choosing the triple-layer chocolate cake with clotted cream.

What dominated his thoughts throughout dinner was not the food and wine but the money. If he made the wrong decision it could haunt him for the rest of his days.

Sated, he walked unsteadily back to his room. After a brief shower, he slipped naked beneath the covers and had a wildly erotic dream that involved a well-appointed gym, clotted cream, and Colleen O'Herlihy wearing lacy white panties.

The bells of a church awakened him at eight in the morning. As the last sounds reverberated over the rooftops there was an imperceptible tap on the door. Harry lifted up his head from the soft white pillow and saw a maid flitting across the room.

"Good morning, sir," she whispered as she set a tray down on the table. As she drew back the curtains, sunlight flooded in. Without another word she vanished as silently as she had arrived.

Harry stretched like a contented cat, pulled back the covers, swung his legs to the floor and ambled across to the table. Cup of tea in hand, he watched as a white-hulled yacht on the river below sent ripples of reflected light across the white ceiling above him. In the thick green ivy right outside his window, little brown birds twittered and fluttered.

To see if there was anything about the attempted murder of Colonel Villiers, he opened *The Telegraph* and scanned the columns. At the foot of page 4 was a short paragraph headed "A Mysterious Shooting in Kensington."

It reported on an incident that had taken place at approximately eight thirty the previous morning. A suspect was in custody, but the motive for the shooting was not yet known. The investigation was being pursued actively.

Well, that gave him a little breathing room. For the moment he was safe. What was more, no one knew where he was.

The battered brown suitcase in the corner of the room was too conspicuous to be carried everywhere. Nor could the cash be easily put in a bank. He had to find some remote place where he could hide it but still have access.

He showered and dressed, took out a bundle of the bills and closed up the case. Down in the lobby he gave a friendly wave to the woman behind the desk.

"Lovely day," she said with a smile.

"Yes indeed," Harry replied.

In the center of town at Barclays Bank he changed two thousand of the dollars into pounds sterling. The Queen stared imperiously up at him from the pile of fifties. Her royal gaze gave him but a momentary pause. The bills were folded over and put in an inside pocket. The bulge they made felt reassuring.

Back in the sunshine he came upon Davidson's Luggage Emporium. A polyester suit came forward rubbing his hands.

"Hi there," said Harry.

"Ah, from America, are we?" said the salesman.

Harry nodded.

"Ah! You've come at the right moment, sir. We have a shop-wide thirty percent sale in effect."

"I am only after a suitcase. The zipper on my old one is broken."

"Ah, sir," the man replied with a sly smile. "You would save money if you was to buy two. May I suggest these?"

To avoid further conversation, Harry agreed and paid cash, arranging for two Tumi cases to be delivered right away to his hotel. As he left, a funeral procession motored past. The hearse contained a black coffin heavily trimmed in brass. The whole interior was festooned with brightly colored flowers. All were on their way to the local cemetery for the internment. The burial.

Here was the solution! He could bury the case! Taunton was surrounded by countryside. Somewhere out there was the perfect spot for temporary underground storage.

A workman, with cloth cap held respectfully in hand, stood beside him at the curbside watching the funeral go by.

"Excuse me," said Harry. "Could you tell me where there's a hardware store?"

"Hardware store?" said the man with a slightly puzzled expression.

"Yes," replied Harry.

"Oh! You mean 'ironmongers.'" He pointed directly across the road. "Over there."

In Bletchley's Emporium, a short salesman in a brown apron produced every conceivable form of gardening implement. Harry chose a small black shovel. To this he added a flashlight and a roll of duct tape. As the case might have to be buried in damp earth he asked for a roll of big Baggies.

"Baggies, sir?" The man's gray eyebrows rose.

"Garbage bags," said Harry.

"Garbage, sir?" They rose higher.

"Yes. Big plastic garbage bags."

The penny dropped. So did his eyebrows. "Oh! You mean bin liners! How many do you require?"

"Er . . . well, one would be fine if it's big enough."

"Well sir, the Council usually supplies those but I should have a spare one here somewhere." The little man rummaged beneath the counter. "Yes, here we are, sir."

Harry flinched. It looked exactly like a body bag.

A stationery store in the high street provided him with a local survey map. Farther down, he was able to rent a compact car from West Country Motors. After a brief look at the map, he drove to the end of town and headed for the hills. Almost immediately the road narrowed. On either side grew high hedge-rows. For a couple of miles the car climbed steadily upwards until he came upon a quaint little village. A signpost identified it as Buckland St. Mary. The weather-beaten church looked down on thatched cottages and the local post office doubled as the general store.

Up a steep hill in about half a mile, a dirt track on the left led to a small group of trees that stood in a hollow. Harry stopped the car and got out. High above him a lark was singing in the sky. Mixed with the birdsong was the rhythmic sound of an axe chopping wood. It came from a thatched farmhouse three fields away. A thin spiral of smoke rose from the weathered brick chimney. No other buildings could be seen in the immediate vicinity.

Harry walked along the bumpy track and down into the hollow. The ground beneath his feet was soft and pliant. An ideal spot to inter the suitcase. Sitting back in the car, he took out the map, carefully marked where he was and drove back to town.

He spent the remainder of the day resting. When darkness finally began to descend, he wrapped the case in the body bag and sealed it securely with the gray tape. At one o'clock in the morning, he carried it out of the hotel by a rear door and made his way to where he had parked the car. The silence of the night was scarcely broken by the soft padding of his shoes on the sidewalk. Scudding clouds crossed the moon and a fresh westerly wind now rattled the leaves in the trees. An owl hooted in the distance.

Nothing passed him in either direction during his drive up the hill. He was alone in the world. Nevertheless, he switched off the lights for the last few hundred yards and parked on the verge at the entrance to the track. Carrying his gear to the center of the hollow, he turned on the flashlight and propped it against a rock.

There were three trees larger than the others. Using them for a rough triangulation, he picked a center point. Kneeling down, he sliced out the first piece of turf. As he cut the second, a dog outside the farmhouse began to bark. Harry stopped digging and the dog stopped barking. Harry waited a full minute. As soon as the shovel hit the ground again the dog broke into a stream of staccato yelps. Moments later a door was opened and a yellow rectangle of light burst across the fields. An irate male voice shouted, "Come here, Betsy, damn it! Get inside!" Moments later a door slammed, extinguishing the light. Peace returned to the farmhouse and the hollow.

As noiselessly as he could, Harry moved the rest of the sod and scraped out the earth beneath. The clouds above cast weird shadows that slithered along the ground. Harry felt like one of the gravediggers in Shakespeare's *Hamlet*. "'Is she to be buried in Christian burial that willfully seeks her own salvation?'" he muttered, and dropped the plastic package into the hole. Shoveling in the loose dirt he tamped it down with his feet. The only thing left was to replace the turf. He knelt down and picked up a clump of grass.

A voice behind him continued to quote, " 'Alas, poor Yorick! I knew him, Horatio. A fellow of infinite jest.' "

Before he turned around, Harry knew who was behind him. He also had a hunch he would be looking at the Browning automatic. He was right about that too.

"After I left you with the car," said Colonel Villiers, "I realized I'd accepted who you said you were, principally because you saved my life. As you know, that's not something a chap takes lightly. But on reflection, I also realized I really hadn't a clue as to who you really were. So I called Max on the hotline. I got the distinct impression he'd never heard of you."

"How the hell did you find me?" asked Harry in panic.

"Wasn't easy, old boy. But you Yanks are so predictable the way you never leave home without it."

Harry was perplexed.

"American Express, old boy" came the explanation. "I have friends in high places. Friends who obligingly kept an eye on your account. At Paddington Station you used it to buy a ticket to Taunton."

Damn! The bloody ticket. In his hurry to catch the train he had used his credit card without giving it a second thought.

"When I got down here I located you in the first hotel I inquired. Saw you from the garden enjoying your fancy dinner. Next day I followed you at a discreet distance. I wondered what you were up to when you went into Bletchley's. Now that I've found out, I don't think I approve."

Harry closed his eyes and his body drooped. "How did you get here? I didn't hear you—"

"You drove me, old boy," said the Colonel. "I've been lying in the back of your car ever since you parked it on the street. Not a lot of room on the damn floor for a big chap like me. Bloody cramped, in fact, but it served the purpose."

Giving Harry a nudge he pointed to the shovel. "Be a good fellow and dig. And while you're at it you can tell me who you really are and who you're working for."

Harry scraped frantically at the earth with his fingers. In an attempt to convince Villiers of his innocence he told him the truth. All of it.

When he had finished, Villiers was skeptical. "You say you overheard a conversation?"

"Yes. Outside a Chinese restaurant."

"Who was having this conversation?" asked Villiers.

"I don't know. I needed to take a leak and when the people inside told me the place was closed, I went out back and pissed against the wall. Above me there was an open window. Through that I heard them talking."

"How fascinating. And what exactly do you do when you're not urinating against the walls of restaurants?"

"I'm an actor."

"On the stage or on the television?"

"Both. And films of course . . . and I've done audiobooks . . ."

"Audiobooks? Oh, we like those. What was your last one?"

"*Passion and Power!*" Harry shouted trying to wake the farmhouse. "A novel by Stan Benedict."

"I must remember to buy it. It would be fascinating to listen to your voice when it's not quite so agitated." He gave a sardonic grin. "Although, somewhat macabre, don't you think?"

Harry unearthed the case and dragged the heavy package out of the hole. Villiers slid the safety catch off the automatic and put the hard metal against Harry's head.

"My apologies, Mister Murphy," he said flatly. "Or whoever you are. I'm afraid I don't have any more time to waste."

Contrary to popular belief, Harry didn't relive his whole life story. He felt angry and sad. As sad as it was possible for a man to feel. And he felt stupid that he had allowed his time on earth to end like this. His mother and father were right. Honesty is the best policy. Harry had tried to be smart and this was the pathetic result. He also knew the bullet wouldn't hurt as his brain wouldn't have time to register the pain. A split second and his life would end. With his eyes closed he thought about the little brown birds in the ivy outside his room. The gun made a hollow thud and he did indeed feel no pain. Only a heavy weight falling against his legs. When he opened his eyes Villiers had collapsed at his feet. Framed in the moon above was the figure of a man holding a thick wooden stick.

"Jesus, that hurt!" the man said, shaking his wrist in pain. "I didn't kill him, did I? I hit him bloody hard."

Harry gave a sudden cry of recognition: "Oh my God!"

His savior was the helpful man in the bowler hat from the train. But the bowler had been replaced by a seaman's cap and the pinstripes by a set of overalls.

Harry said again, "Oh my God!!"

The cap and the overalls! The worker on the roof in the Mews fiddling with the aerial. Harry was looking at the same face. The face of the man who'd driven the Telecom truck. The gentleman who had recommended the Waterside Hotel.

This chameleon gave Villiers a brief examination.

"He'll live," he sighed. "More's the pity. Unquestionably the world would be a better place without him." Gone was the upper-class accent. Now the man spoke with a slightly foreign tongue.

Once he had retrieved the weapon and applied the safety, he pulled Villiers's arms back and snapped a pair of handcuffs on his wrists. "Let's see if his friends in high places can get him out of those. Oh, by the way," he said to Harry, "my name is Ivan. Depending how you look at it, I am one of the good guys."

As he helped Harry to his feet, two more good guys materialized from the shadows. One of them was in uniform and turned on a powerful flashlight. Harry followed as they propelled a groggy Villiers down the hill. Ivan brought up the rear with the wrapped case and tools, which were placed back in the trunk of Harry's car. Villiers and the uniformed policeman got into the rear and Harry in the front passenger seat.

Ivan reversed the little car down the track and swung out

onto the paved road. Two police cars followed behind as they set off down the hill.

As the little posse drew up at the Taunton police station Villiers was conscious but moaning. As he was led away Ivan gave an order to an approaching constable: "No one is to go near that car. Is that understood?"

"Yes sir!" came the smart reply.

Handcuffs were put on Harry's wrists and he was taken into the building. They went quickly up a flight of stairs to an empty office.

"Make yourself comfortable," said Ivan. "This may take a while." He closed the door. A key turned in the lock.

The room into which Harry had been ushered showed signs of heavy daytime operation. Metal desks were piled with folders and the waste bins overflowed. The grimy windows were permanently sealed shut and the air smelled stale. Harry sat down and rested his arms on a desk.

Had he been arrested, he wondered, or simply saved from further harm? Or a bit of both? If he'd only been saved they would hardly have put him in handcuffs. But if they were going to charge him with something, what could it be? So far nobody had read him his rights. Or was it only back home that they did that? The more he thought about it, the more he was sure that he hadn't committed any real crime. Trespassing maybe, but certainly nothing more serious. They wouldn't hold him for long. As soon as someone came back he would insist that he be allowed to make a call. Perhaps he should get in touch with the American consulate? Although at this time in the morning there would probably only be a security officer on duty.

Harry rested his chin on his manacled hands. After several narrow escapes from death he was ready for a nap.

30

Outstretched on the sofa, Max was able to relax his body but not his restless mind. Each of the phone conversations he had just had with the UK kept running through his head. Finally he jumped up and headed down the stairs to the restaurant.

Nino was sitting at the bar reading the *Post*. When he saw Max he slid off the stool. "Where to?" he asked.

"Long Island."

"Lawrence?"

"You got that right."

The house where Sal had lived for over twenty years was at the end of a quiet tree-lined street. The front door was opened by Sal's wife. She stood aside to let him in. "Max! *Che bella sorpresa!*"

Furella de Benedictis Bruschetti had been born and raised in a hilltop village not far from the industrial town of Ragusa in southern Sicily, where her family had lived for several centuries. Furella was the third of six children with two older brothers and three younger sisters. Her father was a successful landowner and adopted an air of self-importance as he strutted around the village streets. Fabio Cesare de Benedictis was equally dictatorial in the running of his household. No one ever complained. It had been that way for generations.

Young children were kept out of sight at the rear of the house. On special occasions such as Saint Joseph's Day, they were taken out and paraded around in their best clothes. The housekeeper, Sofia, took care of the children's daily needs. The young Furella adored Sofia.

On her fifteenth birthday Furella was allowed to eat for the first time with her parents and elder brothers in the front dining room. The occasion was so traumatic that she threw up on the embroidered tablecloth. Her father immediately banished her back to the kitchen until she could learn to control herself.

On a humid day in August almost two years after the dining room incident, Furella's mother collapsed while going up the stairs. Furella and Sofia were the only ones at home. The former was sent to fetch the doctor, who diagnosed heatstroke, wrote out a prescription and ordered Furella to run to the *farmacista* at the *Ospizio dei Preti* to get it filled.

At the *Piazza della Vittoria*, Max Bruschetti had been seated outside the *Trattoria Marconi* enjoying a cool *Campari Soda* while Sal was setting up his tripod to take a photograph of an ornate fountain. Furella came hurrying past. Sal called out to her and she stopped and listened as he suggested that if such a beautiful girl were to sit on the stone wall his composition would be complete. Intrigued by his quaint New York accent she sat down and carefully arranged her dress. Sal snapped the picture.

As she hurried home Sal fell in beside her. Could he please have an address where he could send a copy of the photograph? Worried that someone would see them together, she pleaded for him to leave her alone. Sal acquiesced, but lingered and watched as she went in through a big front door. When she reappeared at a second-floor window, he stepped out into the sunshine and gave her a wave. Furella closed the curtains fast.

Sal spent the rest of the evening raving to Max about this enchanting creature. After half a bottle of *Grappa*, he ran back up the street, leapt over the garden wall, climbed up the ancient vine that clung to the rough stonework and tapped gently on the little window. Furella pushed open the casement. Frightened that he might fall, she let him clamber over the sill.

In whispers he explained that he was from America and he was in Sicily on a roots trip with his younger brother Max. They were driving to Rome that night. But he was totally and madly in love with her and it would devastate him to leave town with only her image in his camera. Would she please come with him to New York?

Furella was horrified. But only for a few seconds. For years she had dreamed of breaking free. Standing on her bedroom carpet was relief from the years of oppression. A way to escape. She impulsively nodded her head and grabbed a coat from her closet. Sal helped her down from the window and together they tiptoed in their bare feet to where Max waited with the car.

Before heading to Fiumicino and the flight to America, the threesome enjoyed four wild days in Rome shopping for her immediate needs and greasing willing palms to procure a passport.

When they arrived back in Brooklyn, a dilemma soon presented itself to the young girl. Her prince was not as charming as he had first appeared. In fact, the whole of his family earned their money doing dirty jobs that no one else would touch. They were smart, efficient and successful crooks.

Her choices were simple. She could return to her family in Sicily and face her father's wrath. She could leave Sal and make a life of her own in America. Or she could become a willing accomplice. She chose the last as it promised the greatest challenge. Salvatore Bruschetti and Furella de Benedictis were married three days after her eighteenth birthday.

On her wedding night she declared that he must never deceive her or keep anything secret. No matter how ugly or brutal his work, they must always talk frankly. As a result, Furella became a steadying influence. When Sal and Max were thinking about linking up formally with an established crime family, it was she who advised them against it. Let the Families band together with their oaths and allegiances; the Bruschettis would be better off with anonymity and independence. She also insisted they refrain from the macho practice of adopting pseudonyms between their first and last names, pointing out that there was no need to glamorize what they did.

She soon gave birth to two sons, Vicenzo and Angelo. When the boys turned sixteen and seventeen Furella told them what their father and uncles did for a living. Angelo was deeply affected but wisely kept his feelings to himself. When the time came to go to college he applied and was accepted at Pepperdine in Malibu. The day he left for the West Coast he hugged his parents on the front steps, took the short cab ride to JFK and never came back.

On the other hand, Vicenzo had visions of taking over when his father and uncles retired. This ambitious young man was intrigued and impressed by the way they managed to avoid even the slightest run-in with the law.

The emergence of the computer set up the path he would follow for the rest of his life. When their electronic devices were in their early stages the young Bruschetti instinctively recognized the potential rewards that could be reaped from their use. He studied voraciously, assimilating everything he could. When he quit college at the end of the first semester he had a comprehensive understanding of computer design and function and had become an ace programmer, surprising even his teachers who marveled at his concise code.

Max turned in the hallway as Furella closed the door and admonished him with a shake of her head. *"Mascalzone!* It's been too long. We haven't seen you since . . . how long has it been?"

"Vic's birthday."

She looked at him quizzically. "Vicenzo's birthday was last week."

"No." He smiled. "Last year."

"Oh! That is terrible, Max. We live so close." She waggled her index finger like an Assisi monk and added, "This is not good for family. Are you hungry? Good. Come in and I'll make us something."

Max pulled out a stool and sat at the kitchen island as Furella poured him a mug of coffee.

"Some fresh pasta?"

Max looked surprised. "I thought you guys gave that up."

She laughed. "For Sal, yes, but for you, no. And it gives me an excuse to indulge too. I picked some beautiful zucchini from the garden this morning. And plum tomatoes. How soon do you have to be back?"

Max just shrugged as he knew Furella was aware he had come unannounced and that meant something was afoot. She also knew that unlike Sal, Max didn't like to include her in matters of business. Her husband would fill her in as soon as he left.

"Sal's taking a nap. He should be up soon."

Furella formed a well in a mound of white and semolina flours on the marble counter and cracked in two eggs. Then she added a little olive oil and salt. With her left hand she deftly mixed it into dough. "Sal is still too heavy. His new diet helps, but I wish he'd take walks, but he says around here that's not safe."

"What about his golf?" asked Max.

"Golf!" she said with contempt, taking out the pasta machine. "They ride around in those stupid carts like kids at a fairground and then end up in the bar for beer."

Max watched as she rolled out the dough and fed it into the machine. "Speaking of kids," he asked, "you hear from Angelo?"

"No," she said, and gave a little grimace.

"How's Vic?"

"Always busy with his computers and his machines. Day and night. Makes a lot of money." She laughed as she draped the strands of pasta over the back of a chair. "Knows how to spend it too!"

A door opened below. Stockinged feet shuffled up the stairs from the basement. Sal's voice asked, "Are you two having an affair?"

Max smiled. "I didn't come for the sex; I came for the food. Did I spoil your nap?"

"That's okay. I got enough." He caressed the pasta machine. "I don't suppose any of that's for me?"

Furella shook her head. "For you I have tuna salad on a bed of lettuce."

The fresh pasta with the lightly cooked vegetables was perfect. Most of the time they ate in silence broken only with small talk. When they had finished, Max poured himself a fresh mug of coffee and followed his brother down the steps to the basement.

When he was not out on the golf course or in bed, Sal spent most hours down in his den. The furnishings were sparse: black leather sofa, coffee table, vibrating recliner and a practice putting ramp. An enormous flat-screen television dominated the room.

Sal closed the door and pushed the newspapers onto the floor to give his brother a place to sit.

Max took a moment to look at the many framed photographs on the walls. Over the years he noticed that Sal had physically changed the most, principally as a result of his growing girth and baldness. Furella had changed the least. Only a few lines around her eyes. In all the pictures, Furella and Sal were always touching, her arm often draped around his neck. Pride of place in the very center of the wall was a faded print of a young girl sitting on the wall of a splashing fountain in the town square with her head held high.

"Fucking amazing what people will do to screw themselves up," said Sal, pointing to the *Post* with his foot. "Every day it's the same. Useless politicians. Beheadings. Wars. Suicide bombers. Guys fighting over who has the best fucking God for Christ's sake! Worst of all, we got goddam Catholic priests molesting kids! What a world!" He dropped into his recliner and pushed back. "So why are you here? Did we fuck up?"

Max gave a shrug. "Could be."

"Tell me about it," Sal grunted, closed his eyes and listened attentively as Max brought him up to date.

When he had finished, Sal gave a deep sigh. "You have any idea who this Murphy is?"

"No," said Max. "But I see it like this. Who knew about the hit? Only Rocco and this guy Eddie Ryan. Stands to reason Ryan's the leak. Shoots his mouth off in a pub. Murphy overhears him and decides to stick his nose in. But all of a sudden he finds himself with a bagful of cash. Right now he's a long way off celebrating his good luck."

"Yeah. Maybe." Sal linked his hands behind his neck. "When did you last talk to Villiers?"

"He called to say he was okay. Seemed pretty pissed off."

"Have the police questioned his wife? What's her name? Rhonda."

"Right."

"Find out," said Sal. "Find out if they've asked her if she knows where he is now."

"Why?" asked Max.

"If they haven't asked her then they already know. They could have taken him in for questioning. Maybe they've been tailing him. Maybe they had his phone tapped. That would explain the Telecom van."

Max looked at his watch. "I'll give her a call."

Sal opened his eyes. "When Villiers hears about Santiago, do you think he'll make a connection?"

"He could."

Sal grabbed the lever, pulled himself upright and flipped open the lid of a humidor on the table by the chair. He cut the end from a Cohiba Millennium Reserve, took out a box of matches and lit up. "What have you told Rocco?" he asked.

"To sit tight. I told him I'd call him."

"Tell him to come home. He needs to do some explaining. If you feel he can still take care of Villiers, then he can go back later."

"So what else? What have we missed?"

Sal sucked deep on the cigar. "Give me a worst case."

Max leaned back in the sofa. "Villiers knows our names and various contact numbers," he said. "If he cops a plea and tells them what he's been doing for us they'll throw him inside for a good long stretch. If the Feds here in the US decide to get involved we could be facing a problem. But according to Carter, the paper trail he has set up is a good one. It would take a lot of man-hours to come up with hard evidence for a prosecution."

"What about this Murphy character?" asked Sal. "You think he could be working for someone?"

"It's possible. But I have no idea who it could be."

"Keep me posted. Let's meet with Rocco when he gets back."

The two men stood up and walked upstairs. Max kissed Furella on both cheeks and left.

Nino waited with the car. Max got in and stretched out in the backseat as they drove off. Maybe somewhere the ideal female was walking around waiting to drape her arms around his neck, make him feel loved and cook him fresh pasta.

Nino took the Belt Parkway to the Brooklyn-Battery Tunnel. Once through, Max told him to pull up at a payphone on Canal Street where he could call Rhonda Villiers. She told him that the police had questioned her briefly, but no, they had not asked her if she knew where her husband had gone.

As Max walked back to the car, a cute blonde in a fuzzy pink sweater and white leather pants walked by on three-inch red patent-leather heels. Max invited her for a drink. She was not ideal, but he needed a little light entertainment.

Some things never change.

31

The sound of a key in the lock woke Harry up. The door opened to reveal Ivan with a clipboard.

"A statement. I need a statement," he said, and clearing a space at one of the desks he pulled over a keyboard.

"Then I sign it and you let me go?" said Harry.

"First things first" was the enigmatic reply. "And slowly please; I don't type so fast."

Once more Harry began with his audition and ended with

his rescue. Ivan was a two-finger typist. When they were finally finished, he got up, removed Harry's handcuffs and walked out. Minutes later, he came back with the young woman from the Telecom truck.

Now she wore a studded leather jacket, a short black skirt that was stretched over shiny Lycra tights that ended in combat boots. At the other extremity, her eyes were heavily lined with mascara and her mouth was daubed with a psychedelic mauve lipstick. Dragging out a chair she sat down. Ivan handed her the clipboard with a printout of Harry's statement.

"I am Detective Sergeant Elizabeth Carswell." She spoke with a Cockney accent. "My friends call me Lizzie. My classification is 'Pain in the Arse,' as I have a special knack for sticking my nose in where it's not wanted."

She turned to the man at her side. "This dozy, idle individual here is Detective Sergeant Ivan Sapinsky. Otherwise known as 'Ivan the Terrible.' His ancestors came from Stara Zagora in Bulgaria. Take my advice, Harry; don't fuck with Ivan."

Leaning back in her chair, she lifted her legs, and her boots landed on the desk with a crash. "On second thought, you'd better not fuck with either of us."

She tapped the clipboard with the back of her hand. "I've read your little story, but I want to hear it from the horse's mouth, so to speak. If you refuse to oblige me, I'll turn Ivan loose. He'll probably grab you where it hurts the most. You get my drift?"

Harry was captivated. He nodded.

Lizzie took out a packet of Camels and lit one with a small jeweled lighter.

"How did you find me?" he asked. "I know how Villiers tracked me down, but how did you?"

"Find you?" She took a noisy drag. Smoke came out of her mouth in spurts as she talked. "We never lost either of you. I spent the last couple of days in hot pursuit of your chum Villiers. Ivan's been glued to your ugly backside like a leech."

"Villiers lost you at the entrance to the garage," said Harry.

Lizzie looked at him as if he were a naughty child. "We knew all about his little getaway car, Harry. The minute you both headed towards that garage we had squad cars all around the place."

She turned her attention to the clipboard.

"You were born Harold Patrick Murphy in Brooklyn, New York, September 20th 1981. You presently reside at 409 West Fifty-sixth Street, New York, New York, 10019. You are a member in good standing of the Screen Actors Guild, the American Federation of Television and Radio Artists and Actors' Equity. You are represented by the Milstein Agency of New York. You have a good credit rating. You flew overnight to London on American Airlines. You checked into the Fabian Hotel, from which you made one very brief call to the residence of one Charles Villiers. You visited the aforesaid residence at eleven-oh-five hours that morning, being admitted to the premises by his wife, one Rhonda Villiers. You returned to your hotel and stayed in your room for the rest of the day.

"Later that night you walked to Soho. After dinner, you patronized the Isle of Capri Coffee Lounge, where you consumed one coffee and two alcoholic beverages and attempted to pick up Policewoman Susan Banks, who had been assigned by Ivan here to observe and report your activities."

Her eyes had a cheeky glint when she looked up at him. "Susie was real surprised. She thought you'd penetrated her cover."

Harry tried to remember if he'd said anything stupid after two Sambucas. Lizzie read his mind. "You don't have to worry. Susie told me you behaved real nice."

The clipboard was dropped to the floor and she peered at him intently. "I've got all the facts, Harry, so, now, as I say, I want to hear you tell it to me. All of it. Every little detail."

Harry felt a disturbing affinity towards this unusual female, so he not only obliged her but also added small particulars wherever he could. When he had finished, she sat silent for almost a minute before getting to her feet. With Ivan the Terrible in tow, she walked out of the room. Five minutes later they were both back. This time she swung the chair around, straddled it with her legs and leaned on the back.

"Who sent you, Harry?" she asked lighting another Camel.

"Nobody sent me!" he answered forcefully. "I'm not working for anyone."

"Ivan thinks that as well as being an actor you're making a little extra money on the side as a courier."

Harry jumped up in frustration. "I don't know anything about being a courier," he protested. "I've never seen Villiers before and I have nothing to do with him or his organization, or any other organization, for that matter."

Lizzie inhaled into her toes. "Prove it," she said.

"Can I go back to the hotel?" he asked.

"What for?"

"I have something there that might help me."

"Okay," she said, and stood up.

"You want me to come too?" asked Ivan picking up the clipboard.

"No," she replied. "You have a kip. We won't be long."

"Do we take my car?" asked Harry.

"No we don't take your car," said Lizzie. "We'll have one of those good-looking young coppers drive us."

She picked up the handcuffs and snapped one end on Harry's left wrist and the other on her right. "It's not that I don't trust you, but I'd feel real bad if I lost you."

When they walked into the hotel, Lizzie pressed against him so no one would see how they were linked. Up in number 14 his new luggage stood neatly wrapped in brown paper. Lizzie took off the handcuffs and dropped them on the table. Harry reached into the closet and pulled out his carry-on. From the side zipper pocket he produced his iPhone. As soon as it was booted up he went to the Notepad app. "As I told you. I made a list."

Lizzie took the phone and looked at the screen.

"Well?" he asked. "Do you believe me now?"

Lizzie made a clicking noise with her teeth and pulled out the pack of Camels. Harry walked past her and opened the window wide. "If we're going to spend time together you'll have to stop doing that," he said with mock irritation.

"Are you a convert?" she asked as she handed back the phone.

"I smoked when I was too young to know any better. I gave up when I discovered just how badly I smelled."

"What about pot?"

"No, never did that," he said, putting the phone back in the carryall.

"Never?" she asked. "I thought everyone in show business did shit."

"Not me."

"Why not?" she asked.

"I never felt the need."

With the bag back in the closet he turned to see that Lizzie had dropped into the armchair and was sitting with her knees apart. "Do I smell bad, Harry?" she said with a provocative smile.

"Yes, you do," he replied. "But it suits you. Goes with the territory."

"Rubbish. I stink because I haven't had a wash in three days. Thanks to your friend Villiers."

"What will happen to him?"

"Good question, Harry. One possibility is that we will charge him with attempted murder. Ivan's a pretty reliable witness so he's certain to be convicted."

"How long before he goes to trial?"

"Why?"

"Will I be allowed to go back home?"

"To America?"

"Yes."

"Depends."

"Am I being charged with anything? Because I should probably get in touch with the Consulate."

"You don't have to do that, Harry. I think you're what you say you are. You are free to go."

A strong feeling of relief swept over Harry. "Can I get you some breakfast?" he said impulsively.

Lizzie walked over to the bathroom and looked inside. "Can we have it up here?"

"Room service? Sure."

"What you going to have?" She yanked the ceiling cord and the light came on.

"The works," he replied. "Coffee, eggs, bacon, sausage, toast."

"I'll have the same, but make mine tea."

As he dialed room service, the water in the bath started to run. By the time he had placed the order, Detective Sergeant Elizabeth Carswell had thrown all her clothes into a small pile in the bathroom doorway. Harry stared at the black underwear with little red bows. The faucets were turned off. He heard her step into the tub and there was then a momentary silence.

"Feel good?" he inquired.

"Great," she replied. Her voice echoed in the tiled bathroom. "What do you know about the Real IRA, Harry?"

"Not a lot. Why?"

"Tell me what you know."

"Just what I read in the papers. It's a bunch of guys dedicated to the unification of Ireland. After all these years it seems like a lost cause to me." Harry sat down on the edge of the bed. "Is that what this is all about?"

"In a way," she replied.

"I thought they came to some sort of an agreement a long time ago. A cease-fire of sorts."

"That was the IRA. I'm talking about a new organization called the RIRA, or True IRA, as they like to be called. Formed in 1998. They didn't go along with the cease-fire and the buggers are still pretty active. Bombings, shootings, assassinations. They tend to operate in covert cells keeping a low profile to avoid being infiltrated by informers."

Water splashed as she began to wash. "You know it takes a lot of money to keep an organization like that going."

"Yeah, I imagine it would."

"And not just for guns, ammo and explosives. Money for fine wines and fancy cigars. After all these years of the money flowing in from the States some of them have got themselves some pretty expensive tastes. Did you know that?"

"No, I didn't," said Harry, wondering why she was telling him all this.

"Trouble is the US government has now declared it illegal for anyone to donate to the RIRA. As a result, the supply of cash has dwindled."

"Really?" He thought for a moment. "What has all this to do with me and Villiers?"

"Ivan and me is part of a group that keeps an eye on known IRA sympathizers in the UK. We are particularly interested in anyone acting as a conduit for illegal funds. We been sitting on our arses in Manchester for the last six weeks watching a man who did nothing except collect his dole and take walks to the local pub. We were just about to give up when we got lucky. One lunchtime he meets with another idle wanker who Ivan recognizes right away. He had arrested him a couple of years back for stealing dynamite from a stone quarry and smuggling it across to Ireland. Anyway, when he leaves we follow and he leads us to Kensington Mews. So we get ourselves a warrant to watch and listen to number four. That's what we were doing when you turned up and put a spanner in the works."

"So you and Ivan are back to square one."

"We never left square one. But now we got their money. Quite a lot of their money. And I've got you."

Harry could see his life getting complicated. "You think I could help in some way?"

"Maybe."

"How long will it take you to make up your mind?"

"Not long. Do you have any shampoo?"

"It's on the shelf by the basin. There's conditioner there too."

"Be a pet and get them for me."

Harry's heart skipped a beat. Her invitation was so blatant. Sure, he found her attractive, but he found this odd in itself. Lizzie was the antithesis of every girl he'd ever known: aggressive, irreverent and vulgar. And she smoked.

She was lying full length in the soapy water. Harry took the two little plastic bottles from the glass shelf and handed them to her. She sat up, unscrewed the cap and poured some onto the palm of her hand. Her wet skin was flawless. Her body muscular and beautifully proportioned.

"Thank you," she said, and worked the shampoo vigorously into her scalp.

"You're welcome," he replied, and returned to the bedroom.

He listened as she washed and rinsed her hair. The plug was pulled and the water gurgled down the drain. Bare feet squeaked on the tile floor. A moment later, she walked in wearing a hotel bathrobe and rubbing her head with a big towel.

"On Thursday morning," she said, "you said Villiers and his wife were expecting someone named Rocky. Right?"

"That's what they told me. Only I think it was Rocco."

"Well, we can be pretty certain that Rocco found out what happened."

"Maybe Rocco is the guy with the Uzi."

"No. The guy with the Uzi was Eddie Ryan. A known villain."

"Was?"

"Someone put a knife through him yesterday in the hospital right in front of the copper who was detailed to watch him. A neat and professional hit. We didn't get nothing out of Eddie."

Lizzie went back into the bathroom. Rummaging around in

Harry's toiletry case, she came back with his hairbrush. "D'you mind?" she asked.

He started towards her. "Let me wash it first."

"Don't be so silly," she said, curling up in the armchair to brush her hair. "By now Rocco will have passed on the news that someone tried to kill Villiers and the cash is missing. After you left Colonel Villiers in Myrtle Avenue, he spent most of the day in the Hampstead Public Library. When he wasn't reading he was making telephone calls, so we can be pretty sure he also passed on the fact that he gave the money to you. As they have not a fucking clue who you are this will not come as good news."

There was a polite knock at the door. Harry opened it and two young maids entered with the breakfast trays. The first smiled politely. "Where would you like us to put them, sir?" she asked.

"Anywhere'll do," he answered.

The first maid placed her tray on the chest of drawers as the second hovered by the table. Harry picked up the handcuffs and threw them on the bed. The maids left in a fit of giggling.

"What do you suppose they thought we were up to?" said Lizzie. The robe had slipped open.

"What do you want me to do?" he asked somewhat ambiguously.

"I don't know, Harry; I don't know. I'm going to need a little time to think." She spoke to him with mock intensity. "Whatever I come up with, do you think you're man enough to handle it?"

"I'll never know until I try," he said with a grin.

With a sudden move she pulled the robe open and pressed her body against him. Her heart was beating like a hammer. He put his arms around her waist and held her tightly.

Lizzie spoke first. "Breakfast's getting cold."

"We'll order lunch," he said, and kissed her gently on the neck and shoulders. When she spoke her voice was husky. "If we're going to work together you'll have to stop doing that."

The robe fell to the floor.

"I should take a shower," he said.

"Stop being so bloody American."

She kissed him hard. There was nothing tentative or hesitant about Lizzie. Desperate to share her nakedness, she tore off his clothes and flung them in all directions. When Harry tried to take the initiative she pushed him back and down onto the floor. She kissed him from head to foot, producing sensation after sensation in every part of his body with her hands, mouth, arms and legs. Suddenly she stood up and put one foot on either side of his chest. With her eyes fixed on his she lowered herself until they made contact.

Contracting and relaxing her muscles, she squeezed him tightly, deep inside her. Then she began to rock back and forward, side to side, rhythmically and smoothly. Suddenly she lost all control and became like a frenetic animal. Her body glistened as she thrashed about on top of him. From her throat came grunts and moans of pleasure. When Harry exploded Lizzie was not far behind and with a final yell she collapsed beside him.

For a few moments she let him hold her but then abruptly jumped up, scooped up her clothes and disappeared into the bathroom closing the door with a bang.

Harry wasn't quite sure how he was supposed to react. Did this crazy woman have some sort of weird sexual desire that needed to be fulfilled? Or was she simply suckering him into becoming a willing accomplice?

At the best of times Harry had never been able to figure out the way women thought. Whether they were instinctively calculating or calculatingly instinctive. Paranoia made him feel he was responsible for their weird and unpredictable ways. With everyone else he was sure they were calm and reasonable.

He picked up the damp robe and put it on. As he knotted the cord Lizzie came back in fully dressed except for her boots.

"Is New York anything like they say it is?" she said picking up a rasher of bacon and popping it into her mouth. "I've never been there." She flopped into the armchair, pulled on the boots and laced them up.

"It can be a pretty lonely place if you don't know anyone," replied Harry.

"I know you, though, don't I?"

She picked up a fried egg with her fingers, swallowed it in one bite and washed it down with milk straight from the jug.

"Time to go," she said and picked up the handcuffs. "Got to go see our friend the Colonel. Find out if he's going to be cooperative."

"He's our friend now, is he?"

"Let's hope so, Harry; let's hope so."

"What about me?"

"You wait here. I'll be in touch. Thanks for breakfast." She grinned. "It was just what I needed."

And she was gone.

Harry walked into the bathroom, closed the toilet seat and sat down. A frothy residue adhered to the sides and bottom of the tub. Discarded towels lay in a heap, one smeared with mauve lipstick. The indent of Lizzie's small wet footprint was still visible on the thick bath mat.

Slipping off the robe, he rinsed off the tub, sat down in it and tried to take a shower. The hand spray was a pathetic substitute for the real thing. Harry could never understand why the British preferred baths to showers. What was the attraction of lying in a tub of dirty water?

British daytime television soon wore thin. He read *The Telegraph* from cover to cover and then tried his hand at the crossword on the back page but was only able to fill in one of the answers, the word "scent" missing from a Shakespearean quotation. Harry had played *Hamlet*'s ghost in high school and could still remember his overly dramatic reading of, "But soft! methinks I scent the morning air!" All the other clues seemed to be the product of a deranged mind. Tossing the paper aside he lay for a time on his back watching a horse spider symbolically weave a web in the corner of the ceiling.

The phone woke him just before three. It was Ivan and he was calling to tell Harry to go to the center of town and meet Detective Sergeant Carswell in a pub.

Harry hung up. So far he'd been shot at, driven in a high-speed car chase, and had more money than he'd ever seen thrust into his hands with the inexplicable words "It's all yours now." He'd almost died from a bullet to the head, been rescued, put in handcuffs and then released. As if this weren't enough, an English policewoman had just ravished him and he was about to join her for a pint.

When he arrived at the pub he spotted Lizzie drinking an enormous glass of Guinness at the saloon bar. The conversation level was deafening. No British reserve here. As Harry came up behind her she saw him in the mirror and asked loudly, "What'll you have, Harry? It's on me."

"Thanks. I'll have a Guinness."

"Right. Let's have a couple of Ploughman's. I'm feeling peckish."

Minutes later, glasses and plates held high, the two squeezed through the crowd and looked for somewhere to sit down. Lizzie nodded towards the rear and shouted, "Let's see if there's someplace to park ourselves out back."

An elderly gentleman in tweeds and his white-haired lady were about to leave a table by the low garden wall. As Harry and Lizzie approached, they insisted on wiping the table clean before they left. Lizzie sat across from Harry and they both turned to look at the river flowing lazily past. Lizzie took out her cigarette pack and Harry watched in fascination as she combined eating, drinking, smoking and talking.

"I was right about Colonel Villiers being pissed off," she said knowingly. "I could tell last night that underneath all the bluster he was real angry. Very upset that someone took a potshot at him. I recognized the type. He'll do anything to get even. He has also filed away in that nasty little brain of his that whoever tried to knock him off in the Mews is going to want to finish the job. Especially when he finds out what they did to Eddie in the hospital. I told him we knew about him calling the States and it wouldn't be long before we got the number from the phone records. I told him it would be better for him if he saved us the trouble and gave it to us now. I also reminded him he faces an indeterminate number of years in a prison that smells of piss and cheap disinfectant. I suggested we make a trade."

"What was his reaction to that?"

"I didn't wait for an answer. Left him to think about it for a few hours."

"Have you figured out what you want me to do?"

"Yes. I would like you to help us. I don't actually know how yet. But I will."

"Where's the money now?" he asked.

"Across the road in the boot of your car. Unless someone's nicked it in the last ten minutes." She pulled his car keys from a pocket and dropped them on the table.

"Have you marked the notes yet?" Harry asked.

She gave him a look of mock innocence and both of them ate for a while in silence.

"So what's my first move in this little game of yours?"

Lizzie wiped her fingers on a napkin this time and leaned over the table. "If you agree, drive me to the station. Train leaves in fifty-five minutes. Then go back to the hotel." She reached into another pocket and, producing a small sheet of paper and a stubby pencil, swiftly scribbled out two addresses.

"Drive up to town tomorrow and drop the car off here," she said, pointing at the first. "Tell them Lizzie sent you. Then take a taxi to that address." She pointed to the second. "It's a café just off Piccadilly. I'll be there sipping a cappuccino at eleven thirty. I'll have talked with my superiors by then."

Harry slowly drank the last of his Guinness.

"Why are you trusting me with the money?" he said. "Isn't that a bit of a risk?"

"No, Harry. You're the honest type. Everyone else out there knows you took it. It stands to reason you've still got it. So that's the way it has to be."

She picked up the car keys and dangled them in the air.

"What do you say?"

Life is made up of choices, some easier than others. In spite of a chilly breeze, around them the men were in shirtsleeves and the girls in light dresses. Bare brown arms and red legs. The work of the day was done and it was time for pleasure, time to take advantage of a beautiful evening, time to walk along the towpath or lie entwined on the grass. Out on the river, boats cruised gently by with their occupants languishing in the sterns. A couple at a table close by laughed happily together.

Harry couldn't help make the comparison between this air of unconcerned enjoyment and the complications that could come into his life if he accepted those keys and did what this unpredictable woman was asking.

"Are you sure you wouldn't like to come up for a nightcap?" he asked lamely.

She jiggled the keys. "And miss my train?"

"You could drive up with me in the morning."

"Nice try, Harry. But I got to go to work." She threw the keys high in the air.

Harry reached out and caught them. Instinct over reason.

Walking back to the car he felt great. There was no going back now. This extraordinary creature had come crashing into his life. He was hooked and he knew it.

The journey to Taunton Station took only a few minutes. As they pulled up at the entrance Lizzie leaned over and gave him a peck on the cheek.

"Thanks for dinner," he said.

She smiled. "One of these days I'll cook you one of my specials."

"I like your specials," said Harry.

Lizzie laughed. "You haven't tasted nothing yet."

He watched her jog up the ramp to the platform. At the top, she turned and gave him a wave.

Back at the hotel and safely out of sight of prying eyes, Harry opened up the trunk. The tools and bags had been removed. The old leather suitcase lay right where he'd left it.

32

Lizzie Carswell lived her early life on a narrow street between the South Bermondsey railway station and the South Eastern Gas Works. Although never actually an orphan, she might as well have been one. How to survive was her first lesson. As a toddler she began by teaching herself how to slide backwards down the stairs. To reach door handles she dragged around a small wooden box to stand on. From early on she had a special place where she stashed food to eat when her mother forgot to feed her. To take refuge from constantly threatening situations, the young girl retired to a bizarre world created by a vivid imagination. Left to her own devices, Lizzie replaced reality with fantasy.

Every day her dad came home smelling of sweat, beer and an assortment of foul chemicals. It was only later she learned these were used in the manufacture of leather. Her mum spent most hours watching television. Neither parent made any effort to stimulate Lizzie's mind, nor did they encourage her to play or even go for a walk. Both of them took out their frustrations by yelling at her. Like a boxer, little Lizzie learned how to duck and weave.

The first day of school came as a revelation. Wearing a uniform and conforming to rules gave her a new sense of order and freedom and she began to relate to others and make friends. Learning came easily and as a result she enjoyed her classes.

Miss Aitken was her first teacher. This kind and dedicated woman took great pride in the appearance and performance of her students. But she soon realized that in Lizzie's case there would be little or no parent-teacher communication. So Miss Aitken took it upon herself to encourage Lizzie's strengths. Over the years they developed a close working relationship.

Lizzie had no time for the facts and dates of History. Geography appealed to her when she was coloring maps and creating imaginary islands. Mathematics fascinated her. The power of numbers intrigued her. Miss Aitken and the headmistress felt strongly that in spite of current educational trends, domestic classes were still important. Lizzie was eternally grateful to them as these came in useful in her later life. They not only allowed her to move swiftly through several dull office management courses at the Police Academy but also provided her with the means to seduce several young men after dinner on the kitchen floor.

When Lizzie was twelve, after a lively discussion with Miss Aitken on Nixon's ignominious and tragic resignation in the United States, she came home to find her mother seated at the kitchen table sipping tea. Her elbows rested on a table amidst jam jars, empty milk bottles and piles of dirty dishes.

"Your dad's gone," she announced flatly.

"Gone?" said Lizzie. She took off her coat and draped it over her arm.

"Yeah. Last Friday. He went out for a packet of cigarettes . . ."

"What are you talking about?"

"You may not have noticed, but he's not been home for over a week."

This was not particularly unusual. "Where'd he go this time?"

"I dunno."

Maybe they'd had another big fight. "Why'd he go?"

"I dunno that either. But knowing him, he's probably gone off on a pub crawl of Europe."

"When's he coming back?"

Her mother never answered the question but shrugged her shoulders and gave a defeated smile. Lizzie could never think of her mum after that without seeing that stupid smile.

Each year on March 5, Lizzie celebrated her birthday with classmates, cake and candles. When she was old enough to drive a car she applied for a temporary license. The local office informed her there was no record of her being born on that day. After an extensive search she found that she had been born on October 5 of the previous year. Her parents had lied to her about the date of her birth.

This odd discovery prompted a little detective work. Their marriage certificate gave her the answer. Little Lizzie had been born only four months after Sydney and Sylvia Carswell were legally wedded. This explained the endless petty bickering. Lizzie's parents were never meant for each other. They had married because of a careless copulation.

Her father's absconding was a blessing in disguise. Sylvia was forced to take a job in a plumbing supply store and brought home a regular paycheck for the first time in her life. Along with government handouts, mother and daughter now had enough money for cigarettes, rent, food and clothing. As both spent little time at home, their paths rarely crossed.

At the age of fourteen, Lizzie discovered she was an athlete. Although of average height she had the perfect build for a long-distance runner. Light, trim and very fast, she began to run cross-country at school. At first she had no idea how to pace herself or breathe properly and often ended up back in the pack. As her technique improved and her muscles developed, she moved steadily closer to the front. Matches were arranged with other schools. Lizzie began to run against unfamiliar faces.

Her first victory came in the last race of the summer term. As she crossed the finish line she felt a euphoric surge of self-satisfaction. She realized in that instant that winning was everything. Winning not only as an athlete but also in every other facet of her life. From that moment on, losing was never an option for Lizzie Carswell.

Throughout the fall and winter she covered long distances through the streets and over the parks. The fitter she became the more keenly her mind functioned. Lizzie joined the local harriers who met every other weekend. Her third race was against a team of cadets from the Hendon Police Academy and she beat out a tall lad from Lancashire by a few feet. The boy was furious at losing to a female and was determined to find out the name of the fucking bitch who had bested him. Their relationship lasted a week. Both lost their virginity and Lizzie chose a career.

Her father would have been disgusted at his daughter's choice. Sydney Carswell had a lifelong contempt for the police. As soon as he was old enough to lift a glass he had a running battle with the law and was constantly hauled in for disturbing the peace. Sydney called the drunk tank his "home from home."

Lizzie applied to the Police Academy and the day she was accepted she announced to her mother that she was moving out.

"No you're bloody well not" came the reply.

"Yes I bloody well am!" Lizzie was ready for a fight.

"Shut the fuck up!" said her mother. "You're not leaving; I am."

"What?"

"You can have the house." She took a deep drag on her cigarette and flexed her neck and shoulders. "It's what you've always wanted! I'm off tomorrow to live with my sister. I wasn't going until the end of the month, but as I'm clearly not wanted here, I think I'll go tonight." Exhaling noisily, she stood up and went into the bedroom to pack.

Lizzie was astonished. Not that her mother was leaving but that she had an aunt. No one had ever mentioned her. As soon as the front door slammed shut, Lizzie rolled up her sleeves and scrubbed the house from basement to attic.

Life at the academy presented little challenge and Lizzie was top of her class in every subject. With a combination of street smarts and good looks, she moved fast through the ranks of the force. Her ultimate goal was to work as a plainclothes officer. Lizzie achieved it in record time.

33

In the morning sunshine, a steady trail of blue smoke drifted from the side window of a vintage gray Renault that stood directly in front of the Parthenon Express.

At first, Harry didn't recognize the woman in the front seat who sat reading *The Guardian* and sipping coffee from an oversize paper cup. As he came closer he was surprised to see Detective Sergeant Carswell in a crisp white blouse and a dark blue skirt, beige stockings, sensible shoes and jacket. As he opened the passenger door she gave him a welcome smile.

"How was the drive?" she inquired brightly folding the newspaper.

"Uneventful," he replied, "I am glad to say."

Easing his luggage into the backseat, he sank in beside her. Lizzie took a last drag on her cigarette and stubbed it out.

"No problem at the garage?" she asked with a slight cough.

"No. All very James Bond," he replied.

"You want to get some coffee?"

"No thanks. I'm fine."

Her deep blue eyes gazed at him as if assessing her next move. Then she spoke. "Do you think you have the makings of a smuggler, Harry?"

"What?" he said, surprised and not a little confused.

She nodded her head towards the suitcase. "If you had to get that lot back into America without anyone knowing, do you think you could do it? You see, Ivan and I have had a little chat.

We've decided we definitely would like you to help us. As I told you, we've had a pretty lousy few weeks. We think if you was to get involved it could make a difference."

Harry wanted to exercise caution, but the plot was becoming interesting. "Tell me more," he said.

"We'd like you to play a part, Harry," she said confidentially. "You should be good at that. Someone very frightened who did something very stupid."

She was asking him to perform. If he was about to negotiate a deal maybe it was time to call his agent.

"Whoever owns that suitcase knows about you from Villiers," she continued. "He probably told them you have something to do with show business, so it would make sense for you to be a bit thick."

"Thick enough to want to give up over a million dollars?"

"Yes."

Some deal.

"In the Police Academy they taught us that fear is a great motivator. A lot of people do a lot of dumb things when they're scared."

" 'I have a faint cold fear thrills through my veins,' " quoted Harry.

"What?"

"It's a line from *Romeo and Juliet*," he explained. "Go on."

"Villiers came to his senses. Gave us his contact's number. We want you to call it."

"From here?"

"No. In the States. You call from somewhere in Manhattan. Ivan thinks if you got on the phone and pleaded with them to take the money back they might listen." She leaned over and laid a hand on his arm. "I'll understand if you want to walk away, Harry. It's just that . . . well . . . this seems to be such a great opportunity. We just might find out who these sods are and where they're getting their cash."

"Wait a minute!" he exclaimed. "You're suggesting I go back to New York, make a phone call to a bunch of villains who will kill me if they find out who I am? Am I alone in this venture or will you be providing some sort of support?"

"Of course we will!" she exclaimed. "I'll be right there with you and before we do anything I'll arrange for an American backup team. Trust me, you'll be perfectly safe."

"How long do I have to think about all this?"

"You could go for a little walkabout if you want," she said. "Think it over for a couple of minutes. I'll wait here."

"What makes you think my calling them will make a difference?"

"You're the real thing, Harry. You're believable. We think it's well worth the try."

"You really think I could do it?"

"All we have to do is make one connection! A name, an address, anything that could take us to the next step."

"But why the hurry?"

"You got to sound genuine. If you're scared you wouldn't wait."

"All I do is make a phone call? That's it."

Lizzie withdrew her hand from his arm. "Well, to be honest, there is a slight possibility you might have to do a follow-up."

"Follow-up!?"

"It's very unlikely. These people are highly skilled at covering their tracks. Most of them don't have driver's licenses, Social Security numbers or anything that would give them an identity. When it comes to communication they use burn phones, pagers and beepers that are registered to anonymous or fictitious names. I know it's a long shot, but it's all we got." She paused momentarily. "Of course my boss will have to approve all this. He's the one who will make all the arrangements with New York."

Harry shook his head. "I'm sorry, but it's a crazy idea. No one would give back all that money. It doesn't make sense."

"You would have to make it all make sense," she said with conviction.

Harry had always had a rule when it came to work. He should take the first firm offer that came to him regardless of the possibility or promise of other jobs. But this was madness. He was about to join a fringe amateur dramatic society performing Kafka. With any luck the final outcome would be a bad review and not an obituary.

"When you said I was part of your team I didn't expect to be so actively involved. I'm not equipped to handle anything dangerous."

"That's my job, Harry. To keep you safe and away from anything unexpected."

"You're sure I'll be okay?"

"Yeah. Absolutely. You can rely on it."

In for a penny, in for a pound.

"Okay," he said, "in that case I'll do it."

"Great!"

Lizzie drained her coffee and threw the paper cup over her shoulder and onto the floor. She started up the engine and let out the hand brake. With a squeal from the tires the Renault headed north.

"Where are we going?" asked Harry, looking for a seat belt.

"Broadcasting House," she said. "My boss is giving a talk on the radio and he'll be there until one o'clock."

"What's he like?" asked Harry, giving up the search.

"He's from the old school. Likes to micro-manage. A pretty decent sort actually."

"What happens if he gives me the Good Housekeeping Seal of Approval?"

"You get to show me New York."

"Now that I would enjoy," said Harry.

At B.H., a landmark circular concrete edifice at the top of Regent Street and the original home of the BBC, a uniformed page met them in the lobby and assisted them through security.

Once down two flights of stairs and along a curved corridor with pale green walls, he ushered them into a small control room. An engineer in shirtsleeves sat at the console. Behind the double glass partition a stocky man in a blue suit could be seen seated in front of the microphone. On a hook on the wall behind him hung his raincoat, a neatly rolled umbrella and a Fedora. He waved to Lizzie.

"Wait here," she said, and pushed through the pair of connecting doors.

Harry watched them mime through the partition. They greeted each other with smiles. The man listened and Lizzie talked. Then she listened as he spoke. A question-and-answer session began and Lizzie became more and more animated, pacing up and down and using her hands and arms for emphasis. Harry could sense her mounting frustration.

At that moment the engineer decided to check a microphone and slid the control open.

Her boss was talking. "All we need is a good cover story, my dear. Shouldn't be an insurmountable problem . . ." The control slid closed and the engineer rose from his seat and walked past Harry into the studio. As the heavy door swung open he heard Lizzie say, "Why can't we make an approach under Section Two-Oh-Six or Two-Oh-Seven?"

"Perhaps," came the reply. "Perhaps. Definitely worth consideration. But if something goes terribly . . ." The door swung shut, cutting off the sound.

Two minutes later Lizzie came out to the control room.

"Trouble?" asked Harry.

She shook her head. "Basically he likes the idea. His problem is the American obsession with privacy. But he thinks he can deal with that. Might take a little time, that's all."

Lizzie's boss came out of the studio. "Thank you, Duncan," he said to the engineer. "Be a good chap and pop off to the canteen for a nice cup of tea. I'd like five minutes alone with these two if you don't mind." Duncan picked up his jacket and left.

The elderly man gave Harry a firm handshake. As he moved, his clothes smelled as if he had been close to a wood fire.

"I understand you're a thespian, Mr. Murphy," he began. "Might I have seen your work?"

"It's possible, but most of what I've done has been in the States," replied Harry.

"Great admiration for you chaps the way you learn all those lines. How you do it is beyond me." He indicated they should both sit and settled himself in the chair at the console.

"It's highly commendable when citizens such as yourself are motivated to assist the authorities. I can assure you that your efforts are greatly appreciated. But I think you should know that what you are about to do falls outside standard operating procedures. We're stepping out on a limb, so to speak, and if the bough happens to break we won't be in the best of positions to stop your hitting the ground. Could be a little painful."

Pleased at his own metaphor, he smiled. Harry felt as if he was in a time warp. It was 1944 and he was about to be dropped into France.

"Electronic eavesdropping devices are extraordinarily sophisticated nowadays," the little man continued. "Once you make contact you should assume that you are being overheard no matter where you are. Detective Carswell will indicate when it's clear to talk shop. She will also be using a cover that we've used effectively in the past, the overseas representative of a package tour company researching restaurants and hotels. It allows her to poke around without arousing suspicion. You, Mr. Murphy, will be working with a different sort of cast and director, and knowing how Detective Carswell operates, I wish you the best of British luck!"

He turned his attention to Lizzie. "I'm going to make a phone call or two. Call in a few favors. Go directly through my office. Tell Freddy to give the matter his personal attention. He has pretty good connections, so it shouldn't take him too long to deal with protocol and the necessary finance. If it becomes necessary I'll make a couple of calls to expedite matters. Meanwhile you both should work out your cover. Make sure you know your relationship to each other and act accordingly. Now if you'll excuse me, I have to wax eloquent on the subject of the *Apis Mellifera*."

Without saying another word he returned to the studio.

As Harry and Lizzie walked back along the corridor he asked, "What the hell is *Apis Mellifera*?"

"The common honey bee," she replied. "The Commander is an authority on beekeeping."

"Aha! That accounts for the smell of smoke."

"What smell?" she asked with a frown.

"Woodsy smell of burning. You burn rolled-up newspaper to keep the bees calm when you handle them."

"How do you know about that?" she asked.

"Played a homicidal beekeeper once," he replied. "Amazing what you can learn in show business."

When they returned to the Renault, a horrendous medieval contraption had been padlocked to the rear offside wheel with a threatening sticker pasted to the passenger window. Lizzie had neglected to buy and affix a parking ticket to the windshield. The parking space was now permanently blocked. Lizzie climbed into the driver's seat, put the key in the ignition and turned the radio to loud pop music. She lit another cigarette and let out a dense cloud of smoke that curled up the windshield. Harry wound down his window.

From the glove compartment she produced a cellphone and a small notebook. Handing him the phone, she wrote down three telephone numbers. Below those she scribbled an odd series of numbers and letters.

"Keep this with you," she instructed. "The first number is if you get into trouble. Don't use it unless it's a real emergency. The second is my direct number. The third is the airline. Call them and make two Business Class reservations to New York on the first flight that leaves tomorrow."

"Do I use our own names?"

"Yes, Harry. We are operating in the real world. We use our real names."

Her finger tapped the fourth line. "If you have any problem with the reservation, give them that as a priority code. They'll know what to do. Leave the mobile on all the time. I'll call you as soon as I have any news."

"What do I do until then?"

"Find yourself somewhere to stay and decide how you would smuggle one million, five hundred thousand dollars into the United States of America. Shouldn't be too hard a problem for a smart man like you." She took the key from the ignition and got out. "Remember, when you meet me at the check-in counter we're supposed to be good friends. Make like you're glad to see me."

"What do we do about your car?" said Harry.

"The fuzz'll tow it away. It'll be a fucking sight safer with them than outside my flat." Dashing across the street, she flagged down a passing cab. As she climbed in and shut the door, she blew him a kiss.

Harry closed the windows and retrieved the cases. With them safely stowed in another cab he told the driver to go to South Kensington where there would be several suitable places for him to stay the night.

A capricious summer shower fell as they passed along Oxford Street, but by the time Harry made his way up the steps of the Five Sumner Place Hotel the sun shone brilliantly. A gentleman with a thick middle European accent was able to give Harry a room on the ground floor.

Inside was sufficient space for the task in hand. The bathroom was small and clean. On top of the icebox were a kettle, tea bags, packets of powdered milk and a plastic spoon. Sunlight streamed in from a bay window that overlooked the little garden. On the right of this was a high wall and along the left was a greenhouse where tables were already laid ready for breakfast.

Harry sat down on the bed, picked up the phone and dialed the airline but was informed that all the flights in Business Class were fully booked. The priority code that Lizzie had written on the piece of paper magically produced two seats.

Lizzie had suggested he figure a way to smuggle the cash, so he lay back on the coverlet and mentally did the math. A hundred and fifty packets of one-hundred-dollar bills needed to be concealed in something that wouldn't cause undue comment. Everything would also have to be taken on the plane, either in the cabin or as checked baggage. What could he use? What would pass inspection by the TSA with their meticulous and often painstakingly slow checks?

Was there anything that actors routinely carried with them when they flew to a location? Or the crew? What about a film unit? Even the smallest carry a lot of gear, and usually in metal cases. It wouldn't be out of the ordinary to travel with one for a camera, and others for lenses and spare batteries. But could such equipment be protected by 5 percent foam padding and 95 percent cash? The weight wouldn't be a problem, as camera cases are notoriously heavy.

Harry locked the room and took the key with him. At a Cyber Café in the King's Road he went online and began to search the Web. It soon became clear that with so much redundancy in the electronic world there was a great deal of old equipment for sale. He chose a seller in Ealing with an Arriflex 16SRII SR2 movie camera complete with lenses, batteries and film magazines plus a Nagra Stereotime Code recorder IV/S. This selection was primarily because everything was packed in "three sturdy aluminium cases." The seller also listed a phone number. Harry called and after a brief conversation ran out and jumped into a taxi.

The cases were piled in the corner of a garage in a semi-detached house. Harry opened all three, ostensibly to check the equipment but actually to again make mental calculations. Each case was padded with almost three inches of dark blue foam.

He quickly realized there would be room to spare. With the time he had left he figured he wouldn't find anything much better, so he peeled off the necessary number of notes and loaded everything into the waiting taxi. To complete the job he needed tools and other paraphernalia, so halfway down the Edgware Road he made the driver wait while he went into drug- and hardware stores.

Back at the hotel he cleared a space in the middle of the room and sat down at the little desk to calculate on paper exactly how many packets of bills he could hide in each case. Then the real work began.

34

When the Murphy family moved to Brooklyn they didn't own a car. Not wanting to waste the space, Harry's father turned the garage at the side of the house into a workshop. As well as doing necessary household repairs, he took up woodworking as a hobby. Many of his tools hung on two sheets of pegboard above the workbench, all outlined in red to indicate exactly where they went. When Harry was old enough to sit on the bench without falling off he was given the task of replacing them. This gave him a respect for every hammer, saw and screwdriver. As he grew bigger he was permitted to use the tools and would spend long hours with his dad making projects of his own. Over time he became quite an accomplished carpenter.

One of Harry's first professional jobs was as an intern to a summer stock theater in Ogunquit, Maine, where he was hired for twelve weeks to oversee the gathering of all the props and furniture for each of six productions. Old glasses, cracked crockery, books, clocks, radios and an assortment of flower vases filled the shelves of the prop room. Everything else had to be begged or borrowed. With the grand title of assistant stage manager he was sent at all hours of the day and night to every corner of town to procure whatever was needed. What he couldn't find he made. By the end of the season, he was an adept electrician, upholsterer, metalworker, plasterer and plumber, so the task before him now was no great challenge.

The camera case linings were carefully loosened, removed and hung over the towel rails in the bathroom. With a black felt pen and a ruler he drew thin lines on the foam where the cuts needed to be made. The slicing and dicing took several hours and he used up an entire box of industrial razor blades. With small sharp scissors he removed all the tiny unwanted pieces of projecting foam and smoothed out the cavity. Great patience was called for throughout as he couldn't leave even the slightest trace that might reveal what he had done.

With demolition complete he cleaned up, packed all the detritus into a plastic bag and on a deserted street corner dumped it into a garbage can. His stomach was rumbling in protest at being neglected for so long so he headed towards the lights at the end of the road and an all-night deli.

Back in his room he lay on the bed and enjoyed two Chicken Tikka sandwiches and a large bottle of orange juice. His energy was renewed and his gut silenced. Pulling on a pair of disposable rubber gloves he turned to phase two.

Each packet of bills was tightly wrapped in several layers of cling-film. Then they were assembled into bundles and put in alternate directions into the precut cavities. Miraculously, they all went in perfectly.

With an awl, a pair of tweezers and a box of Q-tips the linings were gently glued back where they were before and the fabric smoothed flat and cleaned of any surplus glue. The only trouble was that there was now a strong smell from the adhesive. Harry opened all the windows and propped the cases as close to the night air as he could. Exhausted, he flopped down on the coverlet.

Lizzie woke him up very early. The phone rang six times

before Harry managed to locate it in the bedclothes and press the key.

"Congratulations! We are set to go," said Lizzie. "Did you make the reservation?"

"Sure did," said Harry sleepily.

"Which flight?"

"The first one, like you said." He yawned. "What the hell time is it? Where are you?"

"I am in my office" came the reply. "I'm sending someone over to pick up the money."

"What?" Harry asked, slightly confused.

"The suitcase," she said patiently. "I need the money."

"That's going to be a bit awkward."

"Why?" she said sharply.

"I sort of made other arrangements."

"What the hell are you talking about?" She sounded concerned.

"You told me to work out how to smuggle it and I did. I now have three extra cases," he explained, "for camera equipment. I've wrapped and stashed the bills inside them."

"Why did you do that?"

"You told me to."

"I told you to?"

"Yes. You said I was to find a way to smuggle the cash back into the States."

There was a distinct silence. Lizzie gave a little laugh. "Let me get this right. You bought three camera cases and hid the cash inside them?"

"Yes," said Harry. "I removed most of the linings and replaced them with the money. I would have preferred something more modern, maybe video equipment, but this was the best I could find at short notice. All I need to know is what we have to do about the airline."

"How did you pay for all this?"

"I used some of the cash. Don't worry; I can sell all of it in New York and put the money back. I just need to know what happens when we turn up at check-in with three extra bags."

"Just a minute, Harry," she said, and covered the mouthpiece. Muffled sounds could be heard as she talked to someone in the office. Then she took her hand away. "You do what you would do under normal circumstances. You call the airline and tell them what you got. Let them know the bags are properly labeled and can be opened for inspection. They'll tell you what else you need to do."

"Did I do wrong?" asked Harry.

"No, Harry," replied Lizzie with a chuckle, "you did absolutely right." And she hung up.

A wide-awake Harry sat up and called British Airways. After endless layers of computerized menus a human voice came on the line and Harry was able to describe his predicament. The voice told him that there would simply be an additional charge for each extra bag.

"That's all?" asked Harry.

"Yes, sir" came the pleasant reply. "I'm sure you'll have no problem."

Harry was encouraged by her optimism.

35

The girl with the red high heels tucked the money into her bra and picked up her fuzzy pink sweater from the bedroom floor. Max let her out into the street and went back up to the crumpled sheets. Several hours later his eyelids twitched as he heard a knocking. Rocco was tapping on the doorframe.

"I brought us some food," he said. "I thought you might be hungry after your strenuous night's work."

"Very funny," said Max.

"Maurizio made some hash and eggs."

"Yeah. Just what the doctor ordered."

Slowly regaining his equilibrium, Max stretched and ambled through to the dining table. "Bitch fucked like a wild animal," he said, rubbing his eyes. "Made deep growling noises in her throat every time she came."

Rocco handed Max a knife and fork as he sat down. "Where did you find your fuzzy friend?"

"Picked her up on the street. What a body! Not an ounce of fat. And strong legs. Trouble was up top. All pumped full of that silicone. I can't get used to the feel of those fucking things."

As they ate, Max asked, "You never told me. Who gave you Eddie Ryan?"

"Joe Piscarelli."

"Ratface?"

"Yes."

"Have you called him?"

"No need. He'll know what happened. If he has any news he'll call us."

Max shook his head. "We need to know what he knows. Call him."

"Okay. No problem."

"When did you get back?"

"Last night. Just got into bed and watched TV. *Goodfellas*. Great movie. I kept thinking how glad I was that you guys are not like those guys. It's no wonder they all got busted."

Max got up to put on fresh coffee. "Did I ever tell you about the first time I was involved in a hit?"

"No. When was it?" asked Rocco.

"I was sixteen. Papa Aldo came into my bedroom in the middle of the night and told me to get up, get dressed and get myself downstairs. He told me a capo in one of the families wanted a cousin eliminated. A cousin for Christ's sake! Seems the guy had committed 'an unforgivable sin.' The old bastard didn't want relatives or associates involved, so he looked around for an outsider. Papa was the first one he asked.

"I remember sitting at the kitchen table, just like this. He was leaning against the icebox in the corner, smoking one of his thin rolled cigarettes, drinking his coffee. That was the first time I came face-to-face with the reality of what he did. Boy, did I wake up fast."

Rocco leaned back in his chair as Max continued.

"We drove over the Williamsburg Bridge to Manhattan, crossed the island and took the West Side Drive up to Seventy-ninth. Papa never said a word until we parked off Amsterdam and began to walk up the avenue. 'I've been following this guy for the last two nights,' he told me. 'He goes to the same bar and hangs out with the same group of associates until two in the morning. Sometimes he walks home, either alone or with a friend, or sometimes he takes a cab. You can never be sure.'

"Then he pulls this bit of paper out of his pocket and hands it to me. It had a phone number scribbled on it in pencil: 'You call that number at exactly twenty-five minutes past one. When you get an answer, you ask for Vittorio. If they want to know who's calling, you say, "Sandy." Got it?'"

Max poured some coffee.

"We stopped at a pay phone and synchronized watches. He went into the bar and I made the call just like he said. Back then it cost a dime. I looked at that coin in my hand and thought it was such a small price for a man's life. But I dropped it in. Did what I'd been told to do. When I got the unsuspecting Vittorio on the line I heard a soft pop and a loud grunt and that was it."

He sat back down at the table. "I stood on the sidewalk expecting to see my old man come running. Almost three minutes went by. I began to get worried something had happened to him. Then he comes sauntering out of the bar rolling a cigarette. He gave me a friendly wave and crossed the road. Together we walked to the car. You know what he told me on the way back home?"

"What?"

"He said that what we did was like a war. We only fight the enemy. Only the bad guys. Never the good guys. No way would the Bruschettis be asked to kill anyone unless he'd gone real bad. That way no one got whacked that shouldn't get whacked.

"Two days later I read in the paper that the cleaning woman in the bar had found the body of an alleged member of the Mafia slumped in a phone booth. The night before, everyone who passed by assumed the bastard was making a very long-distance call."

Rocco smiled.

"You know what else Aldo told me that night?" said Max.

"No. Tell me."

" 'Never be impulsive or reckless. Think before you act.' Told me it was like sawing wood. You measure twice and cut once."

"He was right," said Rocco. "It's a lot nicer up here than on Rikers."

"Ain't that the truth," agreed Max with a grin. "I'm glad you're back. I don't like it when you're not here."

"It's good to be back," said Rocco getting up and putting their dishes in the sink. "Give me a call when you need me."

Max washed, shaved and put on clean clothes. Out in the street he walked three blocks to a small shop that sold newspapers and magazines. He pulled out thirty dollars from his wallet. The turbaned Sikh behind the counter punched the machine and out flipped six Lotto quick picks. Max handed over the money and left. As he paused on the sidewalk to put the tickets in his wallet an accented voice behind him drawled, "I'm surprised, Mr. Bruschetti."

Max turned. In front of him was a gentleman in a light gray suit, cream shirt and dark green tie secured with an emerald pin. In one hand he carried a Panama hat, in the other a silver-tipped cane, which he used to point at the Lotto tickets. "Or perhaps you purchased those for someone else?"

"Señor Hernandez!" said Max, trying to conceal his surprise at such a direct contact. "I buy them for myself twice a week. I get a kick out of checking the numbers."

"What a coincidence," said the Colombian.

"Our meeting like this, or do you play too?" replied Max.

"Neither," said the other with a slight shake of his head. "I refer to you flying down to South America to make me an offer while I was in North America to do the same to you. Quite serendipitous."

Max took a breath and concentrated fast. Unless Rodrigo had read the English papers he couldn't possibly know what had happened in London. The Colombian began to walk. Max fell in step beside him.

"At precisely the time you have decided to make changes in your organization," Hernandez continued, "we have been forced by events to do the same. But in our situation, we are not contemplating retirement but rather reorganization."

"I don't understand," said Max.

"The factors involved are many. In spite of many changes in our country over the past few years, it is still a wild, chaotic place. Too many factions struggling for power and control. Every one of them has its own paramilitary force. It is too easy to be caught in the cross fire." He gave an expressive shrug of his shoulders. "I am afraid the days we knew when we started doing business together are long gone. In Colombia honor among thieves is nothing but a distant memory."

"So what do you intend to do?"

"As I believe my colleague told you, we have gone into the gold business. It is more manageable. But life is strange sometimes; these days mercury is a greater problem for us than the bullet. We also must diversify. We must think like the farmers in the hills who now plant many small fields beneath the canopy of the trees that go undetected from the air and thus avoid the spray of government chemicals. We must set up invisible organizations that go unnoticed by all who would, at best, control us or, at worst, destroy us. Most significantly, we must change our routes into the United States.

"Which brings me to my reason for meeting with you. Up to now our operations here have been focused on New York, Washington, Chicago, Miami and Los Angeles. As the federal agencies became increasingly sophisticated in the methods they use to enforce the law, our little group made the decision to decrease our involvement in these cities and concentrate our efforts in the less populous centers where I am happy to say there is a well-established customer base. Do you follow me so far?"

"Absolutely," said Max, following the logic but at the same time wondering how it could involve him.

"My business partners and I discussed the issue in depth," said Hernandez. "Your name was at the top of the list as most qualified to take charge of the East Coast—in a purely administrative capacity of course. We all felt that the Bruschetti family has the experience to set up such a network. Specifically to pick the personnel needed to infiltrate existing suppliers, set up the means of distribution, et cetera, et cetera. As to remuneration? A deal will be agreed upon that I can assure you will be acceptable to us both. Naturally we will give you a day or two to think it over.

"As to your brother's concerns, as soon as you have achieved our primary objectives we can discuss the matter of retirement."

A Cadillac Escalade drew up at the curb and the rear door was pushed open from inside.

"As soon as you have thought my proposition over, contact me in the usual manner."

With a nod and a smile the South American ducked into the car and it drove off leaving Max clutching his Lotto tickets.

"*Ma, porca puttana!*" he cursed.

This was the last thing he needed. Just when he felt he was

getting free and clear. He sighed audibly. Why the hell hadn't he told Hernandez right there and then that he didn't want to have anything to do with his damned scheme? It was a no-brainer. But at the very least he owed it to his brothers to let them know about the offer.

Then he would turn it down flat.

36

Lizzie arrived to pick up Harry at the hotel in faded blue jeans and an old denim shirt, with a shaggy sweater tied around her shoulders. "Have to look the part," she announced. "This is what they call 'plain' clothes!" And she did a pirouette and sank to her knees by the cases.

"Is all of it in there?" she asked.

Harry nodded. "I wrapped them in layers of plastic. You suppose a sniffer dog could still find them?"

"Not unless they had been in the same room as pot or coke. Then he'd be on to them in a heartbeat." A broad grin crept across her face. "You are a clever bugger, aren't you?" She rose to her feet. "Come on, let's get 'em loaded."

"What about Villiers's suitcase?" asked Harry. "Should we leave it or bring it with us?"

"Bring it. You never know, we might need it."

Outside Ivan was waiting with an SUV. Once everything was packed in, he drove quickly to the Motorway. At the airport Lizzie called over a skycap. Using a trolley, he wheeled everything up to the check-in counter. But before they could be tagged a customs agent was summoned.

"Are these all yours?" he asked, pointing at the cases and looking at Harry.

"Yes, they are."

"And what do they contain, sir?"

"A camera . . . a sound recorder . . . and some other stuff," he said casually.

"Right. Well, I just need you to turn everything on. I have to see them working."

Harry tried his best to make it look as if he were familiar with the equipment. To his great relief, it all ran smoothly. Within minutes the cases disappeared along the moving belt with the rest of their luggage.

In the departure lounge Lizzie spent a small fortune on glossy magazines and bought four cartons of cigarettes in Duty Free. Harry was still unable to relax, as he knew that everything would be run through an X-ray machine before it was taken to the plane. But nothing unusual happened. Boarding was on time and uneventful. Apparently his plan had succeeded.

As the wheels of the big jet were tucked up into the fuselage, Harry pressed the button on his seat and reclined. Stretching out his legs, he sipped his champagne and gave a chuckle.

"What's so funny?" asked Lizzie, sorting through her recently acquired reading material.

"I was just thinking. I could get used to all this."

"All of what?" she asked.

"You know," he said, popping a cashew into his mouth. "Flying the Atlantic, sitting next to a beautiful girl, sipping champagne. You'll never guess what happened the last time I flew over."

"Tell me," said Lizzie with a slight smile.

"First, the flight was overbooked so I was bumped up into Business Class. Then they sat me next to this gorgeous creature. Just my type. Had the most amazing eyes. I thought about asking her if she wanted a lift into town, but by the time I got through immigration and customs she was long gone."

"I can give you her address if you like."

Harry stopped chewing. Lizzie put down her magazine.

"We knew all about you soon after you made the call from New York to the Mews house. That was the first real connection we'd made in weeks. Right away my boss made a call to a friend of his in the US and arranged to have your phone bugged.

"When you contacted the airline, Ivan dispatched Marisa Vargas to New York to sit beside you. It was her idea to have you both travel Business Class. She likes her comforts. And she may be your type, but she is also Ivan's. They've been together for over a year. He met her on a case in Spain when they were both undercover."

Harry looked at Lizzie in disbelief, feeling cheated and foolish.

"You didn't think I was going to let you run around all by yourself?" she said with a little laugh.

Her flippancy made him angry. He'd agreed to cooperate with this bizarre female but he hadn't bargained with every single move being monitored. Lizzie and her pal Ivan were manipulating him like a puppet. No doubt they would do it until they achieved their objective. Whenever that might be. What an idiot Marisa must have thought him with all his crazy made-up tales. Mercifully, he would never see her again. Once he made the call, Lizzie and her cohorts would all become an amusing memory.

Conversation between them ceased. Lizzie went back to turning pages and Harry stared at the television screen. For a while they both slept. Lizzie awoke first and went to the toilet. When she returned she reached over and shook Harry by the shoulder.

"I don't think I've treated you very nice," she said simply and honestly. "And I'm sorry. I don't want to arrive in New York feeling there's a problem between us. Will you accept an apology?"

"Sure." He nodded, half-awake. "And I'm sorry if I behaved like a jerk."

"Not at all," she replied brightly. "Now. Where are you going to take me when this is over? Tell me all about New York."

Harry sat up. "Ah. Yes. Well, once we've unpacked we're going to walk through Central Park over to Columbus Circle. We'll take a subway to the far end of the island and watch the sunset shining on the Statue of Liberty. We shall then take a cab to Brio, my favorite restaurant. And while you're in New York we must be sure to go to the Metropolitan Museum of Art. You'll love it there."

"Wow!" said Lizzie.

Harry became serious. "First we have to get through Customs and Immigration. What will they do to us if they find the cash in the linings?"

"It would be sodding awkward," she replied. "I've never tried to do anything quite like this." She gave a smirk. "Let's hope they don't."

"You didn't expect me to actually smuggle it, did you?"

"No, Harry, it came as a bit of a surprise. I told you to work out how you were going to do it, that's all."

"What would you have done if I hadn't?"

"Ivan already made arrangements to pop it on an RAF flight."

"Why didn't we just do that?"

"Simple. Your story is so much more believable this way. If anyone asks, you can actually tell them how you did it!"

The plane's nose dipped as they began their final approach. Once they were on the ground the big jet lumbered over to the gate. Harry became progressively more nervous. Immigration was fully automated and went smoothly. In the baggage hall at Carousel 4 their personal bags arrived, but the cases were no-where to be seen. Harry stopped a passing agent and inquired where they might be. The woman took Harry and Lizzie to the oversize section, where all were present and correct. With her help they loaded up two hand trolleys and pushed them up to the counter. An agent looked at their forms and then inquiringly at the metal cases.

"It's camera equipment," said Harry. "I do documentaries."

"What's in that one?" the agent asked.

"Batteries. You always need extras," Harry replied.

The customs agent looked at him with a frown. "Haven't I seen you someplace before?" he asked. "Aren't you an actor?"

"Yes. In this business you make a buck wherever you can."

The agent pointed his finger at Harry like a gun. "I have it. It was that movie about the Marines with Tom Cruise! The one in the snow?"

"Oh, that!" replied Harry, relieved. "I'm flattered you remembered me."

"It was the way you died. Was that you or did you use a stuntman?"

"That was me," said Harry, and then added modestly, "It wasn't quite as dangerous as it looked."

"I see a lot of movies," said the agent, writing on the form. "It's kind of like a hobby." He handed it over. "Nice to meet you. Welcome back."

"Thanks," replied Harry, and added somewhat foolishly, "You too."

Following the signs they headed out of the customs area. Harry called Carmel to request a minivan. They were told to wait at the pickup point.

As they walked over, Lizzie said, "I'm impressed."

"At my brilliance as a smuggler?"

"No. That you worked with Tom Cruise. What he's like?"

"I have no idea, other than his crazy involvement with Scientology," Harry replied. "He wasn't in any of my scenes."

They crossed the Queensboro Bridge onto Manhattan and soon pulled up at the hydrant outside Harry's building.

Harry paid the driver, and making two trips, he and Lizzie carried all the cases up the stairs to his apartment. Taking out his keys he unlocked the two dead bolts, pushed open the door and said, "Make yourself to home."

Lizzie looked around as he brought everything in.

"Are you going to give me the tour?" she asked.

He laughed and pointed in three directions. "Bedroom, kitchen, bathroom."

Lizzie indicated a door next to the kitchen. "What's in there?"

"Junk room."

Lizzie poked her head inside. The closet was piled high with an assortment of cases, boxes and plastic bags.

"It's old props and all the stuff I keep for character parts," he explained. "I always mean to go through it all and sort it out, but somehow I never get around to it."

Lizzie walked over and gazed at the framed photographs on the wall above the desk. "Good God!" she said. "You know these people?"

"I worked with them. It's not quite the same thing."

"And isn't that Madonna?"

"Yes," he replied. "For half a day. Weird movie."

"Holy shit!" Lizzie said. "I'm really impressed." She moved to the next picture, showing a group shot of four men. One of them was in uniform. "Is that your father?" she asked.

"Yes."

"He was a policeman?"

"A cop, yes. He was a cool dude."

"Sounds great!" she exclaimed, and then asked, "Do you have a landline?"

He pointed to the bedroom. "By the bed."

Lizzie opened her suitcase, pulled out a folder, a black dress and a pair of low heels and headed into the bedroom. Harry got himself a Stella Artois and sat down on the sofa. Her call was brief and moments later she shouted out to him. "How do I get to West Tenth?"

"The Drug Enforcement Agency office?"

"Yes."

"Get a cab," he replied. "Take you about ten minutes."

Now looking very official, she came back into the room, picked up her purse and slung it over her shoulder.

"I have to take care of protocol," she said. "I won't be long."

"Oh," said Harry, a little surprised. "You have to do it alone?"

"Yes. Do you have a spare key?"

"Sure," he said, and retrieved a ring of keys from a kitchen drawer. Lizzie slipped them into her pocket. "Don't worry Harry;

once we've got all this official nonsense out of the way we can enjoy the sinful pleasures of New York."

The front door slammed and he was alone. The sound of her heels faded as she went down the stairs.

Harry carried the camera cases into the kitchen and stowed them under the table. In the bedroom he unpacked his suitcase and made two piles, one for the wash and another for the cleaners. The mail was collected from the foot of the stairs and sorted on the kitchen table. All of it was junk. When Lizzie came back, he had been to the laundry, dropped off his dry cleaning and from Whole Foods had brought home olives, pâtés, nuts, cheese and crackers. In the icebox were two bottles of Vermentino.

"Sorry. Took longer than I thought. But Marty turned out to be real busy."

"Marty?"

Lizzie adopted a mock American accent. " 'Special Agent Marty P. MacAvoy.' My contact here. Busted a supply house last night and pulled in half of the Bronx. I had to wait while he filled in the forms. Place was a shambles. They had suspects lined up along the walls in one room and in another they had put those big folding tables. They was all covered with big bags of cocaine. On one side was a huge wooden door with ten locks on it. All smashed in it was."

"What was that there for?"

"Evidence."

She squatted down on the floor by her suitcase. "What have you been up to?"

"I got us some food. I thought we'd have a glass of wine with an appetizer or two before starting our tour of the Big Apple."

"All that will have to wait," she said abruptly. This time she pulled out a print dress and a pair of sensible walking shoes and went into the bedroom.

Her voice rose as she changed.. "Marty said he could spare two agents. They'll be in place at six. That's when you make the call. Then no matter what is said or done you get your arse back here."

So much for showing Lizzie the sights. "No last meal for the condemned man," he commented pointedly.

"We can go out and eat first. We got time." She strode back in and lifted her suitcase up on a side table. "Where shall we go? It's my treat."

"Coffee shop just around the corner. But you're not paying for your first nosh in New York, I am."

"Neither of us is paying, Harry. I'm putting it on Expenses. We're noshing courtesy of Her Majesty. But before we go we need to pick out what you're going to be wearing later. You need something that can be identified at a distance. Nothing overt, but it should be specific. Marty's people have to be able to spot you right away so they can follow you."

This was news to Harry. "Where the hell are they going to follow me?"

"Probably nowhere, but we got to be prepared. We need something simple but distinctive. What have you got in your little cupboard?"

"Bits and pieces. Theater stuff."

"Let's have a look," she said, opening the door.

"Some sort of hat?" he suggested facetiously. "What about a Stetson? I got a big white one. After all, I am supposed to be one of the good guys."

She smiled. "I don't think so."

"A bowler? Some sort of cap?"

"Show me."

Harry pulled out a cardboard box and was about to tip the contents onto the floor when Lizzie reached over him to lift out a pair of red suspenders. "What about these?" she asked.

"Fireman's clip-on suspenders. I wore them in a modern dress production of *Major Barbara*," he replied. "Why not? With the right shirt they would stand out a mile."

"Put them on," she ordered.

ONCE A CROOKED MAN

Lizzie changed in the bathroom as Harry put on a T-shirt, a tattered work shirt, a pair of old blue jeans with the red suspenders and a pair of sneakers. When she emerged she gave him the once-over.

"Perfect," she said. "Now let's go eat."

In the coffee shop, Lizzie took the time to read all five pages of the menu.

"What's Marty like?" asked Harry, watching her.

"Tall dark and handsome with a long thin face. Gave me the impression he would prefer we wasn't here."

Harry suggested she choose the lox with cream cheese and sliced onion on a toasted bagel. It was her own idea to add a chocolate milk shake. Harry settled on a turkey burger, fries and coffee.

"The contact number Villiers gave us," said Lizzie, "is probably a custom portable device. You dial and punch in the number where you're calling from. When it shows up on their little receiver, someone makes a note of the number, calls someone else, and then that someone else calls you back. There are different combinations for the calls, but basically they're all virtually untraceable. So much so that Marty thinks we're wasting our time."

"Really?" said Harry hopefully.

"He says today's villains do all they can to keep their identities a secret. He also said that there is no way anyone is going to blow their cover for a measly million and a half."

Harry's eyebrows rose involuntarily. "Wouldn't they at least be curious?" he asked.

"Not according to Marty. Even if we're on the right track and make a connection, it's more than likely we'll be contacted by someone far from the circle of trusted people."

"Isn't that just as good? I mean, all you want is to make contact."

The food arrived and Lizzie looked in amazement at the huge plate. "My God! There's enough here for the Arsenal football team." Picking up the warm bagel she asked, "Okay, what's the drill?"

"You take the bagel, spread the cream cheese on top, put a piece of onion on top of that, then a slice of the salmon. Then you sprinkle on the capers and add a squeeze of lemon."

Lizzie followed his instructions and took a big bite. "Mmm," she said approvingly. "Well worth the effort."

Harry opened his burger, spread on the mustard, poured on the ketchup and added the pickles.

"You're right about us wanting to make contact," said Lizzie with her mouth full. "But remember, we need something we can follow up. You got to make them think you're crazy enough to cause trouble. They've got to want to meet you. Talk to you face-to-face."

"How long do you think all this is going to take?"

"No idea."

"Shouldn't we put the money back in the suitcase?"

"No. Not yet." She blew the wrapping off the straw into the air.

"What if they ask me for it?"

"Harry," she said patiently, "first you have to get them curious. Then you have to convince them you're going to be a nuisance they can't ignore. Then you have to agree to a meeting. That's when I take over. I'll deal with the money."

Harry put his burger down on the plate. "When we started this charade, I agreed to make one phone call. Now I am being told to make a series of calls in which I have to give an Academy Award performance to convince a bunch of low-level peons that I am a raving lunatic who urgently needs to meet their paranoid boss."

Her head went from side to side. "At this level of operation they wouldn't expect it any other way, Harry. The receivers will make their own determination and report back. That's the way it's done. You have to go through the layers."

"Why didn't you tell me all this before?"

"I did, Harry. You wasn't listening. Or I just assumed you knew. Look, if I made a mistake I'm sorry. Just make the calls one by one. Marty will have two agents watching you the whole time. You'll be quite safe."

"Where will you be?"

"I'll be up in your flat while you make the first call. After that, Marty wants me with him. If anything should happen he doesn't want to be the one making decisions."

"Sounds a bit of a wuss to me."

"Let's hope not. For both our sakes."

In his early career Harry had performed sketches that demanded improvisation. His efforts, although adequate, had given him a healthy respect for the written word.

"What makes you think I'll be able to come up with the right dialogue when I'm dealing with some meathead asking awkward questions?"

"Think about what you know, Harry. Stick to the facts. Tell them about London. About Villiers. About having afternoon tea with the Colonel's wife. About what happened in the Mews. You were there! You know what happened. Not only that, you have names. Mrs. Villiers spoke about an Enzo. The Colonel talked about Max and Rocco. Use that information. You're an actor, Harry, I know you can do it. I just know you can."

37

Harry dropped two quarters into a pay phone on Columbus Circle and dialed the contact number Lizzie had extorted from Colonel Villiers. There was a click and then three sharp beeps. Harry punched in the number in front of him and hung up. The phone rang almost immediately and gave him a start. Picking up the receiver, he listened to resonant silence. Whoever was on the other end was not going to start the conversation.

It was clearly up to Harry. As he was totally unprepared, he hung up.

A short rehearsal was needed. He had to establish a character for himself. If he was someone scared and a bit stupid what would he say and how would he say it? Lizzie had just told him to base everything on what he knew. After making a few mental notes he cleared his throat, put two more coins in the slot and dialed. Once again he heard the beeps and tapped in the numbers. Moments later the phone rang. This time he was prepared.

"My name's Murphy . . . Harry Murphy. I'm back here in New York. I need to talk to Max, or maybe Enzo . . . about the suitcase . . . the suitcase with the money." A touch of hysteria crept into his voice. "Oh God! I hope I'm doing the right thing . . ."

Harry felt as if the success or failure of the entire production was now on his shoulders. A bad review could close the show. "I don't want it! Do you hear? It's all a goddam mistake!"

"Okay, fella," said someone with a serious nasal condition and who was clearly unimpressed by Harry's histrionics. "Call back in an hour."

Harry hung up. The adrenaline overflowed through his system giving him a clear and concise picture of what he was doing. The whole stupid business was insane. "This has to end here and now!" he said forcefully to a passing stranger who proceeded to give him a wide berth.

Back at 56th Street he charged up the stairs and walked decisively through the front door. Lizzie had taken a shower and slipped into something loose and red. She ran over and put her arms around his neck. Without a thought, he put his arms around her waist. She felt warm, soft and silky.

"How did it go?" she asked.

"I spoke to someone who told me to call back in an hour," he answered.

"Great!" she cried. "You did it!"

"I—"

"One more call, Harry."

"I—"

"You can't let me down, not now."

"I was thinking—"

She lowered her voice. "Right, Harry! Just keep thinking about all we can do when this is over." She kissed him lightly on the tip of his nose. "Okay?"

"Okay," said Harry, his resolve obliterated.

38

The Fiery Red Dragon was not particularly busy when the three Bruschetti brothers came in and slid into the corner booth. Rocco followed them, put the Closed card on the outer door and had the neon sign turned off. He then ordered an assortment of appetizers and drinks for everyone. As they munched away they made small talk. As soon as the last of the patrons left, the waiter and cook were banished to the street and the four men got down to business.

"Tell me, Brother, why the hell don't we just say no?" Sal asked bluntly.

"Not a good idea," said Enzo. "We don't want to make the South Americans our enemies."

"What makes you think you can trust them?" asked Max. "Once we set up the organization for them they could get rid of us permanently."

"That would be very bad for business," Enzo replied, chewing on a spare rib. "Even the Colombians know you got to trust somebody somewhere."

Sal took a sip of his Cutty Sark. "What makes you think we can deliver what he wants?"

Enzo leaned back and said forcefully, "Goddam it, Sal! The

man is giving us a one-way ticket to retirement. To a little peace and security."

Max shook his head. "I agree with Sal. It won't be that easy to set up an organization like the one he wants. We have few reliable contacts outside the city. How do you set up a network without manpower?"

"Simple," replied Enzo. "We relocate the guys we know here." He glanced at the doubting faces around him. "Look." He shoved aside the dishes. "It's like this." He illustrated with a finger on the tabletop. "I would be in overall charge from here in Manhattan. We divide the country into sections. We assign someone we can trust to each one and let them pick a team. They will report directly to me here in New York."

"You think he knows what happened in London?" asked Sal.

Rocco spoke up. "If he doesn't know now he will soon. Nothing gets by those guys."

"He's right," said Max. "We need to figure out what to say when he asks."

"Not a problem," said Enzo confidently.

Sal looked over at Rocco. "Did you wait to see the kid come back to his room?"

"What?" said Rocco.

"When you were in London."

"No. I didn't," answered Rocco. "It would have been too risky."

Sal grunted. "I'd sure like to have been a fly on the wall when he opened that fucking closet. What do you suppose the bastard did?"

Rocco smirked. "Packed his things as fast as he could. Put as much distance as he could between himself and his apartment. No way he could ever explain the stiff in his closet. That was the beautiful part of it all. He had nothing to do with Santiago's death, but when they catch him his goose is truly cooked."

"Why did you call the hotel?" asked Enzo. "What was that all about?"

"I did it in case the kid checked to see that Mr. Herbie Smith was a legit guest."

Max tapped on the table. "I think we should reject the offer."

"Well, I don't," said Enzo loudly. "I think we should give it more consideration. Think it out." He stood up and began to walk around the room. "Figure out how many guys we would need. I could buy an atlas. One that has one of those colored maps that show where people live. Make some choices."

"Population densities," said Sal.

"What?" said Enzo.

"Barnes and Noble," said Sal.

Enzo stared at him. "What are you talking about?"

"Barnes and Noble," Sal growled, "the bookstore. They got atlases."

"Every bookstore's got fucking atlases for fuck's sake," said Max.

Rocco's iPhone vibrated. To answer the call he went over to the far side of the room.

Enzo looked at Max and asked, "How you feeling these days?"

"Fine," replied Max. "Never better. Who told you I was sick?"

"I don't remember."

Max stared at him. "Why bring this up now?"

"All this sudden talk of getting out," muttered Enzo. "Go figure."

"And what if he did?" said Sal.

"Did what?"

"What if he thought about himself?" replied Sal. "That if he took it easy for a while maybe he could live a little longer! You got a problem with that?"

Rocco came back over with a puzzled expression on his face. "You're not gonna believe this," he said, sitting in the booth. "You have a call from a Harry Murphy."

For a moment no one moved. Then everyone looked at everyone else.

"No shit," said Max.

"He's asking for you Max," said Rocco.

"For me?"

"Yeah."

"He's here in New York?" said Sal.

"Seems so," said Rocco.

"Are you sure it's *the* Harry Murphy?" asked Max.

"Well I don't suppose there are a lot of Murphys around calling about a suitcase of money."

"A suitcase of money?" said Enzo.

"Yeah. That's what he said. Karl says he sounds pretty crazy. Kind of spaced out."

Enzo shook his head. "I don't believe I'm hearing this."

"Me neither," said Sal. "Are you sure it's not a plant?"

"No, I'm not sure," replied Rocco. "But I can find out real quick."

"Get him," said Max. "I want to meet him."

"One of us should talk to him first," cautioned Enzo. "Let me take care of it."

"Do it fast," said Max. "I can't wait to meet this interfering son of a bitch!"

39

Her instructions were simple. Make the call and then use his initiative. Lizzie took a piece of paper out of her pocket. "That's where you go to make the next call."

The north side of 25th Street, he read. *The short block between Broadway and Fifth Avenue.* He looked up. "Why do I have to go all the way down there?"

"That's where Agent MacAvoy will have his men in position. Trained agents will watch you wherever you go. At the slightest sign of trouble they will move in and take over.

"Promise me one thing, Harry," she said, coming close. "You won't make a move if you think it will get you into danger."

Harry had no trouble crossing his heart and promising to be extremely careful. Thirty minutes later at the appointed spot he went through the now familiar routine with the coins.

Nasal Condition came on the line. "Is dis Murphy?"

Harry replied in the affirmative. The man sneezed and gave him a number to call. Harry dutifully dialed it and was connected to an officious female with a high-pitched voice.

"Is this Mr. Murphy?"

"Yes," he said.

"Mr. Harry Murphy?"

"Yes," he said a little louder.

"I am instructed to direct you to make your way by public transportation to the South Street Seaport where you will enter the main building and go to the top floor. At the souvenir shop you will purchase a rolled-up poster . . ."

"What are you talking about?" said a slightly confused Harry. "I said I wanted to talk with . . ."

"Sir! I am only instructed," she said coldly, "to read you the directions in front of me."

The game was changing. Did this violate Lizzie's mandate to avoid danger? No, he decided. "Okay, okay," he said. "Start again, will you?"

The woman repeated the itinerary. This time Harry made notes. "Purchase a poster," he murmured. "Then what?"

"Outside the store are the doors that lead to the balcony. On the balcony there are several benches. You will sit on the first bench on the left and place the poster on the seat beside you. Is this information clear or would you like me to read it again?"

"Quite clear," he answered. "Thank you."

And she was gone.

The plot thickened. With any luck it wasn't the first act of a tragedy. The Seaport would be very crowded in the evening and the perfect place for an assassination. Someone could walk up, put a gun in his ribs; there would be a muffled thud; his body would fall to the ground; passersby would scream. Harry would hear the wail of the ambulance as he struggled to stay conscious.

The curtain was definitely up. The late afternoon sun shone through the tops of the trees as he walked across Madison Square Park. Looking around, he tried to see if he could spot MacAvoy's trained agents, but there were few likely candidates. Slouched on a bench was a man wearing dark glasses under a Cleveland Indians cap. A security guard in a blue uniform chatted with a woman in a green uniform who was supposed to be sweeping the pathways. A mother talked volubly on her cellphone as she pushed along an empty stroller. A group of students from NYU photographed a boy on a bicycle carrying a huge unfurled Star-Spangled Banner. An inert couple lay entwined on the grass.

From the park Harry headed along 23rd Street to the subway entrance on Park Avenue where he pushed through the turnstile and onto the platform. When the train arrived it was packed. Harry was careful to move aboard slowly to give his invisible minders time to keep up. When the train pulled into the Brooklyn Bridge station everyone squeezed out and headed up the stairs.

At the exit, a Middle Eastern girl with a dirty face sat cross-legged clutching a baby. An older child in soiled clothes lay fast asleep at her side. The mother reached out a hand in supplication. As a rule Harry never gave to the homeless, but right then he needed all the luck he could get, so he reached in his pocket for his money clip and peeled off a twenty.

Once out on the streets and past J&R Music World, he turned left onto Fulton Street and began to walk as if he were upset and angry. Occasionally he slapped his right thigh in frustration. The Seaport came in sight. A row of stanchions delineated the cobbled roadway as a pedestrian mall. On either side were brand stores and open-air restaurants. The crowd thickened and forced him to move more slowly.

As he crossed South Street he wondered about the poster. Why did they want him to buy it? What significance could it have? By now he was no doubt under observation by both the good and the bad guys.

In the center of a group of tourists on the pier an elderly musician wailed on his saxophone. Some clapped their hands; others happily swayed to the music. Above their heads rose the masts of two massive sailing ships. Harry's progress was slow as he weaved his way through the crowd and over to the mall entrance. Once through the two sets of swing doors he found himself in the cool interior and at the foot of an escalator. On the top floor he entered the souvenir shop and picked a poster from the rack in the corner. The exact change was handed over and he ambled outside to the bench on the balcony.

As instructed, he sat down and laid the poster at his side. On any other occasion he would have enjoyed the view of the shores of Brooklyn bathed in the evening sunshine. Now he was more concerned about what was coming next. He didn't have to wait long. A kid carrying a skateboard adorned with bright graffiti popped up in front of him. Without a word, a slip of paper was dropped in his lap. Harry watched the boy whiz away to the escalator and then picked up the note and unfolded it.

Go to the pay phones northwest corner of 62nd and Lexington. Keep this paper with you.

Puzzled, he stared at it for a moment. Back uptown? It all seemed so pointless. Or were they simply being especially careful to make sure he was alone?

Back on the ground floor he crossed the pier and took a more direct route back to the subway station. The doors were just about to close on an uptown express. Harry ran down the stairs.

But halfway down alarm bells sounded in his head. The minders! Using a technique he'd been taught by a stuntman at MGM, he tripped realistically, tucked in his head and arms and rolled down the last few steps to the platform. Jumping to his feet, he cursed audibly at his bad luck at missing the train and dusted himself off.

The next train took him to Lexington Avenue. Two blocks north on 62nd Street, Town Cars and limousines were parked everywhere, their drivers chatting and drinking coffee. A youth in an AIDS Walk T-shirt hosed down the sidewalk in front of the flower stall of the corner Korean market. Harry crossed over to the designated payphones. The right-hand one rang as he stepped up on the curb. He glanced around before taking the receiver off the hook.

"Take a cab," instructed Nasal Condition. "Go to the Delta Airlines Shuttle at LaGuardia. Got it?"

"Got it," said Harry, and he hung up.

Now what? Why the airport? Were they going to ask him to get on a plane? He doubted it. Probably they were going to use the crowds to make contact. A vacant cab cruised slowly past the curb. Harry raised his hand and the driver pulled up. Harry climbed in.

"LaGuardia," he said. "Delta. The shuttle."

The driver waited until the light was green and then cut obliquely across the traffic and headed fast down Lexington as Harry did up his seat belt. Three blocks later they made a left towards the 59th Street Bridge.

Suddenly he was aware that instinct had overcome caution and he was now very much alone. He hoped he hadn't moved too precipitously. What should he do? Best thing would be to get out as soon as they were off the bridge and take a short walk. This would allow his security detail to catch up.

On 21st Street he rapped on the plastic partition. The man ignored him and increased speed. Harry tried the doors but they were locked and unyielding. Suddenly he was thrown against the partition as the driver braked hard and made an abrupt turn into a car wash. The front wheels bumped into the track. The car wash mechanism pulled the cab forward with a jerk.

Long strips of thick wet material swung back and forward, beating, like severed limbs, against the windows and roof. Flailing brushes spun against the side of the cab and cascading water lashed down. The door beside him was suddenly opened. The water sprayed in, soaking his clothes.

"Now just a fucking minute!" yelled Harry as two big arms reached in and dragged him out. A strip of gray tape was slapped over his mouth by an unshaven hulk with vivid red hair. Harry's arms were pinioned behind his back and tied with rope and he was dragged back to another cab that had pulled in behind the first. Both men lifted him up bodily and dropped him into the trunk. As he fell, the lid was slammed shut and his head hit sharp steel.

In the darkness Harry could feel a wet trickle of blood running across his forehead. What was worse, the tape over his mouth partly covered his nostrils and cut off his breathing. Tucking his chin down against his shirt he tried to push the tape free. The nauseating smell of a new tire filled the cramped space. A small amount of air leaked into the trunk from the outside, but this was mixed with exhaust fumes.

Trussed up like a chicken and very short of oxygen, Harry broke into a profuse sweat. His heart labored frantically to pump blood around his system. His skull felt as if it were going to explode. Harry retched a couple of times, partly from the stench and partly from fear.

Panic had to be avoided. Survival would be impossible unless he was in full possession of his faculties. MacAvoy's men would certainly have lost the trail by now, so if he threw up he would probably suffocate on his own vomit.

Above him, whirring dryers blew the moisture off the paintwork. A couple more bumps followed and then a heavy jolt as the cab swung left out of the car wash. The whole exchange had taken less than three minutes. Concentrating on the sounds outside, he sensed the turns and was able to get a rough idea of which way they were going. Across the 59th Street Bridge. Down the ramp and back into Manhattan. Straight for a while. Right on Third and then a left, probably 66th Street, as this seemed to take them through the park to the West Side.

A metal door rattled up. Muffled voices. A man laughed. The engine was switched off. The world became very quiet. The trunk opened. The glare of fluorescent lights above momentarily blinded Harry. Big Arms from the car wash lifted him out. A wiry individual wearing a Mets baseball cap closed the trunk.

The cab was parked in a garage workshop, the floor thick with years of oil and grease. The Mets fan spun him around and pushed him over to a workbench, where he emptied the contents of all his pockets into a manila envelope held open by Big Arms. Both men tied Harry to a metal chair and secured the chair with electrical wire to the bench. Before ducking under the descending door they turned out the lights.

Harry sat in the dark with one eye now completely closed by the congealed blood on his eyelid. They had his wallet, his keys, the pencil and both pieces of paper. His address was on his driver's license. If they went to his apartment they would see the camera cases and the empty leather suitcase. Might they recognize it?

What else could they find?

40

Rocco tore open the envelope from Big Red's Garage and tipped the contents out on the table. The three men gazed down at them. Enzo picked up the wallet and laid out a MetroCard, Visa, MasterCard, American Express and Discover cards, a driver's license, union cards from SAG/AFTRA and AEA, a Health

Plan card, a faded photo of a young man in a police uniform holding a citation and standing beside a pretty girl, a money clip with nine twenty-dollar bills, a five and two singles, a Chase Bank card and a condom.

"You suppose he's a faggot?" said Rocco.

"Who knows?" replied Max.

Rocco picked up the bunch of keys. There were two large and two small. Max smoothed out the pieces of paper.

"That one's from me," said Enzo. He pointed at the other. "What's that one?"

"It says," replied Max, " 'North side of Twenty-Fifth Street . . . between Broadway and Fifth Avenue.' "

"Hall and front door," said Rocco, thumbing through the keys. "Mailbox and what looks like a lockbox. Where's he live?"

Max picked up the driver's license and his eyes met Harry's for the first time. The actor knew how to hold his head and give the right smile to take full advantage of the lighting even in the DMV.

"The famous Mr. Harry Murphy," Max said drily, and threw it down. He picked up the SAG/AFTRA card. " 'Screen Actors Guild,' " he read. "What the fuck is that?"

"A union. It's the actors' union. Actually, it's two unions combined," said Enzo.

"He's an actor?"

"Seems that way."

"Actors have unions?"

"Sure they do," said Rocco. He flipped through the other cards. "One for theater, one for live television and commercials and one for when they work in movies. SAG has always had the best health plan of any union."

"How you know all this?"

"I know a pimp in the Bronx who's one of them. Bastard's always boasting about his benefits." He reached for the license and memorized the address. "What do you want to do?"

Max handed him the keys. "Take these, but let us have them

back. Go there. Take the place apart. See what you can find. Nino can take you."

"Got it," said Rocco, and he hurried out.

Nino drove fast uptown. As they turned onto 56th Street Rocco told him to park on the far corner until he came back out.

"You got your phone with you?" he asked.

Nino reached into a pocket and showed him his cellular. Rocco pulled out his Ruger KSP-321XL. Tucking it in his waistband, he got out and let himself into the building. Inside he read the mailboxes. Murphy was on the top floor. He inserted the small key in the lock and pulled open the box and grasped the letters that had been delivered earlier. Closing the box, he pushed through the inner door and climbed the stairs three at a time, all the while shuffling through the mail. At the apartment he rang the bell. After thirty seconds he let himself in.

Before turning on any lights he took a cursory look in each room to make quite sure he was alone. In the bedroom closet he felt in every pocket, ran his fingers along every seam, checked each piece of clothing and then threw it on the floor. The labels showed Murphy did most of his buying at Brooks Brothers, L.L. Bean and Bloomingdale's.

Each pair of shoes was examined and added to the pile. On the upper shelf were boxes of sweaters, gloves and scarves. A plastic see-through bag contained packets of new socks and handkerchiefs. All of it was checked and tossed on the pile. A blue American Tourister suitcase lay empty. Rocco noted that the flight label on the handle was from British Airways and dated the day before.

He moved over to the bedside table, picked up the answering machine and pressed "Play." Murphy had one new and five old messages. Rocco listened to them all but learned nothing and dropped the device on the floor. He flipped through each book and magazine, emptied the bedside drawer onto the coverlet. The pictures on the wall were taken apart one by one. In the chest of drawers under the window were shirts, socks and underwear. Rocco tore out the lining paper from the drawers but only found an old airline ticket stub to Houston, Texas.

The bedding was dragged off and the sheets and coverlet shaken out. Leaning the mattress against the wall, he felt around the box spring and propped it up against the mattress. Two furry coffee mugs and a belt lay on the floor amidst a mass of fluff and dust.

He strode across the living room into the kitchen, turned on the light, opened all the cabinet doors and emptied out all the jars and boxes. He tipped or dragged out everything from the drawers, icebox and freezer. Glass and crockery shattered as they hit the floor.

Standing up on the kitchen counter, he looked above the cabinets but saw nothing but dirt. As he jumped down, his hip caught the edge of the kitchen table. The impact pushed it to one side to reveal three metal cases.

From the first he pulled out a fancy camera and put it on the table. He bent down to examine the inside of the case. A key turned in the front door and it opened and closed. A girl's voice said, "Harry?"

The living room light was switched on. "Harry, is that you?"

Rocco smoothed his hair back and walked into the living room.

A pretty young brunette stood by the sofa with a purse over her shoulder. When she saw him she gave him a smile. "Hello," she said pleasantly. "Are you a friend of Harry's?"

"You might say that," replied Rocco. "Who are you?"

The girl walked over and held out her hand. "Lizzie. I just came over with Harry from London."

Rocco shook a strong hand. The girl passed him and went towards the bedroom. She immediately saw the mess.

"Oh my God!" she exclaimed, spinning around. "What have you done? Just who the hell are you?"

Rocco reached behind his back and pulled out the Ruger, causing the girl to put a hand to her mouth.

"Lie down," he said, "on the floor. On your face."

"No, please!" she whimpered. "No! Please don't."

"Just shut up! And lie down! Face on the floor!"

The girl meekly did as she was told.

"Don't move a muscle!" he said menacingly. Keeping the gun pointing in her direction, he retrieved a belt and tie from the bedroom floor and used them to secure her ankles and bind her arms behind her back.

"Now get up!" he ordered, and pointed to the sofa. "Sit there!"

With his help, the girl struggled to her feet and sat down. Her frightened eyes never left him as he took out his phone and dialed.

"Benny, get in touch with Max," he said. "Tell him a chick just walked into Murphy's apartment. Says she's a friend of his. Came over on the plane with him. The label on her suitcase shows their flight was yesterday. Yeah, she just came up. No. Everything's fine. I need to know what Max wants me to do with her. I'll wait here."

While he finished his search he put down his phone on the table but kept the Ruger pointed in her direction. The books, CDs and photographs were all checked and dumped to the floor. A Filofax was given a peremptory glance and stuffed in his pocket. Each piece of furniture was shoved away from the wall and the carpet flipped over. A search of the bathroom took less than a minute. In the closet he opened every box and bag and dumped out the contents.

Back in the living room he noticed an old suitcase made of leather. It was empty. On a side table was a black TUMI with wheels. Except for the name, the flight label on the handle was the same as the one in the bedroom. " 'Elizabeth Carswell,' " he read, and looked at her. "That you?"

She nodded.

Rocco opened the case and systematically went through her clothes, throwing each one to the floor. The contents of the makeup and toiletry case followed. The phone beeped and rumbled on the center table and he picked it up.

"How soon?" he asked, looking at his watch. "The keys? No problem. I'll give them to you as soon as you get here."

Rocco made sure the girl couldn't move and then ran down the stairs. Benny drove up a few minutes later and held out a manila envelope at arm's length. Rocco dropped in Harry's keys. As Benny drove off, Rocco waved to Nino to pull over.

Back in the apartment he picked up the girl, draped her over his shoulder and went swiftly down to the street, where he bundled her into the car.

From 56th Street they took the West Side Highway to the Brooklyn-Battery Tunnel. Once through, they made their way to Gowanus and a large warehouse that had been abandoned to vandals, spray paint and pigeons.

Inside, Rocco propelled his captive across a dark floor. The ceiling fittings were all broken, but lightbulbs had been randomly strung across the hallway on lengths of wire. Rows of makeshift shelves were stacked high with an assortment of cardboard boxes. Bundling the girl past them and down a flight of stairs to the basement, he pushed her through a door marked MEN and slammed it shut. There was no lock, so he took a length of rusty pipe and jammed it under the top of the lower panel, kicking the other end hard into a crack in the concrete floor.

As he left he heard the girl sobbing loudly.

41

Lizzie waited until the man's footsteps faded away before she stopped the phony sobs. She looked around but the darkness was total. When her captor had gone into the bedroom to get a tie and belt, she had jammed her purse in the back of her skirt beneath her blouse. Taking out her lighter she flicked it on and held it above her head.

Her prison cell was once a men's toilet complete with rows of urinals, basins and mirrors. Everything was covered in black dirt. With her shoulder against the door she gave it a good shove but to no avail. Squatting on a WC in one of the stalls, she took out a cigarette and lit up.

The end glowed red in the darkness as she took a deep drag and wondered if she made the right decision in Harry's apartment. Her abductor had acted tough and strong but he'd been careless. With her training she could have taken him out at least twice but if she had disarmed him that would have blown her cover. On the other hand, if Harry was in some kind of trouble her decision to play the innocent girlfriend could be one she could live to regret.

42

The big metal door rattled up and jerked Harry to his senses. A man came in, turned on a light and walked over to him. This one wore a dark suit, a pale blue shirt, a dark red tie and in his lapel was an American flag pin. He pulled the leather glove from his right hand, reached down and pulled out a large serrated knife from his leg. The bare bulb above glinted on the blade. Harry tensed, but the man only used it to free him from the chair. Slipping a finger under the tape over his mouth, the man yanked it off. At the sink he pulled down a few sheets of blue paper from the dispenser and moistened them under the faucet.

"Here," he said, holding out the wet paper. "Wipe off your face." A trace of garlic wafted through the air.

Harry got up and stretched his arms and legs. There was little he could do about the deep ache in the back of his neck and shoulders. On the wall above the bench was a dirty piece of mirror, courtesy of Goodrich Tires. Harry leaned close and saw that congealed blood ran from his hairline to his chin. As he sponged it off with the towel the cold water felt good. In the same mirror he saw that a Ford LTD Town Car was parked outside with the back door open.

Harry glanced around as he was pushed out. The workshop was part of a repair facility for yellow cabs. He thought about making a dash for it but in the darkness he had no idea which way to run. Also, he could see that the perimeter fence was topped with coils of razor wire.

As they drove out through the gate, Harry had no idea where he was being taken or who he was going to meet. Apparently Lizzie's plan was working. But only if Agent MacAvoy's men hadn't lost track of his whereabouts. The car bounced over the curbstone. A couple of turns and they were on Tenth Avenue passing a sign for 37th Street. When they reached 79th, the driver turned towards the river and pulled up a few yards short of the on-ramp to the West Side Highway. The driver got out, locked the car and motioned for Harry to follow him.

"This way," he said, and headed towards an underpass beneath the West Side Highway. Bums and vagrants huddled along the walls in the stagnant air of the concrete passageway. Many lay stretched out on sheets of cardboard. Sullen eyes watched Harry and the driver pass. The acrid smell of unwashed bodies, feces and urine was almost unbearable. An old woman cackled like a witch as they passed, her face so black she could have come from the depths of a coal mine.

At the other end of the tunnel was the pedestrian walkway

that runs along the eastern shore of the Hudson. On the far side
of this was a high chain-link fence that insulated the inhabit-
ants of the boat basin from the rest of the world. The driver
pulled out a key, opened a metal gate and pushed it open.

"Go out to the end and wait," he said.

Harry walked through. The driver relocked the gate and
pocketed the key. Harry watched as he disappeared back through
the tunnel.

The voice of Luciano Pavarotti singing "*E lucevan le stelle*"
from the last act of *Tosca* came from one of the houseboats
anchored in the little marina as Harry walked along the boards.
The wooden jetty moved gently beneath his feet. Tied on either
side were cabin cruisers rigged for fishing trips, sleek launches
built for speed and modest weekend boats. Out on the river the
night chill mingled with the sun-warmed water to form a fine
mist that obscured the lights of the Jersey shore.

An engine started up a short distance away and a large boat
loomed out of the night heading towards the dock. The engines
were put in idle and the big craft glided past. A man with a Mets
cap waved for Harry to jump on board through the gap in the
low railing. As he landed, the engines surged and they swung
around and headed back upriver. The little man gestured that
Harry should follow him aft, where he opened a door. A shaft
of light rippled across the water. From inside, the smell of coffee floated on the air.

A small black box with a chrome metal hoop was moved over
Harry's clothes, paying particularly close attention to his crotch
and armpits. The device beeped as it passed over the clips on
his suspenders. Satisfied that he was clean, the man left him
alone and disappeared through a door at the far end.

The aft cabin was a storage area. On the left wall were a
couple of sleeping bunks with crumpled bedding. The windows
were covered with heavy black cloth. At night with her running
lights off the boat would be difficult to see. Judging by the sound

the engines produced, it would also be hard to catch. Boxes and bags of groceries were piled everywhere. Cans of tomato paste, a carton of Comet with a delivery slip that read: *Gazelle, Port Imperial Marina, New Jersey.* The doorway to the galley was behind a high stack of Diet Coke, Mountain Dew and V8 juice. On the counter was the aromatic coffeemaker.

The engines were abruptly shut down and the boat began to drift with the current. Waves slapped rhythmically against the hull. The forward door opened again and Harry was waved through.

In the few steps that took him to the doorway he consciously recalled how he had behaved earlier on the phone. It was imperative that he play the same character as before.

As he crossed the threshold he was surprised to see who was standing by the table in the main cabin. In his mind Harry had imagined he would be meeting with some sort of lowlife hoodlum. This man wore a smart suit over a dress shirt with a striped tie secured with a monogrammed pin.

All the curtains were closed. To the left was a small wet bar. To the right were the television and music systems fixed to long wooden shelves. The lighting was low, with most of the illumination focused on the central table. On this polished surface lay an envelope and the contents of Harry's pockets.

When an actor forgets his lines he is forced to cover the embarrassing silence that follows by making up his dialogue. Harry rarely suffered from such lapses, but when it happened he enjoyed the challenge. His talents for improvisation were now about to be sorely tested. He began strong and continued his role of a man scared and just a little bit weird.

"Are you Max?" he muttered. "Please tell me you're Max. Or that you can tell me where he is."

"No, I am not Max. What do you want with Max?" asked the other.

"To give back the money!"

"Why do you want to give it back?"

"I don't want it! I don't want to have anything to do with it! I know now that I made a mistake. I know—"

"How did you get the money in the first place?"

Harry gave the man a hunted look as if he were trapped. "A guy named Villiers gave it to me."

This produced a visible reaction. There was a pause. Then he was asked, "Why did he do that?"

"I have no idea," replied Harry. "He just said, 'It's all yours now,' and left me."

"Do you know Eddie Ryan?"

If Harry had not met Lizzie he would not know anything about Eddie. The report in *The Telegraph* had not printed his name. He feigned puzzlement. "Eddie who?"

"Ryan. Eddie Ryan."

"No. Who's he?"

"What about Percy Santiago?"

Santiago had been on Harry's list but he simply shook his head. "Never heard of him," he said. "Look, can we cut to the chase? We need to agree on somewhere Max and I can meet so I can give him the money."

"You were in the Mews in London Thursday morning?"

"Yes."

"What were you doing there?"

Harry hesitated. If he avoided the truth it would produce a web of lies. If the man in front of him was as smart as he appeared to be, a cross-examination could get Harry in an awkward tangle. His interrogator moved to the far end of the table and sat down. "Don't you remember what you were doing?" he asked.

"Of course I can remember!" Harry shouted, and then calmed down. "I just don't quite know . . . where . . . to begin." He pointed a shaky hand at four bottles of water on the top of the bar. "Could I have one of those?"

The man nodded. Harry walked over and took a bottle of Vermont Pure, unscrewed the cap and took a long drink.

"I'm an actor. Well, you know that by now," he said, wiping his lips nervously. "I work in film and television and in the theater. I was auditioning in Queens for a play. I crossed the road afterwards to take a leak in a restaurant toilet but some men inside told me to fuck off so I went round the back to piss against the wall. There was a window over my head and I heard that someone was in trouble, so I made some notes of what I was hearing. Wrote them down on my cellphone and then figured out later what they meant."

He took another drink. The man was now listening intently.

"I heard that someone called 'Villiers' was going to be 'dead meat.' I worked out who he was . . . and . . . well . . . that he lived in Kensington in a house in a Mews . . . and I decided the best thing to do . . . was to go to there and warn him. He wasn't there but I talked with his wife. She gave me tea and cakes. Look, I know this all sounds crazy, but that is exactly what happened."

The man stood up. "You heard it all through a restaurant window?" Harry nodded as his interrogator came slowly around the table. "You flew all the way to London and went to the Mews where you talked to Villiers's wife?"

The man was close enough for Harry to read the monogram on his tiepin. The letters *EB*. Could this be Enzo? "Yes," Harry replied. "But I thought it best not to tell her why I was there. I decided to wait for her husband."

"And you say this Villiers just gave you the money? Just like that?"

"Yes. Obviously he mistook me for someone else. I remember he said something about Rocky."

"Jesus Christ!" muttered the man and shook his head from side to side. "Karl!" he called out. The man with the Mets cap came back in.

"Watch him," EB said, and crossed to the ladder. "I'm going topside."

With his jailer standing silent by the door, Harry finished the water and set the empty bottle on the table. As he did so he was able to surreptitiously pick up his wallet, money clip and keys and slip them back into his pant pockets.

43

Max felt reassured. Rocco had searched Murphy's apartment and found nothing incriminating. The girl was safely locked up, and in spite of all the recent glitches, Max felt he had everything under control. Now it was time to deal with the South American.

The paging device on his desk beeped. Max read the numbers. Using a disposable cellphone, he called Enzo. His brother was highly agitated. "You remember when we all met at the Fiery Dragon the other day?"

"Yes. What about it?"

"We talked about Villiers becoming 'dead meat'?"

"Yes," said Max. "What about it?"

"Murphy overheard us. He was the guy that came in wanting to use the restroom. You and Sal told him to fuck off. Remember? Well, he went outside and round the back and overheard everything we said. Pieced it all together. Decided to be a good citizen and warn Villiers. Bastard flew all the way to London!"

Max sat down on the sofa and shook his head in disbelief. "You mean if I had just let this Harry fucking Murphy take a piss, none of this would have ever happened?"

"Yes, it seems so."

"Where is he now?"

"We've got him below in the cabin. Karl's watching him."

"What about the money?"

"He says it's in his apartment, but he's lying. It wasn't there when Rocco looked. What do you want me to do?"

"Scare the bastard. Soften him up a bit," said Max. "Find out if he shot his mouth off to anyone."

"Then what?"

"Then take him to the warehouse. We can interrogate both of them. I need to find out how the bastard got our contact number. I'll meet you there in an hour."

Max tossed the phone into the wastebasket and went into the kitchen to get himself a strong cup of coffee.

"Shit, shit, shit," he said quietly but with great expression.

44

Harry was wondering what EB would come up with next when the little man came back down into the cabin and reached for his coat. "Tell me, Mister Murphy, why did you let Villiers give you the case?"

"What else could I do? People were shooting guns! We were being chased through the streets. I had no idea what was inside until I got to my hotel."

"Then what did you think it was?"

Harry exploded. "Drug money of course! What else could it be? I've seen enough movies to know it was probably that."

"What did you do then?" the man asked, quietly putting on his coat.

"I panicked. Made up my mind to run away. I needed to give myself time to think."

"Where is Villiers now?"

"How the fuck should I know? He wasn't too happy at being shot at."

"And the suitcase of money?"

"In my apartment."

"Are you sure?"

"It was there when I left."

"Why didn't you bring it with you?"

"I thought it better to make the calls and get into direct contact with Max like Villiers said. I didn't think it was a good idea to deal with strangers."

"Would it surprise you to know we already searched your apartment?"

"And?"

"There was no money."

Harry acted surprised. "You're kidding me."

"Maybe your girlfriend took it."

"Why would she? She doesn't know anything about any of this. I just brought her along for someone to talk to. I hate being alone."

"How did you bring so much cash into the States?" EB asked.

"I hid it in the lining of a case."

"Really!" said EB skeptically. He turned to the man in the doorway. "I think it's time to get rid of our friend here. Go get Carlos."

Harry had faced death on several occasions: before a firing squad, as a condemned kidnapper being led to the gallows and as an unfulfilled research scientist with a terminal illness. Each time he had searched his soul for incentives to give his characters a ring of truth. Although these performances were some of his best, none of them had actually prepared him for the real thing.

Carlos was a thug with a thick neck, one earring and scars. Harry made a desperate dash for the ladder but his foot slipped on the narrow rung and he fell backwards to the floor with a crash. EB stood aside as the two men carried him out to the stern and dumped him on the portside seat. While Carlos stood over him, Karl went forward. No doubt to mix the concrete.

Harry was going to be flung into the murky waters of the

Hudson and his lungs would fill with water as he struggled to breathe. How long would the agony last? How long would it be before his brain, starved of oxygen, slipped him into oblivion? Or would it be an instant death as his heart stopped with the valves frozen in sheer terror?

EB came over and sat beside him. Harry could smell his cologne. "Do you remember anything else that might be of use to us?" he said. "Any little detail?"

"I've already told you everything I know!" squirmed Harry.

"No, I don't think you have; I think you're keeping something very important from us."

"No I'm not!"

"That is such a shame."

Karl appeared dragging a length of heavy chain. Carlos leaned over and grasped Harry by the shoulders.

"Hold it!" said EB.

"What?" said Carlos.

"Shut up!" said EB. "Listen!"

A chopper was approaching from down the river.

Carlos pulled out a small automatic from his Windbreaker and aimed it at Harry's zipper.

Seconds later the mist was swept away by the downdraft from the whirling blades. A searchlight snapped on and floodlit the boat. Overhead there was a crackle of static.

"You are operating without lights," said an amplified voice. "Do you have an emergency?"

Up on the bridge the helmsman threw a switch and running lights came on from stem to stern. His laconic reply was also heavily amplified. "Sorry. We had a minor electrical problem. We just fixed it."

The pilot hesitated for a moment as if he was deliberating what to do but then banked away. The helmsman started up the engines and the cruiser went slowly ahead as the helicopter made a complete circle and headed south. Once it was out of sight the helmsman spun the wheel and set a course for Jersey, opening the throttles wide. The hull leaned over in response to the sudden surge. Carlos lost his balance and gave a slight stagger. The automatic was momentarily thrown off target.

Harry had no desire to be listed in the end of year AFTRA/ SAG obituary page so he let out a tremendous scream, kicked hard in the direction of Carlos's scrotum and flung himself backwards over the side. The plunge upside down into the Hudson made him gasp. His mouth filled with water and for a moment he lost control of his lungs and breathing. His clothes became heavy and he had to struggle hard to get to the surface. Once there he was able to recover sufficiently to take a big gulp of air. A searchlight on the upper deck of the *Gazelle* started to sweep the water, but Harry and the boat were moving apart and the beam never came close. Everyone in the boat was yelling as Harry kicked off his sneakers and trod water. Then the light on the boat went off and the boat and its unsavory crew disappeared with a roar into the dark night.

The current was slowly but steadily sweeping him downstream towards the Verrazano Bridge and out into the Atlantic Ocean where New York City once dumped its rotting garbage. Not a problem. Long before he got there he would be swimming with the fishes.

Harry couldn't see the shore clearly through the light mist but he reckoned he was about 250 yards out. He calculated the odds. On the positive side, he was a good swimmer and had frequently swum far longer distances in the ocean or while doing laps in the pool. On the negative side, there was the strong current and the disturbing fact that he hadn't swum a yard for at least ten years.

For the first hundred strokes he could hear the music from the houseboat. Now they were listening to *The Damnation of Faust* by Hector Berlioz. As the devil rode his horse to the abyss, the mist swirled about Harry. As the tide took him along the music faded. Soon his sodden shirt impeded his progress, so he stopped swimming and stripped it off. As he did the red suspenders snapped off and sank into the depths.

He swam slowly and rhythmically, the sound of the traffic on the West Side Highway giving him a rough idea of the direction he should aim. The water was not particularly cold, but after a while his body began to chill. To keep his mind positive he filled it with random thoughts, starting with the names of all the movies he had done and locations he had visited. These images were abruptly halted when something scratched his face and he became entangled in the branches of a drifting tree. At first he struggled to get loose but then found he could support his weight on a submerged limb. Able to lift his head out of the water, he took advantage of a welcome breather.

As he floated along on his improvised raft the mist cleared. As if by magic, the brilliant night skyline of Manhattan came into view. In spite of his predicament, Harry couldn't help marveling at the magnificent sight.

To his relief he saw that he had overestimated the distance. Dry land was about a hundred yards away. However, the tide was moving fast and time was now becoming the dominant factor. Abandoning the branch he plunged back into the open water and swam with his energy renewed.

But not for long. Harry was sadly out of shape and his muscles began to let him down. As he weakened, the weight of his pants increased. Lifting his arms out of the water became a Herculean effort. Lethe numbness dulled his senses. And then to his amazement his body became toasty and warm! He felt fine!

He was unaware that his considerate nerve endings were sending false messages to his befuddled brain to help him overcome his imminent death.

45

The phone beeped again. Max put the coffee down and retrieved the device from the wastebasket.

"Murphy's in the river," said Enzo.

"For fuck's sake!" said Max. "I said soften him up a little, not drop him in the fucking river."

"We didn't drop him in the river. We just wanted him to piss his pants and tell us what we wanted to know. The bastard jumped! I think we scared him a little too much."

"Could he make it to shore?"

"I doubt it. The current is real strong out there. Tide's going out. I don't think they'll ever find his body."

46

Lizzie had managed to make a small indentation with her nail file under the old door. With her head on the floor, she was able to see the pipe that wedged it shut. The trick was to find a way to dislodge it. At the side of the cubicle doors were lengths of rotted molding. She pried off a piece, lay down again on the floor and pushed it under. It was just possible to tap the bottom of the pipe. After several hundred of these her arms and neck ached but the pipe was loosening. A door upstairs banged. Footsteps crossed the hall. Lizzie threw the molding away and hunched down against the wall.

The door was opened by the man who had abducted her. Behind him in the shadows stood a new figure. "Take her upstairs, Rocco," he said. "I can't see a damn thing down here."

Lizzie got up off the floor and put her purse over her shoulder. Rocco propelled her up to the first floor and into what was once the reception office. The other man followed. Rocco slid over a wooden crate and sat her down. A shaft of light from the street shone across her face.

"Where are you from?" asked the stranger still in shadow.

"London," she replied.

"London, England?"

"Yes."

"How long have you known Murphy?"

"Harry? Not long. Only a few days, in fact. He said he would show me around New York."

"Where d'you meet him?"

"In a coffee shop at the top of Regent Street. For your information, that is also in London, England. I was in line to pay when I realized I'd left my change purse in the car. Harry was standing next to me in the queue. He offered to pay for my Cappuccino."

"Go on."

"We got to chatting and he said he was going to America this weekend on business. Would I like to go with him? He said he hated flying alone and would pay for my ticket. Well, I jumped at the chance. I mean, who wouldn't? Usually when I go places it's always for work and the company pays. I don't never have no spare time. This was a chance to come over and have some fun." She grimaced. "Little did I know."

"What do you do for a living?"

"I do research for a package tour operator that sends tourists all over Europe. I go first to make sure all the hotels and restaurants are up to par and not gone all skanky."

"Skanky?"

"You know. Gone off. Hotels where they curry cans of dog food. Pass turkey breast off as Veal Scallops."

"Did he seem nervous on the flight? Jumpy?" asked her captor.

"Far as I can make out, Harry's always jumpy and nervous. That's the way he is."

"What luggage did he bring with him?" asked the other.

Lizzie paused to remember. "He had two bags. One was blue plastic. The other was old and made of leather. Heavy it was."

"Where is Murphy now?"

"Don't ask me. All he said when I left was that he had some business to do and expected to be finished in time to take me to dinner. Look, I come over here to bloomin' New York for a holiday and I go out for a little walk around the shops and the next thing I know your mate here is going through my things and chucking everything on the floor. Then he pulls out a gun and tells me he'll shoot me if I cause trouble. Well, I have no intention of causing trouble to you or anyone else. All I want to do is get on a plane and go home."

The stranger came over and knelt down. Lizzie looked into eyes that were a deep brown. He had strong features but looked tired as if he needed a good night's sleep. He was also in need of a shave.

"I like the way you say 'research' and 'bloomin' New York,'" he said quietly.

"Thank you. I'm glad you like it," she replied flatly.

"I'm afraid your friend Harry won't be taking you to dinner tonight."

"Why not?"

"Because he's dead."

Lizzie gave a gasp. "How . . . ?"

"Mr. Murphy fell into the Hudson River. He drowned."

The man abruptly stood up and walked away leaving her in a state of shock. Almost as suddenly Lizzie found herself taken roughly by the arms and propelled down the stairs. The door to her cell was slammed shut and the pipe firmly dug into the floor.

She stood motionless in the center of the dark, silent space.

Harry Murphy was dead?

For the first time in her life she was totally at a loss. She had fucked up royally. She was a prisoner of a bunch of thugs in a foreign land and she was definitely expendable. The man with the tired brown eyes had openly used the other man's name.

In spite of top-level requests from London, Marty MacAvoy had made no bones about his reluctance to get involved in her scheme.

For all intents and purposes her life was over.

47

The uppermost floor of the warehouse where Lizzie lay languishing had originally been a row of five small storage rooms. Vic Bruschetti now used the farthest as his office. The adjoining one housed the very expensive machines he and his associates used to print out counterfeit credit cards. Once a month, bundles of these were delivered to a network of operatives who used them briefly and then destroyed them before any of the transactions could be traced. To provide space for a new project, the wall between the next two had recently been removed. Only the first room was unused.

The merchandise bought by these operatives went to equally untraceable addresses where it was collected, warehoused and then sold openly through Amazon, eBay and elsewhere. Ninety percent of the cash thus generated found its way back to legitimate commercial bank accounts personally controlled by Vic.

To warn of any unwanted snoopers a thin strand of monofilament was stretched six inches above the seventh tread of the top flight of the stairs. This ran from the balustrade through a small plastic ring on the wall opposite and down to a can filled with an amber liquid. Below this was a plate covered with a white powder. The slightest movement of the filament would tip over the cup. When the two substances mixed, a gas would be produced that induced paroxysms of coughing.

Stepping carefully over this wire, Max went up and along the corridor to the last room. He was about to knock on the door when a voice inside said, "Come in, Max. It's open."

Vic was sitting at his desk typing on his Dell laptop surrounded by piles of papers. Above his head was a row of security monitors. Max pulled out a folding metal chair and sat down. "I don't understand why you keep that goddam thing on the stairs when you have the building on video."

"May I remind you, Max," said the young man as he continued to type, "what you and Dad used to say to me? 'Measure twice, cut once.' I've never forgotten that. Security is an obsession with me. I can't imagine being any other way. Jack drives me crazy sometimes. He can be stupidly careless."

"Where is your electronic genius right now?"

"Jack took in all our RFID readers. He had to re-engineer them because of a bunch of new FBI modifications. Didn't take him long. He's out delivering them. Should be back soon."

"Well, let's hope not too soon, because I have something to run by you." He nodded at the laptop. "Can you quit work for just a moment? I'd like your undivided attention."

For the next ten minutes Vic listened as Max told him how the Bruschetti brothers were about to close down all questionable activities and take an early retirement.

Vic smiled ruefully. "I'm a bit young for a rocking chair on the porch."

"True," said Max.

"I can see why you're doing this and why Dad sent you to tell me. But why does your quitting have to include Jack and me? I don't get the connection."

"I spoke earlier with Carter. He feels if we're going to do this we have to make it total."

"That stupid prick would say that," Vic said with feeling. "But before I answer you, there's something you should know." He stood up and came out from behind his desk. "Your timing couldn't be worse. Jack and I have been branching out with a new project that is close to completion. When that happens I can guarantee a very big payoff."

"How much time would you need to finish it?" asked Max.

Heavy footsteps could be heard down the corridor. Vic glanced up at the monitors.

A tall individual appeared in the doorway with flowing hair, a wide forehead and deep-set eyes. Below these were fleshy cheeks, an enormous nose and large lips. The skin was pock-marked and scarred. To compensate for this grotesque appearance, Mother Nature had made Jack Blackthorn exceedingly smart.

Uncle Sam snapped him up when he graduated from MIT and put him to work in a laboratory deep in the deserts of New Mexico. However, the scientist was unable to submit to what he considered excessive secrecy and in less than a year he was summarily fired. Few were willing to hire him and as his debts mounted he compounded his problems with alcohol. In his favorite bar in Queens he casually struck up a conversation with Vic Bruschetti who offered him a job.

"Hello there, Max, my friend!" said the big man with mock surprise. "What an honor! We always enjoy your rare visits to your humble minions." He looked over at Vic. "Have you told him?"

"Not yet, Jack" came the reply. "Max is here to tell us we have to shut down."

The big man laughed. "You're not serious."

"Very," said Max quietly.

"Why?" Blackthorn took out a cigarette and hung it on his lower lip.

"Never mind why," said Max. "It has nothing to do with you. All you need to know is that the ride is over. It's time to close up shop."

"Whoa! Uncle Max! Just a fucking minute." He lit the cigarette, snapped the lighter shut and sucked the smoke deep into his lungs. "You are going a little too fast. Let's start again, shall we?"

"All you need to know is that this entire operation is over. Finished. *Capish?*"

"We just can't close up shop, Max. You forget, it's not just Vic and me. We got Toshi and a whole lot of guys and gals out there that rely heavily on us. I would hate to think of them becoming suddenly penniless. They might get mad and do something foolish. What do you suggest we do with them?"

"That's not my problem. They'll manage. Tell them what I told you. You've had a great run but it is time to move on."

"Move on. Good idea, Max. To move on. I take it the only connection between us and your brothers is this building. If we were simply to 'move on' somewhere else there wouldn't be a problem either for you or for Vic and me." He gave a snort as he saw the look of doubt on Max's face. "Maxie baby! The digital universe is in the air all around us. It's simple! Relocation! Vic, Toshi and me, not to mention our many enthusiastic young employees, we can operate from anywhere we choose to go. Once we've gone there will be no more nasty connection for you to worry about."

"He's right, Max." Vic nodded. "We could be out of here in a couple of weeks. Probably take more time to find a place than to actually make the change."

Max thought for a moment. Aware that this was an argument he couldn't win he got up to leave. "I'll need to talk it over with Sal. Don't do anything until I call."

"Sure thing," said Vic. Blackthorn gave a theatrical bow. Max went out into the corridor ignoring the gesture. "One thing more. Stay out of the basement. I got someone down there locked in the Men's room."

"Have you really, Max? How fascinating," said Blackthorn. "Don't worry; I'll see to it that Vic only uses the Ladies."

As Max started down the stairs he realized that his nephew hadn't told him what his fancy new project might be. As he turned to go back, his foot hit the strand of monofilament and the little cup tipped over.

"Shit!" said Max quickly pulling out his handkerchief to cover his nose. To get clear, he went headlong down the steps, taking two at a time. In his emotional state and with the added exertion his chest began to throb.

At the foot of the stairs he stood still and, using the wall for support, took deep breaths as he tried to calm his pounding pulse.

48

Eight-year-old Harry Murphy learned to swim at Shawnee Wigwam in the Pocono Mountains. Every year along with dozens like him he was sent off to camp for two weeks.

At the end of his first year at college, Harry came back home for the vacation and was told there would be no more summer allowance. The time had come for him to go out and get a job. For two days Harry trekked around local shops and restaurants. He tried the hospital and library, but nothing temporary was available. On the fourth day the annual flyer arrived in the mail from Shawnee Wigwam. At his mother's suggestion he called them up and asked if they were still hiring. After a perfunctory interview he was taken on as a counselor.

Among his duties was coaching the boys' baseball team. This took considerable patience and a high degree of tolerance. Few could pitch and none could hit. But everyone screamed advice. Runs were scored on walks, missed catches and wild throws. Most of these went to the wrong base. At the end of each week the boys played the girls. The coach of the girls' team was Charlene Louise Bogdanovich from Garden City.

As a baby Charlene had been pudgy and unattractive to everyone except her mother. As a small child she was cute and put on a bewitching smile the instant a camera was pointed in her direction. But for the next ten years she ate junk food in front of the television and swiftly regressed to pudgy and unattractive.

The change to womanhood began at twelve and by her sixteenth year she was well on the way to becoming a slim, silken-haired beauty. At the height of her charms she ravished Harry in the old woodshed.

The game was in the third inning. The girls were ahead by six runs. The wind began to blow. Storm clouds grew large on the horizon. Harry yelled at the kids to run for the Crafts Cabin as huge drops of rain fell. Charlene picked up the bases and gloves, Harry grabbed the bats and balls and they raced together into the equipment shed.

The heavens burst, the wind howled and the rain battered down on the corrugated roof.

As Harry turned from closing the door, Charlene Bogdanovich gave him another image to take to his grave. Dripping wet and with her smooth brown skin visibly steaming, she ever so slowly removed her shirt and shorts. Then she turned away, bent over and ever so slowly slid her panties down her legs. Kicking them away, she released her 36D bra and twirled it over her head like a professional stripper.

Breasts heaved as clad only in her sneakers and socks she walked to the pile of exercise mats where she lay down on her back. Lightning flashed. Thunder roared. Harry wildly dragged off his damp clothes and stumbled across the intervening chasm.

With a jarring crash his head smashed into something solid. The shock brought him back to consciousness. Whatever he'd hit conspired with the river current to suck him under the water. Stroking hard with his arms, he kicked himself back to the surface and found himself bobbing along between what appeared to be the hull of a ship and a floating dock. Frantically he felt for something to grasp on to but his hands just slid along smooth metal. The space between the vessels began to widen and Harry was swept out into open water. A brightly lit superstructure towered over him. He called out but no one heard his weak cry. High above he could make out aircraft wings overhanging what appeared to be the flight deck of an aircraft carrier. Dear God! He was floating beneath the Intrepid Air & Space Museum!

His panic was abated slightly when he saw a forest of stumps sticking up out of the water. The remains of an old wooden pier. As he did as a kid in his first swimming race at Shawnee Wigwam, he put his head down and thrashed towards them until his arms circled a seaweed covered pylon. Like a limpet he clung there for almost five minutes. Then he swam from stump to stump stopping at each to rest. Finally his foot touched friendly concrete and he was able to get a foothold. Then a grip. Harry hauled himself out of the water and onto dry land.

The wire mesh of the fence helped him to stand up and like a big fish he flopped over the rail to the ground. A euphoric sense of elation rushed through his body. With an audible chuckle he rolled over on his back. He was exhausted and soaking wet, but he was alive and for the moment he was safe.

The thought of a hot shower entered his chilled brain and brought him comfort. Back on his feet he shuffled across the blacktop towards Twelfth Avenue, now leaving a slimy trail like a snail.

At the edge of the road he reached into his pockets to make sure he still had his keys, money clip and wallet. They were there. Hopefully he would be able to dry out the contents.

Harry raised his hand to passing cabs. Some slowed down but none stopped. That was hardly surprising. He was soaking wet, barefoot, he wore a filthy undershirt, his pants hung low and his hair was a tangled mess. Screw them. He would walk home. It was only fifteen blocks and the exercise would warm him up.

But as he set out a troublesome thought entered his mind. Lizzie hadn't given him a way to get in touch with her. Was she still with Marty? No matter. Home first. Lizzie later. Block by block he moved north.

Unfortunately his mind was in better shape than his body.

His limbs began to shake as his muscles tried to adapt to the insane conditions in which they found themselves. A prodigious effort was required to put one foot in front of the next. Harry was fascinated to see that no one took any notice of him. He was a homeless drifter, a panhandling bum, one of an army of deadbeats that slept on the streets and begged for spare change. A police car even pulled up beside him at the light but neither of the cops gave him a second look. To the rest of the world he had become invisible. A nuisance to be ignored.

By the time he reached his building he was in a frightful state but somehow he found the energy to crawl up the stairs. No one saw him go up to his apartment. No one heard his horrified gasp as he saw the devastation that was once his home. No one saw him stagger to the sofa and flop down.

The room was warm. The pillow beneath his head was soft. Everything else could wait.

49

Max had stumbled out the door of the warehouse looking very much the worse for wear. Nino had helped him into the car and driven him straight to Mazaras. The ride gave his heart a chance to slow down, so when Nino punched the buttons on the keypad at the back door Max had almost fully regained his composure. Inside, at the end of the corridor, Cora was vacuuming the carpet in the room the girls used for relaxation.

Over the years as each of the women came and went they left behind little touches of themselves. An embroidered pillow. A group of picture postcards tacked to the wall. A tattered teddy bear. Several photographs. Many small ornaments and curios on a long shelf. Even a miniature poodle immortalized by a taxidermist. The furniture was old but amazingly comfortable in spite of its threadbare appearance.

Sitting himself down on the long leather sofa, Max patted the cushion. Cora switched off the vacuum and locked it upright.

"I need your advice," Max said.

"That's a pity," she replied.

"Why a pity?"

"You always ask me for my advice when you're in trouble." With the back of her hand she brushed off traces of cigarette ash before sitting down. "How bad is it this time?"

"That's the problem. I don't know."

There was a moment's pause before Cora asked, "This all started in the hospital, didn't it?"

"Yes, it did."

"That's when you made up your mind to make changes?"

"Yes."

"And that's why you went down to Colombia?"

"I'm shutting down Mazaras," Max said.

Cora stared at him in disbelief.

"When that doctor told me I had to reduce the stress in my life, it didn't take a rocket scientist to figure out it was time to quit. The more I thought about it the more I liked the idea."

"Go on," said Cora.

"I talked to Sal and Enzo and we came to an agreement."

"But it all didn't work out the way you planned. Where did things go wrong?" she asked.

"Sal decided we should cover our tracks in London. But you're right. There was a screwup. Rocco was able to deal with Santiago but he missed with Villiers. Now the Colonel's mad and he's on the loose."

"Rocco missed!?"

"Villiers was warned off by some nut called Murphy. Sal and I yelled at him when he came into the Dragon to take a piss. He went outside and around the back overheard everything we said. Now the bastard is here with his girlfriend in New York. Says he wants to give the money back."

Cora was more than a little confused. "What money?"

"Villiers had a case full of cash. He gave it to Murphy. He thought Murphy worked for us."

"Jesus! No wonder you need help." She got to her feet. "I need caffeine. Let's go upstairs."

Fortified with steaming cups of strong coffee laced with Bourbon they sat down at the table. Max started from the day he left to go to South America and ended with Murphy's untimely leap into the Hudson.

"Before he drowned," said Cora, "this Murphy never told you what he did with the money?"

"No. We have no idea where it could be."

"And the girlfriend's in Brooklyn?"

"I got her in the basement at the warehouse."

"Well," Cora said after a moment of deliberation, "apart from dealing with the girl and the missing cash, you only have Villiers to worry about. When he surfaces, Rocco has to whack him. In fact, he needs to dispose of anyone who knows anything. Present company excepted of course."

She reached over and put her hand on his arm.

"It's going to be fine, Max. You worked it all out great. I'll help you shut this place down. We'll make up a story. I can tell everyone we're doing some renovations. God knows we need them. I'll give them a month's money."

She stood up and asked a little too casually, "What's the Murphy girl really like?"

"Kinda cute. With a Limey accent."

"She might know where your money is. That would solve that problem."

"Why should she tell us?"

"Use your Sicilian charm."

"Then what?"

She snapped her fingers in the air.

"Then she can join her buddy in the Hudson."

50

"Where is Detective Carswell?"

Harry opened his eyes to see a stranger staring down at him. The face was angular, the hair dark, the suit gray and the gun in his belt shiny.

"Where is Detective Carswell?" the armed intruder demanded once more.

"Who?" said Harry.

"The Brit agent in charge of your investigation."

Comprehension returned. "Who needs to know?" he asked.

The man flipped open a badge. "Marty MacAvoy, Mr. Murphy. If you know where Detective Carswell is please tell me now."

Harry propped himself up on his elbows. "I haven't seen her since she left here yesterday. What time is it?"

MacAvoy looked at his watch. "A little after four."

The front door opened and a man with the physique of a bull came in carrying a folder, which he handed to the other. He wore his artillery on the left side of his waistband with a clip-on holster. This weapon was black.

"Thanks, Frank," said MacAvoy giving the folder a cursory glance. "No sign of her?"

The big man shook his head. "Nope."

"Goddam it!" was the succinct comment.

"You still want to hold off on a report?"

"Yeah. For the time being."

Frank looked around. "Boy, they sure made a mess up here."

Next to arrive was a diminutive person in a short-sleeve shirt and green pants. His hair was slicked down and he wore steel-rimmed spectacles.

"Harry Murphy, this is Special Agent Luigi Rienzi," said Mac-Avoy. "Luigi's our IRS Criminal Investigation Coordinator."

The little man took Harry's hand. "Wait a minute!" His face lit up. "*SEALS in the Snow.* Am I right?"

Harry nodded.

The agent broke into a big smile. "I knew it," he said knowingly. "And you played the bad guy in that movie last year with Meg what's-her-name, the one with the hallucinogenic mushrooms. Am I right or am I right?"

"You're right," said Harry.

"Lou!" interrupted MacAvoy.

"Sorry, Marty," said Luigi, and he relinquished Harry's hand. "I see a lot of movies. Nice to meet you."

MacAvoy turned to the first man. "And this is Frank Torregrossa."

"Pleased to meet you," said Frank.

"So. Tell us your side of the story Mr. Murphy," said MacAvoy.

Harry lay back down on the sofa. "When did you lose me?"

"At the car wash," replied Frank.

"But not for long," said MacAvoy, taking out his notepad. "We had this apartment staked out. Our agent saw several individuals enter and leave the premises. One of them was Detective Carswell.

"Subsequently a male individual came out and procured an envelope from the driver of a vehicle. He dropped in what appeared to be a bunch of keys and handed the envelope to the driver of another vehicle that came past. Our agent made the decision to follow the second car.

"He observed the envelope taken aboard a boat. We proceeded to track this boat from a mobile unit on the West Side Highway. You were observed going aboard at the Seventy-ninth Street marina. So I called up a chopper from Governors Island. The pilot radioed a description of you in the stern but reported that you seemed okay, so I told him to leave. The boat was checked when it docked midtown, but you were not on board. Gave us a nasty surprise."

"I jumped off."

"What?" said Luigi.

"I had to jump off."

MacAvoy gave him a quizzical look.

"If I hadn't, I'd be fish food by now."

"And you swam ashore?"

"Yes," said Harry.

"I'm impressed," said Frank.

Luigi gave a whistle. "You must be pretty fit. You work out a lot? I wish I could—"

"Lou!" said MacAvoy.

"Sorry, Marty," said a chastened Luigi.

MacAvoy turned to Harry. "Is there another way in or out of here?"

Harry pointed in the direction of the kitchen. "The fire escape. What's going on? Why did Lizzie come back here?"

The agent frowned. "It was her idea. She realized you didn't have any way to get in touch with us and she figured if you were in any kind of trouble you'd go home. If our agent hadn't followed the car with the envelope she probably wouldn't have disappeared. But then we would never have picked up your trail. Best guess is that she surprised whoever trashed this place. Right now we have no idea where she is."

Harry got up and went into the kitchen. This was a Comedy of Errors. He picked up an unbroken glass from the floor and filled it with cold water. Sitting down, he took a long drink. The cases were as he'd left them except one of them was open. The camera had been taken out and put on the table. Harry glanced down and saw that the lining was happily untouched.

The three agents trooped in. "So what happens now?" Harry asked.

Luigi and Frank looked at their leader.

"We haven't really decided that yet," said MacAvoy. "Why don't you take a shower and get some things together? I don't think it's a good idea for you to hang around here."

Harry was finding it hard to think straight. "And then what?"

Luigi spoke up. "What do you know about the Witness Protection Program, Mr. Murphy?"

MacAvoy gave his IRS agent a disapproving look. "I don't think we need to go into that just yet, Lou," he said sharply.

"I only know what I've seen in the movies," said Harry. "New identity, new background, a new home far from the scene of the crime. A monthly check. Plastic surgery. Boredom followed by paranoia and madness. What makes you think I'd go along with that?"

"You don't really have a choice," said Frank. "Take a look around you. As soon as the word is out that you're alive they'll come looking. And in my experience these guys don't make the same mistake twice."

"Look," said MacAvoy. "Why don't you take that shower? Then we'll all go back to the office. After a bite to eat and a hot drink we can talk this over."

"If that's what you think best," said Harry.

"I really do," said the agent.

Once again the Fates flew in and altered the direction of Harry's life. This time with a toothbrush. In the shower he rinsed the soap out of his hair and reached up to the plastic cup on the wire shelf. But it only contained toothpaste, so he left the water running and stepped out to get the brush he kept by the basin. But whoever had trashed the place had dumped everything on the floor. Donning his robe, he headed barefoot for the kitchen where he kept extras. MacAvoy's voice stopped him two paces from the half-closed door.

"We have to face it, Frank. What started a few days ago as a routine arms deal assist has become a politically sensitive situation. If there is a foul-up and Carswell is injured or made inoperative, I want a total blackout. We know nothing. You hear me? We're not involved. And we never were. And keep the paperwork to a minimum. I don't want anyone asking awkward questions later on."

"Whatever you say, Marty," said Frank.

A routine arms deal assist? This was a new twist. And another piece of the Lizzie puzzle. Harry tiptoed away. MacAvoy's concern for Lizzie's well-being was clearly not as deep-rooted as his. Cleaning his teeth could wait.

Turning off the shower he ditched the robe. In the bedroom he put on some underpants, a pair of trousers and a shirt. As he crossed towards the living room he cleared his throat.

"Look, guys," he said, and pushed open the door. "It's going to take me a little while to get all my gear together. Can you send someone to pick me up in a half hour? Shouldn't take much longer than that."

MacAvoy looked doubtful. "I don't know, Mr. Murphy. I'd hate for anything to happen to you."

"One of us should stay with you," said Luigi.

"No need. I'll be fine."

MacAvoy was unconvinced so Harry feigned emotion. "I need a little time alone," he said quietly. "I don't know when I'll be able to come back here. After all, this is my home."

Luigi was moved by his performance. "Come on, Marty; give the man a break. He swam out of the Hudson for God's sake! And he's right. Who knows when the hell he'll be able to come back here." Reaching into his back pocket, he pulled out a well-worn wallet and handed Harry one of his cards. "If you hear or think you hear anything, call my cell. We'll come running. And for that matter anytime in the future when you need help, give me a call. Twenty-four-seven."

"Thanks," said Harry, and put the card in his pocket. "Tell me, Lou," he asked, "why don't you carry a gun like these guys?"

"But I do!" The IRS agent pulled up a pant leg. "I keep it strapped to my ankle so I get to duck when the shooting starts!"

"Okay, Lou, you win," said MacAvoy. "Right, Mr. Murphy. Thirty minutes. But to be on the safe side I'm going to have Frank here wait for you downstairs and keep an eye on the entryway. You can let him know when you're ready to leave."

As the trio headed for the door Harry called out, "What exactly is Detective Carswell doing here in the States?"

They all stopped. MacAvoy turned. "I thought you knew. The Brits have made a direct link between a possible sleeper cell group in the UK and a terrorist organization in Yemen."

"Al-Qaeda?"

"Most likely. Detective Carswell told us she is here to gather evidence. She said that with your help she would be able to prove conclusively that money donated by individuals here in the United States is going directly to purchase arms and ammunition which are then used to assassinate both British and American targets."

"That was why she came here? The money is for an arms deal?"

"That's what they told us. You know different?"

"No. Thanks. I'll see you in thirty minutes."

Harry shut the door and sat down on the floor.

Lizzie had lied to him. Her beekeeper boss had lied to him. All that talk of the IRA when it was all about weapons going to Al-Qaeda. Or was it?

His watch told him he had twenty minutes to pack up if he was going to leave by himself and thirty if he was going to capitulate and go with Marty and his boys. Did he really want to become a part of the Witness Protection Program? To disappear? To start life anew in Butt-fuck Idaho? It would mean quitting acting. His face was much too recognizable. They might have to surgically change it. Well, there was no fucking way he would ever do that.

To hell with the program. His salvation and the truth lay with Lizzie and she was probably in the hands of the bad guys. Well, he knew as much as anyone else as to where she might be. Perhaps it was up to him to go out and get her back.

With nineteen minutes to go he scrambled to his feet. Digging out a box of lawn-size garbage bags, he threw it on the living room table and strode into the bathroom to collect some toiletries. As he did he caught sight of himself in the mirror. His hair was a wild tangled mess and he needed a shave. But the image gave him an idea.

Every so often Harry was asked by friends if there was any special role that he would like to play. Along with Hamlet, Sam Spade and Scrooge was a desire to play a vagrant. If the part called for him to be mentally impaired, so much the better. Such parts were Oscar or Emmy shoo-ins.

On the walk from the *Intrepid* museum back to his apartment he had experienced firsthand what it was like to be a drifter on the streets. If he adopted such a character and found a place to live rough he could virtually disappear.

Into a black garbage bag he stuffed his oldest shirts and an old tweed jacket that had seen better days. Then he added his raincoat and folding umbrella. In case he needed to look clean and respectable, he threw in a Windbreaker, a clean pair of pants and a couple of button-down shirts. On these he laid his passport, a sharp knife, a spoon, a fork, a can opener and the portable radio he used at baseball games.

Changing into a pair of well-worn blue jeans and a faded "I Love NY" T-shirt, he checked to see if his ATM and credit cards were still in his wallet. They were sticky but usable. Back in the bathroom he climbed on the edge of the tub and reached up to ease aside a panel in the ceiling.

About two years earlier Harry had been hanging up a pair of his socks to dry when a drop of water hit him on the head that wasn't from his socks. Unable to locate the leak or the building superintendent, he called a stage manager friend who was good at plumbing. To reach the pipe the friend cut a square hole in the center of the ceiling. When the repair was done Harry had covered the hole with a panel of thin plywood. Once painted it was hardly noticeable. Now it was the perfect place to hide the money.

Back in the kitchen he took out the camera and sound equipment and sliced away the linings of the three cases. The bundles of notes fitted neatly back into the suitcase. The clock on the microwave showed he had five minutes left. He quickly replaced all the gear, closed the cases and put them back under the table.

Balancing precariously on the edge of the bathtub, he slid the leather case through the opening, pushed it back out of sight and replaced the panel.

Opening the kitchen window, he climbed out onto the fire escape with the plastic bag over his shoulder. Below, the alley was deserted.

As he walked along the road, he realized he had to make himself very scarce while he planned his next move. MacAvoy would come looking. The first rule of battle is know your enemy. Harry had scant knowledge of any of his adversaries. The second rule was to have overwhelming superiority. That was a joke. The third called for an overall strategy. That would have to come later. The fourth demanded he have an exit strategy when everything went wrong. That he had. He would crawl back to MacAvoy, beg his forgiveness and ask for a ticket to Idaho. But first he had to find a secluded spot where he could set up home.

From outside the Food Emporium he purloined the oldest functioning shopping cart he could find. Dumping in his bag, he trundled off along the sidewalk taking deep breaths of the early-morning air.

Harry had spent most of his daily life uptown and had missed the urban change that had taken place along the lower shores of the river. What he remembered as an area of abandoned piers and broken-down warehouses was now gentrified with luxury apartments, office buildings, green grass and wide paths for running, jogging and biking.

The neighborhood may have been cleaned up but not the natives. At Twelfth Avenue and 34th Street Harry was accosted by a vagrant with primeval smells emanating from every pore and orifice. Harry was surprised to see him panhandling so early in the morning.

"Can you spare some small change please!" the man wailed. "I need to get something to eat."

"Where do you sleep?" asked Harry.

The man extended a shaky hand. With glazed eyes he swayed from side to side like a metronome. "Can you spare some small change?" he repeated loudly. "I just need something to eat."

"Yes, I know that's what you need," said Harry. "But I need to know where you sleep."

The bum's demeanor changed "What the fuck are you talking about?" he said angrily, dropping all pretense. "I just want some fucking small change, man! Are you crazy?!"

"No. I am not," replied Harry forcefully. He pulled out his money clip. "I'll pay you."

At the sight of money the man stopped walking and his shoulders jerked. Harry peeled off a bill and tore it in two.

"Shit, man!" he yelled. "What are you doing? That's a fucking fifty!"

Harry held out one of the halves. "Show me where you sleep and you get the other half."

The proposition was considered and after more bodily spasms was accepted. A sooty hand thrust the torn piece into a pant pocket. Muttering something about man's inhumanity to man, the bum walked fast to the end of a narrow alley that led away from the river. On either side were the back walls of the few remaining derelict buildings. The bum pointed up the alley and held out his hand.

Harry said quietly, "Show me."

They trudged to the far end past piles of discarded cardboard boxes, where the bum pushed aside a rusty sheet of corrugated iron to reveal a vertical slit that had been hacked through the wall. Both men edged through the tiny opening. In what had once been a kitchen were signs of recent habitation. Beer cans, piles of newspapers and empty food containers littered the floor. Harry's reluctant companion pointed to an exact spot in one corner.

"There," he said pointing. "I slept right fucking there! Okay? My head was there and my feet was there. Okay? Are you satisfied now?"

Harry looked around. The space was dry and comparatively secure. What had once been the inner door to the rest of the building was nailed tight shut. The narrow hole in the wall was the only way in and out.

"I'll take it," he said. "Here's the first month's rent." The man snatched the other half of the fifty and scrambled away.

Harry followed him outside. Folding up the roomiest cardboard box he could find, he dragged it back through the hole and set it up in the corner. Retrieving the bag with his belongings from the cart, he pushed it into the far end of the box. As he did this his stomach rumbled. Five minutes later at an all-night delicatessen on Ninth Avenue he bought a bacon-egg roll, some cookies and a large cup of coffee and took them back to his new home. The bag made a comfortable rest for his head. Stretching out his legs he ate his breakfast to the sounds of Mozart on his little radio. As he ate the cookies he was reminded of the last time he had tea with the Colonel's wife in London. Later perhaps he would call Rhonda Villiers and tell her where her husband had been taken into custody. It might be productive to put the cat among the pigeons back where it all began.

But where and how to begin in New York?

The contact number Lizzie had given him would allow him to call Max and make threats, but what would be the point? It could endanger Lizzie all the more. The taxi repair garage? If he could locate it he could follow the people who came in and out. No good. That would take too much time.

The label on the box of groceries had told him the *Gazelle* was berthed at the Port Imperial Marina, which was on the other side of the river in New Jersey. If his memory was right it was directly across from his present accommodation. He could go over to the Marina, locate the boat and keep an eye on it until someone came. Again, what was the point? He hadn't the means to follow the boat and it could be days before anyone turned up.

What would they do in the movies? What would George Clooney or the indestructible Harrison Ford do in his place?

Simple. They would blow the boat to bits.

Harry had once played an assistant district attorney on a miniseries. With all the car chases, shootings and pyrotechnics, the special effects department was strained to the limit. Marcel "More Smoke" Forestière was considered one of the best in the business.

A scene in one episode called for a limousine to be blown up on a railway bridge as a train passed beneath. Five cameras were set up to get several diverse points of view. Setting up the shot took all morning and part of the afternoon. Finally the old Mercedes was winched across the bridge on a cable with two lifelike dummies in the front seats. As it reached the center span Marcel hit the switch. Later that evening he admitted to Harry that he made a mistake in his calculations and multiplied when he should have divided. The detonation was so powerful that the huge car rose up high into the sky, spewing smoke and flame but disappearing out of view of all the cameras. All five had been locked off and none of the operators could react fast enough to release the wheels to allow them to tilt up. Fortunately, no one was hurt and the paint department was able to make the Mercedes look like new. Three hours later, the second explosion worked to perfection.

Harry chuckled to himself. If he could blow the boat up at its moorings EB would come running like a gazelle! With any luck Harry could follow the dapper little man when he left the Marina.

Before departing for the Jersey shore Harry put on socks, shoes and a clean shirt, zippered all his valuables into his Windbreaker pockets and slipped it on. With the plastic bag tucked in a dark corner he slid out into the alley and replaced the sheet of metal over the hole.

At the NY Waterway terminal he bought a round-trip ticket to New Jersey and stepped aboard. Standing in the stern of the ferry he watched as New York receded beyond the churning white wake. A little upriver he could just make out the forest of pilings sticking out of the water that had recently saved his life.

The Port Imperial Marina was a short walk from the ferry terminal. Access was through a narrow gate at the far end of a short concrete bridge. At the entrance two security guards kept watch from a small shed. A little way past this was the Marina office and store. The whole dockyard was protected by a chain-link fence.

On the far side was a repair and storage facility. Everywhere Harry looked there were square floodlights on the top of high poles, so it would not be easy to get to the target unobserved. But on the downriver side of the boatyard he came across a section of wall that had crumbled with age. At night it would be in shadow and the river was only a few yards from the other side. Harry ran his eyes down the lines of boats tied up on either side of the jetties. Almost immediately he spotted the *Gazelle* and saw that the distance from the shore to the boat was easily swimmable.

Where could he get plastic explosive, a detonator and a timing device that would allow him to swim clear before it went off? The answer was he couldn't. So what else could he do? Set the boat on fire? Gasoline and matches were readily available and easy to transport. But he might set himself on fire or the blaze could spread to adjoining boats. Harry had no desire to punish the innocent.

Could he sink it?

The hulls of most modern boats are made of some form of fiberglass. Plastic laid over a nylon web of sorts. All it would take would be a few holes below the waterline. A portable drill would do the job nicely and the latest models made very little noise.

The ferry was about to return to Manhattan. Harry ran back and jumped aboard. On the return crossing he made his way inside, and settling down on the wooden seat, he congratulated himself on his creative brilliance.

51

The morning when someone had tried to assassinate her husband, Rhonda Villiers had prepared his breakfast and had just put on the kettle when she heard the staccato sounds of the bullets. Running rapidly up the stairs to the bedroom window she was just in time to see Murphy clamber into the Jaguar before Charles pinned the leather-clad motorcyclist to the wall. As the man's weapon hit the ground and the bullets flew she ducked to avoid being hit.

It was not unusual for Charles to disappear for short periods of time. But when they grew longer he always managed to get in touch and reassure her of his health and safety. This time he hadn't called and she had become worried that he might have been wounded.

When the phone on the kitchen wall rang she hurried over and took down the receiver, assuming it would be her husband.

But it wasn't.

"Mr. Murphy, what a pleasant surprise! How good to hear your voice. I'm glad you called. I'm a little worried about Charles. I haven't heard from him. Do you know where he might be? Oh, really. Yes, yes, of course. Just a moment."

She pulled out a notepad from a drawer and rummaged around until she found a pen. Once ready she said, "Yes, Mister Murphy. I'm ready. Taunton." She wrote on the pad. "Yes. I have that. Who? Sapinsky. Yes. And Carswell, Elizabeth. When was that? I see. Yes I most certainly will. Thank you. I will see what I can do."

Moments later Directory Enquiries gave her the number of Taunton Police Station and she added it to her notes. Before calling she decided it would be prudent to consider everything she had just heard and why Murphy had chosen this particular moment to call her. The gas popped as she put on the kettle. Once the tea was made she settled herself on the living room sofa.

Her basic problem was whether a call to the authorities would help or hinder Charles. Rhonda had a great mistrust of anything that involved the government, both local and national.

Perhaps this would be a good time to ask her father. He always gave her good advice. In fact, he had never failed her. Not once. Bless his heart. Not since that devastating day at Ainsley House Boarding School for Girls when she had been summoned from class and sent up to the see Miss Weatherly.

The headmistress had stood stiffly behind her desk and given an awkward cough before she spoke. "I'm sorry, Evans, but I have some bad news. Your father has died. Quite suddenly, I am told. The funeral will be on Saturday. I've arranged for a taxi to take you to the station so you can catch the next train to London."

Rhonda Evans had fainted on the parquet floor. Matron was summoned and told to cope.

Two days later Rhonda watched as her father's casket was lowered into the cold ground of Highgate Cemetery. The young girl, still in her school uniform, waited until everyone had left and then knelt down on the fake grass that covered the mound of dirt.

"It's me," she whispered. "I only have a moment. I know who they are. I promise I will see that they pay for what they did. No matter how long it takes. I have to go back to school now, Daddy. I'll visit soon. I promise. I love you, Daddy."

Gareth Evans had been a gentle soul, unlike his father before him. Rhonda's grandfather was a Sergeant Major in the Welsh Guards and constantly lectured his son on honor and military tradition. He naturally assumed the boy would follow him into the army. When young Gareth became a chartered surveyor and joined a small architectural firm in Hampstead, communication between them ceased. They met only once when Gareth married his secretary, Elsie.

The newlyweds set up home in a tree-lined street in the suburbs of Golders Green in North London, where they raised first daughter Rhonda and then son Julian. When both children grew up and left home, Gareth and Elsie moved to a mews cottage in Kensington.

For a while all was well but when the British economy went through one of its cyclical downturns cutbacks became necessary at the firm and he was laid off. It wasn't long before he was unable to cover his expenses. One day he was summoned to the local Inland Revenue office and informed that he had overlooked the matter of his tax return. A humiliating meeting precipitated an audit of the previous four years and several negligible amounts were brought into question. But by the time the government added four years of penalty and interest the total owed was considerable.

Gareth Evans had neither the funds to pay nor an income from which he could make an offer of installments. One month later an officious letter dropped with a thud through the front-door mail slot:

> *Unless the above matter is settled to our satisfaction, we shall be required to take measures that may result in a further fine, legal action and possible confinement.*

In other words, dishonor and disgrace.

Gareth dropped the letter to the floor and went to the cupboard beneath the stairs. Opening an old metal trunk, he pulled out his father's service revolver and a box of .455 shells. For a moment he thumbed through old uniforms, shirts, ties and socks, all neatly folded. In the bottom he even found a pair of boots with the toecaps so shiny he could see his reflection.

Rhonda's mother found her husband in a pool of blood on the floor of the living room, the revolver in one hand, the boots in the other. Fragments of his skull, hair and brain were scattered across the photographs, banners, plaques and trophies. The distraught woman put the house on the market, but before anyone could make an offer she dropped dead on the same floor. Autopsy revealed a cerebral aneurysm.

For the second time in a month Rhonda Evans walked behind a casket in Highgate Cemetery. Once again she hovered until everyone had left and then crouched down. "Hello, Daddy," she said. "I'm sorry about Mum. But isn't it wonderful! This means I'll inherit the house! I'm going to have the whole place to myself now! It's a little run-down, but a good cleanup and some paint and wallpaper will soon take care of that. I called Julian and he said he never wanted to see it ever again, so it's all mine! Oh, and you'll be pleased to know he's been made manager of the bank. Think of it! Little Julian a bank manager!"

Brother Julian dropped in unexpectedly one day on his way back from a college reunion in Bristol. He had come for some sisterly advice. At the reunion he had met an American investment broker who was looking for a way to launder money. If Julian agreed to help he would receive a percentage. Although he was now in a position of power his remuneration remained low. Rhonda was the only person he could talk to and she quickly encouraged him to accept. This was the second element to her plan. The final one came three days after her brother returned to the Channel Islands.

Rhonda became the receptionist in a doctor's office in Harley Street. A tall and distinguished man walked into the office for his annual checkup. From his file she learned he was a Colonel who worked for Her Majesty's Diplomatic Service.

The following morning she called in sick with the flu and for two days followed the Colonel wherever he went. On the second day she accidentally bumped into him in Selfridges. To her surprise, he remembered her and suggested afternoon tea.

Once he was hooked the rest was simple and by the end of summer she had reeled him in. On the first of October she became Mrs. Charles Jeremy Villiers. She waited for several months before asking him if he would be willing to carry a little package in his diplomatic pouch for her. "I know I shouldn't ask you to do this, darling, but it will make me very happy." The Colonel had saved little from his army pay and was easily persuaded. After several of these trips, she fully confided in him and he became a willing accomplice. Rhonda called Julian and gave him the good news. She then arranged for his American broker to have the cash delivered directly to her in Kensington, where she would keep it safe until Charles was able to take it to the Channel Islands.

From each shipment she took out a few notes and hid them away. One day she would need them. One day they would come in very useful, when she had planned exactly how she would avenge her father's death.

As Rhonda sipped the last of her tea she looked down at her copy of the *Daily Mirror* and saw a panel on the front page that read: "He Died as Wildly as He Lived!'" Beside it was a small photograph of Percy Santiago.

From conversations with her husband Rhonda knew about the Bruschetti connection with Santiago. Now the man was dead and Charles had been shot at. It was definitely time to act on the information that Murphy had just given her. Back in the kitchen she picked up the phone.

"Good day. I understand you have my husband in your care. His name? Colonel Charles Villiers. Yes that's right. With a *V*. Before I get in touch with our lawyer I'd like a word with him if that is at all possible. My name? Rhonda Villiers. I am also calling to find out with what offense he's been officially charged. Perhaps you can tell me?"

52

The young salesman in the hardware store was surprisingly helpful and demonstrated several electric drills. Harry bought a powerful DeWalt with two expensive bits. One was twenty-four inches long and a quarter of an inch in diameter, the other twelve inches long and about half an inch in diameter.

"I'm in for the day from Connecticut to do a job for my sister. She's pretty sick and I don't want to disturb her." He pulled out twenty dollars. "Could you charge the batteries up for me? I could come back for everything in a little while."

"Sure thing," said the man, taking the twenty. "Be sure to come back before we close."

"When's that?" asked Harry.

"Six o'clock."

The subway took Harry to Union Square where he walked across the open-air market and up Broadway to Paragon Sporting Goods.

"I'm going to the Bahamas for a short vacation and I need a wet suit, a mask and a snorkel," he said to a cute salesgirl name-tagged Eve. "Lightweight and nothing too expensive. I usually swim along the surface. Oh," he added. "I'll need a waterproof bag of some sort. Preferably black."

Eve persuaded him to add a pair of flippers. "You'll find it makes swimming so much easier," she explained with a smile.

Avis was his next stop, where he signed the papers for a Ford Escape and arranged to pick it up later.

Back in the box Harry set the alarm on his wristwatch and dozed for a while, dreaming that he was swimming in clear blue water with a naked Eve who giggled at his efforts to skewer a barracuda with the DeWalt.

A rat rummaging in the remains of his breakfast woke him up. The shock of seeing a black rodent so close to his nose made him gasp. The beast gave him a look of pity, twitched his considerable whiskers and ambled off. Harry smashed his way out of the box and into the light. Homelessness was no longer an option.

Getting the car from Avis took less than a half hour. Parking as close to the alley as he could, he put in enough coins for two hours. He gathered up all his belongings and moved them to the car. The passenger seat was now his home, and he sat there listening to the radio until it was time to go back to the hardware store for the drill.

At the Marina, the *Gazelle* was in exactly the same spot as before but now the jetties were deserted. To his relief, none of the boats showed signs of occupancy or activity. Harry watched as the super locked up the office and drove off in his red truck. The security guard closed up the main gate and padlocked it. Out in his shed he sat down and picked up the newspaper and began to read.

Darkness fell. One by one the lights up on the poles clicked on. Harry undressed, hauled on the wet suit and packed all his gear into the plastic bag. Carefully he locked the car and walked over to the gap in the wall.

On a hunk of broken concrete on the far side he made a brief test of the drill, pulled on the flippers, mask and snorkel. The bag was retied securely.

Putting one foot laboriously in front of the other he flip-flopped over the slimy rocks like an elderly walrus. Once he was waist-deep, he floated the bag on the water and launched himself off.

The journey was not as easy as he had assumed. As he was unaccustomed to taking air through a tube, his breathing became labored. To overcome this he concentrated on exhaling rather than inhaling. As he swam out of the calm waters towards the river the current began to drag him along. Harry panicked and almost let go of the bag but then gave an extrahard kick with both legs. The flippers did the trick and he was able to propel himself safely around the end of the jetty.

Harry swam down the line of boats until he reached the *Gazelle* and, slithering along the smooth hull, he climbed out onto the dock and pulled the bag up beside him. Leaning back against a post, he sat down and pulled down the mask and dragged off the flippers.

How would the boat settle in the water? The engines were the heaviest part and were usually towards the rear. If he made the holes near the front and the boat sank by the stern those same holes would be lifted clear of the water. Not a good idea. A spot near the stern directly below a stanchion would work best. There he could make a series of holes just above the waterline. Once these were made he would angle the bit down and drill through the submerged part of the hull to start the flow.

The long, thin bit was quickly tightened into the DeWalt. Back in the river and with the drill held over his head he made his way to the chosen spot. But even before he turned the drill on he ran into a problem. Each time he pushed the drill against the hull his body floated backwards. If he pressed his shoulders firmly against the dock his arms weren't long enough to reach the hull. A solution was fortunately close to hand. The *Gazelle* was roped fore and aft and from side to side to the jetty. Climbing out and keeping low, he loosened both starboard lines and then crawled around and took a firm grip on the port stern line. By pulling with all his might the boat slowly began to respond. Eventually he was able to take a second loop around the bollard. Once the process was repeated with the bowline the boat was considerably closer to the dock.

He was now able to hold the drill against the hull. But when he turned it on, the bit slid across the shiny paint and made no impression. Harry climbed out, switched to the thicker bit and scrambled back down and tried again with the same annoying result.

"Shit!" he said. "You need to make a starter hole, Harry my boy! You need a hammer and a nail. Well, Rome wasn't built in a day!"

Back up on the dock he was about to swim back and make his way to the car when he noticed that the DeWalt company had thoughtfully provided a small but very pointed Phillips head bit clipped to the base of the handle. Harry took it out and put it in the chuck.

With his feet up against the hull he wedged himself as tightly as he could and turned the drill motor as slowly as he could. After a while the sharp point made a mark on the white paint. Harry got out and put in the thin bit. This time it stayed in place and tiny slivers of the *Gazelle* began to drop into the Hudson. A neat round hole was forming. Suddenly the drill shot through the first layer of hull and hit the second.

By the time Harry had drilled ten small holes above and five below the water line he was very tired. It took a great deal of effort to widen the lower holes. But water was now definitely flowing in and success gave him renewed energy. It might take a while, but this baby was going down!

Eventually all the holes were widened and he was able to climb out, pack up the bag, tie it securely and swim back to shore by the most direct route. Crouching down at the wall, he checked to see that the coast was clear, and then ran swiftly over to the Ford.

As soon as he was back in his clothes, he drove across the lot and up the ramp, where he made a U-turn and parked. The entire Marina was now below in full view.

When dawn streaked in the eastern sky Harry was delighted to see that only the wheelhouse, mast and aerial of the *Gazelle* were above water. Still tied by her portside lines, the hull had settled at a steep angle.

As he continued his vigil he was amazed to see that no one noticed anything amiss. The guard was relieved. The gate was reopened and pushed back. The superintendent opened up the office. People went to and from their boats and many of them walked past the sunken hull without giving it a second glance.

Around noon, a father and son came into the dock from the river in a Boston Whaler. The little boy jumped out and made fast the painter. As the pair went towards the office the boy hesitated and his father called for him to keep up. The boy pointed at the *Gazelle*. The father yelled at him to keep up. The kid began to cry. Both of them disappeared into the Marina office. Moments later they came out followed by the superintendent. The boy led the way back along the jetty. All three peered down at the *Gazelle*. As the superintendent hurried back to the office, the father put his arms around his son and gave him a hug.

The lot was now filling up with cars, trucks and vans. To get a better view of the proceedings Harry drove down and parked by the fence. A few minutes after one o'clock an angry squeal of brakes announced the arrival of a black Town Car.

EB ran over the bridge with his driver close behind. Harry recognized the second man as the one who had driven him from the taxi garage. They both stopped at the *Gazelle*. EB uttered a long moan. His body language was marvelously expressive. Sagging incredulity, pacing frustration, arms raised to Heaven seeking an explanation.

On the other side of the boat his driver picked up a pair of flippers and held them up.

"Hey! Enzo!" he called out. "Look what I found!"

53

Rhonda Villiers was pleased when she heard her husband's key in the front door. Usually she accepted his return with a degree of equanimity, but the last few days were unsettling at best.

"Rhonda!" he called out.

"In the kitchen," she replied, and picked up the papers, passport and money that she had in front of her on the table.

"Where have you been, you naughty man?" She spoke with mock severity as he came in from the hallway.

"Ah!" he said dramatically. "Now there's a tale!"

She stood up and gave him a light hug and a kiss on the cheek. As they parted, Charles Villiers noticed the little bundles.

"What are you up to?" he asked.

"I was checking to see if my passport was up-to-date. I was also curious to see how much cash I'd squirreled away." She held up the thick wad of notes.

"Odd that you should bring that up," said the Colonel. "I've been thinking along those same lines myself."

"Yes, dear, I'm sure you have, but before you say another word, I suggest you go up and use the facilities. You smell as if you've been in the trenches. While you do, I'll make us some food. You must be famished. Then I want to hear all about where you've been and what you've been doing. And there's no need to get dressed; just put on your robe and slippers."

Rhonda followed her husband halfway up the stairs and sat down. She pushed the upper left corner of one of the panels in the left-hand wainscoting. With an audible click it slid back and with gentle pressure she eased it to the side. Built into the wall was a clever space lined with black felt. Putting everything in, she closed the panel.

Back in the kitchen she put a skillet and two pans of water on the stove. Into the former she dropped four pork sausages. Peeling and thinly slicing two King Edward potatoes, she dropped them into one of the pans. A small head of shredded cabbage went into the other.

She could hear the sound of the big tub filling up. She always knew when Charles was actually in the water as that was when he began to hum to himself. But this time there was only silence. This confirmed what she had sensed when he had come into the kitchen. His incarceration had made him ill at ease. Charles would have to be handled delicately. She wished she could go and have a word with her father in Highgate but that was quite out of the question. But then she knew what he would say: "Stand on you own two feet, my love. Take charge as only you can."

Twenty minutes later she and her husband were eating together at the dining table.

Rhonda began, "You say you were thinking along the same lines. What lines were those?"

"I have a nasty feeling the Bruschetti organization is compromised."

"And you base this on what?"

"First that attempt on my life! A total stranger turns up in the Mews to warn me of impending danger. I know now that he clearly wanted me alive so he could get his hands on that suitcase of money. But I outsmarted him and followed him to the West Country. Can you believe it? I caught Mister Harry Murphy red-handed burying the case."

Rhonda watched as her husband got up and walked over to the sideboard, where he poured himself a larger than usual scotch.

"I was about to take care of him but the damn police intervened."

He came back to the table and began to speak faster as if he were relieved to be telling her what had happened to him.

"I thought the game was up, stupidly gave them a phone number, but then I was never charged, just kept in a cell all by myself and away from prying eyes. After a while I asked to speak with counsel. That was refused. So I asked to meet with the duty solicitor. That too was refused.

"By law, this gave them thirty-six hours they could keep me under lock and key. All along I had the feeling the whole business was 'off-the-books,' so to speak. Then this morning I was informed that you had called and without further ceremony I was told I was free to go. I thought it prudent not to ask questions."

"Very wise," she said quietly.

"Secondly, when I called Max he didn't seem to know much about Murphy. I had the feeling there was a bit of a mystery there too."

"How interesting." Rhonda smiled inwardly. The situation was not as bad as she had feared. It was certainly manageable. With careful prodding she was sure she could achieve a positive outcome. One that would work to her advantage.

"How did you know where to find me?" Charles was asking.

"It was Murphy. He called from New York and gave me all the particulars I needed. I was beginning to think of him as your Guardian Angel."

"Guardian Angel be damned!" exclaimed the Colonel. "The man is a thief, plain and simple. Gave me some cock and bull story about overhearing Max talk about us."

Rhonda folded her hands in her lap and then said quietly, "Tell me. What conclusions have you come to?"

"That perhaps it's time to take our leave. Go somewhere quiet and simply disappear for a while. Go to ground, so to speak."

She smiled at him. "Charles, I like what you're saying, but I think you're selling yourself short. You shouldn't give up so easily. You know a great deal. About Max. About all of them. And Max knows this."

"Are you suggesting I demand some sort of severance pay?"

"You could call it that. I prefer to think of it as a way of financing our retirement."

"Max would never go along with it."

"On the contrary. He would have no choice. And there would be no need to incriminate yourself. You could spill the beans anonymously. And Max knows this too. Trust me, I know exactly how to do it."

"But shouldn't we wait . . ."

Rhonda silenced him with a wave of her hand and walked over to the sofa, where she picked up the newspaper and the phone. Returning, she dropped the paper on the table.

"Have you seen this?" she asked.

"Good God!" he said when he saw the lurid headline.

"Read it," she said. "All of it."

When he finished he muttered with feeling, "Poor Percy."

"Yes! Poor Percy. Do you want to end up like him?"

She handed him the phone.

"It's the perfect time to call Max. What you say is simple. You tell him that due to present unforeseen circumstances, the Villiers are going to retire. You then let him know that for inconvenience caused you need to be recompensed."

He stared at her. "How much do I ask for?"

"I don't know," she answered. "What do you think?"

He shook his head. "I have absolutely no idea. I have to leave that to you."

Rhonda Villiers thought for a moment.

"Well," she said. "A million pounds has a pleasant ring to it."

54

On the top floor of Mazaras, Max was slumped on the sofa in his office feeling angry and tired. Since he had made the decision to make necessary changes to his lifestyle all hell had broken loose. To add insult to injury there was now this irritating call from Villiers.

The Colonel and his stupid ultimatum would have to wait. Max had more pressing matters to deal with. First and foremost was the offer from Hernandez. The idea of setting up such a massive new organization was ludicrous. Twenty years earlier Max would have jumped at the opportunity, but not now. It was time to call Enzo and put an end to the whole business.

He opened the desk drawer and took out a phone. There were only two left. A trip to Walmart was needed to restock the supply. As he went to dial the one in his hand, the phone on his desk rang. He reached over and picked it up.

"Yeah," he said.

"Max, it's Enzo . . ."

"What's up, little brother? I was just about to call you. About the Hernandez offer . . ."

"Max . . ."

"I have no idea how he'll react but . . ."

"Max!" Enzo said louder. "The boat sank. Sometime last night. Right at the dock."

"What?"

"I just came from there. The super's been trying to call us all morning."

"It sank?"

"Yes, Max."

"Was it an accident?"

"Boats don't just sink. This was no accident. Nino found a couple of flippers."

"Then how . . . ?"

"I have no idea how! But the *Gazelle* is on the bottom of the fucking river. All I could see was the top, all those mast things; everything else is under the water."

"I don't get it."

"I'm on my way to see Vic. Find out if he knows of anyone who might have a reason to get even with us. And then of course there's Murphy."

"You think it could be him?"

"He certainly has the motive."

Max sat down and cursed. Murphy was a cat with nine fucking lives, a goddam grenade rolling around with the pin out.

"Where are you now?" he asked.

"With Benny on my way to the warehouse. Murphy's girl still there?"

"Not for long," replied Max. "I told Rocco to go get her. He's bringing her here."

"Maybe she knows more than she's letting on."

"Maybe. But leave her to me. I'll make the bitch talk."

55

Lizzie heard footsteps descending the stairs. The pipe against the door clattered to the ground. Rocco came in, grabbed her by the arms and pinned her against the wall, where he secured her wrists with a plastic tie. At no time did he give her an opening to take him down. Silently he frog-marched her up the stairs, along the corridor and outside to a car parked at the curb. The street was deserted.

As they drove through the tunnel beneath the waters of the Hudson, Lizzie couldn't help wondering whether Harry's lifeless corpse was floating above her at that very moment. A shudder ran through her body at the thought.

They emerged on the West Side of Manhattan. The driver turned sharply around two corners, up a ramp into a parking garage and over to a gray steel door marked **Fire Exit Keep Clear**. Rocco got out and indicated to her she should follow him. He pressed the buttons on the electronic keypad and opened the door, keeping a wary eye on her as she crossed the threshold.

The lighting was low and red. The soft carpet beneath her feet was red. The damask walls were red and black. The air smelled odd. Cheap perfume and garlic.

Her captor propelled her down two flights of stairs into a dark basement and over to a door marked WC. Taking a knife from his pocket he cut the plastic holding her hands and pushed her inside. The door shut. A key turned in the lock. Footsteps walked away and up the stairs.

As part of her training at the Police Academy, Cadet Lizzie Carswell had attended a lecture on what to expect if she were taken hostage. The lecturer was a craggy ex-paratrooper who had evidently made the subject his life's work.

"If you have the misfortune to be abducted and held for any kind of ransom," he had intoned, "you should consider your life over and at an end. For all intents and purposes you are dead and buried. The inviolable rule is that no government, be it local or national, can ever enter into negotiations or pay money to terrorists or kidnappers. It just perpetuates the kidnapping cycle."

Supervised drills were undertaken where each of the students was deprived of all normal senses. For several hours they were blindfolded, bound, gagged and placed in a dark and very narrow space. Lizzie had little problem with these exercises. She had just slept.

Now she used the toilet, sat down and made herself as comfortable as she could. She was determined to rest. With Harry out of the picture, her only objective was to escape.

56

Enzo's car sped out of the Marina with Harry in hot pursuit. At the first intersection the light changed as they passed through. Harry risked the wrath of the law to keep up with his one link to Lizzie. The West Side Highway allowed him to keep a little distance between them. They crossed Central Park at 66th Street and pulled up outside an apartment building on Lexington Avenue.

Harry watched from a slight distance.

Enzo was clearly in no mood for pleasantries and brushed past the doorman. The car drove off. The coast was now clear. Harry ran across the road and entered the lobby.

"Yes, sir, can I help you?" asked the same doorman.

"*Buono sierra!*" Harry was now a New York Sicilian. "The guy went up in that elevator. *Dio mio!*" He tapped his forehead. "*Ho forgetta il suo nome! Enzo, Enzo . . . ?*"

The doorman fell into the trap. "Bruschetti," he said.

"Yeah, yeah, thatsa right," said Harry brightly. "Enzo Bruschetti. He lives in the pentahousa, right?"

The doorman hesitated. Perhaps he had just made a big mistake. "What exactly do you want with Mr. Bruschetti?"

Harry looked at his watch. "*Santa Margharita Portofino vecchia Maria!* Is thatta the time!" He wheeled towards the front door. "I see Enzo later. My cousin Vinny's waiting for me. *Ciao bella!*"

Out on the sidewalk he flew across to his car, drove fast around the block and parked. If he was going to find Lizzie he needed all the information he could muster. The IRS agent was a good place to start and at the same time he could find out if they knew anything. Cursing his stupidity at not bringing his cellphone from the apartment, he spent five minutes finding a pay phone that functioned. He took out the card from his wallet and called Special Agent Luigi Rienzi. The familiar voice answered.

"It's Harry Murphy," he said.

"Harry Murphy! What do you know! We've all been wondering what happened to you. You sure know how to disappear. Are you okay? Marty needs to talk to you."

"You can tell your pals I'm fine."

Luigi's tone became confidential. "Between you and me," he said, "until we find your lady friend we're on twenty-four-seven. What can I do for you?"

"I need information. Do you have access to department files?"

"Sure do," said the agent.

"Could you check for a name for me?"

"Sure. Why?"

"I'll tell you all that later. It's Enzo Bruschetti."

"How do you spell it?"

"No idea. I've only heard it spoken. Rhymes with 'spaghetti.'"

"How soon do you need it?"

"How soon can you get it?"

"Depends on the filing date. If it's in the computer I'll have it in a few minutes. If I have to shuffle paper it'll take at least an hour. A day maybe. Perhaps never. Where can I call you?"

"I'll call you," said Harry. "Speaking of my lady friend, I don't suppose you have any news?"

"You got that right. But don't lose heart, Harry, everyone's working hard on it. Look, where are you? We could send a car . . ."

"No thanks," said Harry. "Later maybe."

57

Marty MacAvoy was sitting down to a pizza burger in the commissary when Luigi walked up to him. "Whatever it is, it can wait, Lou," he said pointedly.

"No it can't boss" came the reply. "I just had Murphy on the phone."

"Great! He's coming in."

"No he's not. He wanted to know what we knew about the name 'Bruschetti.' Rhymes with 'spaghetti.' Mean anything to you?"

"No. Is that all?"

"I was wondering if I should find out who owns the boat Murphy jumped from last night."

"Frank's already on it. He's over at the Marina right now." MacAvoy picked up his burger.

"No, he's back," said the IRS agent. "I just talked with him. Guess what? The *Gazelle* was where it was supposed to be but was sitting firmly on the muddy bottom of the Hudson. The Marina super thinks it was sunk deliberately. He said something about a bunch of holes."

MacAvoy thought for a moment and then said, "Do you suppose Murphy did it?"

Luigi gave a short laugh. "I hadn't thought about that. Yeah, you're probably right. He's sure got the balls for it."

MacAvoy said bitterly, "God, I hate all this. It keeps creeping up my ass. All right, Lou, do what you think best. But keep it quiet, okay?"

Luigi drew a finger across his mouth. "My lips is sealed. Enjoy your burger."

Luigi needed to talk with Frank Torregrossa in case he had the identification number of the *Gazelle*. He did. Luigi made a copy and took it back to his cubicle, where he had his nephew Mario at the NYS Department of Motor Vehicles look it up and give him the name and address of the boat owners. With his Windbreaker over his arm, he left the building and took a cab across town.

The offices of Walker, Martin, Pomeranz and Fisher were in a tall glass building on Park Avenue. Luigi pushed open the doors, flashed his badge to the security agent and took the elevator up to the seventh floor. At the reception desk he pulled out his badge again.

"I'm with the Internal Revenue Service," he said politely. "I'd like some information please."

The gray-haired receptionist reacted as everyone did when he announced his affiliation: a startled look that morphed into one of complete innocence.

"Who's in charge here?" Luigi asked, smiling. It always helped to keep it friendly.

"On this floor?"

Luigi nodded.

"That would be Mr. Allinson. But he's not here right now."

A young girl came up to the desk with a bunch of envelopes and put them in the outgoing-mail tray.

"Mr. Allinson?" she said. "He went home already."

The receptionist gave her a chilly look.

"And where would home be?" asked Luigi pleasantly.

The receptionist hesitated. "I don't know if I'm allowed . . ."

Luigi held his badge two inches from her nose.

"Well," she said, "if you insist."

A Lexington Avenue subway took him up to 86th Street and he walked the rest of the way. A white-gloved doorman opened the door as he approached. Luigi handed over one of his calling cards. The doorman told him to wait while he called the Allinson residence. After a brief conversation on the intercom, Luigi was shown into a shiny mahogany elevator with polished brass fittings. The doorman reached in and pressed a button.

"Which apartment?" Luigi inquired taking back the card.

"The one straight ahead" came the patient reply.

The elevator glided up and gently came to a stop. The door reopened. A young teenage girl was standing in the doorway of the one apartment on the floor. Behind her were suitcases and bags. Someone was about to take a journey.

"Hi there!" she said brightly. "I take it you've come to see my pops."

"Could be," replied Luigi, and he extended his hand. "You are?"

"I'm Amanda Allinson," she replied, and gave him a firm handshake. "If you'll just wait a moment I'll go get him. Why don't you go into the living room?"

Amanda ran off as Luigi strolled across the marble floor and into the big sunlit room.

Luigi Rienzi lived in a third-floor walk-up above the Fabiani Pizza Emporium in Queens. He had all the comforts of home. A small but adequate kitchen, a bed, a table with four dining chairs, and a comfy armchair strategically placed in front of his home entertainment center. Slowly turning around he admired the fancy upholstery with the big pillows, the beautiful drapes, the artwork, the luxurious carpet. He was looking at a shelf of art books when a voice behind him said, "Hello there."

Luigi lived alone. Although he was never short of female

company he somehow had never found his other half. The ideal match. Walking over towards him now was his idea of perfection. The archetypal New England woman. Above-average height, short hairstyle, classic features, smart for sure and with a body to die for. Luigi was all too aware that such companionship came at a price. This babe was high maintenance.

"My husband will be here in just a moment," she said. Her voice was kind of sexy too. "Can I offer you anything?"

"No thank you, I'm fine," replied Luigi wondering how long it would take him to earn enough money to make her an offer. Not in this lifetime.

"Charming apartment you have here," he said politely.

"Yes," she replied. "We're very lucky. Do you live in the city?"

"No, ma'am," he said. "I live over in Queens. Been there for over ten years now. It's modest, but it's home."

Footsteps across the hall floor heralded the arrival of the man of the house. Tall, slim and exuding confidence. Luigi handed him his card. The man read it, gave no visible reaction and indicated one of the armchairs.

"Please have a seat, Mr. Rienzi."

Luigi sat down and took out his notepad. The man sat opposite him. His wife settled into the sofa between them.

The agent began: "Last night in New Jersey, a boat by the name of the *Gazelle* sank at its moorings. We traced the ownership to . . ." Still keeping his attention focused on Pops, Luigi glanced at his notes . . . "the Martinson Metal Recycling Company. The address of this company was listed as care of you, Mr. Allinson at Walker, Martin, Pomeranz and Fisher on Park Avenue South. We would like to speak with the operators of the vessel, and specifically about the past two days. Can you furnish us with that information?"

"Possibly. I would have to go to my office" came the reply. "I handle many companies. Tell me, your card here says that you are with the Drug Enforcement Administration but also the IRS. How come you're investigating a boat sinking?"

"I'm afraid I'm not able to reveal that at this time, Mr. Allinson," Luigi replied evenly. "How soon do you think you could give us the information?"

"Do you have a fax number?"

"It's on the card."

Carter looked down. "Oh, so it is. As soon as I'm in the office I'll look it up and send it to you."

"When will that be?"

"Would first thing in the morning be soon enough?"

"Sure. That would be fine."

"Thanks."

All three stood up. Luigi made his way across the hall towards the elevator. Passing the luggage he asked, "Taking a trip?"

"My daughter is," replied Mrs. Allinson as she walked past him and pushed the button for the elevator. "She's off to Florence on a school trip."

"Ah," said Luigi. "Lucky girl." On an impulse he turned and said, "Speaking of *la bella Italia,* Mr. Allinson, do you by any chance know anyone by the name of Bruschetti?"

The tall man stopped dead in his tracks.

"Bruschetti?" he asked.

"Rhymes with 'spaghetti,'" said Luigi.

"No" was the reply. His head went very slowly from side to side. "Can't say I do."

The elevator arrived. Luigi nodded good-bye and stepped in. The door slid shut.

The agent smiled to himself. He loved his job. One word had just revealed to him that Carter Allinson was guilty of something. Luigi had no idea what that might be, but it would be very interesting and possibly rewarding to find out.

58

Carter Allinson was about to go back to his study when Fiona asked, "What was all that about?"

"Nothing. At least nothing to do with us."

"Who's Bruschetta?"

"No one important. Someone I once did business with. It's a long time ago."

He turned to go, but his wife put her hand on his arm to stop him.

"Tell me about it?"

"Why?"

"When you heard that name you turned white as a sheet."

Carter kept silent. He knew if he opened his mouth there would be no going back. But what could he say or do?

"I think I need an explanation," she persisted.

"Fiona, it's a long story," he bluffed. "I'll tell you all about it another time."

"Why don't you try now? I have plenty of time."

"It's also not a pretty story. Are you sure you . . . ?"

"Carter. I'm your wife. The mother of your children. Whatever it is, I can handle it. Tell me why that man was here!"

"I'm afraid it has to do with drugs and a silly, youthful transgression back in college. You remember how it was."

"No, I do not remember how it was," she said with a scathing look.

"Come off it!" said Carter. "We all did a little something back then."

"No, we did not all do something."

"Oh please!"

"What do you mean it has something to do with drugs?"

Carter took his time before saying, "I met a guy who worked in the college commissary."

"The commissary?"

"Yes. He was the guy who cleared the tables. He sold me some marijuana. Made it easy for me to supply my friends. I became very popular, and at the same time it gave me a little pocket money."

"Was his name Bruschetta?"

"No. And it's Bruschetti."

"So, you met a man in the commissary called Bruschetti who sold you drugs. Is that all?"

"No. Look, why don't we sit down and talk . . ."

Fiona flared. "For Christ's sake! We just had a Federal Agent in here asking questions and you're burbling on about college!"

"Look, I'm the one who put us in this mess," said Carter, beginning to get irritated. "So you're just going to have to be patient and let me find a way out of it."

"Patient! What mess? You still haven't told me . . ."

"Will you please shut up and let me explain?"

"Don't talk to me like that!"

"I'm going to talk to you any way I please," he said pointedly. "Because right now we don't have many options open to us."

"Then start at the beginning," she said bitterly. "If my life is going to fall apart I would like to have some idea of just how it happened."

"I need a drink," he said, and walked into the short passageway that served as a wet bar. Fiona followed and leaned in the doorway as he took down a whisky glass and half-filled it with scotch. He added ice from the ice machine and topped it up with water.

"I've done my best to insulate you and the kids from what happened back then," he said turning to face her. "I've done everything I can to bury the evidence and cover my tracks so that no one would ever be able to follow the paper trail. From what we just heard, I must have slipped up somewhere." He took a long drink. "The last thing I ever expected was to see a cop walk in here and use the name Bruschetti."

"Were you using pot when I met you?"

"Good God no! It was all over by then. But that's when all the trouble started. When I tried to quit, I was blackmailed."

"By the man in the commissary?"

"No, not him. He was nobody. It was his boss, Sal, the man who had been supplying him all along. I met with him and he told me quite simply if I didn't agree to work for them and handle their investments he would kill me. 'Dead meat' was the phrase he used."

Carter downed the whisky and banged the glass down on the counter.

Fiona stared at her husband. "You agreed to take care of this man's investments even when you knew you could be handling drug money?"

"What option did I have?"

"Why didn't you go to the police?"

"Would you have married me if you had known I was involved with illicit money? Would your father have taken me into the firm?"

He walked up to her and spoke quietly and intensely. "Let's get realistic. I am extremely successful in what I do. And that success has brought me a large number of wealthy clients. Like it or not, when I was starting up, that 'drug money,' as you call it, made all that possible."

Fiona looked at the agent's card in her hand. "Why was he here?" she asked. "Why is the IRS involved?"

"I have no idea. That's why I should go talk to Max."

"Max?"

"Max Bruschetti. Sal's brother. He's the real boss now. The capo."

"Capo!" said Fiona. She turned away and began to wander distractedly around the living room. "Jesus!" she cried. "The hospital presentation is tomorrow. What should I do about that? And Amanda's trip! Does this mean we'll have to cancel it? What about the schools? How do you think Deerfield is going to react when they find out? And the clubs? How long before they ask us to resign? We're going to be just like Valerie and Geoffrey, aren't we? Everything in the *Post* for all the world to see! Do you think you've been clever enough to make the front page?"

He took a step towards her.

"Don't touch me!" she said, her voice a whisper. "Just leave me alone. Get out of here! Go to your office! Meet with your capo! Do whatever you have to do to save your rotten, filthy skin."

With that she strode away and down the hallway.

Carter sank into one of the big armchairs. Fiona's reaction to the bad news was understandable, but he was surprised that she had become so hysterical. Well, he mused, it had finally happened. The showdown that would no doubt open the floodgates. And all because of that stupid meeting with Sal Bruschetti in that filthy Chinese restaurant in Queens and the smug way in which the Sicilian rambled on about crime paying.

"Yes, Sal, it may pay and pay well," Carter muttered to himself, "but you forgot to mention there's one hell of a downside."

He stooped down and picked up the agent's card from the floor where Fiona had dropped it. Grabbing a jacket from the closet he walked out to the elevator.

In the lobby the doorman asked helpfully, "You taking your car, Mr. Allinson, or should I call a cab?"

"That's okay, Sergio," he replied with a wan smile. "I need some air. I think I'm going to walk awhile."

59

With no idea how long it would be before Enzo left his building, Harry had driven to McDonald's and loaded up with enough food for ten unhealthy adults. A mailbox partially hid his car as he sat waiting, once again across the street. To keep himself awake he spoke aloud lines of the various Shakespearean parts he had done over the years. As he reached the point in Mercutio's Queen Mab speech where "her chariot is an empty hazelnut" the familiar car pulled up outside.

Enzo came hurrying out of the lobby and got in back. Harry started up the engine but sank way down in his seat until they had passed by and then followed as they went east on 62nd Street to the FDR and then south and through the tunnel to the depths of Brooklyn. As they drew up curbside he drove past. At the first corner he turned and slammed on the brakes. Jumping out, he ran back and was just in time to see Enzo going alone through the front door of a big warehouse.

Harry had two choices: wait and follow them when they left or stay and take a look around. He chose the latter as the old building was the perfect place to hide Lizzie and he could pick up Enzo's trail anytime. The sun was now just above the horizon. Prudence suggested that he wait for dark before setting off. At one point in his vigil Enzo reappeared and drove off. Harry calculated that he had been inside for about twenty minutes.

Taking deep breaths he crossed the road and headed down the alley at the side of the building. The walls here were sheer and every window was covered with thick wooden planking securely nailed in place. Without a sledgehammer or crowbar there was no way in. Harry went to the end and looked around the corner. Midway down the back wall was a fire escape. Moving closer he saw that the lower part of the ladder was hinged at the first floor and held up by a counterweight.

From several piles of junk and garbage he was able to dig a piece of old rope and a length of two-by-four. With the wood securely tied to the rope he flung it up over the ladder. It took three attempts before it took hold but then he was able to ease the contraption down. Mercifully for an old piece of machinery it made little sound.

The fire escape was old and rusty but still safe to climb. As he stepped off the last rung the counterweight dropped and the ladder creaked back up to its original position. A stairway now rose up above him. On each landing he found an emergency exit, but each one of them was locked up tight from the inside. Peering through a tiny crack in the top doorframe he could see only emptiness. It was frustrating but he kept going up and was rewarded to see a narrow walkway that ran along the center of the roofline. On one side was a straight drop to the roof of the fourth floor. Parallel to the walkway was a row of skylights. At some time they had been covered in black paint, but much of this was now peeling away. Some were now lit from below.

With extreme caution he crawled out a few feet and looked down through the first dirty pane. The space below looked empty and unused but was a possible place where he might gain access to the building. Time and weather had reduced the putty that held the glass to brittle pieces that could be easily pried loose.

"I need supplies," he muttered to himself.

On the bottom flight of the fire escape he rode down to the alley and secured the ladder with the rope. Back at his car he opened the trunk, grabbed the largest of his drill bits and put it in his pant pocket. Hanging the tire iron on his belt, he retrieved the flashlight from the glove compartment, locked the doors and sprinted back into the alley. Before he climbed up he freed the rope and coiled it over his shoulders.

Entry to the rooms was from the one corridor. Harry decided to check the last room first. Very gingerly he crawled along to the far end of the walkway. Below was an office with a series of surveillance monitors above a desk. A desk lamp illuminated a man sitting there working at a computer.

Spinning around on his stomach, Harry edged his way over to an adjoining pane of glass and peered down through a crack in the paint. The faint nasal twang of Asian music could now be heard.

Below in the dark he could make out an enormous machine. On the front control panel several LED lights showed that it was powered and ready to be switched on. Harry had no idea what it was used for.

The next two rooms had been knocked together to form one large area. One door had been removed and the entrance boarded over. The space was filled with refectory tables that were packed tightly together to create an extensive worktop. On these were nine digital projectors that sent their images to what looked like white bedsheets tacked to the walls. Interspersed between these were a series of laptop computers. Everything was connected by a forest of wires that seemed to terminate at two servers in the corner of the room.

There were two men below. In complete contrast, one was small in stature and wore a white shirt. He sat to one side doing nothing. The other man was huge and had very black hair. He was watching the code that scrolled down on one of the sheets. In his hand was a yellow lined pad where he made an occasional note.

Harry pulled himself back and sat up in the middle of the walkway. Directly below him was clearly an important part of the Bruschetti organization. One they wouldn't want to lose. Perhaps he could find a way of messing it up? But right now his assignment was to find Lizzie. The building had to be searched. The only way inside that he could see was down through the first room at the far end of the walkway.

Nothing ventured, nothing gained. The wood beneath him creaked as he went back to the first skylight. Taking out the big drill bit he chipped off the putty from three sides, eased the tire iron under glass and pried it up. With it wedged he managed to get his fingers underneath the edge. But as he began to lift it up the pane started to slip as the fourth side gave way. Harry tried frantically to hold on but he had thoroughly underestimated the weight. The thick piece of glass slid from his grasp and slithered over the edge. With a loud crash it shattered on the sidewalk.

Harry prayed for a full minute. First that no one was walking below and second that the two men beneath him were hard of hearing. His prayers were answered. There were no shouts, cries or moans and nobody came out to investigate.

With the flashlight tucked into his waistband he secured one end of the rope to the ironwork and, easing his legs over the edge, slowly slid down until his feet touched the floor.

Except for a metal folding chair and an old empty filing cabinet the space was empty. Harry tried the door handle. It was not locked so he carefully opened it. It was fortuitous that he didn't open it fully as the man at the end came out of his office at that moment and went into the room with the bedsheets.

Harry heard the door close.

Now all three men were in the same room. If he could keep them there, he could do a fast search for Lizzie without interruption. Presumably all the doors had the same hardware. The metal chair would certainly be sturdy enough to act as a wedge.

Harry ran fast down the passageway and gently pushed the back of the chair under the brass knob of the door, pressing the ends of metal legs firmly into the floor boards. Tiptoeing away, he took out his flashlight and headed swiftly but cautiously down the stairs.

The floor below was an empty void. On the second floor were the dusty remains of cubicle partitions. Scattered everywhere were discarded folders and papers. The ground floor contained several large rooms, all of them clean and filled with an assortment of boxes stacked from floor to ceiling. Harry opened one up and pulled out a new CD. With overt sexual graphics it had the descriptive title of *Penetentiary Penetration*. Harry threw the disk in the box and headed for the basement.

Like the top floor, this was divided into small rooms. Directly opposite the stairs were two toilets. Harry went into the one marked **MEN**. Inside was nothing of significance until he checked the floor with the flashlight. By his left foot were four cigarette butts. When he leaned over to take a closer look he saw that each of the butts had a trace of mauve lipstick. Lizzie had

been there. But how long ago? There was no sign or scratch on
the tiles to give him a clue.

The fact that Lizzie was being held captive by a bunch of
thugs made him angry and that produced an even stronger desire to go on the offensive. If he could chase the men upstairs
out, he could use the same tactic and follow one of them. But
how to do that? Best thing would be to mess up the fancy computer setup on the top floor. This was kept running by a constant flow of electricity. With so much wattage being used in an
abandoned warehouse it was a wonder that Con Edison hadn't
thought it strange and made inquiries.

It was only when Harry looked in the little room at the end
of the passageway that the answer to that was found. A shiny
thick black cable had been skillfully welded into the supply before it reached the meters. All electricity coming in was unre-
corded. Harry traced the cable and saw that it ran up the side
of the stairs. Cutting it would be the best way to cause mischief.
But how?

Searching around, he came across two red extinguishers
hanging on the wall with a fire axe in a glass-fronted case. The
axe could definitely be used to cut the cable. But if he did that
there was a distinct possibility he would be electrocuted. Insu-
lation was required. And fast. It wouldn't be much longer until
someone tried to get out through the door upstairs.

From one of the rooms he brought a box of nudie magazines
and made two piles on either side of a section of the cable that
lay flat on the floor. Smashing the glass with his elbow, he seized
the axe and used it to splinter the wooden case. Taking a length
of the wood, he wedged the blade between the magazines with
the sharp side down and laid the board on top. Picking up the
heavier of the two extinguishers he crashed it down as hard as
he could on the board above the axe. The force of the blow went
from the steel cylinder through the board and into the axe.

Harry was totally unprepared for what resulted from his
Rube Goldberg efforts. There was a huge flash and sparks flew

everywhere. A fire crackled and hissed where the blade had partially penetrated the cable. Smoke billowed up and the lights went out. Harry flung down the extinguisher and ran up the stairs.

As he headed for the front door he heard shouts and sounds of banging as the three men above found themselves in the dark with the door wedged shut.

Out in the street he flew as fast as he could to his car and drove off. It wasn't until he was three blocks away that he remembered to put on his lights. As he approached the Brooklyn-Battery Tunnel several fire engines passed him going in the opposite direction.

A little while later, on the radio of the Ford Escape the 1010 WINS announcer reported a four-alarm fire at an abandoned warehouse in Brooklyn that had involved the entire block. There were no reports of any fatalities or injuries.

Harry swallowed. He knew better. He had probably just killed three men.

60.

Walker, Martin, Pomeranz and Fisher was closed for the day. Carter crossed the deserted lobby and took the elevator up to his floor. For a while he stood by the window and looked down at the street. Below was a world in turmoil. Everything in his life had changed in less than an hour. If only he had been able to lie to Fiona, to come up with a story to explain the visit from the IRS. But now that was all wishful thinking.

In an odd way after so many years of deceit it had been a relief to come clean. His marriage was over as she was not one to forgive. Her sense of what was appropriate far outweighed any love or affection that she might still feel for him. Divorce was inevitable. Amanda and James would be devastated but were young enough to recover. Carter's future relationship with them would entirely depend on what their mother told them. Charles and Katherine Walker were another matter.

That was his private life. Professionally, he doubted anything would come from the agent's visit. It was a fact that he had established virtual companies to hide large sums of cash. But all of these had been closed up and archived ages ago. Back in the early years when he had accepted money from Sal and Max, Carter had never been told the source. If the need arose, he could plead ignorance.

But forewarned is forearmed. Now he had come to the office to find how the IRS had tied him to the Bruschettis. What was the link? Carter had a vague idea that Enzo owned a boat that he kept on the Hudson. Could that be how the Feds made the connection? Once more he opened the safe and took out several boxes, stacking them by his desk.

With his jacket off he sat down and year by year, month by month, day by day, file by file he examined every page, memo and note. When he was done, he leaned back in his chair, completely baffled.

Where else could he look? Somewhere beyond his office? Each of his closest associates and their assistants had their own systems. So did Joan Hutchins. She had sat outside his door from the day he had arrived at the firm. Carter knew that his assistant kept her records in three cabinets lined up behind her desk and the keys for these were kept in a coffee mug where she dropped them every night before she left. He retrieved them and unlocked the first cabinet, pulled out the top drawer and located the B section. There was nothing there. Fingering through to the Gs, he came across a file marked "Gazelle." This was extremely odd.

Back in his office he laid the file on his desk and opened it up.

Inside were two sheets of paper. A certificate of registration listing the owner of the *Gazelle* as the Martinson Metal Recycling Company.

Carter turned to the second page.

This was a handwritten note written by Joan. For some reason she had penciled in the directors of the company. Salvatore and Enzo Bruschetti. Carter stood transfixed. He remembered setting up the Martinson Metal Recycling Company but had absolutely no recollection of doing anything about any boat. There was certainly no way he had ever personally arranged for it to be registered.

Perhaps Joan had opened the mail when it arrived and taken it upon herself to complete the forms. Or could he in a moment of idiocy have allowed her to do it?

Joan would be the only person to have seen this second page. There was no reason for anyone other than her to look at it. The IRS must have procured the Bruschetti name from somewhere else. But where? He needed an answer. And fast. Enzo was the obvious start. A call and a meeting might give him a clue.

If he was heading into their territory it would be a good idea to have a transcript of any conversations. From his desk he took out an Olympus voice recorder and slipped it into his shirt pocket. As he did, he noticed the little metal box in the drawer that contained his Beretta 3032 Tomcat. The little titanium pistol had been acquired soon after he made the acquaintance of Sal and Max. The questionable individual who had sold him the weapon for one thousand dollars in cash had given him a piece of advice.

"If you draw this little baby, you had better be prepared to kill. Otherwise leave the sucker in your pants."

Carter took the little pistol out and held it in his hand.

What the hell, he thought.

Checking the safety, he slipped it into his pocket.

61

The basement below the dining room at Mazaras was once the scene of many wild parties. Now it was a cluttered, untidy maze. In their younger days the brothers had made part of it into a gaming room with a big octagonal poker table and a shiny mahogany bar with six high-backed stools. In the back wall they had a walk-in vault installed to store the cash earned from every nefarious job.

Max and Enzo grew older. Sal spent more time with his family and the space was hardly used. Storage for the restaurant became a premium. First refrigeration was moved down. Metal shelves were erected to store cans and dry goods. The poker table was piled with outdated menus, phased-out flatware and bundles of faded linens. The shiny bar surface became a dump for plastic bags full of discarded kitchen paraphernalia. Boxes were stacked everywhere and New York dust descended on them like a shroud.

Max came down the stairs and switched on the lights. Unlocking the bathroom door he found the girl seated on the toilet. One shoe lay on the floor and she was massaging her foot. She blinked and gave a sniff.

"Have you any idea what a fucking mess your friend Harry caused before he decided to jump?" Max asked, throwing the door wide.

Her answer was a meaningful moan.

"Shut up!" said Max. "Where's the money?"

"What money?" she replied, picking up her shoe.

"Harry Murphy called earlier and told us he had a suitcase of cash. Money that belonged to me. He said he wanted to give it back. Sounded like he was crazy."

She looked puzzled. "Crazy? Harry? Money? I don't have the faintest idea what you're talking about. I told you. He was a ticket that's all. A chance to come here for free and have a good time."

She looked up at Max and shook her head from side to side. "I don't know nothing about Harry. I don't know nothing about any money. I don't know who you are or why you've got me locked up like this. What is it with you? Some kind of fetish keeping people in toilets? At least this one works!" To prove her point, she flushed it.

Max turned away. There was something unusually attractive about this girl. Under the frailty was a toughness that was appealing. Taking her by the arm he pushed her over to a chair at the poker table.

"You said you work for a travel company?" he asked.

"Yeah," she replied, and put her shoe back on.

As she straightened up Max took her purse from her shoulder and emptied out the contents. He glanced at her passport and then carefully examined everything else. Finally he opened a long business envelope and extracted a sheet of typewritten paper. "'Honeybee Travel,'" he read. "Is that you?"

"Yeah," she replied, and gave another sniff.

Glancing at his watch, he asked, "What time they open?"

"What?" she asked.

"Honeybee," he said, and pointed at the paper. "Are they open now?"

"My boss lives over the shop. He answers the phone all hours. Keeps his clients happy that way."

Max pulled a phone out from his pocket and dialed the number on the letter heading. "Hi there," he said. "I'm trying to locate a friend of mine. I understand she works for you." He covered the mouthpiece. "What do they call you?" he asked.

"Elizabeth." She pouted. "Elizabeth Carswell."

His hand dropped. "Her name is Elizabeth. Yes. Oh. It's 'Lizzie.' I see. That's right. But she still works for you? I see. No, no message. I'll call when she's back. Yeah, sometime next week."

The girl called Lizzie gave him a defiant stare as he rang off.

"Satisfied?" she said.

"Is that your boss?"

"Yes," she replied. "Sort of."

"About your friend Murphy," he said.

"I told you he was not my friend. I knew as much about him as I do about you."

"But you came over together?"

"Yes."

"What did you talk about on the flight over?"

"I told him what I did. He told me about his work. Acting and all that."

"Like what?"

"That he did a movie with Tom Cruise but they never worked together. That he did work on the stage and on the TV. And he reads them books people listen to in their cars."

"Yeah?"

"Yeah."

"Nothing else?"

"No. Just small talk. Look, what's going on? What is this place and why am I here? And how come I got mixed up in your affairs? What sort of business is it may I ask?"

Max came back over and looked straight down at her. "How come an attractive girl like you isn't married? You got a boyfriend?"

"No, not right now."

"How come?"

"Too busy I suppose." She folded her arms. "When you said Harry drowned did that mean you killed him?"

"No. He jumped off my brother's boat."

"Why'd he do that?"

"He was scared."

"So scared that he jumped?"

"Yes."

"So you killed him!"

"If you like."

For a moment there was silence.

"What do you do when you're not working?" Max asked.

"Are you coming on to me?" said Lizzie.

Max paused. Lizzie's frankness and candor was new to him.

"Maybe. Answer my question."

"I run a lot. In cross-country races. Track meets. And I go to the cinema. Listen to music. All the usual sort of things."

"You have a good life."

"Yes."

Lizzie started to put her belongings back in her purse.

"Yet you don't have a regular boyfriend. That surprises me."

She held up her lipstick. "Do you mind?" she asked.

Max shook his head and watched patiently as she painted her lips a weird shade of purple. "If all you came for was a good time, I could give you that."

"What?"

"I could give you a good time," he repeated.

"For what in return?" she asked, and blotted her lips on a Kleenex.

"Whatever you want," Max said lightly. "Just take it as it comes. When did you last eat?"

"What makes you think I'm that sort of girl?"

Max laughed. "Every girl is that sort of girl. Just depends on the price."

"Yeah? You sound as if you've had a lot of experience."

"You could say that."

"To answer your question, it was lunch yesterday."

"You want something to eat?"

"What exactly do you do, Max? When you're not abducting and killing?"

"How do you know my name?"

"Your friend called you Max. Back in that cellar. I take it what you do ain't legal."

"Would it bother you if it wasn't?"

"No. Not really. I mean, why should it? If I was back home it might. But being here makes it all kind of unreal, if you know what I mean."

"No, I don't. Tell me."

"I've been to the films, Max! I watch the telly! I've seen what life is like in America. Especially New York and all the Mafia and all that. I mean it's all pretty wild, isn't it? Look what's happened to me and I've only been here a couple of days!"

"Do you watch much porn?"

"No, not much. I had a boyfriend once that liked it, but it never did much for me. All the people was so unattractive and all pale and pimply. Why do you ask?"

"That's one of our businesses. Sex tapes, magazines, CDs and the like. We have some pretty hot stuff with some pretty good-looking studs and chicks."

"Doing what?" she said wryly.

"You name it, we got it."

"Just people humpin'?"

"Not at all. We market a quality product. You'd be surprised at the difference."

"Do your customers know the difference?"

"Many of them do. They keep on ordering. At least they used to. Things are slack right now."

"That's a poor choice of words, if I may say so."

Max looked her for a moment and then asked, "So what's it to be? You want to come upstairs and eat or shall I put you back in there until we figure out what to do with you?"

"Bit of a Hobson's choice."

"What the fuck is that?"

She smiled broadly, finished filling her purse and threw it over her shoulder. "I can see I'm going to have to teach you a few things."

"Come on," he said, heading out.

Upstairs, Max led the way through the dining room into a brightly lit kitchen. A short, dark-haired man with a mustache was wiping down the steel counters. Max hung up his jacket on a row of hooks and rolled up his sleeves.

"*Ciao, Nando. Buona sera,*" said Max. "*Pochi clienti stasera?*"

"*Sì,*" replied the other. "*Nessuno dopo le nove e un quarto. Maurizio ha mandato tutti a casa. Posso preparare qualcosa per lei e la signora?*"

"*No grazie. Lo faccio io.*"

Nando took off his soiled whites and threw them with the towels into a laundry basket in the corner. Picking up his cap and coat, he wished them good night. The front door was unlocked, opened, closed and relocked.

Max took an apron from a pile of clean linen and pulled it over his head. "I hope you still eat beef," he said. "I'm no chef but I can do steaks."

"Sure," she said. "Sounds great."

The gas popped when it was lit and the jets burned blue beneath a big iron grill.

"What is this place?" she asked. "Where is everybody?"

"It's called Mazaras," he replied. "It's named after the house in Sicily where my family used to live. A little village called Mazzarone. My chef and his staff mostly come from Calabria. Right now they're all on their way home or to their favorite bars getting drunk."

"Your chef? You own all this?"

"Yes," replied Max, opening the door to a large icebox where he selected two thick porterhouse steaks.

"I'm impressed," she said with a smile.

Max brushed them with olive oil, covered them with freshly ground black pepper, gave them a shake of sea salt and dropped them with a sizzle on the grill. A small black skillet was oiled and set on the grill. Into it went thick slices of onion.

A delicious aroma rose as Max opened an icebox and pulled out a bag of washed arugula leaves and a bowl of cherry tomatoes. From the overhead rack he took down two big white plates

and loaded them with the green leaves. A razor-sharp knife
made short work of slicing the tomatoes. Checking his watch,
he lowered the flame slightly.

Max watched the meat. Lizzie watched Max. Then she remembered Harry and a wave of guilt swept through her body.

"Are you cold?" said Max.

"No," she replied. "Why do you ask?"

"You were shivering. We can turn off the air-conditioning."

"No thanks. I'm fine."

"Have some wine. That'll fix you up."

"That'd be great," she replied.

Max unlocked a cupboard, took out a bottle of Sagrantino
di Montefalco and swiftly pulled out the cork, using a device
on the wall.

"You eat here a lot?" asked Lizzie.

"All of the time. Except when I'm at home." He turned off
the gas, scooped the steaks onto the plates and gave each a fresh
grind of pepper. "Bring the bottle," he said, and picked up the
plates. Setting them down on a table in the dining room, he lit
the candles and poured out the wine.

"Blimey," she said wryly as she sat down. "Soft lights, fancy
wine, now all we need is the sexy music . . ."

Max walked over and reached behind a curtain. Soft music
came through invisible speakers. Raising his glass, he said somewhat ironically, *"Santé!"*

"Bottoms up!" she replied, and they both drank. The wine
was smooth and sexy. With her steak knife she cut off a piece
of meat and popped it into her mouth. "If you got your own restaurant, how come you stay in such good shape?"

"I worry a lot," he retorted.

"What about?"

"You ever run a business?"

"Only worked in one."

"You'd be amazed at what you gotta do every day. Decisions

to make. People coming to you for advice. There's always something and every little thing adds up and raises your blood pressure."

Lizzie scooped up some onions. "Who do you talk to at the end of the day? Is there a Mrs. Max waiting for you?"

Her captor's hands stopped moving imperceptibly. His face tensed and then relaxed. "Now there's a question," he replied.

"Does it have an answer?" she persisted.

"Not yet, no."

"Tried it before, have you? Or just not met the right girl?"

"How's the meat?" he said abruptly.

"Fine, thanks," she answered, and then added with a grin, "thick and juicy. Just the way I like it." Then she asked, "Where's home?"

"New Jersey." A small dimple appeared in his left cheek as he too smiled. "You're an inquisitive little fucker, aren't you?"

"I'm having a hard time figuring you out. You're not what I expect when it comes to villainy. And I'm curious about you," she said, and took a drink. "You own the whole of this building?"

"Yes."

"What's all them doors up there?"

"What?"

"When I come in earlier we walked past a bunch of doors with names on them, like Paris, Rome, Berlin."

"Which would you choose?" he asked, and poured more wine into her glass.

"Depends what for," she answered. "Art and all that stuff I'd pick Paris. For nightlife I suppose I'd go to Berlin. For food there would be no contest; I'd go to Rome."

For a moment she stared hard at him.

"You know Max, you're the first man I've met that could do more in the kitchen than boil water."

"Thank you. What about your old man?"

"My dad?"

Max nodded.

"I never ever saw him in the kitchen."

"How come?"

Lizzie waited for several seconds before answering.

"Dad was in the travel industry. In fact, he started Honey-bee. But just when the business was showing a profit he was killed in a car crash. I never really knew him. Sad, really. What was your old man like?"

"Old-school. Strict. Spoke Sicilian most of the time. Gener-ous to a fault. Started every day with a shot of *Grappa* and died of old age."

Dinner was over and Max stood up. "Come on," he said ami-ably, and blew out the candles. "Time for the European tour."

They made their way back up the stairs. Max opened the door marked Berlin and ushered her inside. The theme was dis-tinctly Teutonic, catering to the leather and chain crowd. In the center was a raised bed-like platform covered in shiny black rub-ber. On three sides hung the paraphernalia of sadomasochism and bondage. The fourth wall and the ceiling were both mirrored. The floor was covered with the same red carpet as the hallway. The lighting was strategically placed bare red bulbs.

"I see," she said. "Thirties Berlin, storm troopers, swastikas, Marlene Dietrich with black stockings and red lips."

His move caught her completely off guard. Putting his hands on her shoulders, he flipped her onto the platform. Her purse dropped to the floor. Before she could object or cry out he had slipped her wrists into restraints at the top corners. Tearing off her skirt and panties, he equally swiftly secured her ankles as well. In a matter of seconds Lizzie was spread-eagled on her back and naked from the waist down. Her eyes closed as her whole body screamed. Nakedness meant nothing. The threat of whipping meant nothing. It was the terrifying feeling of being unable to move. Tugging helplessly at the restraints she began to perspire as she rolled from side to side.

"All right, Miss Lizzie Carswell or whoever the fuck you are," he said as he walked slowly around the room, "it's time to cut out the bullshit."

"I've told you," she sobbed. "I met him in a coffee shop. He asked me . . ."

Something stroked her foot and slid up the inside of her thigh. Max had a leather whip in his hand that went up one side and down the other three times, each time stroking her sex. Dropping the whip to the floor, he kicked off his shoes and pulled off his shirt and pants. His erection throbbed up and down to the beat of his pulse. Lizzie's heart was pounding twice as fast as usual as he knelt on the black rubber between her feet, bent down and gently licked his way up and down the same route as the whip handle. Lizzie could feel his warm breath.

For a while she writhed and struggled, but then warm sensations started to run through her body and she tried desperately not to respond. But to her great surprise the restraints holding her arms and legs no longer terrified her but began to heighten what were now waves of pleasure.

With his hands on either side of her shoulders Max slid into her and then put his weight on her whole body.

"Move with me," he said softly into her ear.

The Sicilian was an expert not only with his hands and mouth but also with every fiber of his body. For a long time he moved, constantly changing the strength, depth and rhythm. At first, Detective Elizabeth Carswell clenched her fists and tried to resist, but the four inches of soft foam padding beneath the rubber sheet encouraged her to move with him.

Just the way he asked.

When Enzo's phone rang, he was very surprised to find who was on the other end.

"Enzo, I'm sorry," said Carter, "but I need some information that you may be able to provide. We need to meet."

"Where?" Enzo asked.

"Somewhere safe. Somewhere quiet. What about the club?"

"Mazaras? Sure. When?"

"Half an hour. I'll meet you there in thirty minutes." And he rang off.

In the early years, Enzo had accepted his place beneath Sal and Max and had done what they asked without question. Subterfuge was alien to his nature, as he felt it led to unintended and awkward complications. As a result he was never able to develop an honest or lasting relationship with anyone.

Of the three brothers he was certainly the most industrious, putting in long hours to keep the records up-to-date and to make sure that everything owed was collected. It was he who'd found and hired Rocco. It was he who kept the books in a coded language to which only he had the key.

When Sal brought in Carter Allinson as their financial advisor, more than half of Enzo's smooth-running arrangements were abandoned and he found himself with time on his hands. Not one to complain, he began to read. At first he chose recreational fiction, but this soon paled and he turned to broader subjects. Through his books he traveled and researched the world without leaving his living room. Cradled in the cushions on his sofa he visited the Prado, learned how to fly a plane, use a centrifuge and cook a seven-course dinner for visiting dignitaries. When Kindle came along he tried the electronic page briefly but found holding a real book in his hands more satisfying.

Five years later *The World's Greatest Yachts* gave him the thought that he should bring some light and air into his monastic existence. On an uncharacteristic whim he drove to New Jersey and bought the *Gazelle*.

Now she was on the bottom of the fucking Hudson.

Enzo took out a phone and made two calls. One telling Benny to bring the car around fast. The other to his brother.

63

At five thirty in the afternoon, Sal Bruschetti had taken a Viagra, washing it down with a glass of Frascati. After a light supper Furella took full advantage of his chemically encouraged vigor. After a soapy shower together they climbed back into the rumpled sheets and entwined in each other's arms they drifted off to sleep. Neither heard the first three rings of the cellphone, but on the fourth Furella shook herself awake and retrieved it from Sal's jacket.

"Oh Enzo! It's you," she said, doing her best to sound normal. "You want Sal? Hold on. I'll go get him." She prodded her husband's shoulder until he returned to the land of the living.

It's your brother, she mouthed.

"What? Who? Max?"

Furella shook her head. Pulling himself up against the headboard, Sal took the phone. After a couple of expressive grunts he said, "Mazaras. Okay. On my way."

As he dressed, Furella went down to the kitchen and filled up his travel mug with decaf. At the front door she buttoned up his cardigan.

"Whatever it is," she said, "we can handle it. Call me if you need to talk. I'll be here."

He leaned over and kissed her on the forehead. "Thanks, babe."

The Cadillac was parked out front in anticipation of a nine o'clock foursome. Moving his clubs from the backseat to the trunk, he squeezed his belly in behind the wheel and drove off.

64

The portrayal of killing and violence is an accepted part of motion pictures and television. Over the years Harry had participated in his share. But what he had just done at the warehouse in Brooklyn was not the product of a writer's imagination. It was the real thing. The reality show to end all reality shows.

In preparation for another long vigil Harry stopped at an all-night deli and grabbed a tuna sandwich, a banana, a large bottle of Diet Coke and four tubes of Pringles. Parking directly across from the entrance to the apartment building, he ate potato chips and ruminated whether it was time to throw in the towel and head for the Witness Protection Program. Opening the Diet Coke, he took a long drink. As he did, his quarry came flying out of the apartment and caught him by surprise. The Town Car barely stopped at the curb. Enzo jumped into the passenger seat and they drove off fast.

Harry threw the Pringles over his shoulder, pushed the Diet Coke into the cupholder and set off in pursuit. He had to use all his driving skills to keep the other car in sight as the driver ahead weaved in and out of the traffic. The trip ended in Lower Manhattan on a side street where Harry's quarry drove up a ramp and disappeared from view. Minutes later a cab pulled up and a tall individual in a gray suit climbed out and stood to one side as a Cadillac DeVille swung around and up the same ramp.

The Chiefs were gathering for a Pow-Wow.

Sal pulled up and parked. As he got out of the car, Carter came up the ramp.

"I asked to talk to you alone, so how come everyone's here?" he asked Enzo, who was waiting at the door.

"When there's trouble we all work together, my friend."

"What makes you think there's trouble?"

"You," said Enzo, and he pressed the buttons on the keypad. The three men trooped inside and down the stairs. In the dining room Nino was sitting alone at a table reading *La Settimana Enigmistica,* sipping a Peroni and listening to a Neapolitan CD on the speaker system.

"Ciao, Nino. Max here?" said Sal.

Nino pointed to the ceiling and made a phallic gesture. Enzo turned and ran back up the stairs.

Max's buttocks rose rhythmically up and down atop a spread-eagled girl who was moaning loudly. Several seconds passed before either noticed the intrusion. Then the girl screamed and Max almost fell off the platform, letting out a stream of Italian invectives.

Max slipped on his pants, shirt and shoes. "Let's go," he said brusquely.

"What about . . . ?" Enzo pointed at the prostrate girl.

"Fuck her," said Max. "She's not going anywhere. Who's here?"

"Everyone. Carter wants to talk. Seems there's a problem."

Four tables had been pushed together in the far corner of the dining room. Sal sat at the head unwrapping a cigar. Benny had joined them and was at a table by the entrance to the kitchen where Nino and Rocco were now busy preparing coffee.

Max sat next to his brother and motioned Carter to sit down. "So what's up?" he asked. "Why the panic?"

Carter said abruptly, "Can we lose the damn music?"

"Sure," replied Max, and pointed to the curtain.

Carter pushed aside the fabric and switched off the music system. "The Feds have been to my apartment. Asked me if I knew you guys. The agent used your name . . ."

The phone on the reservation desk started to ring. Carter walked over and picked it up. "Yes!" he said impatiently. "Yes, it is, but it's late. We're closed. What? Oh. Yes, yes, he's here." He looked over at Sal. "It's your wife."

Sal ambled over and took the phone as Rocco came in with mugs on a tray. Nino followed him with the coffeepot and then went back into the kitchen.

"Yeah, babe?" said Sal.

An uneasy tension filled the room as Carter listened. It was odd for Furella to call. Sal replaced the receiver and walked back to his seat.

"Well?" said Carter and Max in unison.

"Peggio di così non si può" was the enigmatic reply. He looked at Max. "The warehouse just burned to the ground. Vic called to tell his mama that he and Toshi got out, but Blackthorn is dead."

"What?" said Max.

"Jack Blackthorn is dead. Furella's in a cab on her way here."

"Why are they coming here?" asked Carter.

"She didn't say. Just said don't do nothing until she gets here."

"For Christ's sake!" exclaimed Carter.

"Take it easy," said Sal. "She means well."

Max looked over at Enzo. "You told us Murphy drowned."

"He did," said Enzo. "There's no way he could have made it to shore. It has to be an accident."

"Don't be so stupid!" growled Sal. "First Villiers is warned, then your boat sinks and now this fucking fire."

"You think . . . ?" said Enzo.

"I don't think; I know. When you heard about the *Gazelle,* what did you do?"

"Got in the car and went to the Marina."

"Anybody follow you?"

"I didn't look," said Enzo.

"Anyone follow you here tonight?"

There was a momentary pause. Rocco moved towards the front door.

"No!" said Enzo, standing up. "I know what the bastard looks like."

"We'll all go," said Max. "But if he's out there I want him back in here unharmed. Understood? I want him in one piece. I need some answers."

66

It was time for Harry to call the Feds. With so many people inside the building, the odds were no longer in his favor. Not that they ever were. He would just take a quick look around and then call for reinforcements.

Climbing out of the car, he crossed the street and went up the ramp. At the top was a parking garage. A Cadillac and a couple of other cars were at the far end. Close to them was a fire door. There was no other way in or out.

He paced out the distance from the door to the right-hand wall. Forty-eight steps. He ran down the ramp and along to the corner of the street. He marched off forty-eight paces and found himself at the door of an Italian restaurant. A faded wooden sign overhead read: Mazaras. It seemed closed, but the lights were on inside. The windows were covered with opaque curtains. Harry pressed his ear against the glass but could hear nothing.

A little farther along the sidewalk was a hardware store. At one side of the doorway was a pay phone. Harry walked over and pulled out Luigi's card. He dialed the operator to call collect, but before he got an answer, four men came out of the restaurant. Two went out into the center of the roadway. One went to the left and the other to the right. A third waited at the curb. Behind him stood the man in the gray suit in the shadow of the doorway.

It's amazing how fast the human brain can process information. It would only be seconds before one of them spotted him. To his right was a brightly lit street with trucks, cars and pedestrians. To his left the cross street was dark and with no sign of life. The man heading to the left was trim. The one heading right was heavier and probably slower on his feet. Harry figured his best chance was to outrun the heavy guy and take his chances in the lights.

Fear gave him speed and he was able to get a head start before being spotted. A sudden squealing of brakes slowed him down as a van swerved to avoid hitting him. This maneuver caused two cars to skid to a stop. The drivers leaned out and screamed obscenities at each other. A vacant taxi drove past, but Harry's pursuer was too close to give him time to get in.

As he ran, he tired. With his stride shortening and his breathing becoming labored Harry could hear the heavyset man gaining ground and relentlessly closing the gap. No matter how many times Harry changed direction, the bastard doggedly followed. When only a few yards separated them the footsteps stopped and Harry heard a loud strangled gasp. Glancing over his shoulder, he saw the man stumble, lean against the wall and clutch his chest in a huge effort to breathe.

It is also amazing how idiotic the human mind can be upon occasion. Harry's first instinct was to go back and help. Reason was soon restored when he remembered that this was someone intent on doing him serious harm. It would be wiser for him to pray the man drop dead.

Free from pursuit, Harry dashed off around the first corner and ran headlong into the man who was thin and fit. The collision sent both of them sprawling to the ground. Seconds later a hard blow to the side of Harry's head knocked him senseless.

67

When he began to regain consciousness Harry knew that his left jaw and cheek had taken most of the damage. He also knew that his arms were securely bound to a chair, one of many arranged around tables. Harry kept very still with his eyes almost shut but saw that each table was neatly laid with white cloths, cutlery, glasses and little vases of flowers. Nobody was near him. No one had noticed he had regained consciousness. The effect was surreal. Film noir.

The individual who had suffered the apparent heart attack sat slouched at the entrance to the kitchen with his face in the shadows. A slim woman with red hair held a wet towel to his forehead. Near to them was a pudgy individual chewing on a cigar butt. Beside him was Enzo Bruschetti, now tieless. The man who had collided with Harry leaned against a far wall. It was Enzo's driver.

The gray suit came in from the kitchen with a glass of water and handed it to the man in the chair. Then he spoke to Enzo.

"What exactly are we waiting for?"

"We are waiting until Furella gets here," growled the man with the cigar. "Why don't you just do what Enzo says and sit yourself down?"

"I don't see where she . . ."

"Shut up, Carter!" said the redhead. "Give us a break. At least give Max time to get his breath back."

So this was the infamous Max.

Carter sat down but continued to fidget. For a long time nobody moved. There was a tap on the front door. Enzo got up and went out into the hall. The door opened and closed. A short woman with strong features and very dark hair came in, pulling a scarf from her head. She glanced around the room and saw Harry. She came over and stood looking down at him.

"Who is this, Sal?"

The man with the cigar answered. "That's Murphy. We just caught him outside."

She nodded and walked over to the man in the chair. "I know how you feel about my being here, Max, but from what I gather we don't have the luxury of time."

"How much does Furella know?" asked Carter.

"She knows everything I do," said Sal.

"Dear God!" Carter muttered.

Furella looked over at him. "Let me make one thing perfectly clear to you, Mister Allinson, Sal and I talk about everything. In private. Just the two of us. He tells me what he thinks. I give him my opinion. He is at liberty to use or reject what I suggest."

Carter ignored her and turned to Enzo. "Listen, I came here to talk to you. Why don't we . . . ?"

Furella's eyes flared. "My son just managed to escape from a fire!"

"What the hell has that to do with me?" said Carter. "I had nothing to do with any of . . ."

"Basta così," said Max coming into the light, and Harry finally got to look at his nemesis. He was surprised to see that Max was nothing like the image he had formed in his mind. "Just get on with it, Carter," he was saying. "Why did you call Enzo?"

"An IRS agent came to the apartment to ask me about the *Gazelle*. Name of Luigi Rienzi. I told him I kept all my files at the office. I said I'd get back to him tomorrow. He gave me his card and left. As he was getting in the elevator he asked me if I knew anyone called 'Bruschetti.' I'm pretty sure he did it to see my reaction. I tried to keep calm. I told him no, but if he's any good, he knows I'm lying."

"What did you do then?" asked Enzo.

"I went to the office . . ." He paused.

"And?" said the other pointedly.

"We made a mistake."

"We?"

"My assistant registered the boat to one of our dummy companies but made the mistake of putting down my firm as the contact address. When the boat sank, the Feds checked the registration. I still have no idea how or where they came up with 'Bruschetti.'"

There was a long and very pregnant pause.

Harry watched in fascination as each of this strange cast of characters tried to figure out how this news would affect their lives. By the expressions on their faces none envisioned a rosy future.

Max spoke first. "Son of a bitch . . ." he said quietly.

Carter wheeled around and stared at him. It was clear to Harry that Gray Suit was now well out of his depth. His forehead had developed a wet shine and his hands were beginning to tremble. "So what do we do, Max?" he was asking pointedly.

"Give it a rest, Carter," said Sal.

"Are you all aware," Carter spoke with a great deal of irony, "I have a wife and kids? What you don't know is that I've lied to them for years. Can you believe it? I've lied to my kids! Ever since they were old enough to hear my voice."

"You know your problem, Carter?" said Furella. "You're hung up on good and bad. Right and wrong. You always have been. You should face the fact that you're human like the rest of us."

Carter said vehemently, "Are you telling me I deserve what I got?"

"Furella's right," said Sal. "You got problems just like us. You gotta learn to take it easy, give it time—"

"Take it easy, Sal?" The decibel level was rising. "I am about to lose everything I've worked for. I am no doubt going to prison. For how long, I wonder? Ten, fifteen, twenty years?"

"Hey Carter," said Enzo, "get yourself a drink. This is no time to lose it."

"If I remember right," said Sal, trying to use reason, "you brought all this on yourself."

Carter banged on a table. "That was way back in college for God's sake!"

"You supplied half the fucking campus!"

"You're right, Sal, when I was going through some of the happiest times of my life! But then I had to go and get myself involved with you. Wasn't so great after that."

"Ma che cazzo, e falla finita!" said Max. "Give it a break."

"I admit I was stupid back then," Carter persisted. "But shouldn't the punishment fit the crime?"

"You came to us," Max said patiently. "I made you an offer and you accepted."

"You threatened to feed me to a pack of dogs!"

"You gave up real easy. And you got plenty of perks working with us."

"I never worked with you! What I did I did under duress! I have never at any time collaborated . . ."

"Oh grow up why don't you!" retorted Max. "Stop thinking only about yourself. You're acting like a spoiled brat."

Harry thought he almost heard something tangible snap inside the tall man.

"Brat?" he echoed. "Yes I'm behaving like a brat. A stupid, idiotic brat! Do you think a sane man would have gone out and bought this?"

A small automatic appeared in Carter's hand. The room froze. Harry felt it an extremely bad time for him to be tied to a chair.

"What about you, Max?" Carter was yelling. "You're not so smart!"

The little gun began to wave around for emphasis.

"All your clever talk about all the little people that work for you? How none of them knows what the others do? Well, someone's talked. Someone's caused a pretty big chink in your goddam armor!"

The gun became a pointing device.

"And now the water is seeping in. Once it becomes a torrent

you'll sink just like the goddam boat. Trouble is you are going
to take us all down with you. Well, I for one do not intend—"

Harry was shocked as an explosion blasted close to his ear.
Carter dropped to the floor with a thud and blood started to
flow fast out of his cranium. The bullet had gone through the
center of one of his intense blue eyes.

Silence and smoke hung in the air.

"What the hell did you do that for, Benny?" said Max.

"Couldn't take the chance, Max," the driver said in the doorway. "Right now we need you a hell of a lot more than we need
him."

"Rocco!" Sal was on his knees by the body. "Get something
from the kitchen, some plastic garbage bags, anything; we don't
want the bastard pumping blood all over the carpet. Why didn't
you shoot him in the heart, for fuck's sake?!"

He picked up Carter's weapon and said, "Benny, go wash
your hands real good. Then come back and give us your coat
and shirt." When Benny hesitated Sal yelled, "Move it!"

Rocco almost collided with Benny as he came back from the
kitchen with a roll of black garbage bags. Sal took one out and
dragged it over Carter's feet while Rocco covered the head with
another.

Benny came back wearing only his undershirt and carrying
his coat and shirt. Sal stuffed them into the plastic.

"Nino!" he called. "Back the car up to the door. Take a bunch
of those bags and line the trunk. Benny! Stay here and take care
of the floor. Be sure to use OxiClean."

"On it!" said Nino and Benny in unison.

Everywhere in the room was action. Sal and Rocco carried
the wrapped body into the hallway and up the stairs. Furella
went ahead of them to open doors. Benny came from the kitchen
with a big saucepan of soapy water and set it down on the floor.
He got down on his hands and knees beside it and began to
scrub.

Harry's heart hadn't stopped pounding since the gun went

off. He'd survived Villiers's attempt to kill him, but this was different. By now they must have figured Harry had murdered one of them. At least when death came it would be quick. Max would shoot him in the heart, being careful to first lay out the plastic on the floor.

But when he had finished, Benny stood up and took the pan with the brush and dirty cloth into the kitchen. After a moment he came back out and headed up the stairs.

Harry was suddenly quite alone. All around him the restaurant was empty and eerily silent. He could turn his head and waggle his fingers but otherwise was totally immobilized.

And then he realized that in all the panic, Max had quietly slipped away.

68

Still bound by her ankles and wrists, Lizzie lay on the soft rubber trying desperately to stop her mind from racing into absurdity. But as much as she tried, she found it impossible to rationalize anything that was happening to her. For the first time in her life a man had forced her into submission and dominated her as no other had ever done, and she had found the whole experience exhilarating. She had also discovered that she was not the woman she thought she was. All those years of schooling and training were gone in a flash. She had failed, both as a woman and as a police operative. She had no idea who she was anymore.

Her thoughts were jolted back to reality when the door to the little room opened and Max came in. Closing it behind him he turned the key in the lock and came over to her side.

"You okay?" he asked quietly. "Sorry I had to leave you so abruptly."

He reached down and quickly untied the four restraints.

"Here," he said, picking up her skirt and panties. "Put these on."

Lizzie sat up on the edge of the bed. As she dressed, Max pulled over a chair and sat down.

"A little while back I had a slight problem in here." He tapped his chest. "And I passed out. Emergency room doctor told me to take it easy. Change my day-to-day habits."

He paused and then continued. "Just now downstairs . . ."

"I heard a shot," Lizzie said.

"Right."

"Anyone I'd know?"

"No."

"Dead?"

"Yes."

"I take it there's more good news?"

"Yes, there is. This morning I had a call from someone in the UK. He gave me an ultimatum and demanded a lot of money."

Lizzie was beginning to catch up. Could this have been Villiers? Might the Colonel have been released? She had to go carefully. A slip of her tongue could be disastrous.

"Why are you telling me all this?" she asked.

"I'm determined not just to stay alive but to get some pleasure from whatever time I have left. Enjoy myself. Relax. I've had enough of this business. I have to get the hell away from here. Away from everyone. From everything. I have a rough idea of how I'm going to do it, but it won't work if I'm alone. I need someone to help me. I want that someone to be you."

Lizzie was dumbfounded. "Me?"

"Disappearing will take cash. I'm going to tell everyone I'm sending money to London to pay off this bastard. They'll accept that."

"But at the same time you'll make other arrangements," said Lizzie.

"Yes. Clever girl."

"How will you get the money to the UK?"

"I haven't figured that out yet. But I have a number of reliable people I can contact."

Lizzie gave him an ironic smile. "It's a pity Harry jumped off your boat. He could have done it. Seems he was quite good at it."

Max stared at her for five seconds and then said abruptly, "Take off your clothes."

"What!?" she answered. "I just put them on!"

He stood up. "Take them all off and lie down on the bed."

Lizzie was very confused.

"Do it!" Max said vehemently. "Take off your fucking clothes!"

69

Harry was no longer alone. Benny had come back and was pouring himself a gin behind the counter as Max came fast down the stairs.

"Where is everyone?"

Benny emptied the glass in one swallow and wiped his mouth. "Sal and Furella have gone to New Jersey. Nino's driving them over to Rutherford. Then he's going to take them home."

"And Enzo?" Max asked.

"He's up in your office with Rocco. Cora's up there too."

"Good. Go tell them to wait. And stay there. Cora can find you a shirt and jacket."

Benny nodded and hurried up the stairs.

Max came over and looked at him. Harry felt as if he were about to throw up. From fear, the blow to his head and the shattering blast of the shot.

Max spoke. "Nothing but the truth," he said. "Okay?"

Harry nodded bleakly. The smell of cordite still filled his nostrils.

"You sink Enzo's boat?"

Harry nodded again.

"How?" asked Max.

"I drilled holes in the hull," said Harry.

"You cause the explosion at the warehouse?"

"All I did was cut a cable," he said weakly. "I never expected anyone to get killed. It was a dumb thing to do."

"That's interesting," said Max.

"How come?"

"Your girlfriend said you were just a dumb actor. Is that a good description?"

"Could be. What else she tell you?"

"Like most actors, you don't make much money, so when you were handed the suitcase you decided to keep it."

"What else?"

"You got scared. Changed your mind and decided to return it."

Lizzie had stuck to the arranged cover story. "All true," he said.

"She also told me that you found an ingenious way to bring the cash with you on the plane without being caught."

Harry shrugged.

"Not so dumb," said Max. "Do you think you could do it again?"

Harry swallowed. Apparently he wasn't about to die. For some godforsaken reason Max needed cash smuggled and he believed Harry could do it. That was the good news. There had to be bad.

"What's the catch?" he asked.

Max slapped him hard across the face, spun the chair around and untied his hands. With fingers of steel pressing into his arms, Harry was marched across the room and up the stairs. Halfway up he stumbled and fell. Max picked him up bodily. The man might have had a heart condition, but he was still physically powerful. They stopped at the end of the corridor before a door marked Berlin. Max turned the handle, kicked it wide open and shoved Harry inside.

A thin woman lay on a raised platform that was covered in black rubber. She was naked and tied down at all four corners. Max pushed him over to the side of the platform. The girl turned her head and their eyes met.

"Oh my God!" said Lizzie. "Harry!"

"That's the catch, Mr. Murphy," said Max, and pushing him back out into the corridor he slammed the door shut and bustled him down the two flights of stairs into the basement. At a black metal door set in the far wall Max spun a dial back and forward five times. As he heaved it open, the light inside went on. Harry was shoved inside.

The vault was lined with shelves. Each shelf was piled with bundles of notes. Most of what Harry could see were hundreds.

"Figure a way to get three million of that to London," said Max, "and you get your girlfriend back."

"You sadistic bastard . . . ," said Harry.

"Well? What do you say?"

"Three million!?" replied Harry. "There's no way . . ."

"You did it before."

Harry hesitated. Lizzie was in deep trouble. Max had a problem. If he could come up with a solution, maybe he could save her. He took a deep breath. "How much time have I got?"

"You don't. It needs to happen right away."

"What if I can't do it?"

Max looked hard at Harry. "I'll just have to find a way without you."

"How do I know you'll . . . ?"

"You have my word," said Max.

"Your word!" scoffed Harry. "That's reassuring."

"My word that you'll both be dead meat if you fail. Do I make myself clear?"

"As crystal," replied Harry.

Max stepped back and closed the door behind him. Automatically the light above Harry's head went out and left him totally in the dark.

70

Max ran up the last flight of stairs, paused to catch his breath before opening the door. Enzo was seated on the sofa next to Cora, Rocco was at the dining table and Benny was in the kitchen.

"Right," said Max. "This is what needs to be done and this is how we're going to do it." He closed the door and moved to the center of the room. "Cora, we have to close this place tomorrow."

"Tomorrow?" said Cora. "Why the rush?"

Max spoke deliberately. "Need I remind you all, an IRS agent just went to Carter's apartment and asked about the Bruschettis. Now Carter has disappeared. Trust me, two days and the Feds will come knocking. It's not likely Carter told his wife about us, so she'll have no idea where he's gone. And if he did tell her anything she'll keep quiet to avoid any kind of a scandal. At the very least that gives Sal a few hours to get rid of him good."

"So?" Cora persisted.

"So you will call everyone that works at Mazaras. Tell them Sanitation has cited us for violations and we have to shut down for a month. Call Maurizio and Nando and tell them the same. Tell them they'll all be getting a month's wages."

"And then what?"

"Take a vacation. Lie low, but let me know where you are. I'll be in touch."

"Just like that."

"Yes, just like that. And before you leave, bring me up some fresh clothes for Murphy's girl."

Enzo smirked. "Yes, I saw how her others got messed up."

Max ignored the taunt. "Enzo, you go over to Macy's, and get a bunch of cases. Get ready to move the cash out of the vault. When you've done that, go home and make sure there is nothing anywhere the Feds could use against us. Destroy everything. Understood?"

"Where I should take it?"

"We still have those apartments?"

"The stash house? One of them, yes."

"Be ready to take the money there."

"When? Why the delay?"

"We have a slight complication. I had a call from Colonel Villiers asking for over a million dollars to keep his mouth shut. I've decided to give him what he wants."

"You got to be joking!" exclaimed Enzo.

"No, I'm not, little brother. What's more, I'm going to use Harry Murphy to make the transfer. He's done it before. Given the right provocation, he can do it again."

Enzo gave an exasperated sigh. "Why send the fucking money? Just send Rocco. He can take care of it."

Max shook his head. "I don't agree. Rocco will go with Murphy. When the Colonel sees the cash, he'll believe everything is going along the way he planned. With Murphy there as an added distraction, Rocco should have no trouble in dealing with Villiers."

"He's right, Enzo," said Rocco. "Villiers will have figured we tried to knock him off once. He'll be on his guard. This way he'll be less suspicious."

The room became very quiet.

Enzo was still skeptical. "What makes you think Murphy will go along with such a crazy idea? What's in it for him?"

"He has no choice. I've told him I'm using his girlfriend as collateral."

"I like it," said Rocco.

"You going to keep her with you?" asked Enzo.

"Yes."

"Where?"

"Out of sight and out of mind," replied Max. "I haven't quite figured that out yet. As soon as I do I'll call you."

Enzo stood up. "Well, if that's what you want, let's get on with it."

Harry lay on the floor of the big safe with a lumpy bundle of cash under his head as a pillow. The Stygian darkness helped him to focus his mind. The bad guys thought he was an accomplished smuggler. If he was going to save Lizzie he couldn't disappoint them.

The last time he had skillfully hidden the notes in camera cases and that had worked well. Why not simply do it again with different cases? They would have to be carried for a specific purpose and whoever went with them would have to be associated with that purpose. All he needed was an agenda that would fill these parameters. The rest would be a matter of logistics.

There was an odd noise above his head. The dials on the door were turning. As it swung open, Harry blinked at the sudden light.

A man stood in the doorway.

"My name is Rocco," he began. "And I'm here to help."

"Great!" said Harry, getting up. "Right now I need a bottle of red wine, preferably Italian. Shouldn't be too hard around here. After I've had a drink I am going to sit and think. If I fall asleep, wake me at five exactly. Bring me a razor and soap and some clean clothes. Mine are in the trunk of a rented Ford Escape that's parked across the road. The keys are in the ignition. Move it to the garage upstairs and bring my stuff down here. Got it?"

"Got it," said Rocco. As he went out of the basement, Benny the driver came down and sat strategically at the foot of the stairs. The man seemed totally unconcerned that moments earlier he had killed the man in the gray suit. The man they had called Carter.

Lizzie couldn't help but relax on the soft warm surface. For a while she dozed off. The door opening woke her. Max came over and began to undo the straps that bound her wrists and ankles.

"That wasn't a ghost, was it? Harry's still alive, isn't he?" she asked.

"Yes."

"You told me he drowned."

"I lied."

"Why?"

Before he could answer her, Cora came in with a dress draped over her arm and a pair of panties. "Jesus, Max!" she cried. "What the hell did you do to her?"

"It was your idea," said Max with a grin. "And it succeeded."

Lizzie sat up. "You got a smoke?" she asked Cora.

"Sure, honey." Cora pulled out a packet of Marlboros and lit one. Lizzie's hand trembled slightly as she took it from her. She took a long drag, let the smoke trickle out slowly and then slid to the edge of the bed to put on the panties.

"What did you mean, 'it succeeded'?" she asked.

"Thanks to you," replied Max, "your boyfriend now works for us."

Lizzie picked up the dress and pulled it over her head. "Doing what?"

"Doing what you said he does well," said Max. "Moving money."

"How come he agreed?"

"I told him I'm using you as security," replied Max.

Lizzie looked around for her shoes and slid her feet into them. She picked up her purse and slowly used her lipstick.

All was not lost. Harry was still alive. How long he would remain that way was another matter. Once again he had man-

ONCE A CROOKED MAN

aged to get himself into a dangerous situation, and this time there was very little she could do to help him.

"You need me anymore, Max?" Cora asked. "I have calls to make."

"No," he replied. "Let me know if anything comes up. I'll be upstairs."

As soon as they were alone, Lizzie said, "Upstairs?"

"Where I live when I'm not at home," said Max. "Come on; I'll show you."

Following Max up to the top floor, Lizzie realized that everything had changed. The worst thing she could do was escape. Now she needed to stay close to Max. That way she might be able to find out what was happening to Harry.

As they came into the apartment she asked, "What are the chances he could get caught?"

"That's a risk I'm prepared to take."

"He's not a cat, you know. He doesn't have nine lives."

"He did it once; he can do it again," said Max.

"How much is he smuggling for you?" she asked.

"A lot."

"What makes you think he can do it?" she persisted. "What if he just got lucky the first time? You stand to lose a bundle of cash. And then what?"

"We move to plan B."

"Yeah? And where does that leave Harry?"

"You ask too many questions."

Lizzie smiled. "Always do," she said. "It's a habit of mine I learned when I was very young."

She walked over and into the bedroom and was surprised to see that the walls were white and bare. An ugly prosaic light fitting hung in the middle of the ceiling. The bed was simply sheets and a blanket. The floor was bare polished wood. Incongruously under the window were unpainted shelves that overflowed with books. Most of them new.

"What's all those?" she asked as he followed her in.

"I like to read in bed. It's a habit of mine," he replied.

She pointed at the door in the far wall. "Is that the bathroom?"

"Yes."

"I need to pee."

"Go ahead," replied Max.

Moments later Lizzie called out, "You don't have a tub, do you, just this bleedin' shower?"

"I only take showers," he replied.

"Mind if I use it? I had a nasty experience earlier and I'd like to wash it off."

"Sure," he said. "Be my guest."

Lizzie was soaping her hair and her eyes were closed when he slipped in behind her. She tried hard to push him away and upturned her face under the cascading water to get the suds off.

"Time for another nasty experience," he said, and reached over for the soap. Working up a lather, he washed her back and shoulders. She gave a slight cry of protest and tried to get past him to the door. Max put his arms around her and massaged her breasts and abdomen. With her arms stretched high over her head and with her body pinned against the tiles he took her from behind. As he moved, their well-lubricated bodies slapped noisily together. Max held back for as long as he could and then drove hard into her and exploded. They both slid down and sat on the floor with the water falling like autumn rain.

"You are a randy old bugger, aren't you?" said Lizzie, holding her mouth open to drink the warm water. "You feed me, fill me with wine, tie me up, rape and ravish me twice in a few hours. Do you treat all your lady friends like this or am I getting the special?"

Max looked intensely at her and said, "I like you, Liz. I like the way you talk."

"So you said."

"Yes. But I also like the way your mind works."

Lizzie gazed hard at him for a moment and then said, "I'm getting all wrinkly."

Max stood up, turned off the water and opened the door. As she got out he handed her a robe.

"You're right about Harry," Max said, toweling himself off. "I don't care what happens to him. I know what I want, and I know how to get it. When I'm through with people it's as if they never existed."

"That's not very nice, if I may say so."

"Maybe. I get the feeling you're the same. You know what you want and you know how to get it."

Lizzie wrapped a towel from the rail around her head and they moved back into the main room. Max retrieved his pants and put them on. Lizzie sat down at the table as he poured them coffee.

Lizzie curled her legs beneath her on the sofa. "So tell me. What are you planning to do with your life? Or not to do?"

"No idea," he said.

"Where would you go?"

"Somewhere far away where it's warm and the living is easy."

"And you'd sit on the beach sipping Mint Juleps, or whatever you Americans drink, and watch the world go by?"

Max walked over to his desk and pulled out a framed photograph from the bottom drawer.

"My father Aldo," he said, sitting beside her. "With one of his trucks. He used to make a big deal about Fate."

"Fate?"

Max nodded. "He told me when you make a choice you make a deal with Fate. He said that Fate is never on your side, so you have to constantly fight to succeed. I realized early on that he was right. I also remember him telling me there is one choice no one ever makes for themselves."

"And what's that?" she asked, a little puzzled.

"He said it all depends on who gets their hands on you first. Where they live, how much money they have, what they do to survive day to day . . ."

"What the hell are you talking about?"

"I'm telling you the first six years of your life determine what kind of a person you are. And you have no choice over those."

He leaned back "I read a book called *Angela's Ashes* and it made me think about how I was raised. How my dad and mom set me up. How I found myself living a life I never chose for myself. It also made me realize I could change. All I had to do was to step out of one story and into another."

"That is your conscience talking, Max."

"No, it's me and the time I have left to me in this life." An odd look crossed Lizzie's face and he shook his head and smiled. "Do you have any idea what I'm talking about?"

"Of course I do," she said. "It's exactly what happened to me."

"To you?"

"Yes. I changed. I got out."

"Tell me about it."

"Not now, Max. One day maybe. Right now I want to hear all about you."

73

Closely watched by Rocco, Harry went up to the kitchen and scrambled himself some eggs, nuked six rashers of bacon, toasted two slices of whole-wheat bread and helped himself to coffee. Back down by the vault he sat munching at the old poker table. In turn, the salt, the caffeine and the fat each hit his system. Blood flowed to his brain and gave him the glimmer of an idea.

"I may have come up with a solution, Rocco," he announced to his minder. "And to make it work I'm going to need someone to go to my apartment and bring back my address book. When I left, it was in the bedroom. Probably by the bed."

Rocco reached into an inside pocket and produced Harry's Filofax.

Harry looked at it in surprise. "Where did you get that?" Then he remembered. "You're the one who trashed my place, right?"

Rocco handed it over.

"I'm also going to need access to a phone," said Harry.

Rocco reached in another pocket and produced two burn phones and said, "When you've done with these give them back to me."

With the little silver pencil from his Filofax, Harry made a short list of actors who had the talents to help him with his scheme. As the cellular signal was low in the basement, he told Rocco he had to go upstairs. As they walked, Rocco took him by the arm and Harry roughly shook him off. "You don't have to do that. Just lead the way. I'm in no mood for heroics."

Up in the dining room a lone figure sat at a table with a bottle of Tequila and a glass in front of him. Harry recognized him right away. It was the man from the warehouse. As he had just tried to kill him, Harry decided this was not the moment for explanations and chose a table in the opposite corner, where he opened up his address book. Rocco stood in the doorway and both men watched him as he made his calls.

"Travis? Harry Murphy. Yes, it has, hasn't it? Yes, I'm very well, thank you. Working? Not right now, but I have a gig I thought might interest you. I won't bother you with it if you're busy. When? Next few days. It's for cable. You are. Great! Right now I have to put a couple of things together and I'll call you back within an hour. On your cellphone? Great. Give me the number."

Harry repeated this offer to another ten candidates. When he had finished he had narrowed the possibles down to eight. Next he made a list of the tools he would need to do the job. As he wrote he gave Rocco instructions.

"Tell Max we need only new bills. Used ones take up too much space. Preferably hundreds. I don't care how you do it but . . ."

"No problem," said Rocco. "What else?"

Harry was impressed. The man had missed his calling. He would have made a great production manager. Tearing off the list, Harry handed it over. "That's what I'm going to need, and by this afternoon. I suggest you go to Home Depot at Fifty-ninth and Third."

As he wrote down another list, Harry continued. "These will require you to use a little ingenuity. I need three guitars with amplifiers and a drum set. A while back we could have gone down to Forty-eighth and picked it all up at Manny's or someplace like it, but maybe they've all closed up shop. Wherever you do find them, be prepared to put down a pretty hefty deposit. We'll need them for one week. Don't take any substitutes. Get exactly what I've written. If there's a problem call me."

"I may be able to help you there," said the man quietly from across the room. "One of the guys that works for me collects guitars. For a price he'd lend them to me."

Harry took a moment to process this new information and then said, "I was sorry to hear about your buddy."

Vic stared at him for a moment and then said, "In a way he killed himself."

Harry couldn't help asking, "How did you get out?"

Vic gave a helpless shrug. "The stairs were burning, but we found a rope in the end room. Toshi and I managed to climb to the roof. If Jack hadn't been so out of shape we could have pulled him up and saved him too. He was just too heavy."

Harry asked, "What were all those laptops and projectors for?"

"You saw them?"

"Yes. From above. Also the big machine. What was it all for?"

Vic smiled before he spoke. "My name is Vic, but they call me 'Ali Baba,' as it is rumored I employ forty people. Among other things, I'm an identity thief. And a good one too. Business was going great. That machine you saw spits out new credit cards."

"And the computers?"

"Those were processing the culmination of three and a half years of intensive and brilliant work that began way back in my college days. I had patiently hacked my way through a maze of European databases to access information that many people would pay a fortune for. All that has just gone up in smoke. My work is what you really killed." Vic raised his glass. "And that's why I'm here drowning my sorrows."

"Didn't you have it all backed up?"

"No. And to explain why would take more time than you have right now. So why don't you just tell me what you need."

Harry gave the list to Rocco who took it over to Vic. Once again Benny came in from the kitchen to keep watch on him as Rocco left. Harry began his calls.

"Trav! You'll never guess what's happened. The network just called back to tell me the project has been given the okay. Yes! Just like that. But it presents me with a bit of a problem. Time is now very short. Could you come over right now? We need to talk. It's a restaurant called Mazaras."

Harry looked over at Vic and mouthed, *Where are we?*

Vic came over and wrote out the address with the pencil. Harry read it out and then added, "It's in the middle of the block. Yes. Italian. Great. See you soon."

"Why did you do it?" Vic asked quietly when Harry hung up. "The fire, I mean."

Harry looked him in the eye. "To explain that would take more time than you have right now. Maybe when this is all over we can meet for dinner. It seems you and I got a lot to straighten out."

Vic pulled a wry face, turned away and pulled out his phone. Harry headed back down to the basement.

74

In his career, Harry had worked with a countless number of actors and actresses. Most of these encounters were uneventful and quickly faded into oblivion. But there were a few exceptions where friendships flourished and often lasted for years. In his first and only Broadway musical Harry had made the acquaintance of a flamboyant thespian by the name of Travis Cornelius Atwell.

Travis always dressed the same: a white shirt and discreet tie under a pinstriped suit with a red rose in the lapel. He boasted that he had more original cast recordings than any of his peers. Most of these were done before the introduction of microphones and amplification and as a result his voice was resonant and perfect for commercial voice-overs. These made him extremely wealthy.

Cora ushered Travis down and as she turned to leave he kissed her hand and bid her adieu.

"Good morning, my lad," he intoned to Harry. "You're up bright and early. Looking a little the worse for wear, if I may say so. Tell me, why are we operating from a dank and dusty cellar? Have you been evicted from your apartment?"

"Interesting you should say that," replied Harry, picking up his cue. "Work has been a bit scarce lately. Not critical, but enough to make me realize I had to find a way to generate additional income."

Travis laughed and pulled out a chair and sat down. "I used to go through that ritual once a week in the old days. Usually on Sunday. Never did find the answer. I take it you have."

"Yes," said Harry. "Cable television. Someone once told me you can sell anything to cable. With that in mind I looked around for a suitable story. I couldn't find one, so I made one up. These days there are so many channels and so many hours to fill it didn't take me long to find a network."

"Capital!" said Travis enthusiastically. "Tell me more."

"I told them that I'd heard about these four middle-aged men from a small town called Stroudsburg."

"I know it. A few miles south of Scranton?"

"The very one. As kids they went to a Beatles concert, got hooked and formed a cover band. They called themselves the 'Jersey Jumpers.' They've played ever since at local gigs for fun and amusement. Strictly amateur and always Beatles music. As the lead guitar is about to turn fifty, the others decided to give him a special birthday present. They made arrangements for the group to perform at the Cavern in Liverpool, England."

"Did the cable guys take the trouble to check out your story?"

"Fortunately, no. They took my word for it."

"Shades of Williams and NBC!" said Travis, and clapped his hands. "You are a genius."

"I told them I thought it would make a great one-hour special. They agreed on the spot and promised me a little up-front money."

"You are a mastermind!"

"Last night, the producer called to say they wanted the finished product as soon as I can get it to them."

"Where do I come in?"

"You're the guy with the birthday."

"George or John?"

"Your choice."

"John of course," said Travis reverently. "Such a tragic end." He rose up and paced the room. "I haven't plucked the strings for a while, but that shouldn't be a problem. Who are playing the other parts? Do I know them?"

"Well, that's why I called you first. I thought while I deal with all the logistics you could help me get a hold of the others. I made some preliminary calls to the guys I know who can sing and play." He produced the list. "But feel free to call anyone you like."

Travis took the paper, put on his reading glasses and gave it a peremptory glance.

"How soon do you want them?"

"By two o'clock today," said Harry. "Do you think you can select three guys by then?"

"This is Manhattan, my dear boy; I could provide you with the entire cast of any musical you can name."

"In that case, get them here for a meet and greet. The instruments will be here and we can try a couple of the songs."

Travis pushed the list into his pocket and looked around the basement.

"What is this place?" he asked. "Friends of yours, are they? Certainly was a pretty filly that brought me down here."

"I've eaten here for years," said Harry casually. "The owner owes me a favor. We can make all the noise we want down here and the food is fabulous."

"When are you planning to leave?"

"Almost immediately. That will mean each one must have a current passport. And I'll need everyone's date of birth."

"What are you offering?" asked Travis, coming to the most important point.

"For two days' rehearsal, two days' travel and the two days in Liverpool I suggest seventy-five hundred dollars for you and thirty-five hundred dollars apiece for the others with Business Class seats and all hotel and expenses paid."

"Return tickets in hand?"

"Absolutely. Cash up-front too. Fifty percent in advance."

"Very generous." His bushy eyebrows rose. "Are you sure this contract is for cable?"

Harry forced a laugh. He had offered more than he should but if Travis turned him down he would be back to square one. The two men shook hands and hugged briefly.

"No need to mention this to agents," Travis suggested as they broke apart. He held up an imaginary cigar. "We ain't no actors. We guys is Pennsylvania coal miners. We don't need no agents."

"Capital!" said Harry, mimicking his friend.

Travis left. Harry called American Airlines to check flights from JFK to Heathrow. He was told he would have no problem getting seats. Next he arranged to pick up two minivans at Avis when they arrived in London. Lastly he made the room reservations in Liverpool.

At eleven Enzo came down, swung open the door of the vault and began the transfer of money out of the vault.

Just after midday, the guitars and drums magically appeared packed in Anvil cases as Harry had requested. Harry opened one of the cases and carefully took out the guitar. His theory would only work if every interior surface was covered with thick padding. It was.

Rocco arrived with a Canon S400 digital camera and a Sony CD player. In another bag were a bunch of Beatles CDs.

"And the tools?" Harry asked.

Rocco pulled out an orange plastic bag from under his coat. "From Home Depot like you said."

Harry put everything up on a shelf. With Rocco's help he cleared the center of the room. As they set up the heavy amplifiers Rocco asked, "We're not taking all these on the flight, are we?"

"No way," said Harry as he plugged one into a wall outlet. "All we need are the instruments. If you want to save the Bruschettis a buck or two you can take these back after the rehearsal and get your deposit back."

Rocco did not appreciate the humor. Harry suggested he sit in a corner out of the way. Then he took out the player from its packing, installed the batteries and ripped the layers of plastic off a CD. A few bars of "Eleanor Rigby" assured him that it worked. In case anyone asked questions, for the next hour he wrote out a brief bio for each of the group, making up names of their families and where they lived and worked.

First to arrive was Mark Masterson carrying his drumsticks in a roll of cloth and with an old briar pipe clenched in heavily stained teeth.

"Hi, Harry," he said as they shook hands. "Good to see you again. How you been?"

"Fine," replied Harry. "Just fine. Saw Val in McCabe's last month. Told me you were going on the road with some rock-and-roll musical?"

"I went. It didn't. So here we are!" He walked over and eyed the drum set. "What's this one all about?"

Before he could get an answer heavy footsteps on the stairs heralded the arrival of Paul Appleton.

"Whassup, Murph?" he said, giving Harry a bear hug. The two broke apart and high-fived each other. "This is quite a gig, man. Nice trip to Ye Olde Country with all expenses paid! How did you swing this one?"

"It wasn't easy," Harry replied, and seeing Paul glance over at Rocco, he added, "Oh, I'd like you to meet Dino Saldutti. He's going to help with the gear. I should warn you, Dino is a man of few words."

The three shook hands as Travis appeared at the foot of the stairs with Joey Konecsny, who had a shaved head, goatee and mustache.

"Oh my God!" he exclaimed. "Mark Masterson! And Paul! You guys in on this? Hi, Harry!" Everyone hugged and back-slapped one another. Unaccustomed to such demonstrative affection Rocco withdrew to his chair.

Travis headed for the instrument cases. "What magic have

we here?" he said, and pulled out a guitar. "Shit, Harry!" he exclaimed. "You got me the real thing!"

"You have to look the part."

"A Höfner bass!" said Paul, opening another. "It's not left-handed, is it?"

"Could you play it if it was?" laughed Harry.

"I can't wait to play this baby," said Joey, putting a Gretsch Tennessean over his head. "What time are we on?"

"Between the opener and the main act. Around nine."

"How long do we play?" asked Mark, repositioning the drums. Even in the dim light the mother-of-pearl shone brightly.

"They're expecting four songs," replied Harry, amazed how easily he could lie. "I reckon it'll be about a half hour. Enough for the documentary."

"Who's going to shoot our sterling efforts?" asked Travis.

"BBC Midlands. I have a crew meeting us at the club. I figure the easiest way to get going is to listen to the music. It's pretty simple stuff melodically. You've heard it a thousand times. Shouldn't be too hard for you. If anyone has a preference . . ."

"Let him speak now or forever hold his peace," said Travis.

The group chose "Can't Buy Me Love" as the opener, followed by "When I'm Sixty-Four" and "A Hard Day's Night." They would close with "Norwegian Wood." The encore would be "Ticket to Ride." Harry played the first song a couple of times. One by one the musicians picked up their parts and joined in. By the third time they were ready to try it without the CD.

Harry watched as the Jersey Jumpers played and sang. With so little rehearsal the result was astonishing. Cora came down and listened for a short time. Harry sensed she would have liked to dance.

They rehearsed for a further fifteen minutes and then Harry lined them up against the wall holding their guitars. He took a photograph using the digital camera. Before the four men left he gave them details of the flight, instructions as to where they should meet at Kennedy, a hundred dollars for cab fare and each of their fictitious bios.

As soon as he was alone he put in a call to a friend whose brother Fred worked at the *Post.*

"Alan. Harry Murphy. I need a favor." He gave Alan the details and then said, "Cool. Thanks. It's on a SanDisk, so I'll messenger it over to him right away with a note." He took a pen and paper, scribbled out a message and removed the disk from the camera.

Giving it to Rocco, he said, "Get these over to the *Post* at 1211 Avenue of the Americas. Tell them it's urgent and should go direct to the desk of Fred Christianson. He's expecting it. And I'll need a suitcase for my clothes."

75

The telephone next to the bed rang. Max picked it up. It was Rocco.

"Yes?" said Max.

"Murphy has come up with a scheme."

"Yeah? Will it work?"

"The odds are good. We leave tomorrow. He's already checked the flight."

Max hung up and lay back on the pillow. A prone Lizzie beside him smiled. "Harry's done it again, hasn't he?"

"Seems like he has."

"Now what?" she asked provocatively.

"Time to get going," Max said, and jumped off the bed.

In the living room he flipped back the rug and opened up the safe.

"Now, let me see," he said, taking out the passports. "Who are we going to be?"

76

Rocco came back down the stairs. "Your disk has been delivered."

"Great!" replied Harry. "Now get me a flask of coffee. I'll be ready for the cash in about an hour."

His estimate was optimistic. Detaching the foam from the fabric in the case without tearing it proved more difficult than he had thought.

Heels clicked on the stairs. Cora came down to collect the dishes.

"That was quite a performance," she said, picking up the tray. "They play together a lot?"

"No. First time," replied Harry.

"Really? Sounded damn good."

"It was also the last."

"Pity," she said, and left.

Rocco came down with another tray. This one was piled with bundles of new notes. Harry wrapped each one tightly in clear plastic and glued them into the case, rotating every other bundle. The lining was replaced and smoothed down. Finally the material was edged back into the groove around the top.

With the guitar back in, he closed the case and picked it up. It felt exactly as it did before he started. The added weight made little significant difference.

Four cases were dismantled, packed with money and restored. Once again Harry's only concern was the smell of the adhesive. Rocco fetched a commercial fan from the kitchen and set it up to blow a stream of air across the room. Harry was pleased with himself. He lay down on the floor and listened to the whirring of the fan.

Rocco shook him awake. It was time to leave.

Kneeling down beside him, Rocco said, "Just for the record,

Mister Murphy, if you make an attempt to contact anyone, by any means, at any time, I will kill you. Understand?"

"Yes. I know the drill," said Harry. "I'll be dead meat."

Rocco looked blankly at him.

"Forget about it." said Harry. "It's an inside joke."

The fan had done the trick. No more smell. The instruments were carefully replaced, the cases closed up and labeled.

After he had washed, shaved and packed his new suitcase, Harry helped Benny and Rocco load everything into a panel truck out front and they set off. Once past the Van Wyck Expressway they sped to the terminal and turned up the departure ramp. The luggage was unloaded and Benny drove off as Harry summoned a skycap.

The Jersey Jumpers were waiting at the counter. Harry gathered the passports and checked everyone in. The cases were tagged, replaced on the trolley and wheeled over to baggage security. Harry watched as everything went through the scanner. As the cases came out the other end they were simply moved over to the conveyor belt. As Harry had hoped, the carefully arranged metal strips in the money had again been taken for webbing in the padding.

First hurdle cleared.

Everything continued to go smoothly until Travis went through the metal detector. In spite of his removing his shoes, watch, keys, small change, money clip, cellphone, belt and jewelry, the red light flashed and there was a loud beep. Travis was told to stand to one side and spread his legs. An electronic wand was waved over him from head to foot. He leaned over and whispered to the TSA agent. She put down the wand and patted him down with her hands and then let him pass.

Harry was putting on his belt and shoes. "What was all that about?" he asked.

"Don't ask," replied Travis.

"I am asking."

"Well, dear boy," he confessed, "I am wearing a corset. Evidently the manufacturers thought fit to use metal stays."

"Metal what?"

"Precisely. For one horrifying moment I thought that woman was going to get me to strip."

Harry laughed. "I'd have paid money to see that."

"To see what?" asked Mark from the other side of the table.

"Enough!" Travis called out and they headed for the food court.

Harry didn't eat. His nervous stomach advised him to avoid all food. At a newsstand he bought a *Post*, opened it up and smiled at what he saw. Tearing out the page, he folded it and put it in his pocket.

Rocco watched every move he made.

The journey across the Atlantic was bumpy but uneventful. In Immigration the passport line was long but moved quickly and the group soon descended the escalator to the baggage claim area.

One by one the luggage from their flight came slowly round the moving beltway. Mark, Travis and Paul retrieved their suitcases. Harry's was the last. As he pulled it free a small terrier appeared with his handler, sniffing his way around.

Travis leaned down to pat the little fellow on the head. The dog snapped. The actor backed quickly away. Harry waited until the dog had gone to the next carousel before he walked over to the oversize section. Rocco followed. The cases were all there. Safe and sound. So far so good.

"All these belong to you, mate?" said a cheerful porter.

"Yes," replied Harry.

"Got the claim checks handy, have you?"

Harry took out his passport and extracted the baggage tags. Together they checked all the numbers. The porter loaded Harry's and the band's luggage and the cases onto a trolley and pushed it toward the exit.

"Got anything to declare?" he asked.

"I can't think of anything," said Harry. He looked at Rocco. "Can you?"

Rocco shook his head.

"Right you are then," said the helpful man. The whole group passed beneath the green sign.

An officer stepped forward and motioned for them to stop. "What's all this then?" he asked, looking at the metal cases.

"We're a band," said Harry with a friendly smile.

"Bound for Liverpool," added Travis.

"Where we are playing in a club," said Joey proudly.

"Really?" was the flat reply. "What are these? Guitar cases?"

"Not just guitar cases!" exclaimed Travis. "But cases containing the exact kinds of instruments played upon by the Beatles back in the sixties." He pointed at the bottom case. "That's mine. A three-five-six Rickenbacker. Would you like to see it? It really is amazing."

Harry prayed his group would shut up before they were all marched off for interrogation. Out of the corner of his eye he could see a second officer approaching. This man's shirt was starched and his hair was close-cropped. On his upper lip was a handlebar mustache.

"What's up, Jack?" asked the new arrival.

"They're musicians. Going up north. These are their instruments."

Both men looked at the cases. There was an awkward pause. Harry said calmly, "Here. Take a look at this."

Digging into his pocket, he pulled out the page from the *Post,* unfolded it and handed it over. At the top was the photograph of the smiling group in the basement of Mazaras. Below it a headline proclaimed "Big Beatle Birthday Bash!" Beneath was the story of the trip just as Harry had written it. The supervisor compared the faces on the page to the faces in front of him.

"Who are you then?" he asked Rocco.

"I work for him," said Rocco, pointing at Harry.

"He's our techie," said Harry smoothly.

The supervisor made another circle of the cases. "How long will you be in the United Kingdom?" he asked.

"Just a couple of days," murmured Harry as nonchalantly as he could.

"All these will be returning with you to the States when you leave?"

"Absolutely." Harry smiled.

"All right," Jack said with a wave of his arm. "Off you go then."

Relief swept over Harry as they passed from the customs area, and he felt almost euphoric as he made arrangements at Avis for the two vans to be brought around to the passenger loading area. A slight drizzle fell as the porter trundled the trolley outside. Harry pulled his raincoat from his suitcase and put it on.

The group's luggage went into the first van and the instruments with Rocco's and Harry's suitcases into the second.

Joey had been selected to drive. "You okay on the left?" Harry asked.

"No problem," replied Joey.

"You have the address of the hotel?"

Travis eased himself into the front passenger seat. "Do not worry, dear boy," he stated imperiously. "I have all the pertinent information and the latest Michelin Guide. I shall navigate."

A police officer with an automatic weapon across his chest was coming towards them. The doors slammed shut and Joey drove off with everyone waving and smiling. Mark sang, *"It's been a hard day's night . . ."* and they disappeared around the corner.

Harry drove the other van through the tunnel out of the airport, around the traffic circle and over to the Motorway.

He turned on the wipers and they thumped to and fro across the windshield.

Rocco took out a satellite phone, switched it on and dialed. "We're through customs," he said succinctly and closed it.

"I need to use that phone," said Harry.

"What for?"

"To cancel the gig. Here, dial this number." He took a piece of paper from his pocket.

"What's that?" asked Rocco.

"The hotel in Liverpool."

Rocco dialed and handed the phone to Harry. A thick Liverpudlian accent answered, "Hello? How can I direct your call?"

"Front desk please," said Harry, and waited a moment. "Hi there. I want to leave a message for four guests who will be arriving at your hotel in a few hours. The reservation is in the name Murphy."

"Of course, sir. Not a problem."

"Tell them the performance is canceled. They should make their own arrangements to return to America."

"'Return . . . to . . . America.' Got it. I will inform them when they arrive."

"Thank you."

Harry had begun to drift to his right. A loud horn from a big lorry behind him blared. Quickly he threw the phone into Rocco's lap and pulled out into the fast lane.

Harry's hands gripped the steering wheel. His options were dwindling. He had sent four good friends on a fool's errand. Lizzie was in quadruple jeopardy. He had committed murder. Next to him was a ruthless killer. Ahead was a distinctly dubious future.

77

The front door of 4 Kensington Mews opened as Harry pulled up. The Colonel came out in his shirtsleeves carrying a large black umbrella. Harry wound down the van window,

"Mr. Murphy," Villiers said jovially. "We meet again." He turned his attention to the back of the van, where Rocco had opened the rear doors.

"Rocco, my dear fellow," Villiers said with a broad smile. "What a pleasant surprise."

"Where do you . . . ?" said Rocco.

Villiers looked in at the cases and then over at Harry. "So that's how you did it? Fascinating. Now then, let's just get 'em inside. Excuse me a moment while I get some rain gear. Would you care for a coat, Rocco?"

"No, I'm fine," said Rocco flatly. "Let's just get on with it."

Together they carried the cases into the hallway. The Colonel said, "Stack them up here." Once everyone was inside, Rocco closed the door.

Rhonda Villiers appeared from the living room with the evening paper tucked under her arm, her reading glasses perched on the end of her nose.

"Mr. Murphy! How nice to see you," she said with a smile. "Would you care for a cup of tea?"

Well at least she hadn't changed. The thought of her cakes made him almost accept. "No thank you, Mrs. Villiers," he answered. "We have too much to do. Maybe later?"

"A rain check. Isn't that what you Americans call it? Very appropriate in weather like this. Oh, do please call me Rhonda. The other sounds so formal."

The Colonel examined the cases. "The loot is in the linings?"

Harry nodded.

Villiers pulled out the snare drum and took it into the kitchen.

The others followed. Taking out a knife from a drawer, the Colonel sliced through the fabric and extracted one bundle.

"Excellent," he said. "Very ingenious, very ingenious indeed." Dropping the knife down on the table with a clatter, he took the bundles out. Opening another case, he ran his fingers around the linings.

"All told, how much is here?" he asked.

"What you said on the phone," Rocco replied. "Give or take a few thousand. We didn't have time to keep an accurate count."

"Good. Shall we all go into the living room?" Villiers said pleasantly.

Harry was unable to fathom what was going on. Rocco was being helpful. The Colonel was all smiles. The latter was easy to explain. He had just got his hands on three million bucks.

Rhonda was sitting in the corner of the sofa. "All shipshape?" she asked.

"Signed, sealed and delivered," replied her husband.

"Wonderful!" she replied, getting up. "Let's give these two a drink before we send them on their way. Charles, come with me into the kitchen. I'll get the glasses while you get us some ice. You know how Americans like ice in their drinks."

Harry watched them go and turned to Rocco. "Isn't it time we called New York?"

Rocco pulled out the satellite phone. Rhonda came back with four crystal glasses and set them on the coffee table.

"Now what will you both have?" she asked, pulling open the doors to a liquor cabinet. Villiers came back with the ice bucket and banged it down on the bar. Rhonda Villiers took out a bottle of Scotch, popped the cork and waved it back and forward in front of Rocco.

He shook his head. "I don't . . ."

Before he could utter another syllable, Charles Villiers had stepped behind him and whipped an arm around his neck. The phone flew across the room and smashed on the hearth.

Rocco kicked and flailed to get free but the Colonel clung on tight.

Harry got the picture in a flash. Of course! This was the reason for the whole charade. Rocco had come with them to finish what he had tried to arrange in the Mews all those days ago. But the Colonel had moved first. Harry took a step forward.

"No, Mr. Murphy!" said an odd voice.

When he turned, Rhonda Villiers had a gun in her hand and it was pointed at his head.

Rocco fought back. He reached up and pulled hard on the Colonel's hair. This infuriated the big man, so he reached round and thrust his a finger into the closest eye socket. There was a wet sound and the eyeball popped out and dangled on Rocco's cheek. He gave a horrible scream and fell limply to the floor.

Villiers put a knee on his quarry's throat and applied his full weight. With the air supply completely cut off the body flailed briefly and then abruptly lay still. The Bruschetti enforcer was dead.

The Colonel stood up and pulled an antimacassar off the back of one of the armchairs to wipe his hands.

"Charles! Don't use that!" Rhonda exclaimed. "Get a cloth from the kitchen."

"Later," he replied. "I'll clean it off later." He nodded towards Harry. "What about him?"

Mrs. Villiers looked hard at Harry. Gone was the little old lady with the tea and cakes. "We need to keep an eye on Mr. Murphy. He can make himself useful," she announced. "He can drive us."

She pointed to the body on the floor. "We can't use the van. It's too conspicuous. We'll take the Escort. I know a good spot where we can get rid of him."

Harry was unsure who she meant.

"Take his feet," said Villiers to Harry and folded Rocco's arms over his chest.

Harry put his arms around the buckled knees and the two men half-carried, half-dragged the heavy body across the living room and through the kitchen. With the gun still in her hand, Rhonda went ahead and held open the door to the garage. Inside were both the Jaguar and the Ford. Rocco was heaved into the back of the latter, eased upright and firmly secured with the seat belt. As his head lolled back, wet foam started to come out of his mouth and a foul stench filled the car.

"Start up, Mr. Murphy," said Rhonda. "I'll tell you where to go, as we go."

Harry got in and turned the key and the engine sputtered to life. Rhonda Villiers sat beside him as her husband settled himself next to Rocco. Villiers pressed a button on the visor and the garage doors rolled up and over their heads.

Outside, the rain was still pelting down. Rivulets of water ran down the center of the road and into the overflowing drains. The familiar fuzzy dice hanging from the rearview mirror swayed from side to side as Harry pulled out and turned right. The remote was activated again and the door rattled down behind them.

This trip with the Colonel was more bizarre than Harry's last. Next to him was a woman with a Beretta pointed in his direction and there was little doubt she knew how to use it. Behind them was his late minder with his brains seeping out of his eye socket and Villiers beside him happily humming his regimental march.

Harry tried to take note of the route they took but the roads and highways became a blurred and rainy mess. Silence prevailed most of the way other than when Rhonda gave him directions.

Suddenly Villiers gave a chuckle. "I have to hand it to you, Murphy," he said. "I've been looking forward to my retirement for many a long day. And it is now here. Not only that, I have the means to enjoy it! All thanks to you." He gave another little laugh and looked over at his wife. "Hell of a way to show our gratitude, don't you think?" he said ironically.

"Be quiet, Charles," said Rhonda firmly.

"Where would you like to retire?" asked Harry.

"Interesting you should ask," said the Colonel. "Italy is my first choice. Somewhere in Umbria or Tuscany. A villa with a nice garden would be nice. My wife does not agree with me."

"Why is that?"

"She has other ideas for the money. We earlier were unable to come to any kind of agreement. She believes we should be more altruistic with our newfound wealth."

"Perhaps she's right," replied Harry. "In my experience it's the woman in most relationships who knows what's best when it comes to money."

"Quite possibly, old boy. But in her case it's not just a matter of dollars and cents."

"Go down there," said Mrs. Villiers, indicating left. Harry glanced in the rearview mirror and turned off the main road.

"Did you know my wife has a cause?" continued the Colonel.

"No I didn't."

"Yes. She's had it for some time. Ever since her father died. Lately it has become somewhat of an obsession. She blames the petty British bureaucracy for his demise."

"Really?" said Harry, feigning interest.

Rhonda turned to face him. "Yes, Mr. Murphy. And soon they will be taught a lesson thanks to the money you have brought us from America." She glanced at her husband. "Money that is not going to be frittered away on grapes." Her eyes gleamed as she added, "Yes, I will give the British something to remember. Now shut up, both of you, and turn up there."

Harry peered into the darkness where she was pointing with the gun. A dirt road that ran across a common. There were few lights and no buildings in sight.

Mrs. Villiers indicated a gap in the trees. "Go that way," she said.

The car rattled and bumped over the ruts in the road. The headlights illuminated shrubs and trees moving violently in the wind. A wooden fence loomed a few yards ahead and forced them to stop.

"Turn off the engine," said Mrs. Villiers. "Charles! Take the keys."

Her husband reached over and took the keys from the ignition. This time their faces came close and the Colonel's oily hair brushed against Harry's cheek. As he jerked away, the dice swayed again, prompting Harry's brain to recall the first time he saw them.

"Leave the car in Myrtle Road," the Colonel was saying. *"It's close to Hounslow East tube station and from there it's only a short ride to the airport. Throw away the keys. I have others if I need them."*

The keys. The keys to the car Harry was in now!

He'd never thrown them away! He'd put them in a coat pocket and it was the same coat he was wearing. But that was a long time ago.

Both his captors were getting out of the car. Harry eased his hand down and ran it over the fabric and felt a lump. When he slid his hand in through the pocket opening his fingers closed over a ring with two little keys!

"Get out, Mr. Murphy!" shouted Rhonda, waving the gun. "We are going to need your help to carry him."

But Harry was ready to help himself. Climbing over to the driver's seat, he put the key in the ignition, started the engine and rammed the gear lever into first. His foot banged down on the accelerator and the Escort shot forward.

Rhonda Villiers was directly in front of the car. She leapt out of the way, aimed the Beretta at Harry and pulled the trigger.

The semi-automatic Beretta Cougar 8000 holds ten rounds. The first seven did minimal damage to the surrounding leaves and trees. The eighth shattered the front window of the car. The ninth accidentally struck Colonel Charles J. Villiers in the base of his sternum and tore open his heart.

The last bullet was the only one to find its intended target. The projectile entered Harry's left arm through the infraspinatus muscle and broke his humerus into several pieces before it passed through surrounding tissue and lodged itself in the doorframe.

As the last of the ejected shell cases hit the ground, the car plowed through the old fence and disappeared from sight.

Harry's life now went by in slow motion. In the rearview mirror he saw Colonel Villiers slam against a tree and drop. Harry felt the thud below his neck and the searing pain that swept through his body. Rhonda was screaming with her hair blowing wild in the wind. Chunks of wood flew up in the air from the shattered fence. The bottom of Harry's world dropped out as the little car plunged downwards and into a muddy pond.

Rocco's body slipped free of the restraining belt and pinned Harry and his seat against the steering wheel, causing the horn to add its penetrating cry to the wild sounds of the night.

Icy cold began to come up around his ankles, legs and thighs. His whole body shivered and he began to lose consciousness. But his brain continued to process sounds and images. The wail of an ambulance. Or was it a police car? Bright lights. A floating sensation. Voices. Shouts. Wrenching metal and the face of Marisa Vargas from the plane. Violet eyes. Above her the face of Detective Sergeant Ivan Sapinsky. His savior! Why was Ivan there? Where had he come from? Of course! He was with the cavalry! He had come to rescue him again!

Harry shook his head from side to side and said hoarsely, "Too late, my good friend. This time you're too late. It's all over."

Looking upwards, he saw the big red curtain slowly descending as the lights dimmed. When it rose again he heard the applause and instinctively tried to bow from his waist.

The curtain came down again. The final act of the play was over. It was time to go to the bar for a drink.

78

As he was being wheeled into the operating room, Harry regained consciousness long enough to acknowledge that he was in neither Heaven nor Hell but in a hospital and to realize that his body had been seriously damaged.

Five hours in surgery, seven in recovery and very slowly comprehension returned. With it came the pain.

The next day he learned from the surgeon that he had been lucky. Only his left upper arm had been shattered. The bullet had missed all the vital bits. The surgeon also told him that before he performed the operation his fellow doctors had suggested a plastic replacement. The older man had listened to his younger colleagues but opted to attempt to rebuild Harry's bones. The recovery would be long and the results uncertain, but if all went well there was every reason to believe he would have full mobility of both the arm and shoulder.

Various medications were added to his drip tube to keep the pain level within acceptable limits and to accelerate the healing process. All these drugs conspired to dull his already depleted senses.

Eventually he was transferred to a private room with a window overlooking the tops of trees. For his first solid food he was given a bowl of pale liquid with floating colored lumps. As he slept off the effort of lifting the spoon to his mouth the door opened and a small woman came in carrying an arrangement of flowers. Behind her was a thickset man clutching a brown paper bag.

"Harry?" the woman said in a hushed voice. "Guess who's here? Guess who's here to see you?"

"He's asleep, Bridget," said the other. "We should leave and come back later."

Harry's limbic brain connected with the low tones of this

voice and his eyes jerked open. At the sight of his parents he tried to sit up. This made him moan.

"Don't try to move, my darling," said his mother. She came over and kissed him gently on the forehead. "We only came to stay for a few minutes. We wanted you to know we were here."

"How did you . . . ?"

"Read about you in the paper," said his father. "Said you'd been pulled from an automobile just before it sank. We thought you might need us, so we jumped on a plane. Nice flight. Food was great."

"That's enough, Mike," said his mother taking the bag. "Here, Harry, we brought you some fruit."

They stayed for a further ten minutes, during which time Harry learned that the spare room in their little house in Boca Raton was aired and ready. As soon as he was able to travel they were going to take him home. His immediate reaction was to politely decline, but good sense prevailed. His mother's chicken soup might be just what the doctor ordered.

For most of the next twenty-four hours Harry slept. He was awoken in the late afternoon by the smell of burning leaves. Opening his eyes, he beheld Lizzie's boss by his bed with his hat in hand. Smiling down, he gave a friendly nod and pointed to the armchair with his umbrella.

"Do you mind?" he asked before sitting down. "Are you up to a little chat?"

Harry was about to be interrogated. In spite of his weak condition, it was imperative he find out as much as he could before he gave too much away.

"How's Lizzie?" he asked.

The beekeeper raised both eyebrows and said with an expressive sigh, "I had hoped you might be able to tell me."

"You haven't heard from her?"

The answer was a shake of his head.

Harry sank deep into the pillows. Knowing the Bruschetti

methodology, Lizzie Carswell was six feet under the marshy ground of New Jersey.

Harry had genuinely felt great affection for the crazy woman and he had failed miserably. Every decision he had made had been wrong. Why the hell had he done it in the first place? Lizzie had tricked him for sure, but he had made his own choices. He had fooled himself into thinking that what he knew about organized crime, that what he had learned from the virtual world of film and television, was enough to keep him alive and even help others to survive. How stupid! How futile! Many people had died and absolutely nothing had been accomplished or gained.

The beekeeper was talking and Harry wasn't listening so he asked his visitor to begin again.

"I suppose I should start at the moment when I received the call from the States asking for confirmation of Detective Sergeant Carswell's undercover identity. I was most encouraged. I felt her scheme was going according to plan and she had gained access to her target. From then on we had no further communication. This is not unusual in this type of operation, so I saw no cause for alarm and I decided to wait. It came as quite a surprise when you were shot.

"Soon after this I received a communiqué saying that Detective Sergeant Carswell's passport had been flagged at Heathrow, but of course by the time we arrived there she had long since left the airport."

"Then she's alive!" cried Harry. "She's here in the UK!"

"I doubt it, Mr. Murphy," the little man said. "There is a strong possibility the passport was used by someone masquerading as Miss Carswell. Security cameras show a female of similar height and build, but the face is completely obscured by a hat and scarf."

"You think she's dead?"

"I'm afraid I do. If she weren't she would have got in touch with us by now. She was well trained and very resourceful. The Americans think we should assume the worst. Such a shame."

He stood up and looked out the window. "Of course I immediately informed Detective Sapinsky of her possible appearance and he returned with Agent Vargas to watch the Mews premises in Kensington. It was the one location we knew was connected to our investigation. By doing this I saved your life. They observed the arrival of the minivan and saw the Ford Escort leave. When they saw that you were driving they followed at a discreet distance and called for backup.

"When the shots were fired both ran forward and observed the Escort crashing into the pond. They pulled you free before the vehicle went under."

He put down his hat and pulled out a small notebook. He flipped it open.

"A second man was later recovered from the rear seat and a subsequent autopsy revealed that strangulation was the cause of death. A third individual was recovered from the riverbank and he has been identified as Colonel Charles Villiers. Records show he was retired from the military but currently employed by the European Parliament in Brussels.

"It's all a bit of a puzzle," he said, closing the notebook. "Apart from yourself, the only person who could throw some light on the affair is the Colonel's wife, and she has apparently gone insane. When anyone goes near her she screams obscenities. Left alone, she has long, rambling conversations with her dead father. We checked and found the poor fellow had committed suicide when she was about fifteen years old. Some petty dispute with the tax authorities.

"The only relative of Miss Carswell we can trace is her mother. Although they were estranged from one another, I will see that she receives all the appropriate benefits."

So far he hadn't mentioned the bundles of cash, so Harry asked. "Did you check the Mews cottage?"

"Oh yes" was the reply. "And that added to the mystery. Several metal cases were found with their linings ripped out. Beside them were three valuable guitars and a set of drums."

Harry was careful not to flinch.

"In one of the lids was the address and telephone number of a man who apparently owns the instruments. He was unconcerned about the state of the cases but keen to know about the instruments. I informed him that they were undamaged and assured him everything would be returned as soon as it was practical."

"What about the Americans?" Harry asked. "What did they tell you?"

"I'm afraid they weren't very cooperative. The whole business seems to have been a thorn in their collective sides. They did tell me they had been to an establishment known as . . ." he referred to the notebook, "Mazaras."

"What did they find?"

"Painters and plasterers. The place was undergoing a renovation. They carried out a thorough search, found nothing and left. Your apartment was thoroughly checked and seemed to be as you left it. Their attitude is that no crime has been committed. As far as they are concerned, it's all over. I personally would appreciate anything, anything at all you can tell me. Mainly to put my mind at rest."

Harry stuck to the facts. "We flew to New York. At Lizzie's prompting I made a phone call to the people who controlled Villiers and made contact. She encouraged me to follow this up and at the same time assured me DEA agents would be watching. But they lost me. I was abducted and held hostage. Miss Carswell made an unsuccessful attempt to rescue me and was herself taken. When I saw her she was gagged and bound and we never had the chance to speak. That's the last I saw of her."

"I see," said the beekeeper.

"I was told to get the money to London. If I succeeded she would be freed. Otherwise they would kill her. The money was in the cases you found in the basement. The dead man in the car was sent over to make sure I didn't run off with it."

"How did he die?"

Harry thought it best to let this one alone. "I have no idea," he lied.

"What were the names of the individuals in New York?"

Harry wanted it all to end. He wanted his life back. Lizzie was gone. If he gave names his testimony would be forwarded to Marty MacAvoy. The investigation would be reopened.

"Again, I have no idea," Harry said weakly. "They were all careful to keep all that from me."

"How much money did you bring over?"

Harry shrugged. "More than a million. I arranged for friends of mine to come with me posing as a rock band." He paused for effect and then added dramatically, "I can't believe I'm saying this. It sounds so crazy!"

"In my experience life often is, Mr. Murphy. The scheme apparently worked."

"Perfectly."

The two men sat in silence for a moment.

"Tell me," said Harry. "What was the real reason we went to New York? With everything that happened I got confused."

The beekeeper took a little time before he answered.

"To achieve national security, Mister Murphy, many governments have special forces that remain in the shadows. They perform operations that are not regulated by normal rules. They are 'off-the-books,' so to speak. Budgets are provided. No questions are asked of anyone.

"I am head of such a task force that works with MI5, MI6 and GCHQ. When necessary, we cooperate with similar clandestine operatives worldwide. Specifically, our unit was formed three years ago to fight cyberterrorism, as there was a suggestion that someone had hacked into several highly classified and sensitive areas at the European Defence Agency.

"As Miss Carswell was one of our senior operatives, she was given the lead on the case. After months of painstaking work tracing back through various sites that had been compromised, we were able to narrow down the primary source to New York.

Other avenues of investigation led us to the Villiers's Mews cottage in Kensington.

"Her argument to use you to make the connection between London and New York was very persuasive, and as you know, I readily agreed. Perhaps I shouldn't have been so hasty. Possibly had I questioned her more thoroughly she would still be with us."

He picked up his hat. "I'll leave you now. Get some rest. If I hear anything further, I will get in touch, and I'd appreciate it if you would do the same. Incidentally, I have persuaded the authorities that Her Majesty should take care of all your medical expenses. It's the least we can do."

Taking a card from his top pocket he laid it on the table. "My telephone number," he said gently. "Call anytime."

"Thank you," said Harry, and he picked up the card. "Before you leave," he said quietly, "tell me, was it all worth it? What did you and your covert operatives achieve in all this?"

The beekeeper said simply, "Nothing, I'm afraid. It was all a complete waste of time and money. I realize it may be difficult for you to accept, Mister Murphy, but in our business you win some, but you lose most."

He walked over to the door and turned.

"No one complains because what we do never happened."

With a final nod he left the room and closed the door.

Harry was too exhausted to process so much information but he also was too upset to sleep.

Nothing Lizzie had told him was true. All along it was about cyberterrorism. She was just a fucking liar. And nothing had been achieved. She had failed. He had failed. The money had gone. No one knew where.

All that effort. Zero. One complete fucking failure.

But then he smiled as he remembered that it all had happened because he had needed to take a leak!

79

"Bloody hell, Max!" said Lizzie in frustration. "Look out there! You got it all! Just what you said you wanted. Sunshine, golden sands, wavin' palm trees and a view of the beautiful blue sea. What more do you want?"

Fernando Perez, aka Max Bruschetti, and a well-tanned Lizzie stood in a big empty room on the top floor of a vacant house half a world away from New York and London. The tropical scene outside the big window was lit by a dramatic orange sunset.

"We've been here on this island paradise for five fucking months. I've had enough of the golden sands and waving palm trees," said Max. "I need some goddam action. I am sick of doing nothing."

Lizzie pointed a finger at him. "Well, it's not going to be the same sort of action like what you was doing in New York. From now on everything's got to be straight."

"What do you mean, straight?"

"Straight! Not bent, not crooked, on the level."

"So tell me! What the fuck am I going do?" he persisted.

"Not just you! Both of us, Max. In case you haven't noticed, you're not alone anymore."

"Well, I got a problem. I don't know how to do anything 'straight,' as you call it."

"Don't be daft; of course you do!"

"Like what, for instance?" he asked.

"You ran a very successful business," she answered.

"Yes, but . . ."

"I'll give you it was a bit dodgy, but it was a business none-theless. All we have to do is find out what's needed around here and set it up. Thanks to Harry we certainly have enough start-up money. I never realized how easy it was to move cash around this world."

"Nothing to it if you know how. And anyway, if we need more

I can get it from Sal. He has full access now. Carter was smart enough to make it so he could."

"What did you do with Carter's body? You never told me."

"Deep down in the muddy marshes of New Jersey. Just beside the turnpike. Sal took care of it."

"I wonder how he's doing?"

"Last I heard he's doing great." He laughed. "Furella wrote that he broke ninety and almost had a stroke as he lined up his last putt."

"What else did she write?"

"Not a lot. Feds took a good look around Mazaras and didn't find a thing."

"Nothing from the South Americans?"

"No. Poor old Hernandez must have better fish to fry."

"So what are we going to do?"

"Run a restaurant?" he suggested helpfully.

"Do you really want to do that, Max? You really want to tie yourself down twenty-four hours a day? All the shopping, the cooks, the waiters?"

"I never had any trouble before. You get yourself a good chef and he runs it for you—"

"Then you're not running a restaurant!" Her voice echoed in the empty space. "You'll just end up sitting there drinking with the customers! But wait a minute. Do you want action for your mind or your body?"

"I don't know."

"Well, I do. I need something physical. Did you know I was once a runner?"

"No."

"I ran cross-country. I was thinking we could build a gym. You know, like one of them spas. Where people come to exercise. It could have a trendy little restaurant. We got enough property right next door."

"I'd like that."

"There are a lot of tourists in this part of the world and not a lot of places to work out. They could run on the beach. We could have bikes to rent. There are lots of roads around here for that. The word would soon get around. All the chicks would come by in their skimpies and you could check them out."

"I'd like that too."

The front door opened and closed on the floor beneath. A woman's voice called out, "Anyone home?"

Lizzie leaned over the balustrade. "Up here," she answered.

Footsteps clicked up the bare stairs. A tanned woman in a wrinkled seersucker suit came into the room carrying a manila folder.

"Have you seen the sunset? Gorgeous!" she gushed.

"You got the papers?" asked an anxious Max.

"Hello, Lucy," said Lizzie, and shook her hand. "Forgive my husband; he's not in the best of moods today."

"Not a problem, dearie," Lucy said easily.

The real estate agent showed the contents of the folder to Max. "I made them all out in just your name, but I can easily change them if you want to make it Mr. and Mrs. Perez."

"No!" said Lizzie. "They're fine the way they are; we don't need to change anything."

"Right you are." Lucy handed over the folder. "You can look at them tonight. I'll collect them from you tomorrow. You're paying cash, so there are no financials to bother with. You should be able to move in within a week."

"That soon?" Max thumbed through the typewritten pages.

"I'll be off," said Lucy. "Enjoy!"

Lizzie gave her a wave. After a moment the front door closed beneath them. All was quiet.

"Why did you have to say that?" said Max.

"That you was not in the best of moods?" she asked.

"That I'm your husband."

"Don't you think we look like a happily married couple buying their dream home?" she said with a laugh. "I did it so we'd appear normal. I wanted her to go away thinking we are just like all her other dumb clients, nothing special, nothing out of the ordinary. Nothing to remember."

"Then why did you snap at her?"

"When?"

"When she suggested she put both our names on these," he answered, and held out the folder.

Lizzie took a moment and then said, "I made a mistake. I thought she was asking me to sign as Lizzie Carswell. I forgot that I'm Lizzie Perez now."

She came back over to him. "*'The time has come, the Walrus said . . .'*"

"What?"

"I got to tell you something."

She sat down on the floor, pulled up her knees and wrapped both arms around them. "I am not what you think I am."

Max gave her a penetrating stare.

"I don't want to spoil what we have, Max. I want us to have a real relationship. One that's honest. No secrets."

Max was motionless.

"I've got a horrid little secret. It's the story of my life. Only problem is, it has a bit of a surprise ending."

"I like surprises," said Max. "Try me."

"I wanted to tell you on the flight from New York. And again in the car going down the Motorway. I came closest in Kensington Mews when we was in the basement stuffing the money in them duffel bags. Somehow, I couldn't find the courage."

"Courage for what?" he asked, dropping the folder on the floor.

"I'm a police officer. A cop."

"Really!" said Max.

"Yes, really. I came over to the States with Harry on an on-going investigation."

"Well, well, well," said Max. He walked over and sat down beside her. "So that's your horrid little secret."

"I worked in special ops. Headed up a cybercrime unit. Spent my time chasing hackers."

"You don't say," said Max impassively.

"By now they will have given up on me. The report will say that I am presumed dead."

"A cop." He put an arm around her shoulders. "Well, I suppose I should tell you my little secret."

"You?" said Lizzie, surprised.

"Yes, me. You see, Miss Carswell, I knew from the minute we met that you weren't what you said you were. I also saw your pal Harry was a total fake. It was pretty clear both of you were lying. Getting me to call your boss! At . . . where was it?"

"Honeybee Travel."

"Right." He grinned. "What genius thought that one up?" He gave her a kiss on the cheek. "Your cover was a piece of shit. And you are much too skinny to be running around checking on restaurants. And too smart. People who poke around to find fault with others do it because they can't come up with anything to do for themselves. Overweight failures. You are neither."

"Why didn't you say anything?" asked Lizzie.

"I liked you. You made me laugh. I realized that I didn't care what you really were. Because you were the most interesting and fascinating woman I'd ever had the pleasure to stumble across." He laughed at the look on her face. "God! You cops are all alike. You think you're so smart, got everything sewn up. What you don't get is that you only catch the dumb ones."

"And Harry?"

"Harry was harmless. I could deal with him anytime. So naïve. Such an innocent. It's a wonder he's lived so long." He gave her shoulder a squeeze. "A cop. Who'd have guessed? You got a uniform?"

"Yes. For special occasions. Most of the time I was in plain-clothes."

"I'd like that," he said with a grin.

"What?"

"To see you in your uniform. I bet it makes you look sexy. We got to get one and have you wear it one night."

"Max!"

"All this talk about the straight and narrow and it's you that turns out to be crooked."

"I should have told you sooner."

"What for? We're a good team. I've waited a hell of a lot longer for you than you have for me. What difference does it make what you were before we met?"

Lizzie looked into his eyes. "What a wonderful man you are."

"Thank you," he replied. "You're not so bad yourself."

"You're right about Harry," she said. "I picked him right off the street and used him. Such a sweet guy. I feel badly about the poor bastard. He did us quite a favor."

"He was trying to save his skin," said Max.

"No," replied Lizzie. "He was trying to save *my* skin. I think he had a bit of a thing for me." She stood up. "On the subject of Harry, you remember that leather case with the money?"

"No. What case?"

"The case the Colonel handed over to Harry. Right after Harry warned him about Eddie Ryan. The one you never found."

"What about it?"

"I think he's still got it somewhere. He's a clever sod and he could easily have hidden it."

Max gave her a quizzical look.

"We owe him one, Max."

"What?"

"Without him we wouldn't be buying this place."

"Oh yes, we would," replied Max. "If he'd fucked up, I'd have found another way."

"Well, he's probably still got the money but doesn't dare touch it. I'd like to let him know he can spend it."

Max stared at her again.

"Well, what do you say?" she asked forcefully.

"I've a lot to learn about you." He raised his hands in mock surrender. "Okay, if that's what you want."

Lizzie went to put her arms around his neck and Max pushed her away. "It's time we christened this place. Take off your panties."

"You mean knickers," she replied with a grin.

For the next hour they had creative sex in every room of the house. As the moon rose they ran naked down to the ocean and rinsed themselves off in the surf. Still sticky with salt, they dined beneath the stars in the little bistro that overlooked the fishing boats in the harbor.

80

Fiona Allinson had expressed outrage when Carter revealed the misdeeds of his college days, but she never thought for a moment that the man she had lived with for so long was spineless. The only rational explanation she could come up with for her husband's disappearance was that he had run rather than face the consequences.

For weeks she expected a letter or a call, but nothing came. Her mother advised her to file for a divorce. Her father advised her to file a Missing Persons Report. A few days later IRS Agent Luigi Rienzi came by. Fiona told him she and Carter had quarreled badly the night he disappeared, but she had heard nothing from him since. The agent left, apparently satisfied.

Away at boarding schools James and Amanda were not directly affected by the sudden gap in the family. Both believed their dad would return home soon. Both worried that they might have been responsible for their father's departure. Fiona assured them that this was not the case and infuriated them by saying she would reveal what had actually happened when they were old enough to understand.

The hours alone in the evenings were the toughest for her. Life suddenly seemed pointless. Once again her mother counseled Fiona and warned her that if she didn't take care of herself she could end up in a depression that could take several years to shake off, by which time it would be too late to start over.

In spite of not feeling her usual self, Fiona attended the dedication at the hospital and accepted the thanks of the staff and the good wishes of the donors. Her husband's absence was accepted as quite normal. Everyone assumed his work took precedence over a social engagement. As the evening progressed, Doctor Richards came over and asked her how she was feeling. She sensed he had heard about her husband's odd disappearance. Welcoming the attention, she revealed that there was indeed a slight problem at home. Over lunch the next day she elaborated. They parted that afternoon with a mutual promise to keep in touch.

Discreet inquiries revealed that the doctor was neither married nor divorced nor in a serious relationship. Fiona didn't waste any time and picked up the phone.

"Doctor Richards, it's Fiona Allinson."

"Mrs. Allinson. What a pleasure. What can I do for you?"

"I have two tickets for the opera tonight. I was wondering if you're free to go. I know it's very short notice, but . . ."

"I should be delighted."

"Wonderful. It starts at eight. Would you care to come over for a drink first?"

"That's sounds perfect. What time would you like me to come?"

"Why don't we say six thirty?"

"I'll be there."

In the opera house they smiled at each other as the chandeliers rose and the lights dimmed. The three loud chords of the overture to Verdi's *La Forza del Destino* burst forth. The irony of the title was not lost on either of them.

81

The month in Florida was not easy. Harry's mother fattened him up as his father regaled him with endless stories of their past. Calories and nostalgia finally drove him out. With hugs and kisses he took his farewell.

Using his coat as a pillow, he slept for most of the flight to New York and put it on as he left the terminal at LaGuardia. Snow was falling and a northeast wind blew the big flakes into little drifts. Back on 56th Street he found his mailbox full. Harry cradled the papers, magazines and envelopes against his chest, picked up his suitcase and slowly went up the stairs. Halfway up he had to pause to catch his breath. On the top landing he extracted his keys and opened the door. The big iron radiators greeted him with a welcoming hiss of steam.

The apartment was just as he had left it. A demoralizing scene of chaos and destruction. His first instinct was to leave. But the thought of finding a room for the night was less appealing than the cleanup. At least the place was warm.

Out of habit he went into the bedroom to check his answering machine. The phone was on the floor with the receiver off the hook. Harry put it together and pressed the play button. He listened to five very old messages. One of them was from Richie, telling him he'd been picked for the Mueller's Mayo commercial.

Harry replaced the scattered clothes in the closet and drawers. Found a set of sheets and made up the bed. As he smoothed the coverlet he had trouble resisting the temptation to lie down. The living room took longer as his challenged arm made it difficult to lift the books and ornaments back onto the shelves and tables.

All the pieces of broken glass and china went into the trash. Tossing all his theatrical paraphernalia back into the cupboard he pushed the door shut. In the bathroom he looked up and saw that the panel in the ceiling was undisturbed. Above it was over a million and a half dollars in cash. But to spend one note would be an invitation to disaster.

The smell in the kitchen was subtle but nasty. Green mold covered scattered food on the floor. Sweeping everything into a pile, he scooped it into a garbage bag from the box in the living room. Apart from the Stella Artois, the contents of the icebox and freezer went the same way. The camera and recorder were repacked into their cases and slid into a corner of the living room. Once the cushions were straightened, he sat down and looked around, pleased to see that his apartment was beginning to look like his old familiar home.

Over the next weeks Harry's physical recovery was gradual but steady. He went to the therapist every Wednesday and Friday morning and built up his stamina by walking the six and a half miles around Central Park. This regime caused him to lose weight. He applied for unemployment as he didn't yet feel strong enough to go back to work. Several residual checks arrived giving him sufficient funds to get by.

One cold and frosty morning, he returned from his walk, collected the mail and jogged up the stairs. Laying everything on the living room table, he hung up his coat.

A handwritten envelope with the postmark "Lawrence NY 11559" caught his eye. He tore it open and pulled out a single handwritten sheet of paper.

Harry,
I am real sorry you went through so much shit. I know it was all my fault. Things just didn't turn out the way I expected. Life is pretty strange sometimes. Max and me owe you a lot. Without you we wouldn't be here. The weather is glorious, with lots of sunshine and not a lot of rain. We got a house right on the beach. We ride bikes and take long walks. Hope your arm is better. I have given up smoking and Max hasn't had a cup of coffee in weeks. This makes

both of us irritable and we have glorious fights! In case you still got them, the notes in the suitcase you brought over were never messed with. I never did nothing to them. You can spend them and nobody will be any the wiser. Max agrees with me that you should have them. Just thought you'd like to know. Take care of yourself.

In place of a signature was an imprint of Lizzie's mauve lipstick. Harry was stunned. Lizzie was alive and safe. And wealthy.

Well, that was one mystery solved. Max and Lizzie must have taken the money from the cases.

But when had she gone over to the side of the bad guys? Or at least to the side of one of them? What could possibly have made her do that? And when? And why were they suddenly paying him off? Could the note be a hoax? From a desk drawer he retrieved the note Lizzie had written to him on the first day she'd been in his apartment. One glance showed they were both written by the same hand.

Lizzie had used their names. So she knew the letter was untraceable even by the FBI lab. But then Max and Lizzie knew every trick in the book. How the hell had they ended up together? Answers were called for.

With the stepladder from the kitchen straddling the toilet, Harry opened up the bathroom ceiling and pulled out the suitcase. Dirt and dust fell to the floor. Carrying the suitcase over to the bed, he flipped it open, took out one bundle, closed the lid and pushed the case back into the ceiling. Once the panel was replaced he swept up all the dust and dirt.

From the closet he retrieved his coat and headed out. Fifteen minutes later when his cab pulled up in front of Mazaras, Harry was convinced the driver had made a mistake. Gone was the overhead sign and the bricks had been cleaned and the wood trim painted a dark red. Then he read the lettering on the front window.

Pushing open the door he went inside. Delicious smells greeted him. The ground-floor layout was the same, but the wall coverings, carpets and curtains had all been changed and there were fresh flowers everywhere. Harry walked into the dining room and took off his coat.

A new bar with four stools had been built across the far corner. A man in his shirtsleeves was polishing glasses and sliding them on an overhead rack.

"Excuse me," said Harry as he made his way through the tables. "Am I too early for lunch?"

The barman turned around and both men did a take. Benny dropped the cloth and thrust out an arm. "Holy shit!" he said loudly. "How are you, Harry? You look great. How do you like the new place?"

"Pretty neat," replied Harry, and putting his coat on a stool, he leaned over to shake hands. "I thought it was time I came to visit. Maybe get a bite to eat."

"First things first. What would you like to drink?" asked Benny. "How about a Jamesons?"

"Great," replied Harry and he looked around. "It feels very strange to come back and see everything changed. As if it all never happened."

Benny poured out the Irish whisky with a flourish. "Tell me about it!" he said with a shrug. "Imagine how we all feel."

"Who's here beside you? Anybody I know?"

Benny lifted up the bar flap. "I'll let the boss tell you."

He hurried across the room and up the stairs as Harry poured a little water into the whisky from the jug on the bar. Not so very long ago he'd witnessed Benny shoot someone dead three feet from where he sat. If he chose to go to the cops and tell them what he knew the man would be arrested and could spend the rest of his life in jail. This didn't appear to enter Benny's head. He had accepted Harry as one of the guys. A member of the family. Or was he just making a show of welcome? Harry glanced down to where Carter had fallen. The whole floor had been stripped bare and highly polished.

"Well, well, well," Cora's voice drawled behind him. "Will you look what the cat brought in. The walking wounded."

"At least I'm walking," replied Harry. "More than we can say for some."

"Carter? The bastard got what he deserved. How are you, Harry? We heard you were hurt pretty bad."

"It was hard for a while. It's better now. How about you?"

Cora pointed to a table over by the window. "Come and sit down over here; my ass is too small for those stools."

"Whose idea was the bar?" asked Harry, getting up and grabbing his coat.

"Mine," replied Cora. "I used to tell Max it was a good idea, but he never liked it. Now he's gone . . ." She grimaced.

"For a minute I didn't think I'd come to the right place," said Harry. "But then I saw your name on the window."

"Cora's! Pretty cool, huh?"

"Very. So you're the new boss."

"It was a parting gift," she said wryly. "For services rendered." She pulled out a chair for him to sit.

"What happened here after we left?" he asked.

"Everyone scattered like pigeons. Left town as fast as they could. For the first week this place was empty. Sal and Furella went to Florida. Vic went with them. Enzo took a cruise to Alaska, sold his apartment and dropped out of sight."

"And you?"

"I flew to Vegas to visit with old friends for a couple of days. Then I came back here to get the work started. Max wanted the painters to come in as soon as possible in case anyone came snooping around."

"So you keep in touch with him?"

Cora paused. She sat down opposite him. "Kind of," she said.

"How did you feel when he went off with the English chick?"

Cora feigned surprise. "What makes you think they're together?"

"Answer my question," insisted Harry.

"I always hoped that one day Max and I would end up as a regular couple. But I'm a realist, Harry. I knew deep down it would never happen. Max took me for granted. I became one of the fixtures."

"How long were you guys together?"

"A long time. We met in Vegas."

"So what happened, Cora?" said Harry. "Where did they go?"

Cora stared at him for a moment and then asked, "How much do you know?"

Harry took out the note from Lizzie and handed it over.

"What's this?" asked Cora.

"Read it."

Harry sipped his whisky. Sounds of preparation came from the kitchen: voices and the clatter of the dishes. Cora looked up at him. Her face was a mask.

Harry set his glass down. "Max had it all worked out from the beginning, didn't he? He knew what he was going to do before he sent me to London with Rocco. He got there first and was waiting and watching in the Mews.

"I was the setup for Villiers. Then Rocco was going to take care of me. That was his plan. But Villiers had figured it all out. That's why he strangled Rocco."

Harry thought for a moment and then added, "Max waited until we left and then he waltzed in and made off with the cash."

Cora was impassive.

Harry took the note back and put it in his pocket.

"There's one thing I'll never understand, Cora. When I was taken upstairs, Lizzie was naked and tied up. Max used her as a hostage. And yet that night she went with him of her own free will. The only conclusion I can come up with is that she must have been in on his plan from the beginning."

Cora's eyes flared. "I've seen Max react to a lot of women,

Harry. There was something different about the way he behaved with your friend Lizzie."

"So when I saw her tied to that bed. That was a setup? All that drama was for my benefit."

"Yes, it appears it was. We'll never really know."

He paused to assimilate what was he was hearing. "I still don't get why she went away with him," he said. "What the hell happened? What magic did the bastard perform?"

"Surprised the hell out of me," Cora said. "After he took her out of here that night, I never saw either of them again. It all happened so fast. I suppose in some weird way they hit it off."

"Yes," said Harry. "I don't suppose she could be still working?"

"Working at what?" Cora asked with a frown.

"You don't know?"

"Know what?"

"Elizabeth Carswell is an undercover cop. She came here on a cybercrime investigation."

Cora gave him a look of amazement. "A cop?"

"Yes," he said, and added, "Complicates things quite a bit, doesn't it?"

"Does Max know?"

"Not unless she told him. She came here trying to track down a hacker who had penetrated the European Defence System. She never knew it, but young Vic Bruschetti was the man she was after."

"How do you know that?"

"Vic told me. Right in this room."

For a moment they both sat with their own thoughts.

"Do you have any idea where they went?" asked Harry.

Cora abruptly stood up. "No, I don't." She pushed her chair under the table. "It's all about survival, Harry. In this world it's not the survival of the fittest but the survival of the smartest. You got to know when to fight and when to give in."

"That's a pessimistic way of looking at life"

"It's the way Max saw it. And obviously the way your cute little friend Lizzie saw it. They both saw an opportunity and took it. Good luck to them."

She put her hands on the table and leaned close to him.

"It won't last, Harry. I know Max. He gets bored. With people and places. He's never stuck with one woman for more than a month."

Harry picked up his glass. "That rather depends on the woman, doesn't it?" He finished his whisky. "We have to face it. They fell for each other. Found a little happiness. Can't grudge them that, can we?"

"We should be so lucky," she replied, and turned away.

Harry watched her as she walked away and into the kitchen. Cora had an attractive body. Maybe he'd come back sometime and talk some more. Now it was time to move on. The bad guys had won. The villain had gotten the girl and ridden off into the sunset.

Harry's phone rang. It took him a moment to find it. The call was from his agent.

"Hi there, Harry!" said Richie. "How are you doing? Look, I know you're still taking it easy and I'm real sorry to bother you, but they just called to ask your availability next month to read the new Stan Benedict novel. They loved what you did with *Passion and Power* and really want you to do the sequel. It's called *Violent Vengeance*. What do you say? Are you up to it? It's two days' recording and they're offering you the same money. I tried to get more but they said no way. Budget's pretty tight."

Harry hesitated and that in itself was unique. For the first time in his career he was being offered work and he was wondering if he wanted to accept.

"Can I call you back on this one?" he said, needing a little time.

"Sure thing, sport. I'll be here at the office until seven."

Harry closed the phone and laid it on the table.

Why had he hesitated? Was it money in his pocket? Was it the countless bundles of bills back in the bathroom ceiling? Did so much money give him a sense of superiority? An excuse not to work? Suddenly he realized he was behaving like an idiot.

Nothing had actually changed in his life. He still craved the excitement of a new script, the challenge of creating a character, the intellectual exercise of rehearsals and the almost unbearable nervousness of opening night.

Lights! Camera! Action! Harry Patrick Murphy picked up his phone and dialed his agent.

It was time to earn an honest living.

ACKNOWLEDGMENTS

For the most part, the creation of this book was a long and solo effort as I tried to learn how to write a story, but many individuals contributed their time, wisdom and expertise. Special thanks must go to:

My English teachers at University College School, London, for setting me on the right track.

Katherine, my wife of almost fifty years, with her loving encouragement and eagle eye for details that everyone else misses.

Assistant US Attorney Bradley Tyler, who helped me find whomever and whatever I needed to begin and complete my research.

Special Agent Gerald McAleer (Retired). At the time I met him in New York he was the Special Agent in Charge at the US Drug Enforcement Agency. "Gerry," as he is affectionately known, gave me a glimpse of the inner workings of the intricate and sometimes perilous ways of undercover assignments.

Special Agent Jim Christy (Retired), who took me into the world of cybercrime and showed me the way agents are trained to do battle against it. Jim is currently the President and Founder of the Digital Forensics Consortium.

Charlotte Herscher, who taught me the Basics of Novel Writing 101.

Scott Williams, Senior Executive Producer and a writer on *NCIS,* who gave me a reassuring smile as he welcomed me, as he put it, "to the world of self-doubt."

My new friend Will Anderson, a kind and gentle editor at Thomas Dunne Books, who help me guide this effort to fruition.

• • •

The poem "There Was a Crooked Man" has its roots in British history and originates from the ill-feeling between the Stuarts and Charles 1.

The "crooked man" is reputed to be the Scottish General Sir Alexander Leslie who signed a Covenant securing religious and political freedom for Scotland.

The "crooked stile" refers to the border between England and Scotland.

"They all lived together in a little crooked house" refers to the fact that the English and Scots had finally come to an agreement.